# My Name
## is Anton

# Also by Catherine Ryan Hyde

# My Name is Anton

*A Novel*

# Catherine Ryan Hyde

**LAKE UNION**
PUBLISHING

Published by Lake Union Publishing, Seattle

www.apub.com

Amazon, the Amazon logo, and Lake Union Publishing are trademarks of Amazon.com, Inc., or its affiliates.

ISBN-13: 9781542014342 (paperback)
ISBN-10: 1542014344 (paperback)

ISBN-13: 9781542023481 (hardcover)
ISBN-10: 1542023483 (hardcover)

Cover design by Shasti O'Leary Soudant

Printed in the United States of America

# My Name
# is Anton

# WINTER OF 1965

## ANTON'S FEDORA

# Chapter One

*Merry False Christmas*

It was December 10, an odd day to celebrate the Christmas holiday. It was not even quite six in the morning, and Anton "Anthony" Addison-Rice was fast asleep and dreaming about his right hand.

He dreamed he was swimming in the Olympic-sized pool off his high school gym, which, suddenly and for no apparent reason, turned into the open Atlantic Ocean. He raised his right arm in a powerful stroke, breaking the surface of the water. Then he raised his head to look, which his coach would have disciplined him for doing, and his right hand surprised him . . . by being there. It was backlit by a hazy sun, and appeared completely real. Whole and perfect. As though nothing had ever happened to it.

He allowed himself to bob upright in the dream swells, treading water, just staring at the hand. It struck him as an unexpected visitor. It felt similar to the way his late grandpa Anton had come into his dreams a few months earlier. It had the same too-vivid, sharply defined feeling to it—an image that would be slow to fade.

So he spoke to the hand, much the way he had spoken in his dream to Grandpa Anton.

He said, "There you are. I thought you were gone. Why was I so sure you were gone?"

Then the dream let him go and he opened his eyes. It might have been a sound that knocked the dream away. It might have been his mother opening his bedroom door. Because, now that his eyes were open, he could see that she had.

He was holding his right arm aloft, the way he had done in the dream. But the background to the scene was not a hazy sun, but his mother, standing in his half-open bedroom doorway. And the hand was not there after all. That most important factor had only been true in the dream.

He sighed deeply and shifted his focus to his mother. She was watching him silently. Watching him stare at the stump of his right wrist. She had a taut look of disapproval on her face, as if she preferred he ignore the situation. Well, she did prefer that. He knew it from experience. Ignoring situations was her number one life skill.

"You have to get up," she said.

"It's awfully early." His eyes narrowed as he attempted to focus on the clock beside his bed. "Can't I just say goodbye to you from here?"

"We have to celebrate Christmas."

"We can't celebrate Christmas."

"Why on earth can't we?"

"Because it's only . . ."

But he was too close to asleep to grasp the date.

"It's the tenth of December," she said.

"Right. I knew that. Who celebrates Christmas on the tenth of December?"

"We do, this year. Now listen. Your father went to great lengths to buy you a present he knew you would like. And you will come out to the living room and open it and show some appreciation for his troubles. You get me, Anton?"

"Anthony," he said.

He should have known better. He should have given it up long ago, at least at home.

She crossed the room, taking his chin in the right hand she was fortunate enough to have—and probably didn't even appreciate. Her fingernails dug into the skin of his face, hurting him.

He did not say "Ouch," though it would have been easy and natural to do so.

"Now you listen to me, young man. Your father lost his own father not even a year ago, and you will not dishonor the memory of your grandfather by suggesting that his name is not good enough for you. I won't have it. Now get dressed and get out to the living room, pronto. Your father and I have a plane to catch."

———

His father was on the phone, its long cord stretched into the living room. His mother was in the kitchen, making a pot of coffee. She looked at Anthony's face, then down at his pajamas and robe, her own face darkening.

"I told you to get dressed."

"You also told me you had a plane to catch. Do you have any idea how long it takes me to get dressed?"

"Never mind. Coffee?"

"Yes, please."

"Abel!" she shouted. "Get off the phone. We're having Christmas."

"I'm on hold with the airline," he shouted back. "I can't just hang up!"

She sighed a loud, theatrical sigh.

Anthony sat at the breakfast counter between the living room and kitchen, and watched her pour him a mug of coffee.

She had first offered him coffee nine days earlier, on his eighteenth birthday. Before that he had poured himself many cups of coffee, and she had not outright prevented him from doing so. Did she think it would have been contributing to his delinquency to offer coffee even one day before he reached that magical age of adulthood?

She set cream and sugar in front of him, followed by the mug of fresh coffee. The cream and sugar seemed odd to him, because she should have known by then that he took neither.

"Your grandma Marion will look in on you." It was a statement that didn't seem to leave room for discussion.

"I don't need anyone to look in on me," he said.

"You like your grandma Marion. Don't you?"

"Of course I do. I love Grandma Marion."

"Then don't argue. Think of them as visits. And in her presence there will be none of this Anthony nonsense. You are not free to break that woman's heart. Am I understood?"

He nodded vaguely and sipped at his coffee. She had brewed it too weak.

"I want to hear it out loud from your lips. Am I understood?"

"Yes," he said, enunciating clearly. "You are understood."

He looked around to see his father standing beside him, beefy arms across his chest. Tapping one upper arm with the fingers of his opposite hand. Which meant everybody had better hurry up for him.

"They will not be delaying the flight again," his father said. More to Anthony's mother than to Anthony. "A word to the wise. We need to leave in five minutes, tops, or we're going to miss our plane."

—

Anthony sat in the living room, alone on the couch. A dizzying mountain of suitcases sat stacked in front of the door. Anthony's mother sat in the print wing chair, watching him. His father paced. Now and then his mother shot her husband a withering glance, but each one slid off him unnoticed.

The coffee table in front of Anthony had been cleared. On it sat two wrapped gifts. Nicely large. He already knew what was in them. The telescope was not boxed, and its shape was evident through the candy-cane-printed paper. The second gift was a long rectangular box which Anthony assumed would be the telescope's tripod.

It was a gift he had hinted at relentlessly. He would have been surprised had it been anything else.

He reached out and began to tear away the paper with his left hand.

Apparently he was too slow for his father, who dove in and began to tear with him.

"I'll just help you open this," he mumbled.

"Abel!" his mother shouted. It actually hurt one of Anthony's eardrums. "Sit!"

It was fairly unusual for her to speak to her husband that way, but not unheard of. On the occasions when she did, he would not mount a defense.

Abel sat.

"It's just that there's a cab waiting downstairs," Abel said, sounding almost meek. "And the meter is running."

"So let it run. We're having Christmas."

Abel only sighed.

Anthony continued to tear at the paper one-handed until the telescope emerged. It was more impressive in person than it had appeared in the catalogue. It looked bigger and more technical. More expensive. More desirable even than he had imagined.

"It's just what I wanted."

"Well, of course it's what you wanted," his father said, his voice hurried and gruff. "Like you didn't make it clear a hundred times exactly what you wanted."

Anthony's mother shot her husband a stern glance. He fell silent.

"We figured this way you'll have something to play with while we're gone," she said.

"He's not going to play with it," his father shot back. "Stop treating him like a boy. He's going to learn. Explore. Enrich himself. He doesn't play anymore. He's a grown man."

"He's not a grown man."

"He's legally an adult."

"Legally an adult does not make you a grown man."

"Well, he's certainly not the child you—"

"Could you guys please not fight over me?" Anthony asked, interrupting.

"Fine," his father said. "There's no time, anyway. We have a plane to catch. We have to go. There's a cab waiting downstairs, and the meter is running. Or did I say that already? The other package is the tripod. You're smart. You'll figure it out. Now come on, Vera. We don't want to miss that flight."

"How are we getting all of these bags downstairs?" Anthony's mother asked, a sentence that felt like it wanted to be the start of another fight.

"I can help," Anthony said.

Although, he noted, none of the bags had shoulder straps. So he could take only one at a time.

"Nonsense," his father said. "I asked the super to come up."

As if this scene were only a stage play, and as if the super had heard the line of dialogue that was to be his entrance cue, there was a knock at the door.

Anthony's mother swooped across the room and kissed Anthony on the head, blocking out most of the world with her large and solid self.

"Be a good boy," she said. "Well . . . a good man, if your father has anything to say about what I call you. Then again, this time he might be right. For a change."

She stepped away, and Anthony looked up to see the apartment door standing open. No bags. No super. No father. They were all gone.

"Have fun in South America," he said to her.

But she only smiled in reply, and the smile looked tight and sad.

Then his mother stepped out, closing the apartment door behind her, leaving Anthony entirely alone.

For weeks.

For the first time in his life.

———

He was fast asleep when the knock came at the door, but had been dreaming of nothing as far as he could remember. He stumbled out of bed and shrugged awkwardly into his robe on the way to the door.

"Grandma Marion . . . ," he called out. Then he began the tedious job of undoing the locks one-handed. "You know I love you, but they've only been gone a few hours. I mean, really."

A deep male voice boomed through the door. "If I see Marion, I'll pass your message along."

Anthony swung the door wide. Standing on the welcome mat was his uncle Gregor. Or, at least, the man he had always called Uncle Gregor, despite his being a great-uncle—the late grandpa Anton's brother.

"Oh, hey, Uncle Gregor."

Uncle Gregor was a stooped man in his late seventies with wire-rim glasses and a neatly trimmed beard. He wore an expensive camel-hair coat, and looked Anthony up and down as he spoke, rubbing his beard with the heel of one hand.

"You were asleep, Anton?"

"I . . . actually was."

"It's almost one thirty in the afternoon."

"Is it?"

They stood awkwardly, all four of their eyes trained onto the door-mat. As if it would have something weighty or amusing to say. As if it had said "Welcome" every time before, but might say something surprising just this once.

Then Uncle Gregor—who was, inconveniently, a psychiatrist— said, "This is a thing we associate with depression—changes in sleep patterns. I'm guessing you must know it, at least on some level."

"No. It's not that."

"You're not depressed? After the year you had, that would be a miracle."

"I'm not saying I'm not depressed. I don't know what I am. But I mostly haven't been sleeping all day. I just did it today for a completely different reason. My parents gave me that telescope I've been wanting. I want to try it out when it gets dark tonight. So I thought I'd sleep as much as I could today. You know. So I can stay up."

"It's in there somewhere, Anton."

"I'm sorry, what?"

"Trauma and grief. It's in there somewhere. I worry about you."

He felt a deep, sickening flutter down in his gut, as he often did when Uncle Gregor challenged him about his feelings. But he talked around it until it settled again. Behind the wall he'd built to contain it.

"What's wrong with sleeping during the day so you can stay up late?"

"It's the dead of winter, Anton. It gets dark around five p.m."

They stood without talking for a time.

Then, much to Anthony's surprise, his great-uncle turned as if to go.

"Well, I'll leave you to that," Gregor said.

"Wait. You're not coming in?"

"Not if you're trying to sleep."

"But you came all this way."

"Ten minutes on the subway." He raised his hands, turning them palms up for reasons Anthony did not understand.

"You should come in. You'd be doing me a favor. I need help with that telescope. It needs some assembly . . . getting it properly on the tripod and everything. It's a job that takes more than one hand."

—

"Let's set it up on the balcony," Anthony said. "It's heavy. Once we get it all together it might be hard to move it."

Anthony rolled back the heavy glass balcony door and they stepped out into the winter cold together.

Uncle Gregor frowned at Anthony's bare ankles, and his slide-on slippers with no heels. "Go inside and get yourself dressed properly for the weather, son."

"I don't know. It takes me forever."

"No matter. I'll be right here. Where did you think I would go?"

—

When Anthony arrived back out on the balcony, his great-uncle was smoking a cigar and peering closely at the instruction manual.

Anthony sat on a cold metal chair beside the older man and wondered what, if anything, it was currently his job to do.

"So, did my parents tell you to come check up on me?"

"Let's just say I came to wish you happy holidays and leave it at that. Though it's not the holidays quite yet."

"It is around here. Mom forced us to celebrate this morning."

"It made her uncomfortable to leave you."

"I wish she wouldn't still think of me as a child."

"She doesn't. No, I honestly don't think so, Anton. She's knows you're responsible enough to be alone. It's your morale that concerns her. After such a disastrous year. Your parents felt bad about asking you to brave the holidays alone."

They sat briefly in silence. Uncle Gregor smoked. Anthony gazed out at the windows of the apartment building across the street. A light snow had begun to fall. Anthony could feel flakes of it settle into his hair. The sky was a flat, steely gray with an even cloud cover, utterly unsuitable for sky watching.

"Then why did they?" he asked, surprising himself.

"Oh, I hate this part, my boy, because I'm not supposed to say. But I'm going to anyway. But you didn't hear this from me, all right? If anybody asks, you're to say you picked it up on your own."

"Okay. What?"

"Your parents' marriage is hanging by a thread."

"Oh," Anthony said. He had not picked that up on his own. While he was wondering why he hadn't, he noticed that his nose had grown painfully cold. "For how long?"

"Well, since your brother died. Not to give you the impression that they don't care about what happened to you as well. But . . ."

"I get it," Anthony said, jumping into the pause. "I get why Greg dying was worse than me getting hurt. Anybody with a brain would."

"And you kept telling them you were fine if they went away. Which I was stunned to hear they'd used as justification. Let's just say I would've made a different decision if you were my son. I don't want to speak ill of your parents, so I'll leave it at that. But I came to ask if you're really fine. It's a terrible thing to lose your only brother. Even for me, when your grandpa Anton passed, and I was seventy-six. So why did you convince them it was fine to leave you? Did you need the time alone?"

"Not really, no. I would've liked it if we'd had Christmas as a family this year. Actually."

"But you didn't tell them so."

"No."

"Hmm," Uncle Gregor said. Anthony got the impression that the man was trying to figure him out. But a second or two later he realized it was the telescope's instruction manual that held the older man's attention. "I think I see how this mounts. But we need this little gizmo." He pointed to an illustration of a palm-sized, wheel-like piece of metal in the manual. "You know where to find that?"

"I saw it. I put it in the zippered pocket of the carrying case so it wouldn't get lost."

"Wise. You are a wise young man. Except . . . ," he added as he took the wheel-shaped piece from Anthony, ". . . and don't take this wrong. Don't feel like I'm insulting you, please, because I know people three and four times your age who are no better at this than you are. You're not expected to have life down to a science at age eighteen. But I'm going to say this anyway, if only to give you something you can aspire to. A human life is a very different place when you can tell people what you need. I'll just say that and no more."

"I hear you," Anthony said.

"So what do you expect to see through snow clouds, and with all these city lights washing out the stars?"

"I don't know, really. But I still have to try. At least I have to try to look at a plane or a far-off building. To see how powerful it is. I'm really anxious to see how powerful it is."

"You should let me drive you out into the country with it. Sometime."

"I'd love that. When?"

"It'll have to be after the holidays. Your great-aunt will shoot me if I make one more plan."

It was a surprising letdown—just reaching out for something and then having it pulled back, even for only a medium space of time. But he didn't let on. He didn't say what he needed.

Changing one's whole modus operandi of communication wasn't as easy as just hearing a piece of advice and then starting over.

—

Before he walked out and left him alone again, Uncle Gregor sur-prised Anthony with an enthusiastic embrace. He held on tightly and kissed Anthony on the side of the temple, his lips holding firm for a second or two.

"Your family loves you," he said into Anthony's ear. "And I don't just mean your parents. I mean all of us. The whole extended family. We're very proud of the way you turned out. Nobody is blind to the difficulty of your adjustment or your losses. There's support here if you want it." Then he stepped back, and seemed to pull himself together. To draw inward again. "Now, I need to get home to my wife."

"Thank you," Anthony said.

He was not accustomed to crying in front of others, and he could not have said more without crying. More accurately, he was not accus-tomed to crying, period. He had not indulged that release because of a deep fear that, having allowed the tears to start, he would never find the end of them, or would find they had no end at all.

# Chapter Two

## Third Window from the Left

Anthony woke after nine o'clock in the evening. Of course, it was already dark. He fairly leapt out of bed, as if a dark night sky were a precious and dwindling commodity, fleeing as he dressed.

It was not easy to get dressed.

Pants are best grasped by the waistband on both sides, and pulled into place. To pull them up on the left, then shift your left hand around to the right, was to invite them to fall down around your knees again. He had learned to hold them in place by reaching around with his right wrist and pressing them against his hip, but in his hurry that night he made several mistakes.

The T-shirt was easy enough, but then came the flannel outer shirt. Of course, it had buttons. There was an art to doing up buttons one-handed. Especially left-handed. Anthony was only about halfway to mastering that art.

He slipped into his loafers—all his shoes with laces had been discarded and replaced—but he only stamped and folded the heels of the shoes down under his own heels, and he had to sit on the bed and sort both shoes out with his left hand.

He shrugged into his coat and stepped out onto the balcony.

The telescope was covered with its nylon case, just the way he and his great-uncle had left it—to protect it from the moisture of the snow.

He pulled the cover off.

Then he looked out over the city landscape and chose a target to view. Stars were out of the question—there might as well have been none in existence anywhere in the universe. But in the far distance he saw a building with a high point, topped with what might have been a lightning rod, or some kind of communications antenna. Whatever it was, it was currently wrapped in a spiral of red and green Christmas lights.

He would point the telescope at those lights, and learn how to focus on them. Learn how close a night view his new gift could offer him.

He carefully undid the knob that allowed the telescope to sweep horizontally on its tripod. He centered it on the building and tightened the knob again.

Then he loosened the knob that would allow him to raise the angle of the scope. But he loosened it too much, too fast, and without any thought for the weight of the scope and the effect gravity would have on it. He had no counterweight for the back of the scope. Not yet, anyway. He felt it going. Not off the mount—it couldn't literally fall to or off the balcony floor. But the front end was falling, or appeared to be falling. It filled him with an instinctual alarm.

He tried to catch it with his right wrist, because his left hand was still desperately attempting to tighten the knob again. The weight of the scope caused it to slide off his wrist again, scraping as it did, causing a shocking jolt of pain.

He stood a moment, doing his best not to cry out. He held the wrist between his thighs, tightly, though he wasn't sure why he thought that would help.

It was not as though the wound of the amputation was exceedingly fresh. It was more than seven months old. Though, a wound of that severity is fresher and more tender at seven months than a person outside the body in question might imagine. But the issue was more in the nerves. The end of his wrist contained bundles of nerves that had been cut. Pressure on them was excruciating, and left Anthony with the eerie sensation that his hand hurt badly, despite the fact that it was no longer there.

He stood that way on the dark balcony until the pain slowly faded to bearable. Then he centered himself over the telescope, and prepared to do a better job setting it in place.

Before he could, an image caught his eye: a white wall with a mantelpiece, and an abstract painting on the wall above it. It was captured in the eyepiece of the telescope, which was now pointing downward at the building across the street. Anthony's eye had accidentally hovered at just the right distance above the eyepiece. The scene was in perfect focus.

Realizing he was looking through somebody else's window, and uncomfortable with the idea, he moved to correct the angle of the scope quickly. Or, more accurately, he prepared to move. He gave his various limbs and their muscles a signal to move. But, before they could, something happened.

A figure streaked into the scene, clearly captured by Anthony's new telescope.

It appeared to be a woman, though it all happened very fast. She was running. Scrambling. Her body was bent forward, as if to accelerate getting out of the way of something. Something behind her. Her head was bent slightly forward, her arms raised, hands hovering behind her head as if to protect it.

Then, just as quickly, a male hand and arm entered the view. It was a bare arm, save for the short sleeve of a white undershirt. It was noticeably hairy. In a disconnected and more or less inadvertent thought, it struck Anthony that he owned a very good telescope, because it could reveal hair on the arm of a man across the street.

The man's hand grabbed the woman by her hair.

Anthony sucked in air with an audible gasp as he watched the woman's head jerked backward. It was a breathtakingly violent gesture.

Then the woman disappeared from his view. Backward. Pulled back out of the scene. By her hair.

"I have to do something," he said out loud.

His first impulse was to fly. To leap the distance between the two buildings. He was drowning in that much panic.

Of course, he thought better of flying. But he still had to do something.

He froze there a moment, waiting to see if anything else would happen. His nose and the stump of his wrist tingled painfully with the cold, and he was vaguely aware of his rapid breath filling the air as clouds of steam.

Nothing moved in the apartment across the way.

*What would Uncle Gregor or Grandma Marion tell me to do?*

He let himself back into the apartment to call the police.

———

Anthony never spoke with an actual police officer that night, as far as he could tell. Instead he had a conversation with a woman who, he gathered, was some type of emergency dispatcher.

"What's your emergency?" she asked, without saying hello.

There was something hard and brusque in her tone. Anthony found it strangely comforting. She struck him as a person who could take charge—take hold of everything and wrench it back into control—exactly what was needed in any kind of disaster.

"I think I just saw a woman being assaulted," he said, surprised to hear that his voice was shaking. He knew the scene had affected him, yet was still shocked to hear the effect with his own ears.

"You *think* you saw this?"

"Well, no. I don't think. I know. I saw it."

"Where did this assault take place?"

"In an apartment across the street from where I live."

"And you were in the apartment when it happened?"

"No, ma'am. I saw it through the window."

"All right. Give me the address, and I'll have a couple of officers go by and see what's what."

Anthony said nothing. For an embarrassing stretch of time.

"Son? You still there?"

"Yes, ma'am. Sorry. I don't know the address. I should have gotten the address before I called you. I wasn't thinking clearly. But I can give you my address, and the building where it happened is right across the street. Or I can go outside and get the address and call you back."

He wondered why he didn't know the address of the building across the street. Not that he had ever needed to know it. But he had been walking by that building daily since he was fourteen. It struck him as unobservant never to have noticed the street number.

The woman's voice pulled him back to the moment again.

"That actually might work. Just give me your address, and then the apartment number where this happened."

He remained frozen in silence again. He thought he heard the woman sigh.

"Right," she said. "You don't know that, either."

"I'll call you right back," he blurted.

Then he quickly hung up the phone.

He pulled on one glove with the help of his teeth, stuck his right wrist deep into his coat pocket, took the keys off the hook by the door, and prepared to brave the evening cold.

He took the elevator, which was overly heated, thirteen floors down to the lobby, then stepped out into the night.

He peered at the building across the street as if it were an enemy preparing to ambush him. Its street number, 3359, was clearly lit. He repeated the number over and over in his head, hoping it would stick.

He had no idea if the building had a locked outer door. His own building did not, but that was all he knew. He had heard of buildings with locked outer doors. Some of his friends from school lived in such buildings. But he had no idea what was most common.

He crossed the street in the middle of the block, dodging a speeding cab that seemed to come out of nowhere, and tried the door.

It was open.

He ignored the elevator and trotted up the stairs to the second floor.

He should have taken the elevator, he soon realized. Because it would have left him clearer on which direction he was facing when he arrived on the landing.

He walked along the second-floor hallway, unable to secure his bearings. There were no windows in the hallway—just apartment doors, and a long runner of well-worn Persian carpet. He had no way of knowing if the windows of these apartments faced onto the avenue. And, even if they did, he had no way of knowing *how many* windows in each apartment faced the avenue, so the third window from the left could be the first apartment on the left—from the point of view of Anthony's building—or the one next to it.

He sighed and took the elevator back down to the lobby.

He stepped out into the cold again, and walked to the south end of the building—the end from which he had counted windows from his balcony. He looked up to be sure that the first-floor windows lined up exactly with the windows above it. Then he paced off the distance from the corner of the building to the third window, counting his steps.

He took the elevator back to the second floor, knowing he was facing the avenue the whole time.

He stepped out and paced off the hallway from the south end of the building, realizing as he did that he had no idea how much difference in length there might be between the end of the hallway, inside, and the end of the outside of the building.

When he had finished pacing it off, he found himself in between two apartment doors, 2D and 2F, with no idea where the wall between the two apartments was located.

But he saw no more that he could do.

He trotted briskly back to his own apartment building, rode the elevator up thirteen floors to the "14th Floor"—yes, it was called the fourteenth floor, quite purposely incorrectly numbered to put superstitious tenants at ease—and let himself back inside.

He called in the assault again.

He was hoping for the same woman, but got a new one. One who did not sound nearly so able to bring everything back into control. He gave her the address of the building where the assault had taken place. When she asked for the apartment number, he calmly and unapologetically gave her two. Either 2D or 2F.

She sighed, much the way the previous dispatcher had sighed. But she promised to send someone out.

—

Anthony hauled his new telescope in off the balcony and into his bedroom, because it was simply too cold to stand outside all night.

It wasn't easy.

It weighed well over a hundred pounds with all of its elements assembled. And he damn sure wasn't going to take it apart again and risk being unable to reassemble it.

He opened the sliding door, wrapped his arms under the scope where it mounted to the tripod, and dragged it in across the carpet. He was strong enough to lift it, but not confident enough of his grip on it, and too afraid it might end up dropped.

Then he closed the sliding door, shivering in the winter cold he had just invited in, and continued to drag the scope until it was sitting by his bedroom window.

He trained it down to the entryway of the building across the street. It required raising the center post of the tripod to give the scope more room to tilt downward. When they arrested the man with the hairy arms and led him handcuffed into the street, Anthony wanted to see him. He wanted to see for himself, close up, what kind of man could do such a thing.

He pulled up a chair and waited.

And waited.

And waited.

———

He popped awake, sitting upright in his chair, amazed that he had ever fallen asleep.

A police car sat in the "no stopping" zone across the street, its roof lights flashing red.

*So they're inside,* he thought. *So they'll be bringing him out any minute.*

He positioned his left eye over the eyepiece of the scope and waited.

Several minutes ticked by, with Anthony learning one of the first lessons of using his new telescope: it gives one an eyestrain headache to squint-focus through one eye for any extended length of time.

Then he saw the two officers step out of the building.

They had no one in handcuffs. They had no one with them at all.

Anthony had an amazingly close and detailed view of them. He watched one take off his blue policeman's uniform cap and scratch his head, and he could see the bald spot on the very top of the officer's scalp. The other officer lit a cigarette, and Anthony watched the smoke billow out of the man's mouth and nose in clouds, mixed with frozen breath.

They stepped back into their patrol car and turned off the revolving roof lights.

They drove away.

Anthony repositioned the telescope, back to the third window from the left on the second floor. He stayed awake the rest of the night, watching, to see if anything else terrible would happen there.

He never saw anything more than a white wall with a mantelpiece and an abstract painting.

———

In the morning Anthony dressed slowly, his plan forming in his mind as he buttoned his shirt and stepped into his shoes. Though, that description makes the plan sound effortless, as though it appeared in his head voluntarily, when in truth he felt as though he were dragging it in, one detail at a time.

He dug around in his father's office, hoping for nothing more elaborate than a yellow legal pad, but found something better. A clipboard. It had no paper on it, so he grabbed a few sheets from a notebook in his own room and clipped them in. He slipped a pen into his pocket, donned his coat, and walked across the street.

He trotted up the stairs to the second floor, clipboard under his left arm, his right wrist deep in his coat pocket.

He stopped first at 2F. When he knocked on the door, the action of raising his arm even slightly caused him to drop the clipboard onto the Persian carpet. When he had retrieved it and straightened up again, a very old man was standing in the open doorway, watching him.

"Can I help you with something?" The man's voice sounded gravelly and deep, as though it had been used too hard for too many years. It had a wet quaver to it, as though the man were drowning inside, where Anthony couldn't see it.

"I'm taking a survey," Anthony said, surprised by how frightened he felt. His hand was shaking. "I'm hoping you wouldn't mind telling me how many people live in your household."

Because, though it would appear this was not the right apartment, Anthony could not leave without being sure. This could be the father or grandfather of one of the people he had seen the previous night.

"Just me," the old man said.

"Okay. Thank you. That's all I needed."

"That's the whole survey? Just one question? What kind of survey just wants to know how many people live in an apartment? What good does that information do, and for whom?"

"No, sir," Anthony said, hoping his face wasn't reddening. It felt hot. "There's a whole survey. But it's for the lady of the house."

"Oh. Oh, I see."

"Thank you anyway for your time."

The man waved vaguely in Anthony's general direction, and swung the door closed.

Anthony knocked on the door of 2D, his heart hammering.

At first, nothing happened. Then the door swung inward so suddenly that it startled him back two steps.

The man in the doorway was small but wiry looking and probably strong, with dark hair slicked back, showing wet comb marks. He was wearing black dress pants with suspenders that hung free from his waist, as though he'd forgotten to hoist them onto his shoulders, and a white shirt with the cuffs rolled back two turns.

His arms were hairy.

He barked a single word at Anthony. "What?"

"Sorry to bother you, sir, but I'm taking a survey, and—"

"I have no time for a survey."

"Well, actually, this survey is for the lady of the house."

The man froze a moment. Saying nothing. Doing nothing. As if there were a struggle going on inside him and he was waiting, a passive observer, to see which side would win.

Then he turned halfway into the apartment and shouted a name. "Edith!"

The man walked away, leaving the door wide open.

Anthony waited for what seemed to be a full minute or two. He began to wonder if what he was waiting for would ever happen. For reasons he didn't fully understand, his fear seemed to deepen with each second that ticked by.

Then a woman appeared, walking slowly to the open door, not looking at Anthony yet. Her eyes were trained down to the carpet, as if negotiating a minefield. Her hair was a soft brunette with auburn highlights, gently wavy, and Anthony knew it. Recognized it. From having seen it in the eyepiece of his telescope the night before. It fell forward onto her face, especially on the left. Anthony assumed it was because her head was tilted forward and down. But when she arrived at the doorway, and raised her face to him, he got the impression that it had been brushed or combed over her left eye.

She stood in front of him, looking much the way Anthony felt—as though she would just as soon beam herself away to some distant galaxy as stand here and weather a human interaction. She stood cupping her left elbow in her right hand, her left hand raised to her face. Her fingers rested on her forehead, her palm loosely covering that left eye. She seemed to be trying to create the appearance of a casual pose. If so, the attempt failed badly.

Anthony looked at her face and found it hard to breathe. The interior of his chest tingled. He had no time to wonder why. He had to talk.

He had summoned her here, and now he had to talk to her.

"Thank you for your time," he said.

"Oh, it's no bother." Her voice was light, both in volume and . . . well, Anthony couldn't quite explain it, but her voice made his chest feel lighter, in a couple of different senses. Both less weighty and more illuminated. Her voice was making his world lighter. "My husband said you were taking a survey. When I was in college I made extra money with a door-to-door survey. I got lots of doors slammed in my face. I know how that feels."

"Thank you," he said again. But differently this time. A deeply heartfelt statement, because he was grateful she had said something kind, intended to put him at ease.

"What's the survey about?"

In the brief silence that followed, Anthony marveled at the flaws in his plan. The idea had been simply to bring the woman to the door. Just to see with his own eyes that she was okay. Of course, once she was there she would ask questions, and he would have to answer them. A conversation was bound to ensue. He couldn't just run away. It was hard to imagine that he hadn't prepared more carefully for this inevitable moment. Somehow since witnessing that act of violence he had been unable to unscramble his brain.

"Art," he said. Because he had blinked his eyes and seen a visual memory of the abstract painting over the fireplace. "It's about the art that people choose for their homes."

"So why is it a survey for the woman? Men buy art."

"Sure. I'm sure they do. But the organization who's funding this survey feels that the woman is ultimately in charge of how the home is decorated."

"And what organization is it?" she asked, in that voice. That voice that lit up the world. She didn't sound as though she were giving him the third degree. She seemed genuinely curious. As if his work interested her. Then again, it was hard for anything to sound troublesome when spoken in that voice.

"The National Art Council," he said.

She nodded seriously. As if the probably nonexistent council deserved her respect.

"How many pieces of art do you have in your apartment?" he asked her.

As he did, he had to prepare to write down her answer. So he pulled his right wrist out of his coat pocket and braced the clipboard on his

right forearm, securing its bottom edge against his waist. He took hold
of the pen with his left, preparing to write with it, as he had been teach-
ing himself to do for months.

Her amber eyes moved to his nonexistent right hand. To the space
where she had been so sure she would see it. Of course her eyes did
that—everybody's eyes did. Anthony had to witness this moment with
every new person he met, or even passed on the street, which is why he
tended to keep his right wrist buried in his pocket.

He didn't blame her for it. He didn't blame anyone for it. It was
just a human reaction.

But with this woman—Edith, the man had called her—the
moment felt more complex. Because, in the moment she looked, she
forgot to halfway cover her left eye with one supposedly casual hand.
Either that or she felt compelled to look with both eyes at once.

So while she took in Anthony's missing right hand, he was able to
see her left eye, despite its being half-covered with wavy auburn hair. He
could see segments of the dark ring of discoloration underneath it. He
wondered, in a disconnected way, why people call it a black eye when
it tends to be purple, yellow, and green.

"I think six," she said, jolting him back into the moment.

He wanted to ask her if she was safe, but he was afraid her husband
could hear them.

He silently wrote down the number six.

"And here's the most important question," he said, quickly pulling up some phrases he had learned in his eighth-grade art class. "Is it
representational? Or abstract?"

"Mostly representational. There's only one abstract, but it's my
favorite one. It's the most valuable one, too. I inherited it from my
great-grandfather. It's a Valenowski. The artist is dead now, so, even
though I haven't had it appraised, I think it might be worth something."

Anthony nodded as he wrote it all down.

Then he heard, from deep in the apartment, what sounded like a shower turning on. But the sound was muted—clearly coming through a closed bathroom door.

It was the first time he had been able to get a bead on her husband's whereabouts.

He lowered his voice. And, in a move that surprised him with its boldness, he looked directly at her left eye. While she was looking at his face, and would notice.

"Are you okay here?" he asked her.

Her gaze cut immediately down to the carpet again. She stammered a few unintelligible sounds before any actual words came forth. "I . . . ," she said, then seemed to go no further in that direction. "You need to go now. I mean, *I* need to go now."

And she closed the door.

But it was *how* she closed the door that Anthony would always remember. She didn't slam it. Almost the opposite. She eased the door latched with a deliberate caution, a gentleness. As if the door were installed directly into Anthony's chest or gut, and she might hurt him if she mishandled it.

And it mattered a great deal to Anthony, because she did have the power to hurt him, though as yet he had no idea why.

# Chapter Three

*Who Are You?*

Anthony sat in a chair by his bedroom window. His back was getting stiff and a little sore, but he didn't want to move. Because, in that position and that position only, he had a view through the eyepiece of the telescope into the living room of apartment 2D across the street, and also an unaided view out through his window and down to the entrance of the building.

It was the following late morning. He hadn't eaten breakfast because he felt too unsettled. But he sipped intermittently at his second cup of coffee, setting it on the desk in between sips. There was a book open on his thighs, a hardcover edition of a book about planetary alignment, but he couldn't concentrate well enough to read much of it.

A motion caught his eye, but not through the telescope. It was a couple entering the building from the street below. But not *the* couple.

Then, several minutes later, he saw a movement through the eyepiece of the telescope. His heart jumped and skipped about one and a half beats.

He leaned over the scope and peered more closely through its lens. Edith was moving in a jerky pattern, first forward across his small field of vision. Then backward. It filled him with a frightening sense of déjà vu. Then she came forward again. Then backward.

It took him a good minute or more to understand that she was vacuuming the rug.

When he did realize this, he sat up straighter and squeezed his strained eyes closed, calming the beating of his heart. As he opened them, he saw a man leave the building across the street, and felt ninety percent sure it was Edith's husband. Granted, the man was far away, and Anthony was looking down from above. And the man was wearing a hat. Still, there was something in his movements, his body language, that felt familiar.

Telling himself he was probably wrong, he adjusted the scope to point down at the entrance. By the time he had it set and refocused, the man had hailed a cab and was gone.

Still Anthony sat, watching the entrance and waiting. He didn't look away for what might have been more than an hour. Then he glanced at his watch. It was ten minutes to noon.

When he looked back, Edith was stepping out onto the street.

He knew it was her because she was clearly focused in the eyepiece of his telescope. He recognized her wavy auburn hair, which had already become something of a familiar flag in his life. It spilled onto her shoulders from under her big hat. She was wearing a red coat that made her stand out like some sort of beacon in the winter grayness. She seemed to be the only part of the landscape that existed in living color.

She made a right turn and began to walk down the boulevard.

Anthony ran down thirteen flights of stairs, two at a time, because he was afraid he would miss her if he waited for the elevator. He stepped out onto the sidewalk and ran in the direction he had seen her go. But she was nowhere. He seemed already to have lost her.

He kept running, then stopped at the corner and whipped his head in both directions. He saw a flash of her red coat.

She was just disappearing into the little coffee shop and soda fountain around the corner from where they lived. If he had run even the tiniest bit slower, if he had taken one second longer to reach the corner, he would have missed her.

He leaned on a shelf of the corner newsstand, feeling the chill on his coatless upper body, and waiting to catch his breath again. He was not about to step into the restaurant panting, betraying the fact that he had run after her. He was already uncomfortable enough about seeming to be stalking her. But he wasn't stalking her, and in his gut he knew it. He wanted to accomplish one thing, and one thing only: to tell her that he was across the street in apartment 14A, and that she could show up at his door if she needed help or protection. And that he would do his best to help and protect her if she did.

She wouldn't like hearing it. She would probably react with the equivalent of closing the door on him again. It might be painful for her to hear that someone was witness to her abuse. Of course it would be. For anyone. But maybe she would need to take him up on it, and then, in retrospect, it would be worth it.

Or maybe she would be too ashamed to take him up on it, and something terrible would happen to her. In that case, Anthony would need to know that he had done what he could. There would be no living with himself otherwise.

A voice startled him out of his thoughts.

"Hey! Boy!" It was the bark of an impatient man. Anthony turned to see the owner of the newsstand—or its clerk—staring at him through narrowed eyes. "You gonna buy? Or you just gonna lean?"

"I'm going to buy."

He counted out the money in his pocket. Not to see if he could afford a newspaper—he knew he had that much. To see if he could afford lunch. He had plenty of bills stuffed into his jeans. More than he had realized.

He bought the paper not because the man said he should, but because it would give him something to stare at while he was not approaching her.

His plan was to see if she would notice and recognize him. To see if *she* would approach *him*. And if she didn't, well . . . he wasn't sure. He didn't know how much boldness he might be prepared to muster.

He walked to the door of the coffee shop, the newspaper tucked under his right armpit. Just as he reached for the door—just as he pushed it open—he was hit with an uneasy thought. What if she wasn't alone in there? What if she came here to meet somebody? Another man, maybe. It would be hard to blame her, given the man she had.

But Anthony had come that far, so he stepped inside. It was warm. Nearly oppressively warm after the cold of the outdoors. It felt good, though, following that deep chill. She was sitting in one of the red vinyl-upholstered booths, at the far wall, her back to him. Reading her menu. Alone.

Anthony chose a booth in the center—which consisted of two rows of booths side by side—and more or less level with hers. There was only one other couple in the place, in the far corner, out of the scene as far as Anthony was concerned. The world seemed to consist of only Edith and him, alone together on some potentially hostile planet.

It felt strange to call her Edith in his head. It felt strange to know her name when they knew so little of each other. Then again, what he knew about her felt crucial. Maybe it was all he needed to know.

He sat down and began to read his paper, spreading it out on the table in front of him to make the turning of its pages more manageable.

A waiter not much older than Anthony came by and brought him a menu.

He stared at it for a time, realizing he really was hungry. Also that he was already tired of sandwiches and canned soups, now that he was on his own to prepare food. Hot food, well prepared and made from scratch—the type of fare his mother would provide—sounded like a treat. Like enough of a reason to be here, even if Edith had been removed from the picture.

But she wasn't.

Her voice made him jump. At least, he felt as though he had jumped. He hoped it had not been obvious.

"Hey." He would have known her voice anywhere. He could have picked it out of a noisy crowd. "Art survey guy. That's you, right?"

He turned his eyes in her direction. He was prepared to meet her gaze head-on. But she was wearing oversized sunglasses, and her hat brim swooped down over her eyes. Which he knew was likely why she had worn it.

"Guilty," he said.

"So you live around here."

"Right across the street from you. Apartment 14A."

He figured it was better to get that in right away, in case she cut the conversation short.

A silence. He couldn't tell if she was still watching him. Her eyes were too completely hidden. He didn't know if the conversation was over.

"I apologize for yesterday morning," she said.

"Why? You didn't do anything wrong."

"I slammed the door in your face. That was rude."

"You didn't slam it at all. You closed it really gently."

"In the middle of our conversation."

"I get it, though—why you did. I embarrassed you, and I'm sorry about that." *And I'm sorry I'm about to embarrass you again,* he thought. But of course he didn't say it out loud.

She opened her mouth to answer. Before she could, a middle-aged couple came in, and walked right between Anthony and Edith. Anthony waited impatiently for them to pass, but they never did. They paused there, then settled in the booth right beside Anthony, completely blocking his view of Edith. Cutting off the connection.

It irritated him, and he almost said something to them. It reminded him of the days when he would go to the movies alone and some creepy older man would come sit right next to him, even though every other seat in the theater was free. Not that he thought this couple was being purposely creepy. Purposeful or not, they were violating the unspoken social contract that states you must offer a stranger as much personal space as you reasonably can.

Then again, he thought, he was a fine one to talk.

He did not say anything. They had a right to sit where they chose, even if it was rude.

He picked up his menu and his newspaper and moved into a booth in the front corner of the restaurant, looking out onto the street. He stared at the cars and cabs flashing by, and the people bustling along the sidewalk, still unable to shake the aggravation of having his conversation with Edith interrupted.

A moment later she sat down across the table from him, setting down her menu and a glass of iced tea. His belly jolted slightly at the boldness of the move. It felt as though she was about to confront him over something.

Then she opened her mouth and proved him right.

"So here's a question, art survey guy, and hold on to your hat, because it's a big one."

"You're the only one here wearing a hat," he said. He felt his face redden, because it had been a lame and silly attempt to defuse the moment with humor. "Okay. Sorry. Go."

"Is there really an art survey? Because I looked up that art institute at the library. And it doesn't seem to exist."

"No. There was never any art survey. I just wanted to get you to the door to see if you were okay."

"Then who are you?"

"Nobody. I'm just the guy across the avenue. Who doesn't want to see you get hurt."

"But we're total strangers. Why would that guy even care?"

"We're not total strangers. We know each other well enough that we're sitting here getting ready to order lunch together."

Actually, he had no idea if she would stay at his booth through lunch, or even the ordering of it. But she had brought her menu and her iced tea. That felt like a good sign. Anyway, it was worth a try.

"And how well did you know me when you knocked on my door yesterday morning?"

"Not at all," he said, his gaze cast down to the shiny metal table, heavy with something like shame.

"So back to the original question."

"No," he said, finding his voice and his strength again. Because he was trying to do the right thing, no matter her opinion about it. "No, *I* have a question for *you*. And hold on to your hat, because it's a big one. How well do I need to know a person before I'm allowed to prefer that nothing terrible happens to them?"

She let the question sit on the table in silence for a beat or two. Then the waiter showed up, pad in hand, to take their order.

"The usual?" he asked Edith.

She nodded slightly, still silent.

The waiter turned his eyes to Anthony, who ordered the chili with chopped onions and extra cheese.

When the waiter left, Edith raised her face and pulled off her sunglasses. The bruising under her eye was lighter than the previous morning, but still sickening to observe. Less deep purple and more light yellow and green. He looked away from it, noticing her nose instead, which was straight and narrow, and fairly long. It made her less than fashion-model pretty, but he thought it looked dignified and refined. He liked it because it was different. Something by which to know her. A way in which she was purely herself and not anyone else he knew.

"Okay," she said. "I hear that. I get that. I'll give you that much. You're a good guy. You're just trying to be a good person. And I give you credit for it. But there's still a big part of this that doesn't add up."

"What part is that?"

"You came to my door. And you saw I had a black eye. And so you wanted to know that I was okay. Which I get. But I don't get why you came to my door in the first place. Why were you worried before you knocked?"

"Because what happened . . . you know . . . night before last. It happened in front of the window."

For a time, no answer. She set her face in her hands, her eyes hidden from his view. Quite a bit of time passed. Anthony began to wonder if she was ever going to speak again.

The food arrived, breaking her spell. His chili and her turkey sandwich on wheat bread. She lifted her head out of her hands, possibly for lack of other reasonable options.

"They make the best turkey sandwiches here," she said, seeming to shake herself awake again. "With cream cheese and cranberry sauce." She lifted the top slice of bread to show him the cranberry sauce. It was a streak of deep red that he found unnerving. Like a gash. Like blood. "I try to make them myself at home, but they just don't come out the same. So I have one here every day for lunch. Well . . . every weekday."

He said nothing. He was trying to decide if she was purposely telling him her whereabouts every day at lunchtime. If there was an overt message there. And, if so, why. He wanted to say he'd gathered as much already from the waiter's reference to her "usual" order. Though of course he couldn't have known it was every weekday.

"You never think anybody will be looking in on a thing like that," she said, her voice more hushed. "That hit me pretty hard. No pun intended. That's pretty damned humiliating."

"I don't know why," he said, picking up his soup spoon and stirring the half-melted cheese into his chili. "It's not a reflection on you."

But it might have been, he realized—depending on how many times her husband had hurt her, and how many times she had forgiven him and stayed. He wanted to ask how long she'd been married to the man, but of course he didn't. He couldn't. It was none of his business. Any fool would know that.

"I'm surprised you could even see in any detail from the fourteenth floor," she said.

Which was interesting to Anthony, because it meant she had been listening when he told her where he lived, and she had remembered.

"Well, it's really only the thirteenth floor. They just call it fourteen because some people are superstitious." When she didn't answer straight away, he added, "Are you superstitious?"

He took a bite of chili. It was amazingly good. It woke him up inside. It had spice. Heat. It was interesting. Suddenly everything in his life felt interesting, though he realized the chili might be only a small part of that big feeling.

"Not about things like that. But you avoided something there, and I think you know it."

He sighed. "Look," he said. "There's a reason why it happened the way it did—my being able to see what I saw. And it might not sound like a thing that makes sense to somebody else, because it has to do with getting used to doing things one-handed." He paused, noticing her gaze flicker to his stump again. "I know it doesn't sound like the two are related, but you have to trust me on this. I swear on my grandfather's grave, I was not trying to be nosy by looking through your window. It was a weird accident. I'll swear on a stack of Bibles, it was just this weird thing that I didn't mean to have happen. I know you don't know me very well, but I'm not a liar. I'm not a perfect person, but you can count on me to tell you the truth at least."

He pitched back into his chili, waiting to see if she trusted him or not. If she absolved him or not. If it seemed she could forgive him for violating her privacy, accidentally or not.

"Oh." She smacked herself on the forehead with the heel of her hand. "*You* called the police. I just now got that. I'm a little slow, I guess. We thought it was the old man next door."

"I had to do *something*," he said.

Time stretched out without an answer from her. She ate her turkey sandwich as though it required her undivided attention. Anthony never stopped being unsettled by its flashes of deep blood red, even though he knew in his head it was only cranberry sauce.

"So you lost your hand *recently*," she said after several minutes. "When you see a thing like that, you always figure it happened years ago, and that the person is totally used to it."

"I'm not sure you ever get used to it. Maybe you do, but I don't know. It hasn't been long enough to know. Seven months, eleven days. Sounds like a pretty good amount of time to get used to a thing. But you just have to be inside the situation, I guess."

"No, I get it," she said, in between bites. "I mean, you have things a certain way for . . . I don't know how many years . . ."

In the pause, it dawned on him that she might be asking how old he was.

"More than seventeen. I just turned eighteen recently."

"And then everything changes. No, I get it. How long ago did your grandfather die?"

Anthony stopped chewing suddenly, his jaw muscles frozen in shock. "How did you know my grandfather died?" he asked, his mouth still rudely full.

"You just told me."

"When did I tell you that?"

"You just swore on your grandfather's grave."

"Oh. Did I? Oh. Okay. Well . . . it was less than a year ago. Ten months, I think."

"Were you close to him?"

"Very close. Everybody was. Everybody loved Grandpa Anton."

He glanced up, and their eyes locked for a moment. Anthony found it difficult to hold her gaze. And scary. As though someone were slicing into him for a better look. But he held it anyway, because it felt like something important. Like something too good to throw away.

"So you've had a very bad year, then," she said.

He broke off the gaze and stared down at the table. "You have no idea."

He thought she might ask more. But he didn't want her to. So he tried to put out a vibe to keep more questions away. Some variety of psychic fencing.

She didn't ask more.

They ate their food for a surprisingly long time in silence. What was most surprising about it, Anthony thought, was that it never felt awkward. It was a comfortable silence, as if they already understood each other well enough to get by.

—

"So what are you superstitious about, then?" he asked.

He spoke up because he knew their time together was almost over. Because he knew he had to get the conversation started again or nothing would ever get said.

"Oh, I don't know. Just weird little things. Like you see something, or feel something, and it feels like an omen. Like it has meaning. And then you put a lot of weight on it in your mind, because it feels important."

"I don't think that's superstitious. I think that's knowing what feels important."

"I should go."

It was a thing he had been expecting her to say all along. In fact, he now realized, he was surprised she hadn't said it much sooner.

"One thing before you go," he said, feeling uncharacteristically bold. "Well, two things, actually. I'm on my own for the holidays, and I'm having to cook for myself. I'm not completely hopeless at it, but what I've been making is lousy and this chili was good. So I might be back tomorrow to get more. And even the next day. And I don't want you to feel like I'm stalking you. It doesn't have to be about you. I might just be hungry."

She was on her feet already, fishing dollar bills out of her purse to leave on the table. She had her sunglasses on again. "I might be tempted to think it's a little of both." Her voice sounded flat and expressionless. Giving away nothing, except a trace of defensiveness. "What's the other thing?"

He felt relieved that she had followed that first statement with a question. So he could ignore that first statement.

"I told you where I live. Do you remember what I told you?"

"Apartment 14A in the building across the street."

"Right. Good. Thank you for remembering that. Because if you ever felt like you weren't safe, and you needed help, you could show up at my door. Anytime. Any hour of the day or night. And I would help you."

"And then my husband would tear you limb from limb."

"I could take him with one hand tied behind my back."

She didn't laugh, or even smile. Anthony knew why not. Because it wasn't funny. It wasn't a thing that was there to be laughed at—neither of their sides of the thing. And because he likely could *not* take her husband. Seven and a half months ago he would have stood a good chance. Now the man might tear him limb from limb.

"I really should go," she said. And walked away from the table.

He sat watching her go, hating the way the meeting ended. But she paused at the door, one gloved hand on the handle, and turned back to him.

"But thank you," she said.

Then she pushed through the door and she was gone.

# Chapter Four

*Foreigner*

The following morning Anthony made himself a small pot of coffee and sat by his bedroom window with a mug of it. He did not look through his telescope, or even position it. He just watched the entrance of the building across the street, waiting for Edith's husband to leave. As soon as that event was over, Anthony found himself fighting a war he had not seen coming.

He wanted to position his telescope to look through her window. Simply to see her. To watch her performing the simplest daily tasks. To rememorize her long, straight nose and wavy auburn hair, so he could see them clearly behind his closed eyes again.

He wanted this with a surprising fever, like an itch on the one part of his back he couldn't reach to scratch. It felt like a compulsion. Something deeply hard to battle.

But of course he couldn't do such a thing. Her husband was gone, so she could not be in danger. It was one thing to watch out for her safety, quite another to be her Peeping Tom.

He stepped away from the window and read an astronomy book in the living room instead. Forced his mind down different avenues. And, in doing so, barely won that war. But it might have been better for him to view it as a single battle, because any reasonable person could imagine that it was only the start of a much longer and more challenging war.

———

She stepped into the coffee shop and soda fountain at 12:05. He had been waiting for her since 11:30. He had been drinking coffee as a way of postponing ordering. It was making him jittery.

She was wearing her red coat but no sunglasses and no hat. Her eye looked better, but it still did not look good.

She sat in a booth close to his. It was across from his booth, but it was *not* his booth.

He experienced a sensation of his heart falling, as if literally. He now knew what it meant when someone said their heart fell into their shoes. He had always thought it was a strange thing to say, but now he understood.

He shook off the feeling as best he could, determined to speak and function through it.

"Edith," he said, and her head jerked slightly. "Really? You're going to eat your lunch over there?"

He almost said more. Something along the lines of "After all we've been through together." But it would have been a laughable statement, because they had only spoken on two occasions. Still Anthony could not shake the feeling that what they had shared was monumental.

"Well," she said. And seemed undecided as to whether to go on. "I wasn't sure if I was welcome at your table. You didn't invite me yesterday—I showed up uninvited. Maybe you're just here for the chili, and it has nothing to do with me."

He sensed a slight sharpness to the edge of her tone on the last sentence, as if she were poking him with a needle or some other pointed object. He wondered briefly if he had hurt her in some unimagined way when he'd made that statement the previous day.

"Edith," he said, his tone gentle. "Would you please come sit at my booth and have lunch with me?"

"I will," she said. "So long as you asked me so nicely and all."

She sat down across from him. Their gazes met briefly, then careened away again, almost as though under force or pressure, like the north poles of two magnets.

She stared at the table as she spoke.

"It's a little creepy that you know my name. How do you know my name?"

"Your husband called you by it."

It felt surprisingly hard for Anthony to make that simple statement—that the man who jerked her back across the room by her hair was her husband. He wanted the man not to be, and it bothered him to have to admit that he was.

"When? I don't understand. When did you even talk to him?"

"When he called you to the door that first day."

"Oh." She sounded confused. As if she had only just been dropped into this unfamiliar territory, and hadn't yet found her bearings. "I actually don't remember that. But I'll take your word for it."

The waiter brought their menus, and they both picked them up and studied them in silence. Which Anthony thought was odd, because she was here for the turkey sandwich and he was here for the chili, and they both knew it.

"I did the same thing yesterday," he said, his menu blocking any view of her.

"What thing was that?"

"I said something that let you know my grandfather died. And then I was really shocked that you knew my grandfather died. I still don't remember saying it. But, like you said . . . I'll take your word for it."

"I guess I'll have the turkey sandwich," she said in reply, though it was not a reply to anything he had said.

"I guess I'll have the chili."

They set down their menus and waited in awkward silence.

He glanced at her in his peripheral vision, trying to decide how old she was, but he had no talent for such guesswork. She might have been in her late twenties. But she also might have been in her early thirties. Or even late thirties. He really had no idea how to judge. She was younger than his parents, so not a generation older than he was. But she was closer to being a generation older than she was to his own age.

"I'm at a disadvantage," she said.

"I don't know what that means."

"I mean nobody ever yelled your name in front of me."

It took him a minute to sort out that she was asking his name.

"Oh. It's . . ." But then he paused. Froze.

"I didn't think it would be a tricky question," she said. "I thought you would know."

"I go by Anthony. But my real name on my birth certificate is Anton."

"After your grandfather."

"Wait. How did you . . ."

"Here we go again. You told me yesterday. I asked you if you'd been close with him and you said, 'Everybody loved Grandpa Anton.'"

"I'll take your word for it."

They fell silent for another minute. A young man walked by on the street carrying a transistor radio, blasting a Donovan song that was loud even through the restaurant glass.

"Anton is such a beautiful name," she said when the noise faded.

"You think so?"

"I really do. It has a dignity to it. It's unusual. It's distinctive. It sounds like a soldier in the Great War who served with honor, but I have no idea why I say that. I just love the sound of it. Why don't you use it? You don't like it?"

"It's not that I don't like it, exactly. It's a good name, I guess. I don't know. It's hard to explain. But I've had people . . . when I tell them my name is Anton, they actually ask me where I'm from. I was born in Flushing, New York, and they're asking me where I'm from."

"Why do you care if they think you're from somewhere else?"

"I don't, really. I don't know if I can put words to it."

"Okay."

They fell silent. Anthony assumed she would say no more about it, because there was no more to say. But she surprised him.

"Let me see if I can put words to it *for* you," she said. "Little bit of guesswork here, but I'm going to give it a try. It makes you feel foreign. Like a foreigner. Am I anywhere close to the right track? Like you don't really belong in this place. Like all these people around you are native to this place and you're not. Like you were beamed down here from some other planet, but you can't even go home because you don't know where home is."

When she finished speaking, he was aware of his mouth. It was embarrassingly open.

"Now . . . you can't tell me I told you all that and then forgot."

"Of course not," she said.

He didn't ask her how she knew if he hadn't told her. It was obvious that she owed him an answer to that. It didn't require his stating so.

"Because *I* feel that way," she said after a time. "Sometimes. Well. A lot of the time. So I guess I just figured, I'm human and you're human. I'm experimenting with the idea that maybe the things I think are so different about me are more common than I realize."

"How's the experiment going?"

"So far, so good. You seem to be with me on it."

"Have you ever asked anybody else if they feel that way?"

She shook her head, her eyes coming up and past him. Focusing on something behind his shoulder. He didn't turn around to see what was there.

"People don't like to talk about things like that," she said quietly.

By the time she finished the sentence, the waiter had walked up from behind Anthony. He stood at their table, pen hovering over his pad. Poised to take their order.

"The usual," Edith said.

"The usual," Anthony said.

"Wait," the guy said. "Let me see if I remember. Chili with onions and extra cheese?"

"That's it. You're good."

The young man scribbled on the pad and walked away.

"So here's a question," he said to Edith. "And hang on to your hat, because it's a big one. If this is only the third time we've talked, why are we already talking about the things people don't like to talk about?"

Her eyes came up to his. Drilled in. He felt a rush of adrenaline. As if he had just jumped out of a plane. A scary feeling, yet something he felt he could grab onto. And then, having grabbed on, he might never want to let go.

"I have no idea . . . ," she said. She paused. Then she added, ". . . Anton."

She looked away again.

They ate lunch together, but did not say anything more about the things people don't like to talk about. Just small-talked and ate.

It was comfortable. But also disappointing.

—

When Anthony arrived back at his apartment, he saw he had visitors. Two of them. Sitting on the welcome mat, punching each other on the shoulder with surprising force.

"Duncan," Anthony said. "Luke. What're you guys doing here?"

He felt something sink inside himself. His heart, or his gut. Or his heart sinking into his gut. They were his closest friends, or at least among the closest, so it made no sense that he should be less than happy to see them. But the plan had been to come home, lie on his back on the bed, stare at the ceiling, and think about his lunch with Edith. To roll every detail over and over in his head, wearing down a sweet, comfortable rut where his mind could rest until he saw her again.

"Tony!" Duncan shouted, and launched to his feet. "My man!"

He grabbed Anthony in a rough embrace, a sort of shoulder-pounding man hug, and shouted the words "my man" directly into Anthony's ear. Anthony winced, wondering if his friends had always been so loud and he had failed to notice.

He couldn't shake the feeling that he had changed since he'd last seen them. Turned into someone new, someone who couldn't understand their buoyancy anymore. Maybe even someone named Anton who couldn't understand.

"What've you guys been doing?" he asked when his friend had let him go.

"What else would two college guys do on semester break?" Luke asked, also too loudly. "Drinking."

So that explained a lot, Anthony thought.

He dug his keys out of his coat pocket, then dropped them onto the mat.

"I got it!" Duncan shouted, when no shouting was necessary. "I got you covered."

He grabbed up the keys and began sorting through them, as though trying to discover by sheer guesswork which key fit into which deadbolt.

"I can do it," Anthony said. "You should have just let me do it. I can pick up keys after I drop them." Duncan seemed to be ignoring him, so he raised his voice. But it burst out louder and sharper than he had intended. "Just give me the damn keys and let me do it!"

All motion stopped in the hallway. His friends stood staring at him. Luke seemed a little wobbly on his feet.

"Okay, fine," Duncan said, dropping the keys into Anthony's hand. "You don't have to bite my head off."

Rather than feeling apologetic, Anthony felt more irritation wanting to rise up through his gut and burst free.

"And don't call me Tony. I've told you, like, a hundred times, I don't like it."

"Fine. Anthony."

"Or Anton. I don't know. I might go back to Anton."

Another silence. Anthony set about unlocking the apartment door.

"Jeez, guy," Duncan said. "If *you* don't even know what you want to be called, how am *I* supposed to know?"

Anthony swung the door wide.

"I guess you guys had better come in," he said.

———

By the time he'd led Duncan down the hall toward his bedroom, Luke had disappeared somewhere into the apartment. Anthony thought maybe he'd gone to the bathroom, but it wasn't worth it to him to check.

They passed the closed door of Greg's old room. Even though Anthony was walking ahead of his friend, he could feel Duncan stop there, though he couldn't have explained how he felt it. He turned back, walked to his friend's side, and they stood staring at the door together. It had a sign bolted to it, custom made on blue-and-white painted metal. It read, **GREGOR THE TERRIBLE SAYS "KEEP OUT!"**

"I still can't believe he's gone," Duncan said, seeming sobered by the moment. "Can you believe it?"

"Unfortunately I believe it."

"What's in there? Anything?"

"Everything. It's just like it was before."

"How can it be just like it was? Didn't that crew of guys have to take everything out to clean? And paint the walls, and put down new carpet and all?"

"Yeah, but they took pictures of how it was before, and they put it all back together just the same way. I mean, everything that was salvageable at least."

"Can I look?"

"Can't you just take my word for it?"

"I just want to look."

"Fine. Look. But I don't want to look."

He walked three steps down the hall and waited while Duncan peered into his late brother's room. Then Duncan closed the door so softly that Anthony could only describe the behavior as reverent.

"That's so weird," Duncan said, catching up with Anthony.

They walked together to Anthony's room.

"Why is it weird? It's just like it always was. It's just like nothing ever happened."

"Right. That's what's weird."

They stepped into Anthony's bedroom and Anthony flopped onto his back on the bed.

"Ooh," Duncan said. "Cool telescope! They got it for you! I didn't think they'd get it for you. It's pretty expensive, even for them."

"They felt guilty."

"About what?"

"Going to South America for the holidays."

"Oh, that. Are you kidding? The whole apartment to yourself for three weeks? That's a gift. We should have a party."

"I'm not going to have a party."

When Duncan didn't answer, Anthony raised his head and opened his eyes. His friend was examining the telescope, peering at it close up, and touching it lightly with the tips of his fingers—but not looking through the eyepiece, which seemed odd.

Anthony set his head back down and sighed.

"What're you seeing with this thing so far?" Duncan asked.

"Not much. It's been cloudy. And the city lights wash out every-thing. Uncle Gregor is going to drive me out into the country with it after the holidays. Until then it's not doing me much good."

"Well, I think I found the problem!" Duncan fairly bellowed. "You're supposed to point it up at the sky, idiot. Have you been look-ing through other people's windows with this thing?"

Anthony raised his head to see Duncan looking through the eye-piece and—he now realized—into the apartment across the street. Or *an* apartment across the street. He knew he hadn't looked through it that morning, but he couldn't remember if it had been left trained on her window. But even the *possibility* that his friend might be looking in at Edith was more than he could bear. He launched himself off the bed in one sudden motion and plowed into Duncan, knocking him away from the scope.

"Hey!" Duncan bellowed. "What the hell? Why were you looking down there? Is there a lady down there?"

"None of your business, Duncan."

"That's kinky, Tony. I didn't think you were into stuff like that."

"I don't want to talk about it. And don't call me Tony."

"Does she walk around naked or something?"

As he spoke that last horrible sentence, Duncan moved toward the eyepiece of the telescope again.

Anthony charged at him with a surprising rage. He wrapped Duncan up in his arms and used his full weight, their combined weight, to throw his friend onto the bed. He landed on top of Duncan, arm raised to strike. But old habit had caused him to raise his right arm. As he instinctively attempted to make a fist, he found himself plunged into the ice water bath of his new reality. Both Anthony and Duncan stared at the raised stump in silence. Neither moved a muscle.

Then Duncan said, "Isn't that gonna hurt you more than it hurts me?"

Anthony let his arm fall again. He pitched himself off Duncan, landing on his back on the bed next to his friend. They both just lay there for a minute or two, saying nothing.

"So, what was that about?" Duncan asked at last.

"I don't know. Nothing. I've just been under a lot of pressure."

"Well, duh. We knew *that*. Why do you think we came and visited you?"

"Thank you," Anthony said, and actually halfway meant it.

"But it was still weird."

"Yeah, okay. It was weird. I'm sorry."

"You should've started college with us. I hate that you'll be a year behind now."

"I might not even go to college here. I might go out of state."

"I didn't know anything about that. When did you decide that?"

"I've just been thinking."

"I know you can get in pretty much wherever you want, but just . . . I don't know. Go anywhere, but just go. You know?"

"I needed the year off."

"I know you think so, but I think it's just giving you too much time to think about everything that happened. Seriously, Tony. I mean . . . Anton? You're seriously going with Anton again? Why?"

Before he could answer, Luke appeared in the bedroom doorway. They had been staring at the ceiling, but Luke ran into the doorframe with an audible thump that brought them both into an upright position.

"Where've you been, Luke?" Anthony asked, feeling irritated again.

"Trying to see if I can get into your parents' liquor cabinet with a hairpin. But, wow. That lock is locked."

"You were trying to steal liquor from my parents?"

"I would've filled the bottles up with water. I'm not stupid."

"Neither are they, Luke. I can't believe you did that."

"Sorry," Luke said, but he didn't sound sorry. More rushed and impatient. "Ask him, man," he added, apparently to Duncan.

"Ask me what?"

"We were hoping you'd go to the liquor store and buy us something," Duncan said.

Anthony sat in silence for a moment, feeling the sting of that sentence settling down into his chest. "Just a minute ago you said you came to see me because you knew I was under a lot of pressure."

"Well . . . yeah," Duncan said. "Both."

Anthony squeezed his eyes closed and allowed another long silence to fall.

Anthony knew Duncan and Luke from having grown up together, since the fifth grade, in a class for academically gifted students known as "Special Progress." They had all skipped a grade. So now, despite having a semester of college under their belts, neither Duncan nor Luke was eighteen, which was the legal drinking age in New York State. Duncan had nearly seven months to go. Luke was short by only a few weeks.

Only Anthony could legally buy liquor. And that was why they were here.

"You guys need to go now," he said.

Another brief silence.

"Does that mean no to the liquor store idea?" Luke asked, sounding like a hurt child.

"Out," Anthony said.

"Jeez," Duncan replied.

But he got himself up and headed toward the door. Anthony walked them out, to be sure they made no detours to the liquor cabinet. And because he didn't want to treat them so rudely or so coldly that there was no chance of their still being his friends.

"Seriously," Duncan began. "We just—"

But Anthony cut him off again. "I just need to be alone."

"I think being alone is just what you *don't* need."

"Well, I'm sorry, but I'm me, so I figure I know what I need better than you do."

"Just one bottle of vodka," Luke said. "Then we're out of your hair."

Anthony didn't reply to that comment. They wouldn't have liked what he had to say. Instead he unlocked the door and threw it open wide. To make it clear that their exit was definitely the next thing on the agenda.

On his welcome mat stood Grandma Marion, right hand poised to knock. So being alone was not in the cards for Anthony that day, and in that moment he chose to sigh and accept it.

———

She made tea in the kitchen as Anthony sat at the breakfast counter watching her work. Coffee sounded better. But it was an old tradition, tea with Grandma Marion. It had been part of his life since he was a small child. She brewed strong chamomile flowers in mesh tea balls, and it had a soothing quality. And maybe he'd had enough caffeine already.

"How are you getting by, Anton?" she asked, without looking up at him.

"I'm okay."

"On the inside, I meant."

"Pretty okay, I think. How are *you* getting by on the inside?"

She looked at him then, and her hands stilled. She looked ten years older since Grandpa Anton died. Her white hair seemed thinner and more limp. Her skin, which had been creased as long as he'd known her, seemed thinner and more limp as well, as though it had lost the will to remain elastic.

"That's a thoughtful question," she said. "It's very hard since your grandfather passed away, I won't lie to you about that. But as you get older, you learn about the whole 'life going on' concept. Well, it's not even a concept. It's real. It just is. You learn to absorb losses. This year you had your first big losses, so I worry about you more than me. But you had your friends here to see you. That's good, anyway."

"You would think so," he said.

He was staring down at the tile of the countertop, running his thumbnail along the grout in between tiles. A mug of tea appeared under his face, at the end of Grandma Marion's hand. The smell wafted up and filled his head, and felt surprisingly welcome.

"Meaning what?" she asked, sitting on the high stool beside his.

"I don't know. I just . . . have you ever felt like . . . like you've known people for a long time, and they always seemed to fit with you before, but then all of a sudden you feel like you don't have anything in common with them anymore?"

"I have. Absolutely I have. I suppose we all have. It happens when people grow in two different directions, or one grows much faster than the other. Great tragedy brings great growth, Anton. It wakes us up. It makes us into someone a little different from who we were before. You're more mature now. I know it feels like a bad thing, but it pays to let life grow you up. I'm not saying it's good when tragedy happens—of course it isn't. Only that we would do better not to resist its effects on us. Now show me this new telescope of yours. I heard a lot about it from your great-uncle Gregor."

"Okay. I'll haul it out onto the balcony so you can see how it works."

But he really hauled it out on the balcony so she would not see what he had been viewing from the privacy of his room.

# *Chapter Five*

## *The Ghost and the Fedora*

It was a handful of days later. A handful of lunches.

Edith had set her half-eaten piece of turkey sandwich back on her plate, the bitten edge facing him. Anthony stared at it for a moment. He wasn't getting over the shock of that blood color. It jolted him every time. It seemed to drive him out of their lighter, more pleasant conversation and into a deeper place. He wasn't *creating* a conflict or problem. It had been right there all the time. They had been eating lunch while bobbing on the surface of everything more important. Now Anthony held his nose, figuratively speaking, and allowed himself to sink.

"Can I ask you a question?"

She looked up sharply, catching his tone. She was wearing an off-white silk scarf loosely wrapped around her hair. He missed her hair, but thought she looked beautiful in the scarf anyway. The darkness under her left eye had faded to a shadow.

"Should I hold on to my hat?" she asked him.

He could feel her wanting to make light of his mood. To pull him back up into more buoyant territory.

"Definitely," he said, not allowing himself to be pulled.

"Okay, go ahead." But she squeezed her eyes shut as if she'd found herself standing in front of a firing squad.

"Why do you stay with him?"

She pulled a deep and fairly loud breath. She did not open her eyes. "You don't understand about that," she said. Quiet, breathy words.

"Of course I don't understand. It goes without saying that I don't understand. That's why I asked. So help me understand."

She opened her eyes and turned her face away, then sat still and silent a moment, looking out the window. The whole world seemed to be striding or driving by, but the world outside the window meant nothing to Anthony. This felt like his world now.

"The first thing you don't understand," she began, quietly, "is that he's still the man I married. He's not some inhuman monster. Some people have a rough past and then they don't know how to handle things well the way people do when they were raised better. He's not the villain from one of those old melodrama plays, with the handlebar mustache. He's a real person. He's the person I fell in love with, and a lot of the time that man is still there."

Anthony tried not to wince or otherwise betray his feelings as that truth burned down into his scarred gut. He wanted to move the conversation back to the bad side of the man.

"Did he hit you before you were married?"

"Oh, no. They never do. Everybody's on their best behavior during courting. That's just how the world works. It's how people work. Then, when they figure they've got you for keeps, that's when you find out what you've really gotten yourself into. But there's more you don't understand than just that. When you live with a person like him . . . a man who wants to control everything so tightly . . . he cuts off your options. He tightens your circle and cuts you off from the people you used to know, until there's nobody left but him."

"He couldn't cut you off from your own parents. Could he?"

"Both my parents are dead," she said, still staring out the window.

"Oh. I'm sorry."

"But here's what you really don't understand, and it might be the key thing. He controls me by controlling the money. I have no money unless he gives it to me. Even these lunches go on a tab and he pays it. So what are my options? How do I get anywhere else? How can I take my things, just on my back or whatever, and go someplace new? I don't even have money to hail a cab. Hell, I don't even have money to get on a bus. Where would I go?"

"If it's just about money, I could help you."

It seemed to wake her in some undefined way. Pull her out of whatever world she was visiting outside the window. She shook her head. Too hard. Vehemently hard. She raised her gaze as if to look at his face, but missed his eyes by several inches.

"No," she said. "Absolutely not. I can't take money from you."

"Why can't you?"

"How could I do that? It would be taking advantage of you."

"Whatever," he said. "Whether you would take my money or not. You can't really use that excuse anymore. You can't really say you have no place to go because you have no money. Because I'm right across the street and you don't need a single penny to walk over."

She may have said something in return. In the back of his mind he thought he heard her voice. But his attention was jolted completely out of the scene when he looked out the window and saw Edith's husband staring in at them.

Edith was facing Anthony, and giving him her full attention, and she didn't see. The man outside was staring at the side of his wife's head, and not making eye contact with Anthony.

"What?" Edith asked, and he heard her clearly this time. "You look as though you just saw a ghost."

She craned her neck to look, but the ghost was already gone. He had turned suddenly away, flipped his collar up against the December cold, and had already moved out of view of the window.

She looked back to Anthony. "What? What was it?"

"Your husband."

Her face blanched with alarming speed. Anthony had never seen all the blood drain out of a face so fast. She sprang to her feet and ran outside without her coat. Anthony watched as she turned the same way the man had turned, and wondered how she knew which way he had gone. Maybe Anthony's eyes had told her by following his retreat.

He moved quickly to the door and opened it just enough to peer down the street. They were standing close and seemed to be talking near the end of the block. It looked constrained and civil, their talk. Anthony saw no signs of rage in the man, or fear in Edith.

"Hey!" a voice shouted at Anthony, startling him. "You want to close the door? You're letting all the cold in."

Anthony looked around, but couldn't see anyone. It must have been one of the line cooks in the kitchen, because the waiter was nowhere to be seen. And there were no other diners, because he and Edith had begun meeting earlier, around the time the place opened at eleven, when it was least busy.

Anthony had no idea what to do. If he stepped in and closed the door, she might get hurt and he wouldn't know. And if he didn't know, he couldn't help her. If he stepped out and closed the door, her husband would see him watching—keeping tabs on the situation—and that might enrage him, and make it more likely that she would get hurt.

"I mean it, kid," the booming voice said. "Heating bills don't pay themselves."

He stepped back into the restaurant and allowed the door to swing closed. He stood for a handful of seconds, but they felt like hours. His gut roiled and strained under its load of stress. Then he pushed the door open for a flash of a second and looked. The scene of their conversation still appeared calm.

He forced himself to go back to their table and sit down.

A few moments later Edith stepped back inside, alone, rubbing her arms to ward off the cold. She sat across from him again.

"What happened?" he asked immediately.

"Oh, nothing."

"Wait. What? How is it nothing? You just said he tries to cut you off from everybody. How is he not upset?"

"Well, he was. At first. When he came down here, he was. Somebody he knows from work saw us having lunch together and told him, and he came rushing down here thinking I was seeing another man. But he recognized you from that day you came to the door. You know. Art survey guy. So I just told him we have lunch and talk about art."

"And he just believed you and let it go? That seems weirdly reasonable."

"No, it wasn't that. It wasn't like that at all. It wasn't anything I said. He'd already decided that it wasn't anything he needed to worry about."

"How? Why?"

"Oh, Anton. Please. Let's not do this. Don't make me do this."

Anthony sat holding his own head for a moment, as if his hand and wrist were the only forces holding it together. "I don't understand this at all," he said, feeling he had neared the end of some sort of mental tether, but having no idea what would happen when its end arrived.

She sighed. She didn't speak for what might have been a full minute. Then she did.

"It wasn't really reasonable. At all. It was more like . . . he was sort of . . . sneering at the whole thing. Like it was funny that he'd ever thought you might be a threat to him. But the stuff he said was very bad, and you would *not* like hearing it, and I'm trying not to repeat that stuff and make you hear it. Because it was bad."

"Bad about you? Or about me?"

"Both," she whispered, her voice barely audible.

"Go ahead and tell me."

"That doesn't feel—"

"Tell me."

For a moment he could hear her breathing.

"He just thought it was funny, the idea that you would be a threat to him, like I said. To the marriage. Because you're so young. He thinks you're, like . . . just a kid. He's all into the manly thing. Like there's one certain way to be manly. And he thinks women are really mostly looking for a man who can protect them. You know. Physically. That's just how he thinks."

"So by calling me a kid he made himself feel better?"

"I guess so."

"I would think he'd be mad anyway because you were with . . . you know. Anybody. Because you were talking to anybody."

"What do you think he was trying to feel better about? Yeah, it bothered him. But he chose to handle it like this. By laughing at the fact that you couldn't possibly threaten him."

"Because I'm young? Doesn't he know young people are strong? I used to be a pretty good athlete until this year."

Her gaze flickered down to his right hand—or, more accurately, to the lack of it—which in the heat of the moment he had forgotten to discreetly hide under the table. It seemed as though she hadn't meant to. As if her eyes traveled there without her permission. Maybe she had tried hard not to look there, and it ended up being one of those situations like trying not to think of a white elephant.

"Oh," he said. "Got it."

"He just has these old-fashioned views on men and women. He doesn't know it's 1965 and nothing has to be so rigid anymore. In his mind it's still about who can beat up who. So he figures you're young and he doesn't think you could hold your own in a fistfight, so he laughed you off. Like I couldn't possibly be interested in you. But that's just him. Don't take it personally. That's just how *his* mind works. *I* don't think like that."

"So you're saying you *could* be interested in an eighteen-year-old with only one hand?"

It was a stride too far, and Anthony knew it immediately. The moment it was out of his mouth he would have done anything, given anything, traded anything, to grab it and haul it back in again. He saw her face shut down. He felt their connection slam closed.

"I should get going," she said, and stood. And began to struggle into her coat.

"You didn't eat your sandwich."

"I lost my appetite."

She took one step toward the door, but he stopped her, using only words.

"Wait," he said. "I need to ask you one more question."

She stood still for him, but said nothing. Neither of them seemed to be in a mood to make their signature joke about hats.

"Is there ever a line . . . like . . . of . . . hurting you . . . that he could cross? And then that would be it for you?"

She hovered a moment, clutching her coat around herself but not moving. And not answering. "If he does it again, I think I'll need to leave," she said. Finally.

"Why now? What's different?"

He asked because he was afraid that, without a new and compelling reason, it might be all talk on her part. He worried that maybe she always thought—and claimed—that she would leave "next time," but then never did.

She looked straight at him for the first time since they'd seen the ghost. He didn't know why. But she seemed to expect him to know.

She gestured in his direction with her chin, but still said nothing.

"What? I don't understand."

"Because it used to be just him and me. There was nobody else around. Now there's somebody watching it happen. And that's just . . . unbearable."

Before he could speak, she had hurried out the door and was gone.

———

Anthony walked around for hours, up and down the snowy streets, staring into shop windows and trying to get the roiling in his gut to settle. He looked into model train stores, and record stores, and clothing stores displaying mannequins with the latest miniskirts and bell-bottom jeans. He looked into the eyes of the stuffed elves in their Christmas displays.

The roiling in his gut never did settle.

After an hour or so of this, he found himself staring through the window of a men's hat store. It hit him, almost like a sudden key to his salvation, that he must have one. That he would buy himself a hat. It would be a grand joke between Edith and himself. He would wear it whenever he met with her. She would ask him why he wore it all through lunch, and he would say something light and wry. Something like "Well, I never know what you might be just about to ask." And she would smile, or even laugh, and he would have succeeded in lightening the moment, which would then erase the terrible mistake he had made. In that moment, he could honestly believe that a hat would redeem him. It would repair everything.

He stepped inside.

A woman of about thirty stood behind the counter, reading a section of newspaper. She glanced up at him briefly and smiled. He smiled in return, feeling as though the worst of the day's devastation might be over.

He walked around and began trying on hats. He also began stealing a look at the price tags before settling them on his head and striking a pose in the mirror. They were expensive.

"Looking for anything in particular?" the woman asked him.

He opened his mouth, and was surprised to hear that he *was* looking for something in particular. He hadn't known it until she asked.

"My grandfather had the nicest hat. I guess I'm trying to find one that looks like it. He wore it the whole time I was growing up, and I guess that set some sort of an example in my mind for what a man's hat ought to be."

It made him feel better to speak of men's hats, underscoring that he was a man. He *was* a man now, and maybe it was time to step up. To step more fully into the role.

She set down her paper and joined him by the mirror.

"Can you describe it?"

"Like the one Bogart wore in *Casablanca*. And in those old Sam Spade movies."

"Oh, a vintage film buff," she said, sounding impressed.

"Little bit of one, yeah."

"That's a fedora. A real classic in men's hats."

"Do you have one?"

"We have these."

She led him to a rack of hats that turned on its base, and spun it slowly, and showed him a few fedoras. They cost over forty dollars. And they were *almost* like his grandfather's hat, but somehow didn't quite ring that same bell for him.

"They're nice," he said. "But I think I liked my grandfather's hat better."

"He doesn't have it anymore?"

"What's this, now?" he asked, not understanding.

"You said he *had* the hat. And you *liked* it. Past tense."

"Oh. I didn't mean it like that. It's my grandfather who's past tense. He died this year."

"I'm sorry," she said.

"Thanks. Me too."

He set a dark gray one on his head, but it was too big. It fell down to his eyebrows and made him feel like a little boy, so he quickly took it off and set it back on the rack.

"Have you asked your family if it's still among his belongings? Or did someone go through his things and get rid of everything? Because if it was well cared for, a vintage piece from the heyday of men's hats can be a real find."

"It's still around. I see it when I go visit my grandmother. It's hanging on the rack by the door, like he's just about to pop it on his head and go out for a newspaper or a quart of milk."

"I realize I'm a terrible saleswoman for saying this . . . and I work on commission, too, but . . . maybe she would let you have it."

"Huh." He stood frozen, letting the thought swell into his head until there was no room for anything else. "Yeah. Maybe. Maybe she would."

———

Grandma Marion answered the door with her half-glasses drooping down onto her nose. She looked even more surprised to see him than he had expected.

"Sorry I didn't call first," he said.

Grandma Marion lived in a row house in Astoria, with a real front door that opened out onto the street. He was aware of the cold and whirling snow he was allowing into her foyer as they stood regarding each other.

"Always happy to see you, Anton, I'm just surprised. Because I saw you only yesterday."

She had stopped by the previous evening to bring him some homemade soup.

"Right. I know. I wanted to ask you a favor. Kind of a big favor."

"You couldn't bring yourself to ask yesterday?"

"I didn't know I wanted it yet."

"Come in, come in," she said, tugging at his coat sleeve. "We're letting all the heat out."

He stepped into her warm foyer and found himself at eye level with the hat. Somehow it looked more fine and valuable and perfect than he had remembered. If he was wrong to think it could solve all of his problems, he was incapable of seeing the error in that moment. It was in perfect condition, too. A little softer and more broken in than the ones he'd tried on in the hat shop, but not noticeably more worn looking.

"You miss your grandfather, don't you?"

"Of course I do."

"I see you staring at his old fedora. He loved that hat."

"It looks nearly new."

"It does, and he had it since . . . oh, I'm not sure now. Sometime in the forties. Definitely before 1950. But he took such meticulous care of it. He had it cleaned and blocked every year like clockwork. It was something of a signature piece of apparel for him."

He unbuttoned his jacket as she spoke, because he was too warm.

"Would it be all right if I tried it on?"

"Of course."

He took it off its rack almost reverently, and settled it on his head. It didn't fit perfectly. It was maybe a quarter of an inch too big. But it didn't literally fall onto his eyebrows. It just felt a little insecure there. He wouldn't dare wear it outside in a blustery wind.

He stepped over to the decorative mirror, and sucked in his breath when he saw himself. He looked like a new person. Like a fully grown man. Like an adult man named Anton. It was too perfect. He knew he couldn't let it go now—not now that he'd seen who he was in it.

Grandma Marion sucked in her breath, too. Audibly.

"What?" he asked her, when he'd torn his eyes away from his own reflection. "Is something wrong?"

"You look so much like him when I first met him. It took my breath away for a second."

"It looks so good on me."

"It's not a perfect fit. A little loose. But you can buy a strip of fitting material to place inside the band to make it fit more snugly. It's very close." Then, before he could ask if that meant she was giving it to him, she said, "Would you wear the hat if you had it? Really wear it?"

"If I had this hat, I would never take it off."

"Then you should have it. It will make you feel closer to your grandfather. Now come in the kitchen and I'll make us some tea, and you can ask me this big favor."

———

"I want to ask your advice about something," he said as he watched her fill the whistling teakettle, as she called it. "Not advice, exactly. Your thoughts on a situation. A life situation. I never ask my parents about things like this, because . . . well, I hope you won't take this the wrong way, because I know he's your son and all, but I feel like they don't really know, either. Like they don't understand life a whole lot better than I do."

"Nobody truly understands life," she said, lighting the burner under the kettle.

She was wearing a thick blue cardigan sweater over her print house-dress. She was a knitter, so he assumed she had made it herself.

"I feel like you and Uncle Gregor do. Maybe because you've been around a long time. I'm sorry if that sounded rude. I didn't mean it in a bad way."

"You can't surprise me with how long I've been around," she said. She sat across from him at the kitchen table, a huge, heavy antique made of wood distressed by the years. "I was there every second of my life, so I know. What are you hoping I'll tell you?"

"Why do people stay in relationships with a person who's terrible for them? Someone who's just a terrible person? I don't understand that at all."

"Many reasons," she said after a big sigh. "As many reasons as there are people who will stay with someone terrible. But I think it might be fair to say that all the reasons intersect and have one thing in common: too many people can't believe they deserve someone wonderful."

They sat in silence for a time, until the teakettle whistled.

"Does that help you at all?" she asked.

She rose to turn off the stove.

"I think so. It's something I'm going to have to think about."

"That can't be the big favor, just telling you my thoughts on a human foible."

"No."

"What did you want, then?"

"Grandpa Anton's hat. I came to ask you if I could have it, but I thought you probably wouldn't want to part with it."

"In some ways I don't want to. And for anyone else the answer would have been no. But you're his namesake, Anton. You're growing up in his image. And he's no longer here for you to emulate. So it seems as though you are its rightful owner now."

He knew, in that moment, that he was wrong to ever have called himself Anthony, and that he must never do such a thing again.

———

He stopped at the hat store on the way home, and showed his new fedora to the woman clerk, who was suitably impressed. He felt even better then, nearly elated, because he knew it was not just him. It was a great hat. It was *the* hat.

She sold him a band of material that sized it perfectly, and was not in the least expensive.

When its fit was as perfect as its look, he felt as though his world had been righted again. That he had been foolish to believe all was lost.

———

The following day he wore the hat to their usual meeting place. He showed up at 11:00 a.m. and sat in the booth by the window, waiting. He did not take it off as men tended to do indoors, and when they were eating.

He sat drinking coffee, feeling more and more jittery, until nearly two o'clock in the afternoon.

Edith never showed.

When he left, it was not because he was positive she would never come, nor did he feel inclined to give up on her. He left because he realized she might have been hurt, or otherwise unable to get out of the apartment.

He ran all the way home, wondering how he would feel if she was not okay, and also how he would feel if she was. Though her welfare obviously mattered a great deal to him, learning that she had been perfectly able to come meet him, but hadn't chosen to, would be its own brand of disaster.

He rode up on the elevator, panting and tapping his foot.

As soon as he'd let himself into the apartment, he ran to his room, trained the telescope on her window, and focused on her little world across the street. He sat that way for a long time, maybe as long as an hour, biting his thumbnail and even the skin around the cuticle.

Then he saw her walk across the living room.

She seemed okay.

He spent the remainder of the day trying to force himself to accept the plain fact that he had lost her. He knew he'd sit in the coffee shop again the next day, just in case. But it was time to admit that it would probably come to nothing again.

And he knew it was nobody's fault but his own.

He lay awake until after two in the morning, mentally wrestling that truth.

—

Anton Addison-Rice was fast asleep and dreaming about seeing someone off on a train—but he didn't know who it was or where they were
going—when a noise jolted him awake.

He sat up in bed, wondering if he had really heard a pounding, or
only dreamed it.

Then it happened again, and he felt it as a jolt through his gut.
Someone was banging on the apartment door.

His eyes flew to the bedside clock. It was after three in the morning.

He jumped out of bed, pulled on his robe, and strode to the door,
his heart hammering. He squinted through the peephole and saw a
woman who could well have been Edith, but her face was turned away,
as though she might be about to retrace her steps to the elevator.

"Wait, I'm here!" he shouted through the door.

He began undoing the locks, but his haste made him clumsy.

When he finally swung the door open, he was deeply relieved to
see that she was still there. Then he focused on her face in the soft light
of the hallway. Her lower lip was swollen to more than twice its normal
size, and had a split that looked black in that lighting. It had clearly
bled, but wasn't bleeding now. But there was a distinct maplike stain of
blood on her collar, which plunged him back into upsetting memories.

She looked directly into his eyes.

She didn't cry, and didn't look as though she'd been crying anytime
recently. But her eyes conveyed so much sadness that it felt like an anvil
dropping through him, pulling his stomach down and then crashing
through the floor beneath his feet.

"Hold on to your hat, Anton," she said, her words muddied by the
swelling. "I think I might have just left my husband."

# Chapter Six

## A Story of Hell

He dressed quickly—all things considered—then made tea in the kitchen, using Grandma Marion's stash of chamomile flowers. Coffee seemed wrong at 3:00 a.m. Sooner or later it might do Edith good to sleep, if such a thing proved possible.

"Define *might*," he said, raising his voice to call in to her.

"I don't understand the question." Her voice was still muddled by the swelling.

She sat in the living room—possibly purposely far away from him—in his father's leather recliner. Her face was lost in shadows. He had given her a few cubes of ice wrapped in a clean dish towel, and he could barely see the outline of her holding it to her lip.

"You said you *might* have left him."

"Oh," she said, moving the ice. "Not might. Not really. It was just sudden and new, and I was confused, and I didn't know what to say about it. And I was being kind of jokey and trying to be light. This can't be your own apartment, right? You live here with your parents?"

"For now," he said, feeling uncomfortable with the line of questioning.

"Where are they?"

"South America."

"For how long?"

"Another two weeks or so."

"What am I going to do?" She sounded utterly panicky and just at the edge of tears.

He left the kettle on the stove and went to sit with her. He sat on the couch because it was a respectful distance away, and tugged at the knee of his jeans, and dared to tell her his thoughts on the matter.

"You're going to hide here for a few days, because at first he'll look for you close to home, or at the airports, or at the train or bus stations. We'll give him some time to give up on that and figure he missed you. And then I'll give you some money and we'll sneak you out of town. Do you have anywhere you can go?"

"I'll have to think about that. Sure, there's always somewhere, but you have to have train fare and a shot at getting there. But I insist on paying you back." Her voice had settled some. Whatever jolt of fear had gripped her seemed to be easing as they spoke. "Thank you. Really, thank you, because a person can't have nothing. You have to have a friend to go to or a place to go on your own. You can't just step out into the world with nothing. You have to have a safe place to lie down at night."

Her mention of train fare reminded him of his dream, in which he had seen some faceless person off to some unnamed location by train.

"You can sleep in my room," he said. But, as he heard it, it rang in his ears like another mistake. "Oh, hell. I didn't mean . . . I mean, you sleep in my room and I won't. I'll sleep in my parents' room. I wasn't—"

"Anton," she said, interrupting. Her voice was soft in the half dark. She surprised him by leaning across the space between them and briefly touching his cheek. "I know you're a gentleman. You don't have to convince me of that. I wouldn't have come here if I didn't think so."

She sat back, and of course took her hand with her. He sat alone on the couch and continued to feel the touch of her skin on his, even though it was gone.

"Oh, wait. I can't sleep in my parents' room. What am I thinking? I'll have to sleep on the couch. They'll know if I touch their things. They always know. They have eyes in the back of their heads, and they'll be all offended and they'll want to know everything."

"I could take the couch."

"No," he said. "I wouldn't hear of that. You need your own bathroom and a door that locks, so you can have your privacy and feel safe. I'll lay out a clean pair of my pajamas for you. And a towel and washcloth." *And point the telescope back up at the sky*, he thought. "I could sleep in my brother's old room, except . . . no. I can't do that. I just couldn't bring myself to do it."

"Is your brother away at college?"

"No. He died."

The kettle whistled, and he jumped up to pour the tea. It was light in the kitchen, and it made him blink excessively. He poured boiling water into the pot and stood too long, waiting for it to steep and kicking himself for mentioning his brother. Because when he carried it back to the living room, she would ask how Greg died.

But he was also afraid of ruining the tea by brewing it too strong, so in time he rejoined her with the pot and two mugs. He set them on coasters on the coffee table because he would never hear the end of the subject if he left a ring.

They sat sipping tea in the mostly dark for what felt like several minutes.

When she finally opened her mouth, she didn't ask how Greg had died. She asked only, "Recently?"

"This year, yeah."

"Wow. You weren't kidding when you said I had no idea what a bad year you'd had. You lost your grandfather, your brother, and your hand all in the same year?"

For a moment he only sipped his tea in silence. The smell of it reminded him of Grandma Marion, which felt bracing and comforting, and made it just a tiny bit easier to be bold.

"It's not quite right to say I lost Greg and my hand in the same year. I mean, it's accurate—strictly speaking. But it gives the wrong impression. I lost them both in the same fraction of a second."

She didn't answer for a time. The soft light from the kitchen framed her chair from behind, and made it impossible to see her face. Maybe she liked it that way. Maybe she was smart enough to understand that she wasn't the only one who found it disturbing to have someone peering deeply into her life. Anyone.

Because all she said, when she finally answered, was "That must be a hell of a story."

*Or a story of hell,* he thought. But he didn't say it.

———

He was lying awake on the couch, staring at the ceiling, when he heard her soft movements in the kitchen.

"I'm not asleep," he said. He spoke gently, so as not to startle her.

A minute later she came out and sat in the wing chair on the other side of the coffee table from him. The only light was the glow from nearby buildings shining through the living room windows. He couldn't see her beyond just a dark shape.

"I was getting a glass of water," she said. "I hope that's okay."

"Of course it is."

"Are you *trying* to sleep?"

"Not really."

"Good. I kind of needed someone to talk to. I tried looking through your telescope, but there are no stars. Are there *ever* stars in the city?"

"On a clear night, I suppose you can see the brightest ones. But I haven't had it very long, so I'm not sure yet."

"I know that's how you saw us. But if you say it wasn't on purpose, I believe you."

"I lost control of it. I was trying to adjust it with one hand . . . well, how else would I adjust it, right? It was brand new, and I didn't know how fast it would drop when I loosened the knob. And then when I went to angle it up again, it was pointing at your window."

"What are the chances, right?"

"Astronomical," he said. "No pun intended."

They fell silent for a time. He could hear her sipping her water. He still couldn't see her clearly—there simply wasn't enough light for his eyes to adjust to. As he opened his mouth to tell her his story, he made a mental note: if Uncle Gregor got his way, and talked his parents into sending him into some kind of therapy, Anton would ask his counselor to turn off the lights before any serious sharing occurred.

"My brother had some kind of mental illness," he said. "But it was never diagnosed."

Then he waited.

It was a testing of the water. To see if she really wanted to know. Or if she would change the subject, or shift the conversation into lighter territory. She did none of that. Only listened, as far as he could tell.

"My great-uncle is a psychiatrist, and he wanted to get Greg some professional help, but my parents wouldn't hear of it. They wouldn't believe him. They were sure it was some kind of phase—something he'd grow out of on his own. Any fool could see it was worse than that, if you ask my opinion, but they don't ask my opinion. And they don't face things head-on. Well, actually, they don't face things. But anyway, that's a whole long backstory for another time."

He paused again, wondering if she would stop him. *Hoping* she would stop him. When she didn't, he plunged on.

"Our parents were out for the evening. They had tickets to a play. Greg was in his room, and I could hear him talking, but there was no one in there, and he didn't have a phone in his room. I knew that was a bad sign. It meant he was hearing voices. I banged on the door but he wouldn't let me in, so I got scared and broke the door down. I knew it was worse than usual. I knew something was seriously wrong."

He paused again. The curtains had been left open, and he could see lights on in windows of other buildings. A few people who couldn't sleep, or had to work late. He envied them their lives, which he imagined to be comfortable and uneventful compared to his own.

He had only ever told this story one time before, to two police officers who came to his hospital bed after the amputation surgery. *They* had told his parents. Thank God.

"Greg was sitting on the floor, and he had his back up against the end of his bed, and he had one of my father's shotguns. My father likes to hunt upstate sometimes. Or at least he used to. They were supposed to be locked up, but Greg had one. He had the butt end of it braced on the floor between his feet, and he was holding it really tightly between his bare feet and between his knees, and he was holding the barrel in both hands. And he was looking up at the ceiling, with his chin stretched up really high, and he had his eyes closed. And the gun was pointed at the underside of his chin. Like the top part of his throat. That really soft, vulnerable spot under the base of his tongue. But it wasn't right up against his throat. It was a few inches away. If it had been pressed up to his throat, like right between his jawbone on each side, I might've known better than to think I could knock it away. But it was just pointed there, with lots of air in between. So I figured it would knock away easy. And I didn't see how he could reach the trigger anyway, so I thought I could change the way things turned out. I guess I thought my chances were pretty good."

He let a silence fall, and, in it, he found something remarkable: He felt fairly at ease because the person he was talking to was her. He could finish the story. Or he could not finish it. But beneath all that, he believed he might be okay. For the first time in over seven months, he believed it was possible to be okay.

"It's up to you how much you want to tell me," she said.

Which he thought was nice. It was nice because it was supportive, but it was also nice simply to hear the sound of her voice again.

"When I broke in, he looked at me. Just completely calm. It was eerie. And then he looked up at the ceiling again and closed his eyes. And he put his toe on the trigger. And I thought I saw that toe move. Like . . . press. Or it started to—or I knew it was just about to. That part's confusing, because it happened so fast. But I saw his toe move. So I flew. I flew over there. I swear I did. I didn't run, or jump. In that one split second I could fly, so I flew over there and tried to knock the gun out of his hands. But it wasn't very good thinking on my part. Or . . . I don't know. Who had time to think? Anyway, here's what went wrong: He had such a tight grip on the thing. With his hands and his knees and his feet, he just had it so tightly. So I knocked the gun over, but it just knocked him over, too. With it. So it didn't change the aim or the results at all. The only thing I managed to do was get my hand in front of the muzzle."

He heard her mutter a word, but he was not able to make out what word it was, and he never asked. It was some type of breathy exclamation, possibly religious in nature.

"If that was more than you wanted to know," he said, "I apologize."

"We're quite the pair," she said after a heavy pause. "A couple of walking, talking trauma zones. Except . . . all of a sudden my stuff doesn't seem so bad. I have no idea how you're still walking and talking."

"I'm not really sure what other option I had."

"That's a brave statement."

"I'm not trying to be brave."

"What are you trying to be?"

"I don't know. I'm just trying to get through it. I don't really know what people want from me. I don't mean you. People are always acting like I should be . . . I don't know. Feeling more, or being some way I'm not. I don't know how to do it the way they think I should."

"Do it any way you can do it."

"Thank you."

"Wait. And then you're here by yourself for the holidays? Why did your parents go away and leave you alone?"

"I don't know. I mean . . . I sort of know. They're just having problems of their own."

"But that's . . . how could they *do that*?"

Several thoughts, mental observations that could almost have been feelings if he had let them be, warred inside him. One was an acknowledgment that her outrage was appropriate. Another found her disapproval quite surprising and, directly contradicting that, he agreed, and was aware that he had felt the same way she did all along. Finally, he realized it was unsurprising behavior on his parents' part. It was simply another link in a long chain of errors that most parents would know better than to make. At least, he hoped they would.

"You would just have to know them," he said. "They can barely even take care of themselves. I don't want to speak ill of them," he added, realizing it was a phrase he'd borrowed from Uncle Gregor. It was not the first time his great-uncle had said those words. And yet only in that moment did it dawn on him that Gregor had many ill observations about Anton's parents that he was withholding.

"Whew," she said. "No way I can go to sleep after that."

"Stay up and talk to me, then."

And she did.

She asked him every question she said she could think to ask about astronomy. And he told her everything he knew.

———

Just as dawn began to break, and they had both begun to yawn, she asked him, "Is that your hat hanging up in your room?"

"It is," he said, inordinately pleased that she had noticed it. "It belonged to my grandfather."

"It's such a nice hat. Why don't you ever wear it?"

"I've only had it since yesterday."

"Oh. I see. Well, now you'll have something to hang on to when we talk."

"That was the idea," he said. "Yeah."

"Maybe I could manage a little nap now."

"Did this . . ." He spoke quickly to stop her, but then felt unsure about phrasing his question. ". . . this last thing that happened, when he split your lip. Had it already happened before we were supposed to meet for lunch?"

He was afraid of her answer. And yet somehow the time for holding back seemed to have passed. It was too late to be shy or keep secrets from each other. They had been thrown together. Their lives were utterly entwined now. She was here with him, and that's all there was to it.

He figured he knew what she would say, because he had seen her after lunch, through the telescope. But now he couldn't remember for sure which side of her face he had seen. And he needed to know. Good or bad, he needed to.

"No," she said, and her voice rang with something like shame. "It happened at nine o'clock last night. I waited until I was positive he was asleep, and then I came over. I'm sorry. I'm sorry I stood you up. I had a lot of thinking to do."

"I understand."

It was true, and it wasn't true. Part of him understood, and part of him didn't. And all of him hurt to hear it.

———

He woke on the couch and, even before he opened his eyes, felt assaulted by light. Sun poured in through the windows, making him guess it was midday.

He sat up, blinking too much, and looked around. Edith was on the other side of the living room, in front of the windows. She was dancing. Freely and wildly. Dancing.

The sun lit her up from behind, and washed out all detail, making her into some kind of fast-moving silhouette. Now and then she fell into a few short movements from some recognizable modern dance—the Watusi or the Swim. Mostly she just moved free-form. Her hands rose into the air and swayed, then fell to her waist and swung. Her hips gyrated. Her steps moved to some beat only she could hear.

There was no music. The apartment was completely silent.

He squinted, and was able to see that she was wearing the headphone set to his father's stereo. It was the cord that tipped him off.

He sat forward and watched her for a time, arms wrapped around his bent knees. She looked . . . some unexpected way. Something for which he couldn't find a word. Then he settled on *joyful*. No wonder he'd had trouble defining it. Joy had been absent from his world for so long. And, he had thought, from hers, too.

She saw him then. He could tell because she stopped moving. She stood still in the spill of light and pulled off the headphones, looking sheepish.

"Anton. I hope I didn't wake you."

"Nope. Woke up on my own."

"I was listening to some of these records. I hope that's okay."

"You need to stop asking if things are okay," he said, not even attempting to keep the admiration—even adoration—from his voice. "Because everything you do is okay."

"Are you the guy who likes big-band swing music? Or someone else in your family?"

"I don't *dislike* it. But they're my father's records."

She stepped over to the stereo and unplugged the headphones. The living room filled with swing. She motioned him over. Asked him to join her with a wave of her hand.

He spoke up to be heard over the music. "What, me?"

"You're the only one here," she shouted back.

"I don't really dance."

"Neither do I."

"I just saw you dancing."

"Yes, but I don't really know how. I just do it anyway. I was just dancing the same way you'd be dancing if you just came over here and did it anyway."

He rose, and walked to her, still in his pajamas. They were both still in his red-and-blue flannel pajamas.

He tried to move with the music, but it felt too awkward. Especially with her watching.

"I'm closing my eyes," she said, and she did, squeezing them shut in an exaggerated motion. "I'm not looking. So just dance however you want."

And for a minute or two—a fairly miraculous minute or two, considering how self-conscious he tended to feel—Anton danced. Probably badly, but he did it anyway. He didn't move his feet much. Just struck a pattern from the waist up—torso and arms—that he figured he could live with. It did not allow him to keep his right wrist down and more or less out of sight, as he preferred to do. But her eyes were closed—and anyway, it wasn't as if she hadn't seen, and didn't know.

The song ended. They waited for a new song to begin but instead just heard the scratch of the needle at the end of the record.

She opened her eyes.

"You seem . . . ," he began.

"Happy?"

"Yeah."

"I'm free, Anton. I woke up and it hit me that I'm free. And not just from being hurt, either. I can do whatever I want. I can listen to whatever music I want and talk to whatever person I want and state any opinion that comes into my head and nobody is trying to rein me in. Do you know how long it's been since I've been able to do whatever I want? It's a ridiculous time to get all excited about it, because I can't even go out on the street, but I just woke up and felt free. Like I had my life back. I was all caught up in how sad I'd be if my marriage was over, and there's some of that, yes, but I had no idea how boxed in I'd been. He turned up the heat on it a little at a time and I didn't know I was roasting until just now, when I jumped out of the oven. And I owe it all to you."

She pitched forward and covered the few steps between them, took hold of his head by both temples, and kissed him hard but briefly on the forehead.

"I'll cook us something . . . if you have food in the house. Are there eggs?"

"There are."

"Cheese? Any vegetables?"

"Yeah, there's all that good stuff my parents hope I'll eat. I haven't touched any of it because it seemed like too much work."

"I'll make omelets."

"I'll go get dressed," he said, still lost in the feeling—the warm imprint—of her lips on his forehead.

—

When he got back out to the kitchen, Edith had a bowl of broken eggs on the counter in front of her, along with the cheese grater. Shallots and washed spinach sat on the cutting board. And Edith sat on one of the high stools, ignoring it all.

She was crying.

She looked up and saw him, and immediately tried to hide her emotion, quickly swiping her tears on the sleeve of her pajamas. *His* pajamas.

"You must think I'm an emotional basket case," she said, sniffling. "Bouncing up and down like a yo-yo."

He paused in the kitchen doorway, leaning his shoulder on the frame. He wasn't sure if it was okay to approach her. "I don't think that."

"I just got scared again because I have nothing. Nothing familiar here at all except what I jammed into my big purse—makeup and grooming things and a few pictures of my parents that I didn't want to leave behind. I couldn't really pack suitcases because if I accidentally woke him up, it had to look like I wasn't leaving. He might have killed me if he'd known I was leaving. At least put me in the hospital. He already put me in the hospital once, with internal injuries, and over something pretty small in comparison. So that's all I own and I have no idea what my next move is, and the fear kind of ganged up and overwhelmed me after all that happy freedom stuff. I guess freedom is a two-edged sword, right?"

She allowed a pause. But not enough of one for him to respond.

"Can I stay through Christmas?" Her eyes came up to his and shone wet again. "I really like Christmas and I don't want to spend it on a train or with some old friend I haven't seen for ages and who might not have forgiven me yet for cutting ties. I just want to be someplace where I feel okay for Christmas."

"Of course. Stay as long as you like." Then it hit him—the flaw in his plan. "I mean, up until the first or second day of January, because after that my parents come home."

"You must think I'm a basket case," she said again.

"I don't. I know all about roller-coaster feelings."

She jumped up and moved across the room to him, and for a flash of a second he thought she would embrace him. But, if that had been her plan, she thought better of it before she arrived. She stopped a step or two in front of him and looked earnestly into his face.

"We'll help each other until it's time for me to go," she said. "Now I'll just run get dressed, and then I was serious about those omelets."

# *Chapter Seven*

*Where?*

Anton stared at the chess pieces, which sat on their board at his eye level. He had his chin down on the back of his left hand, which was flat on the table. He was wearing his new fedora, in the house, at her suggestion. So his view of the chess game was a narrow one—just what he could see between table and hat brim. He liked it that way. It made the game his whole world in that moment.

He saw her hand grasp the top of her queen and move it diagonally across the board. It hovered there on the chess piece, that hand, as she—he assumed—checked to be sure she wanted to leave the piece there. Then the hand disappeared.

Anton sat up and surveyed the board.

She was planning something big with that queen. He could tell. There was an energy, a gravity, to the move. It hovered in the air. But it would take him some time to think three, four, five moves ahead. Even then he wasn't sure he was a good enough player to anticipate her plan of attack. He stared at the board for several minutes. Then he worried he was holding up the game.

"Am I taking too long?"

"No, it's fine. Take all the time you need. I love not playing with a timer."

Her husband had taught her to play. She had told him that much. But when you played chess with her husband, an hourglass egg timer limited the minutes you were given to plan.

"But the game would be over much faster his way."

"Oh, yeah. It would have been over a long time ago. He would have upended the board because I wasn't losing fast enough."

That brought an awkward silence. Anton was unable to think clearly enough to figure out his next move.

"Do you think . . . ," he began. Then he stalled.

"What?" she asked after a time. "Do I think what?"

"Was he still upset about seeing us together? Is that why . . . ?" He indicated on his own lip the place where Edith's husband had damaged hers.

"Maybe. I don't know. I mean, yes. It bothered him. He pretended he wasn't upset, but it bothered him more than he let on. But if you're asking so you can feel guilty, like it was your fault, don't even do that to yourself. Because it's totally unpredictable. *He's* totally unpredictable, so who knows? Anything can set him off at any time, and he holds on to things before they come bursting out, so why even try to pretend we know why he does what he does? Let it go. None of this is your fault. You didn't tell me to marry him."

Anton sat up straighter and angled the brim of his hat slightly up, to better see her face. She glanced away—out the window, into the late-afternoon dusk, as if suddenly lost in thought.

"Do you know where you'll go now?" he asked.

He had been wanting to ask all day. Ever since she had, with his permission, made a couple of collect calls on his parents' phone. He had purposely left her alone to make the calls in private. But it had been eating at him. The not knowing.

Still, he hadn't been sure it was his business to ask.

"I think so," she said.

"Where?"

A long pause. In it was something difficult. An unwelcome truth, something he would hate hearing. He felt it coming.

"Don't take this the wrong way," she said. "Well, you will. I just know you will, but I still have to beg you not to. Please don't hear this as a personal thing, all right? I'm not going to tell you. Because you live right across the street from him. Of course, he doesn't know where you live. If he did, he would have been over here tearing up the landscape a long time ago. But he knows you when he sees you. And he knows we were talking. Sooner or later you'll run into him on the street and if he thinks you know where I am, he'll hurt you to find out. And I can't live with that. I can't let him hurt you. So after Christmas I'm going to go away and you're not going to know where I've gone."

He sat a minute, feeling the words in his belly. They tingled in a sharp series of tiny wounds that left him feeling slightly singed inside. "Ever?"

"It's better this way."

"That makes no sense. I could just lie to him and say I don't know."

"Could you?"

"What does that even *mean*? Of course I could. Anybody can lie."

"How often do you lie?"

"Almost never. I mean, when I was little I might've lied to get out of something. Or I might tell a little fib to keep from hurting someone's feelings. But I don't really lie."

"So what makes you think you'll be any good at it? How often is anybody good at something they almost never do? If you had touched a piano maybe half a dozen times in your life, would you sit here and tell me you'd play a concerto for him? Things take practice, Anton. Don't get me wrong. I adore the fact that you're so . . . uncomplicated. About the truth, I mean. You don't have all these different layers of what you're willing to reveal. I love that because it makes me feel safe with you. And it's a really lovely quality in a person. But it also leads me to believe that you would be a terrible liar. So let's just keep you telling the truth, shall we? It seems to be where you fit the best."

She fell silent, and they sat for a time. They had turned on no lights since dusk had fallen. The light in the room had taken on a dusty feeling, as though nothing could be seen with absolute clarity. He tried to digest the fact that this situation, this dense collection of moments—the amazing gift of getting to know her—had an ending, looming. A real ending. A finality. It would not end with postcards, and the occasional visit. It would simply end.

"Maybe we could finish the game later," he said.

"I'm sorry I upset you, Anton. But I know him better than you do, and I really think it's for the best. It's the only safe way."

"I'm just going to go lie down," he said.

"Okay. I'm sorry. Please don't be upset with me."

"I'm going to lie down in my room. I'll be out of there before you need to go to bed."

"Of course. It's your room. You'll be up for dinner, right? I was going to make pasta for dinner."

"Okay. Just tell me when you want me to get up for dinner."

———

He lay on his bed, staring out the window as the dusk turned to pitch-dark. The snows had finished blowing through the city, and the sky was clear. Perhaps the recent snowstorms had left the air cleaner than usual, because he was fairly sure he could see three twinkling stars.

He never got up to view them through his telescope. He just couldn't bring himself to care.

———

It was the telephone that finally roused him out of bed.

He trotted to the kitchen to answer it, because there was only one phone in the apartment—bolted to the kitchen wall.

Edith was standing at the stove, stirring a boiling pot of pasta with a wooden spoon. The steam had made her hair look limp. The kitchen windows fogged with that moisture. She appeared to have been expecting him, which should not have been too surprising since the phone was ringing. She smiled at him, but the smile looked so despondent and sad that he quickly looked away.

He grabbed up the receiver.

"Hello?"

"Were you sleeping, Anton?" Grandma Marion's familiar voice asked. "Or were you out on the balcony with your telescope?"

"Oh, hey, Grandma Marion. I was just in my room."

"I thought it was time to discuss where you'll be for Christmas. I kept waiting and waiting for you to bring it up on your own, but you never did."

"Where I'll be?" he repeated, as though unfamiliar with her language.

"You were to choose between my house and your uncle Gregor and aunt Mina's, but now they've invited me to come to their apartment unless we're celebrating just the two of us, you and me. I was thinking it would be nicest if we both went to their place so we can all be together."

"Wait," Anton said.

"All right," she said. But she didn't wait long. "I'm not sure why you sound so confused. Are you positive I didn't wake you?"

"Nobody told me I was supposed to choose where to spend Christmas."

In his peripheral vision he saw Edith's head come up, then angle in his direction. He had caught her ear by saying something he did not want her to hear.

"Your parents didn't tell you to choose a relative to spend Christmas with?"

"I don't think so."

A long silence fell on the line. He didn't know what to make of it. When he finally heard her voice again, he understood that she had been attempting to compose herself.

"Sometimes I swear," she said, her voice breathy, "I just want to wring those people's thoughtless necks."

It was the harshest thing she had ever said about his parents, and it left him feeling stunned. Not because she felt that way—the undertone of those emotions had always been there to absorb. But it was unlike her to express such thoughts out loud.

While he was thinking and feeling these things, he did not answer.

"So where do you want to be, Anton?"

"Here," he said. Firmly.

"By yourself?"

"I won't be by myself. I'm spending Christmas with a friend."

"What friend do you have who doesn't need to be with his own family?"

"I have a new friend. She just left her husband and both of her parents passed away and she's going to spend Christmas here with me. You understand. Don't you?"

In the silence that followed, he wondered if he'd made a mistake. Would it have been better to keep Edith a secret? It was something he hadn't thought through.

"Well, I don't know," she said. "Gregor and I were just assuming we'd see you on Christmas, but maybe we shouldn't have made assumptions. Are you absolutely sure you wouldn't rather be with blood family?"

"Here's the thing," he said. He turned his back to Edith, as if for more privacy, even though he knew she could probably still hear. "Right after Christmas she's moving away. Out of the city. So this is my last chance to spend this time with her."

"Why don't we know about this friend?"

"She's a new friend. I said that."

"Oh. Yes. I suppose you did, didn't you?" He heard her pull a deep, audible breath. "Well, you think it over, Anton. If that's really want you want, well . . . you're not a child anymore, and I won't interfere in your decisions."

"Thank you."

They said their goodbyes, and he hung up the phone and turned to face Edith, who met his gaze directly. She brushed a strand of limp hair from her eyes.

"You should go have Christmas with your family," she said.

She sounded like an adult talking to a child. Offering the benefit of adult wisdom. It hurt Anton. It ached and stung going down, like hot peppers burning their way into his belly.

"No. We have a plan. We're spending Christmas here. We agreed. Because then you have to go and I'll never see you again."

He listened to his words as they hung in the air. There was nothing overtly wrong with them. But maybe it was the way he had spoken them. Somehow he couldn't shake the feeling that he had stepped over the line again and was now standing in uncomfortable territory.

"Anton . . . ," she said, and he hated everything about it. The way she said his name. The words that would follow, even though he hadn't heard them yet.

"Don't," he said, and tried to leave the kitchen.

"Stop."

He did as she had asked. He had to. It was Edith.

"I need to say this," she said.

"Please don't."

"I need to. So listen. Please."

He held still, feeling as though he were somehow hanging there in the air. As if he were a marionette on strings, utterly unable to control his own movements. All of his nerves tingled. It even felt as though his nonexistent right hand was tingling.

"You need a girl your own age," she said.

He'd more or less known to expect it, or something like it. Still, it hit him like a sucker punch.

"We're just friends," he said.

"Are we? I'm glad. That's good if that's true for you. Because otherwise this is not right. I don't want to be leading you on. That's not fair to you and you deserve better. If I thought that was the case, I'd leave sooner. I'd leave right now, so as not to do you any more harm."

He hung a moment longer, feeling as though he were swaying. But he wasn't sure if his brain was exaggerating the feeling. His head felt spongy and a little fogged in, as though he might be a fraction of the way to passing out. Her words had rained onto him like body blows, leaving him reeling.

"No. Stay till Christmas, like you said you would. We're friends."

"I definitely want to be your friend. But—"

"Then stay," he said. Quickly, before she could finish.

"Okay. If you're sure we're just friends."

"Of course we're just friends. How could you even ask that?"

He broke free of his strings then, his body capable of motion again. He tried to hurry out of the room. But she stopped him again with her words.

"Wait. Don't go."

"Why not?"

"The pasta is ready. It's time to sit down to dinner."

—

"I'm making some popcorn," she said, calling in to him from the kitchen. "I thought we could watch a movie."

"Okay. What movie do we want to see?"

"I have no idea what's on. Look and see what's on, okay?"

He reached out to the coffee table and grabbed the TV listings. He had been sitting on the couch with his legs pinned underneath him. The left one was experiencing the pins and needles of falling asleep, but he had not been motivated enough to move.

He sat back and rearranged himself into a cross-legged position, holding the TV magazine without looking at it. Purposely without looking. The light in the room was dim—just a spill of light from the kitchen. He sat still and listened to the sounds of her work. At first he could only hear the shaking of the pan on the burner. The constant back-and-forth movement that allowed the popcorn to heat evenly and not burn. Later he heard the first few kernels begin to pop. He listened until there were no pops left for him to hear.

"I like to sprinkle Parmesan cheese on mine. After I toss it with butter."

Her voice made him jump. He looked up to see her leaning in the kitchen doorway. The light from behind her seemed to halo her, hiding her features but elevating her presence to something larger than life. As though her presence needed further elevating.

"That's fine," he said.

"You want to try a little first? Before I put it on all of it?"

"No, it's fine. I'll try it your way."

"What's wrong?" He saw a slight tilt to her head in glowing silhouette. "Are you still upset about the talk we had earlier?"

"Here's the thing about me and movies," he said. "But I'm afraid it's going to sound silly and pathetic."

She walked across the room and sat on the couch beside him, a suitable distance away. Just the right amount of distance to once again make the point that she knew the difference between a right thing and a wrong one. Which hurt. Again.

"Try me," she said.

"It can't have any violence in it at all. Not even the really fake-looking kind of movie violence where people are getting shot but you don't know who they are and you know it's not real and anyway they're the bad guys so you don't even care. If it has any blood in it at all, I'm out. I can't look. Even if it's in black and white. If it's in color, well . . . I just . . . then my dad went and bought a color TV this year, so that threw a live grenade into everything."

"That doesn't sound silly. Not at all. I'm not exactly a fan of violence myself. We'll watch something light."

On the word "light," she reached for the lamp and clicked it on. Anton winced and blinked into all that light.

"No wonder you couldn't find a movie, Anton. You have to turn on the light to see, sweetie."

"Maybe a comedy or a romance," he said. "Or both in the same film."

"I think we'll skip the romance, too. Maybe just a comedy. Ooh!" she shouted suddenly, as if she had looked down and found a diamond ring lying in the street. "The Marx Brothers! Ever watch the Marx Brothers?"

"Never."

"Do you not like them?"

"I don't know anything about them."

"Well, you will. It starts in ten minutes. I'll just butter and Parmesan the popcorn and then we'll be ready."

She sprang to her feet and headed into the kitchen. But he stopped her with a question. One he hadn't realized he'd been about to ask out loud.

"Why is everything in life such a minefield?"

She leaned in the doorway again and watched him, but this time he could see her clearly. See her expression. She was wearing her own clothes, the slacks and blouse she had arrived in, now clean from their trip to the basement laundry room. She was wearing thick gray crew socks that he had loaned her, and no shoes. She wore no makeup. Neither did she need any. She seemed to be considering what he had asked.

"That's how it is when you've been hurt, I suppose. We have that in common. But still, getting hit in the face now and then is nothing compared to what you lived through."

"It's not nothing."

"I meant in comparison."

"It's still not nothing. At least my brother didn't hurt me on purpose. He only meant to hurt himself."

She didn't answer for a time. He nursed that uncomfortable feeling again, the one that said he had crossed some invisible line. When she finally spoke, she seemed uninterested in following his thread of logic.

"I still don't know how you're managing so well with that."

"I told you."

"You told me you didn't have any other choice but to manage. And I didn't press you on it. But it's just kind of a glib answer, really. I mean, things need to be dealt with."

"What if you don't know how to deal with them?"

"In that case I guess you just keep away from it for a time. You just make it wait until later, when you have more tools. People do that all the time, especially with stuff from childhood. Because children don't have much in the way of tools to deal with things."

They froze that way for a few beats. Him sitting, her leaning. Just a couple of seconds, most likely.

Then he said, "I get why we need to stay away from anything violent. But what was wrong with a romance with some comedy?"

"Oh, honey. Nothing hurts like romance."

"I guess I don't have much to go by."

"When you get to be older, like me, you'll know a lot more. And then you'll probably be every bit as confused by it as you are right now. Now, I have to go finish that popcorn or we'll miss the start of the movie."

—

Anton took a huge and unwieldy handful of popcorn from the bowl she held in his direction and watched Chico Marx playing a long piece on the piano. Watched Groucho listen to the piece with obvious, eye-rolling impatience.

It was right around the time Anton had been thinking the music was going on too long.

So far he had been enjoying the film without laughing. But suddenly he heard himself laugh. Out loud. It was a sharp bark, like the sound a seal might make. It surprised him, and sounded foreign to his ears. It made him wonder how long it had been since he'd laughed. He couldn't even begin to remember.

"What's the part that struck you funny?" Edith asked, seeming pleased. "Was it the thing about going past the ending of the song?"

"Yeah. That. That just struck me funny. I mean, how can you pass the ending?"

"It's nice to hear you laugh," she said.

Anton thought so, too, but he wasn't sure how to say it.

The scene cut off abruptly and a noisy commercial came on. Edith jumped up and ran to the set to turn the volume down.

"I can't stand listening to the commercials," she said. She came back and sat with him, and took a handful of popcorn. "So, you like them?"

"Commercials?"

"No, silly. The Marx Brothers."

"Oh. Yeah. I like them. They're funny."

"It was nice to hear you laugh. I don't think I ever heard you laugh."

That seemed to bring about an awkward silence.

He looked at her sock feet, braced against the coffee table, and wondered what her feet looked like. What he would see if they were bare. They weren't particularly dainty or small, those feet. Not huge either. Just long and sturdy looking. It felt strange that someone could have filled his world so completely when he didn't even know what her feet looked like.

"Tell me something about your brother," she said.

It jolted him to have it brought up suddenly, but he tried not to let on.

"Like what?"

"I don't know. Anything. Just something you remember about him."

He listened to his own breathing for a moment before answering.

"He loved comic books. He collected them. Some pretty valuable ones. He made his own comic books, too. Drew the illustrations and wrote the stories. Nobody knew that but me. He wouldn't show them to anybody else."

"Do you still have his comic book collection?"

"No. They mostly had to be thrown away. Because of the . . . you know." He hoped she knew. But she didn't seem to. "Blood. And other bad stuff." He rushed on, talking fast to try to replace that image. "He had a turtle. One of those dumb little turtles the size of your palm that you can get for hardly any money at the pet department. Thor, he named it. Nobody could figure out why he loved that silly little turtle so much. Like, more than he loved us. Or it seemed that way, anyway. But then my dad stepped on it and that was it for Thor."

"On purpose?" she asked, her mouth full of popcorn and her eyes wide.

"No. Not on purpose. But just in his usual way. Like he only sees himself. You know what? Can we talk about something else?"

"Sure. I'm sorry. I'm sorry if that was the wrong—oh, it's back on. We'll just watch and not talk about sad things."

She jumped up and ran to the TV, turning the sound back up. Then she sat back down and they finished the popcorn and watched the rest of the movie.

Anton didn't laugh out loud again.

# Chapter Eight

*Include Me*

They were sitting on high stools at the kitchen counter when the knock came at the door. They were eating second helpings of waffles Edith had made from scratch in his mother's waffle iron, and reciting all the funny lines they could remember from the previous night's film.

Edith had served the waffles with raspberry jam instead of syrup. Anton had been wondering why his mother only served pancakes or waffles with syrup when the knock startled him out of his thoughts. At first his heart seemed to jump up into his throat, as if he were sitting at the kitchen counter tallying up the cash proceeds of a daring bank robbery, and somehow knew it was the police at the door.

Then he breathed deeply and reminded himself that he had done nothing wrong. So what if he was here with a lady from across the street, without her husband's knowledge? He was helping her. Like a gentleman. And besides, they were only friends.

Unless it was her husband.

His heart jolted again at the thought. But no. It couldn't be. He didn't know Anton's name, or where he lived, and neither he nor Edith had gone outside since she had arrived at his apartment door. They hadn't even gone out on the balcony, where they might be seen.

He glanced at her in his peripheral vision. She seemed to have picked up on the tension.

"Who is it?" he called without getting up.

"Your grandmother." The words came to him faintly from the other side of the door.

He looked at Edith and she returned his gaze.

"Should I make myself scarce?" she asked.

"No. We're not doing anything wrong. We're friends."

"Right. Friends. I wasn't sure how your parents felt about guests while they're gone."

"They didn't tell me not to have guests."

He was less sure than his words seemed to suggest. He had no idea what his grandmother would think. But he was about to open the door and find out. If he told her to hide, and Grandma Marion somehow found out about her anyway, that would appear to be consciousness of guilt. He reminded himself that he had nothing to feel guilty about.

It took a minute. Longer than it probably should have.

He answered the door.

She was wrapped in a warm woolen muffler, twisted around and around her neck and chin. She unwrapped it as she stood on the welcome mat and spoke to him. He was surprised she had left it on in the overheated elevator.

"I came to make a suggestion," she said.

"Okay."

"Mind if I come in?"

"Oh. Sorry. Of course come in."

She stood in the living room and shrugged out of her coat, which he dutifully took from her and hung in the coat closet. She left the woolen muffler hanging down in front of her dress like a drape or a boa. On her, it looked like a fashion statement. Almost everything did.

She looked around, her eyes landing on Edith. She did not look surprised to see that he had company.

She crossed the room with her right hand extended for Edith to shake. It was a gesture that was so familiar, so automatic in the culture, that it stung him every time he witnessed it. Because that simplest of gestures had been taken from him. He could hold out his left, and he had, a few times. But it always forced a correction on the part of the other person. It was awkward, and only drew attention to a situation he would have preferred to leave in the background when meeting somebody new.

This is what people didn't understand, he thought—it was the littlest, most insignificant losses that stung the most, and he didn't even know why that should be.

"I'm Anton's grandmother. Call me Marion."

"Edith," Edith said, and shook the offered hand. "Waffle?"

"No, thank you. I've had my breakfast. But it looks delicious. Thank you all the same."

Grandma Marion hoisted herself onto a high stool at the counter and sighed. Her eyes scanned the kitchen, then the living room. He wasn't sure what she was looking for. Her gaze landed on the couch and seemed to stick there. Anton had folded his blankets, but not put them away. They sat on one end of the couch, his two pillows perched neatly on top. Anton wasn't sure if it was a good or a bad thing that he had left them out. On the one hand, it made it clear that Edith was not simply a brief daytime visitor. Then again, it also clarified that the sleeping arrangements were chaste.

"You make your guest sleep on the couch, Anton?"

"No. No, I gave her my room for the few days she's here. I'm on the couch."

"Good. I'm glad to hear that. That's the gentlemanly thing to do. So, listen. I'll get right to the point. I have a proposal. An invitation. I hope your guest will understand the thinking behind my saying this. This has been a very bad year for our family, Edith. Very hard in many ways. We wanted to have Christmas as a family, pulling together what's left of us. But my son and his wife blew that to smithereens with this crazy South America trip, which makes it feel more important than ever that we cobble together what family we have. So we would like to enjoy the holiday with our dear Anton, but I understand he's made a commitment, so we're inviting you as well, Edith. You're his friend, so that should be all the recommendation we need to open our home to you. You two can spend Christmas morning in whatever way you had planned and then come over in the afternoon for dinner."

Marion stopped talking. Fairly abruptly, leaving Anton thinking there would be more. In the gap that followed, he glanced up at Edith but could not read her expression.

"Here's the thing, though," he said. "We're trying really hard not to go out of the house, because Edith is from the building right across the street. Her husband still lives there. So until she leaves town, we want to make sure he doesn't see her, or know where she is. He could be dangerous if he knows where she is."

With no pause at all, not even a beat to think over her response, Marion said, "All right, then. No problem." He was surprised that she had let the idea go so quickly. Then she added, "We'll have Christmas dinner here. Mina and I will bring the food and heat it up on your stove."

He looked again to Edith, who looked back. Her face seemed relaxed.

"Is that okay with you, Edith?" he asked.

"Of course. I'd love to meet some of your family."

"Then it's settled," Marion said. "You know . . . If I'm still allowed, I've changed my thinking on that waffle. If it's not too much trouble to make another, I'm wondering who says I don't get to have two breakfasts if I want. All I had was toast and yogurt and now I'm thinking, Who am I trying to stay thin for? Who am I trying to impress? I never tried waffles with jam, but it looks lovely. We'll sit here and talk and get to know each other a little."

—

He helped Grandma Marion on with her coat, thinking he would just walk her to the apartment door. That seemed gentlemanly enough. She had other ideas.

"Walk me down to the street, Anton. You can help me by hailing a cab while I wait in the warm lobby. I don't handle the cold as well as I did when I was young. Oh, wait. You said you didn't want to be seen outside. Well, walk me down anyway."

As he told Edith he would be right back, Anton could feel the weight of knowing his grandmother wanted to speak to him in private. Edith seemed to know it, too. Then again, it was hard to know what someone else was thinking. He could have been reading his own misgivings into her.

He and his grandmother stepped out into the hallway together and he rang for the elevator.

"I'm surprised you didn't just call," he said as they watched the floors light up one by one. "Such a long trip."

"I wanted to see who this person was, that I was inviting. But she seems like a lovely woman."

Anton had no idea what to say.

"The only comment I have is . . . and I apologize in advance because I think you won't want to hear it . . . she's a woman. And you're a boy, Anton. I'm sorry. I know you bristle at that assessment, and it's true in some senses and not true in others. But compared to her, you're a child. She's a grown woman. Probably in her thirties. You must understand what I'm saying."

"So? What difference does it make how old she is? We're just friends. I can have an older friend. There's nothing wrong with that."

The elevator doors opened with a bing. They stepped on. The doors whooshed closed, and they watched the lighted floor numbers as the elevator descended.

"Here's the thing about love," she said.

His stomach jumped at the word. He felt revealed. He said nothing because his voice was not working. All he could do was freeze while she said more. So much more.

"There is one thing in this life you can never hide, and that's love. When you're in love, you can't disguise that. No one I've known can conceal it, so far as I could tell. It's like that old saying about trying to hide your light under a bushel basket, except in this case all that happens is you get this very shiny basket that glows with a light people can see from miles away."

Anton watched the floors, feeling dead inside. Seven. Six. Five. The elevator stopped at five, and the doors flew open but there was no one there. In time they closed again, and the elevator moved down.

"So you got that just from having waffles with us?"

"I got that on the phone yesterday."

The elevator stopped at the lobby and they stepped out. The doorman was standing just inside the revolving door, probably to stay warm.

"You know the doorman would have called you a cab," Anton said.

"Of course I know that. My brain is still sharp."

She had stopped in the middle of the ornate lobby and was not moving. Anton knew she would not move, could not be made to move, until she had said her piece.

"I'm not going to apologize for something I feel," he said. "We're just friends. I didn't do anything wrong."

"I didn't say you did. I saw with my own eyes that you've been sleeping on the couch, and I'm willing to believe she's not the kind of woman who would take advantage of a young man. She's done nothing to cause me to mistrust her."

"So why am I getting a lecture?"

"Here's my concern. You had such a dreadful year. And you don't seem to be processing the emotions of it, which worries me. And first love . . . oh, you poor boy, first love is so hard, almost always. So heartbreaking. And here you've gone and chosen a love that can't be, that has no space in the world to exist. I worry about you when she goes away. How will you feel when she goes? Granted, I know it's already too late. Still, I have to ask."

They stood without speaking for a time. Anton was trying to hide inside himself, like a turtle retracting into its shell. It wasn't working as well as it usually did. Grandma Marion's sharp gaze seemed to have him hooked, and it wouldn't let him go. He looked up to see that the doorman had walked halfway across the lobby in their direction.

"Cab for your grandmother, Anthony?"

"Yes, please," Marion said. "Wait. Anthony?"

"It's Anton," he told the doorman.

"I thought it was Anthony."

"No. Anton."

The doorman shrugged his shoulders, turned up his collar, and stepped out into the cold. They stared through the front windows, watching him try to flag down a taxi. Anton kept hoping one would stop for him. So this conversation could be over.

"I don't want her to go," he said, surprising himself.

"Of course you don't want her to go. But it's what has to be. For her safety."

"Maybe there's some way she doesn't have to go."

"Ah. I see. So it's not really love."

"What? Why would you say that? That's a terrible thing to say."

"I'll tell you what love is, Anton, since—I'm sorry—but you're inexperienced and young. Love is when you can make the following statement, and mean it: 'What's best for her, even if it doesn't include me.' Otherwise you just love the way you feel when she's around, and you want to be selfish with that—hang on to it at all costs, even if it harms her. You said yourself that her husband lives across the street, and he's dangerous. So, do you love her enough to put her welfare first? If not, what you feel is what ninety-nine percent of the world is satisfied to call love, but for me it's not good enough. I may be an opinionated old woman, but that's the way I feel."

"'What's best for her, even if it doesn't include me,'" he repeated, his voice sounding stunned to his own ears. "Wow. That feels impossible. How can anybody do that?"

"It's the hardest thing in the world. I doubt you'll be able to do it at your tender age, but I've quite purposely planted the idea in your head all the same. Most grown-ups can't even get close to that kind of unselfish love. I'll tell you a secret, Anton, something that nobody knows but me. And you must never tell a soul. Your grandfather could have lived longer, but he was in so much pain. It wasn't really the cancer that finally took him, though it would have in a few weeks more. It was that he stopped eating. He wouldn't even drink water. I could have reported this to his doctor, and the doctor would have ordered him to be put in the hospital and fed through an intravenous drip. Do you have any idea how badly I wanted him to stay with me, Anton? Even for a few weeks more? But he was in pain. And it was *his* life, not mine. *His* decision. So I loved him enough to stand out of his way. I let him make a decision to go forward to a future that did not include me. Because I loved him that much."

The doorman stepped back inside and waved to them. Anton hadn't noticed that the man had managed to get a cab. He'd been too caught up in his grandmother's words. He opened his mouth to answer, but nothing came out. His brain had been switched to off.

"Be careful," she said, touching his arm. "You're about to put pain and loss on top of pain and loss, and this holding-it-together act you've been doing might become untenable. I'm worried for you. Just take care, and we'll see you at Christmas."

Then she was gone. Ushered out to the curb on the doorman's outstretched arm. And Anton hadn't managed to utter a word. Not even goodbye.

—

Edith was washing the breakfast dishes when he got back upstairs, and she seemed out of sorts. First he told himself he might only be imagining it. Then he decided it might be best to trust what he observed.

"So what was that all about?" she asked, her voice tight. It confirmed everything. He promised himself that, in the future, he would trust his observations. "Did she say something about me?"

"Nothing bad. She said you seem like a lovely woman."

She froze all motion, her hands poised above the sink, dripping soapsuds. "Then why do you look like you've just seen a ghost?"

"Oh. She just told me something. About my grandfather and how he died. But I can't tell you what it was because nobody else knows, and she made me promise not to tell a soul."

He watched her relax and return to washing the coffee cups.

It was true and it wasn't true. She had of course spoken well of Edith. And she had shared that secret about Grandpa Anton's death, but it had not unduly upset him. It was a strange thing to know, but it also felt right. Comfortable, almost. It had indeed been Grandpa Anton's life and decision. Why ask him to endure unbearable pain? The part that made him feel—and look—as though he had seen a ghost was something he was not about to share.

"So are you really okay with my family coming over for Christmas?"

"Of course. It's wonderful. Bad enough that I'm hiding from my own family. Well, you know what I mean. My husband is all the family I have. It made me uneasy to feel like I was hiding from yours."

He leaned his shoulder in the kitchen doorway, watching her work. His mind felt miles away but he could not have said where it was.

Then she spoke again. "I thought I'd leave the day after Christmas. Maybe really early in the wee hours of the morning when we can be pretty sure he won't be up."

A door slammed shut inside Anton. He could feel it in his gut and chest. It felt so familiar in the closed position. The only surprise seemed to be that he had ever allowed it to drift ajar. And without even realizing it. He looked up to see her staring at his face.

"Are you going to be okay when I go?"

"Can we please not talk about that right now?"

He was surprised to hear that he was raising and hardening his voice against her.

"I've been trying not to bring it up. But I just want to be sure you have help here until your parents get back. You know. Just in case—"

"Edith," he shouted. "Please! I'm begging you!" He was fully out of control now, actually yelling at her. He didn't want to be harsh with her, but felt unable to stop. "Can we just let the day after Christmas be the day after Christmas? I have a couple of days left and I don't want to be forced to deal with it now. Can't we just do *now* now?"

He ran out of steam, and they stood, watching each other indirectly, peripherally. She didn't seem as upset as he had imagined.

"Of course," she said. "I'm sorry."

"No, it's not you. It's me. *I'm* sorry. I really didn't mean to yell at you. I'm so sorry I yelled at you, Edith. I never meant to do that and I'll never do it again."

"Anton," she said, and reached for a dish towel to dry her hands. "If you don't mind me offering my opinion, I think you need to get upset and yell about what you need *more* often. Definitely not less."

—

In his dream, Anton was standing outside his brother's door, listening. Their parents were gone. And something was wrong in there. Greg was shouting back at the voices. The walls were thick, and sound didn't carry well. Anton had to press his ear to the door to hear.

It was not entirely unusual to hear Greg talking back to the voices. But this level of disharmony was disturbing and new. And there were other things. Other strange occurrences that told him their whole world was out of kilter. He could see the clock in the kitchen, and its hands were racing, as if hours passed every time he gasped a breath. And the square glass covers on the light fixtures were wrong, impossible some-how, bent into a perspective that did not exist in the normal three-dimensional world. Somehow the energy of his brother's pain and fear was warping the entire apartment.

He pounded on the door, but nothing happened. Nothing changed. The shouting continued without so much as a missed beat. It made Anton feel as though he didn't exist in Greg's world. Maybe even as though he didn't exist at all. Maybe he had only imagined himself as a way of believ-ing he could change the arc of Greg's life in some unlikely way.

Still, he had to try. He had to do something.

He backed up as far as the hallway would allow, got a strong run-ning start, and hit the door with his right shoulder. The wood around the door lock splintered, the door burst open, and his momentum car-ried him in. He cried out in pain because it hurt his shoulder, just as it had that night. It left him rattled and shocked, just as it really had.

But what was inside was nothing like anything he had seen in the real world. It was space. The great vacuum of outer space. And it was sucking him out of his familiar world, as if drinking him through a straw.

Just before they were both pulled out into the freezing darkness of the universe, Greg gave him that look. That soul-searing look. It was not upset, that spooky look in his brother's eyes. It was eerily calm. The shouting was over. The upset was over. Because his brother had found a way out.

They were flying out into space, and Greg's toe was moving against the trigger.

"No!" Anton screamed. "No, no, no!"

A strong light shone into his face, and he felt a pressure like a human hand in the middle of his chest. Anton's eyes shot open.

Edith was sitting on the edge of the couch beside him. She had turned on the lamp and was holding him down with one hand, as if he might be about to fly away. He half sat up, but the hand kept him partway down.

"What? What is it? Did you have a bad dream?"

"Oh. Yeah."

He put his hand on hers. She immediately pulled her hand out from under his. She got up and dragged a footstool near the couch—but not too near. She sat a foot or two away, leaning forward and hugging herself with her own arms.

"Are you okay now?"

"No," he said, without thinking to filter his reaction. "But you did me a big favor. You woke me before it was over. Before the gun went off. I hate it when I don't wake up before the gun goes off. Then I see it all over again. It's like living through it all over again, and then I can't shake it for days. So thanks for that. It could've been so much worse if you hadn't been here."

He sat up and swung his legs around, placing his bare feet on the floor. He leaned forward and wrapped himself in his own arms, unconsciously imitating her body language.

"Do you dream about it a lot?"

"At first I did. The first few months. Three or four months, I think. But I hadn't for a while, so I guess I was thinking it was over."

"Nothing's over till it's over," she said.

He sat with that for a moment, not really thinking. Then he said, "I'm not even going to ask what that means."

"It means what it sounds like it means. Are you going to be able to go back to sleep?"

"No. No way. I can't sleep after that. I wouldn't even dare try."

"Okay. I'll stay up with you. We'll watch something on TV. No, not TV. Too unpredictable, what might come on. We'll play cards, or a board game. Do you have any board games?"

"We have Monopoly. And Clue."

"Ooh. I haven't played Monopoly in ages." She jumped to her feet and trotted around the living room, turning on all the lights. "We'll make it nice and bright in here. And I'll put on some music."

"Wait, you shouldn't have to stay up. Don't you need to get some sleep?"

"Don't worry about me. I'm pretty much a night owl anyway. I can take a nap tomorrow. Besides. You made me feel safe when I needed it. Now's my chance to return the favor."

———

"Park Place!" she said, her voice thick with delight. "And with a hotel. Oh, boy. Sorry, my friend, but that's going to cost you big."

Yet Anton felt inordinately good.

When the roll of the dice had come up, when he'd counted out the spaces in his head, he had felt nearly euphoric that she would be landing on his most valuable property. He wanted to see her happy, even if only over a silly game.

He counted out his money carefully. He could barely afford it. Next time he would have to mortgage one of his measly properties.

He looked up to see her staring at his face. He couldn't quite get a bead on the emotion he saw in her eyes, but it was not the Park-Place-with-a-hotel happiness he had wanted for her.

"What? Why are you looking at me like that?"

"I still can't believe they went off and left you."

"Yeah, well. Having kids makes you a parent, but it doesn't automatically make you good at it."

"Maybe I should stay until right before they get back."

He felt a leaping in his chest, but he tamped it back down again. Sat on it, levered it back into place, might be a more apt description.

"I don't know," he said. "You know I love having you here. But we're going to run out of food soon. And the minute one of us steps out onto the street, we're taking a risk with your safety. What if I went to the store and he followed me back here? How can I take chances with something like that? You could get hurt."

"Wow," she said.

"Wow what?"

"That's pretty unselfish."

He looked down at the board, dotted with tiny green houses. The piece she had chosen to represent herself was the little metal Scottie dog. She had chosen the top hat for him because hats were Anton's symbol now.

"Well," he began. "Here's the thing. Here's how I feel about it. I want what's best for you. You know." A pause to gird himself for the tough part. "Even if it doesn't include me."

He felt as though he were literally forcing the words up and out. Marching them out into the light at gunpoint. By most measures, they weren't even entirely true. He didn't want anything that involved her leaving. But he thought maybe those difficult words could be true by the morning after Christmas. And, even if not, he was doing it. He was doing what was right, whether he wanted to or not. And that was the important thing. Wasn't it? He looked back up into her face. Her eyes had changed again, but still he could not quite read them.

"That is the sweetest, most unselfish thing I've ever heard. You're a really special young man, you know that?"

He felt the heat of his face reddening. "No. I don't know that. I figure I'm just like everybody else."

"Well, you're not. Not even close."

They froze there a moment, considering each other in a manner that fell just short of true eye contact. Then she rolled the dice and they moved on with the game. She won by a big margin, which pleased him.

# Chapter Nine

## *Actual Christmas, Fake Merry*

Anton woke and sat up, blinking. She was in the kitchen. He could hear her opening and closing the refrigerator and the cupboard doors.

He rose and slipped into his bathrobe, then joined her there.

"Merry Christmas!" she said. Her face seemed genuinely bright and elated.

"Merry Christmas."

His frame of mind felt heavy compared to hers. It was their last full day.

She seemed to catch his mood.

"Well, this is perfectly ridiculous," she said, "but we're about to have a lovely, fancy, celebratory Christmas breakfast of . . . cornflakes. We're out of most everything else."

"I don't care what we have," he said, plunking down on a high stool at the counter. "I just care that we're having it together."

Once again he had stepped too far, and he knew it. It had become a familiar feeling, stepping across the line only to have her push him back to his own side again. He had known before he did it this time. There had been no accident about it. He was almost out of time and he didn't care if he said too much. She didn't push. She didn't say anything.

Just finished setting out the coffee and cereal and milk for them in utter silence.

Maybe she knew the same thing he did—that it was a waste of time and energy to lay down boundaries for someone who's about to be gone from your life forever.

She sat on a stool beside him, clutching something in her right fist. Something small enough to hide in her palm completely. He knew it was there only because nobody holds so tightly to nothing. "I want to give you a gift," she said, her voice sober and low.

"You don't have to give me a gift."

"But I want to. You've been so kind to me, and I wanted to give you something. But I can't exactly go shopping, and I don't own much right now. But I do have a gift for you. It's something I brought from the apartment in my purse, and I want you to have it."

"But I don't have a gift for *you*."

"Are you kidding me? What do you call what you've been doing for me since I showed up at your door? What do you call train fare, so I can get out of the city and be safe?"

He remained silent, because he had no idea what to say. He wanted something tangible from her. Anything. Any evidence that she had truly been here with him. That he hadn't just imagined her. Something he could hold on to after she was gone.

"I couldn't wrap it or anything," she added.

"That doesn't matter."

She held out her right hand, and he held out his left. She dropped something small and light into his palm. He stared closely at it. It appeared to be a woman's diamond ring.

"It's my mother's engagement ring. She brought it with her from Poland right before the war. After the accident the police released all my parents' belongings to me. I was pretty young. Nineteen. But I saved this. I didn't use it for my own engagement. I guess it felt too special for that, which should have been a clue about my upcoming marriage."

"How can I accept this, though? It was your mother's. It's a family heirloom."

"Please, Anton. I want you to have it. And when you meet the right young woman, I want you to give it to her. It'll be almost like I'm there giving my blessing to you and the person you really should be with. Some nice girl your own age."

Something broke inside him. He could feel it. "No," he said, his voice thick with anger and hurt. "I won't give it to somebody else. I can't. I want to give it to you."

"Please, Anton. Let's not do this on Christmas. And it's our last day."

"I could come with you."

"Don't be silly."

"Why is it silly?"

"You have your college years coming up. And you need to meet someone who's eighteen, like you, and get married, and start a nice family. Like you deserve."

"No," he said, dangerously close to the edge of tears now. Aggravated, angry tears, but probably the anger was hiding something that would have been harder to feel. "Never. I won't meet somebody else and start a family."

"Anton," she said, and leaned in slightly. Her voice was soft, which he liked. But it also sounded—again—as though she were schooling a child, which he hated with a fresh, motivating passion. "I know it feels that way. Love always feels that way—like it will never be any different than it is right now. Love always tells you it's forever. But we all have first loves, and they're almost always with the wrong person, and hardly anybody is still with that person when they get older. I know it doesn't feel that way now, but you have to trust me on this."

"I want to come with you." His voice sounded miserable and desperate, which humiliated him.

"You can't."

"You don't feel the same?"

It was a brutally hard question to ask, but he was almost out of time. Later, if he hadn't asked it, he would have regretted his cowardice.

She surprised him by letting loose a burst of anger of her own. "I don't *get* to feel the same! Don't you understand that, Anton? I don't *get* to! I can't feel the same and still be a decent person and hold my head up. It wouldn't be right!"

It struck him in a disconnected way that they were fighting. Part of him was shaken by that realization, but it carried a certain satisfaction as well. They both cared enough to raise their voices. They had enough investment to get intense and upset.

But she was still speaking.

"Do you know how old I am, Anton? Well, I'll tell you. I'm thirty-three years old. Thirty-three! Your age plus *fifteen years*! Women can have children when they're fifteen. I could be your mother—that's how much older I am. Don't you know what people would say? They'd have terrible names for me. They'd call me a cradle robber."

"What do you care what they say?"

"Because they would be right!" She barked it out with unprecedented volume. It seemed to sink onto the counter between them and sprawl there, ruining Anton's world. "People can say anything they want to me, Anton, if they're just being judgmental. If I know it's not true. But this is true. It's not right. You need a girl your own age, whether you see it now or not. I'm sorry. I know that feels hurtful to you, but I want what's best for you in the long run. What was it you said? 'Even if it doesn't include me.'"

A long, stunned silence fell.

"Now let's have some cereal," she said.

He did not eat any cereal. He retreated to his room and lay on his bed for an hour or more, thinking nothing. Or, at least, thinking as little as possible.

He held the engagement ring clutched in his hand.

—

They arrived all together, like some sort of herd. They had the super with them, who hauled a dizzying number of food containers on what appeared to be a luggage cart—the kind Anton had seen in big hotels.

His great-aunt Mina kissed him on the cheek, and her lips felt cold from the wintry outdoors. "Grab some food, honey," she said, "and we'll move it all into the kitchen."

"Don't make him do that," Gregor said, following his wife inside. He stood in the entryway and unwrapped his muffler. Snow flew off it and onto the hardwood. "It's hard for him to grasp."

"He's adjusting," Mina said. "He's learning to carry things."

"There's nothing to grasp the containers by," Grandma Marion said. She was hanging up her own coat on a hanger as she spoke. "You need two hands. No offense, darling." She hurried over and gave him a firm kiss on the forehead, standing on her very tiptoes. "I just don't want to see anything dropped. We're not in our own kitchen. There will be no second chances."

"I can carry something," he heard Edith's voice say.

He looked up to see her standing in the archway between the entry hall and the living room. Everybody else looked up at her as well. Gregor, Marion, Mina. Maybe because they had mostly not yet been introduced, they said nothing.

"Everybody," Anton said, worrying that he was being too informal, "this is my friend Edith. Edith, this is my great-uncle Gregor and my great-aunt Mina. And you know my grandmother."

Mina stepped forward first, shaking Edith's hand with an almost alarming vigor. Then each of the women grabbed a stack of food containers and disappeared into the apartment.

Anton turned back to the door to see the super tapping his foot, telegraphing impatience. Gregor and his grandmother moved the food containers from the wheeled rack to the hall table. He heard Uncle

Gregor say "Merry Christmas" quietly, as he slipped a bill into the super's hand.

"How did you get all this over here?" Anton asked. "On the subway? No, you must've taken a cab. But still. In the trunk? Or did you hold it on your lap, or . . . ?"

"Don't be silly," Grandma Marion said. "It's too much. Gregor took the car out of the garage."

*"He took the car?"*

As he spoke, his voice full of awe, he saw Edith come back into the entry hall for another load. She smiled at him, and he smiled back. She seemed surprisingly at ease—as though the sudden chaos of family fit right into her world.

"He never takes the car out," he told Edith. In case she was wondering what they were talking about. "Only when they drive out to the country. Which is only once or twice a year."

"It was a special occasion," Gregor said. He stepped in to shake Edith's hand, and then they each picked up a stack of food containers. "I'll get the turkey," he said. "Nobody else try to take the turkey. It's heavy." As he and Edith walked toward the kitchen together, Anton heard his uncle say, "We're very pleased to meet you, Edith. We adore our Anton, and any friend of his is a friend of the family."

He watched them go for a moment. Then he looked around to see his grandmother staring at him. In all the commotion, he had forgotten she was there—forgotten to mask his emotion with a poker face. To whatever extent he owned one.

"Are you all right?" she asked him.

"Yeah. Why wouldn't I be?"

"I'm worried that I embarrassed you by telling you not to carry anything. If so, I apologize."

"She knows I only have one hand. Besides. It would have been a lot more embarrassing if I'd dropped something."

—

"This feels weird," he said to his uncle Gregor.

They were sitting together on the couch, watching the Christmas parade on TV. But not really watching it. At least, Anton was not genuinely watching.

"What feels weird about it?"

"The women are in the kitchen getting dinner ready. We're sitting here doing nothing."

"Feels too much like gender stereotypes to you?"

"Kind of. I guess. I mean, it's not 1940 or anything."

"They thought you would feel awkward trying to help. And they wanted me to stay out here and keep you company. Is it too much?"

"Is what too much?"

"Are we sheltering you too much? Would it be better if we gave you harder things to do? Let you make your own mistakes? We just want you to have more time to make the adjustment. Fully, and on your own time. But maybe it's too much. We don't mean to treat you like you're disabled—any more than necessary. You just have to tell us if it's too much. We mean well, but that doesn't guarantee that we've found the right line to walk."

Anton opened his mouth to answer. Even though he wasn't sure what the answer should be. Yes, in some ways he wanted to be treated more normally now. On the other hand, he didn't want to drop some important part of dinner. Especially not in front of Edith.

He never got the chance to respond.

Grandma Marion came barreling out of the kitchen as if she had just made some monumental discovery. As if she couldn't wait to share her excitement. "I almost forgot! Everybody get in here! Anton has something he wants to show you."

Anton only sat, blinking too much. He had no idea what he wanted to show them. He looked to his grandmother. Watched her eyes as she waited for him to get it. He did not get it. He did not feel close to getting it.

"Something that used to belong to your grandfather," she said.

"Oh!" He almost shouted it.

He jumped up from the couch and trotted to his bedroom to get the hat.

He smoothed his hair down with his hand and stood in front of the mirror, snugging it into place. He angled the brim slightly down toward his right eyebrow. Because Grandpa Anton had worn it that way.

He stepped back out into the living room.

Everyone was there. Gathered. They all looked up. Stared at him as though they had never seen him before. Even Edith, who had seen him in the hat many times.

Aunt Mina sucked in her breath audibly.

"Unbelievable," Uncle Gregor said.

"I told you," Grandma Marion said to him. "Did I tell you on the way over?"

"But he looks *so much* like him. Yes, you told me. But still I wasn't quite prepared."

Anton knew part of the reason the hat transformed him so fully into his late grandfather's look-alike. It was because their hair had been so different. Grandpa Anton's hair had been black and coarse, and noticeably wavy. Still it felt strange, seeing the transformation mirrored in his family's eyes. It reminded him of the Superman episodes on TV, in which a pair of glasses seemed to stymie anyone from identifying Clark Kent. It always seemed to Anton that more of a disguise should be required. It felt unrealistic.

He looked to Grandma Marion, who seemed to have the beginning of tears in her eyes. She seemed to notice him noticing, and brushed the emotion away.

"Well, enough of this," she said. "Let's get dinner on the table."

The three women disappeared into the kitchen again. Anton perched on the edge of the couch. He kept the hat on because he liked the way it made him feel.

"You're right," Gregor said after a minute or two. "It does feel a little strange. I'll go help them. You stay here and watch the parade."

———

He was just coming out of the bathroom, and Grandma Marion was just going in. They bumped into each other, almost literally, as he stepped into the hall.

"Oh, Anton. Sorry. I didn't know you were in there." She paused in the doorway. He waited, because he could tell there was something she wanted to say. "So how long has your friend been staying?"

He moved closer to her, so no one else would hear. "A few days."

"If it's a dangerous situation, as you said, and the dangerous man is right across the street, wouldn't it have been better to get her out of town straightaway?"

"We thought it would be best to wait until he'd given up looking for her and figured she must've left town and he missed her."

He watched his grandmother's left eyebrow lift. Just slightly. "*Who* thought that?"

"I'm sorry. What?"

"*You* thought that? Or *she* did?"

"I guess . . . looking back, I guess it was my idea. She was upset and didn't know what to do, and I suggested it." He stood awkwardly, waiting for her to respond. The longer he waited, the more he felt himself filling with a sense of shame. "I wasn't being selfish," he added.

"I didn't say anything."

"At least, I didn't mean to be."

"And now? When do you think you can safely see her away?"

"It was supposed to be tomorrow morning. Really early. Like almost the middle of the night. But then it occurred to me, earlier today . . . I have to go to the bank so she has a little money for train fare and food and to tide her over until she can get a job. So we'll need to wait until the bank opens tomorrow."

"Tomorrow is Sunday."

"It is?"

He stood dumbfounded for a moment, wondering when he had last given a thought to the days of the week. His time with Edith had seemed utterly free of such constraints. Open and unrestricted, like a sheaf of unlined paper: draw or mark anywhere. He felt himself flooded with relief. Because tomorrow was Sunday, and he could not go to the bank. So Edith couldn't leave.

"And this bank account you were going to tap? Where do you have all this money?"

"I know you won't approve, but—"

"You were going to take it out of your college fund."

He wondered how seriously he should hear her use of the past tense "were" in this case.

"Not much of it. Just a very small percentage of what I've got in there. Maybe one semester's worth of textbooks. I know college is important, but . . ."

"And I know she's important to you. And I'm not without the spirit of helping, especially on this holiday. But let's leave the college money where it is, shall we? I have a little cash. I'll quietly see what Gregor and Mina have on them. Gregor tends to carry cash in his wallet—more than I would dare, I'll tell you that. We'll see what we can put together for an early morning departure. I really believe that the longer you put off seeing her to the train, the harder it's going to be."

She disappeared into the bathroom, closing the door before he could thank her.

———

He was sitting on the couch, alone in the living room, when his grand-mother swooped back into the room. He immediately pretended to be watching the parade, because that's what he was supposed to be doing. She put one finger to her lips to signal that this would be a silent trans-action. Then she reached out her hand, and Anton saw the flash of green in it. She had forgotten to reach with her left—everyone forgot that. So the transfer was awkward. But he took the money.

He mouthed the words "Thank you," and she hurried back into the kitchen.

He took the money into his bedroom, closed the door, and counted it out on the bed. She had given him three hundred and ten dollars. A generous sum by almost any measure. He made a mental note to ask his uncle why he walked around the city carrying so much cash.

———

"Another helping of turkey, Anton?" Uncle Gregor asked.

Gregor sat at the head of the table grasping the good carving knife, which he held aloft like a sword. Like Excalibur.

"I couldn't possibly," Anton said.

"Edith?"

"I'll explode."

"No one could possibly eat another bite, Gregor," Mina said. "And the more you push, the more you're making sure that my dessert will go uneaten. No one will have room for that beautiful crème brûlée."

Anton absorbed the dessert idea for a moment before speaking.

"I don't think you can do crème brûlée here."

"Why can't we?" Mina asked.

"We don't have those little cups."

"Ramekins," she said. "They're called ramekins, and we brought them."

"And we don't have that torch you use."

"We brought it," Mina said.

"Wow."

"Wow what?"

"It's just a lot of stuff to bring across town."

"It's Christmas," she said. "And you're worth it. And besides, don't argue with anything that gets the car out of the garage. He needs to take the car out more. Stubborn man. Cars need to be driven to stay in good repair."

"I know what cars need," Gregor said. "No one needs to teach me what cars need. So no more of anything for anybody?" He let a beat or two fall, but everyone gestured their fullness, mostly with rolled eyes or hands on bellies. Or both. "So what we'll do, we'll take a nice break and digest what we've eaten, and then we'll think about dessert. Now, if no one minds, I'm going to step outside on the balcony and enjoy a cigar."

"I miss going outside," Edith said.

It stopped the conversation in its tracks. They all sat in silence for a moment. Anton caught Edith's eye and she smiled. A little sadly, he thought.

"You have such a wonderful family," she said, directing her words to Anton. She seemed to want to raise the mood again. "I'm so glad I got to see you with them. I feel better about leaving, knowing you have them. It must be nice to have a supportive family."

Uncle Gregor snorted. "You haven't met his parents." Then he looked around at the faces, and his own face reddened. "I'm sorry. I apologize. That was not a proper thing to say, especially not at the holidays. There are good things to be said about my nephew and his wife. I guess I'm just angry with them for going away and leaving Anton on his own."

"I am, too," Anton said.

It seemed to surprise everyone. Anton had steadfastly maintained the opposite to each and every one of them. But no one was more surprised than Anton himself.

"I guess the idea," Gregor said, talking through the moment, "was that *we* would be his family for Christmas. Those of us in the extended family would step in. But then . . . and this is really hard to believe . . ." He turned his face to Anton. "Did they really not tell you that the plan was to spend Christmas with us? To choose one of our houses? It seems incredible, even for them. Is it possible you might have forgotten?"

Anton sat back and wiped his mouth with his cloth napkin. He set the napkin on the table near his plate, not back on his lap, because he was done eating.

"I haven't been forgetting things," he said. "That I know of. That's not to say that my mind never wanders when Mom talks, but . . ."

Uncle Gregor shook his head in disgust. He pulled one of his signature cigars from his breast pocket and stormed off toward the entry hall, presumably to get his coat.

"I'll help clean up," Anton said.

"You will not," Grandma Marion said. "You will go keep your great-uncle company. He's upset at your parents. You can help by convincing him you're all right. And Edith, you did enough already by helping so much with the preparation. Mina and I will clean up. You go outside and enjoy the night, and we'll take care of everything else. We'll leave you all the leftovers, Anton, because you must be getting low on food by now."

Anton caught her eye, hoping not to have to say anything in front of Mina. He didn't want to share their situation—the fact that they didn't dare be seen outdoors—with anyone else if he could help it. His grandmother nodded slightly at the concern in his eyes.

"It's very cold out there," she said, "so we'll get Edith bundled up properly. She can wear a couple of woolen scarves. You should wrap them all around your face, darling, so the air you breathe is warmed.

And we'll get you some kind of hat. There'll be hardly any of you left showing, but we don't want anyone catching pneumonia. And Anton, you be safe, too, dear. Wear your father's balaclava."

"His what?"

"You know. The balaclava. It covers your face except for your eyes."

"Oh, the ski mask."

"It's not exactly a ski mask, but anyway, put it on. You'll be safer from the cold."

———

He stepped out onto the balcony, into a cloud of cigar smoke. He instinctively waved it away.

"Sorry," Gregor said, and waved with him. Then he looked up at Anton's face. Or looked *for* it, anyway, under the balaclava. "Isn't that overdoing it a bit? It's not the South Pole."

"I wanted to be warm," he said, pulling up a chair.

They sat quietly for a minute. He watched his uncle smoke and thought about what his grandmother had said. That he should put Gregor's mind at ease by convincing the older man that he was fine here without his parents. But there was a problem with that request. He didn't feel fine. In fact, he felt as though he were standing with his toes at the very edge of a steep precipice, and was unable to know what his next move would bring. So, for an extended time, he said nothing.

Then he asked, "Why do you walk around with so much cash? I mean, if you don't mind my asking. Most people are too afraid of being robbed."

Gregor sighed, blowing out another huge cloud of smoke mixed with his frozen breath.

"When you've lived through the Great Depression," he said, "it changes you."

Anton waited for his great-uncle to say more. He never did.

In time the sliding glass door opened, and Edith stepped out. At least, he assumed it was Edith. It would have been impossible to say for a fact. Only her eyes could be seen above her two wrapped mufflers and below her huge knitted hat. She had been outfitted with every bit of outerwear the two women in his family had brought.

"Hey," he said.

Then, after saying it, he worried his tone might have been too intimate and familiar.

"Hey," she replied, in the same tone.

"So you get to be outside."

"I do."

"Because you missed the outside."

"Your grandmother is very kind. I think she took note when I said that."

"So where will you go?" his great-uncle asked Edith.

An awkward silence fell.

"I'm sorry," Gregor said. "Just making conversation. It's really none of my concern." He set his cigar down in the ashtray he'd placed on the arm of his chair. "I'll just go inside and make use of the little boys' room. I'll be back to finish this cigar."

He let himself back into the apartment. Anton looked at Edith and she looked back at him. But there wasn't much for either of them to see.

"You okay?" she asked him.

"I think so."

But he didn't think so.

"I really do like your family."

"They're not too chaotic for you?"

"Oh, no. That's a perfect amount of chaos. That's just what a family should be. A bunch of beautiful chaos. I wanted kids so I could enjoy all that commotion."

Then she fell silent, and he didn't feel he should ask why she'd never had them. It was probably a question that answered itself anyway.

"I have something to give you," he said. "I have some money for you. But you have to promise me if I give it to you now, you won't leave in the night without saying goodbye. You have to let me see you to the train in the morning."

"I would never leave without saying goodbye."

He pulled the wad of cash out of his pocket and held it in her direction. She reached out. With her left hand. She got it. Nobody else got it.

"Promise?" he asked, still holding the cash tightly.

"Cross my heart and hope to die."

He opened his hand. But for a moment she didn't take what he offered.

"What?" he asked her.

"I hate taking money from you. It feels wrong."

"It's fine. Really. Please."

"I guess it has to be fine, because I have no other options."

He heard a softening in her voice. Felt a softening in the air between them. As if they had stepped back into some comfortable state of understanding. She took the cash from his hand, and it made him shiver slightly, because her skin brushed against his. Neither of them wore gloves.

"Thank you for the Christmas gift," she said. "I still feel bad taking it from you, but it's the best gift you could possibly have given me, because it's my freedom."

"I'm sorry about this morning."

"What about it?"

"You know. That argument we had."

"That was hardly an argument."

"I feel like I put you on the spot."

"You don't have to be sorry. You shouldn't have to apologize for what you want. We just don't always get what we want in this world. That's the thing about life. That's the way it is."

He opened his mouth to answer, but as he did the balcony door slid open and Uncle Gregor came out and sat again, picking up his cigar. It didn't really matter, Anton decided. Because he had no answer, anyway, to the way life is.

—

He walked his grandmother to the elevator when they guessed that Mina and Gregor had been given enough time to bring the car around.

"Thank you," he said, when they were alone in the hall together.

"For what, darling?"

"I just thought . . . I don't know. I expected something different. Something not so comfortable. I guess I thought you'd all ask Edith a bunch of questions about herself and kind of . . . give her the third degree. But we just small-talked and it felt comfortable and nice."

"Darling," she said, and rested one warm hand on his cheek. "We're your family. We're not here to give you a hard time."

A brief beat of silence. Then they both burst out laughing. Because what is your family, really, if not the people whose job it is to give you a hard time?

But they didn't need to say, out loud, what they were laughing about, which is probably the best side of family right there.

# Chapter Ten

## The Man in the Moon, Really

While she changed into a clean pair of his pajamas, Anton dragged the telescope to the living room window. The moon was rising over the city skyline, nearly full and surprisingly clear.

He positioned the telescope, then focused both the lens and the eyepiece. He let out a sharp breath when he saw the magnification and clarity of the image.

"Wow," he said out loud to nobody. To an empty room.

At least, he thought it was an empty room.

She answered him, and her voice made him jump. "What? What do you see?"

"I'm just looking at the moon."

"May I see, too?"

"Of course."

He stepped away from the scope and allowed her to step in. She bent over slightly and peered through the eyepiece.

He stood a step or two beside her, watching the way her hair fell forward around her face. It was hard not to look at the shape of her through his soft and drapey pajamas, but he forced himself not to. At least, not for more than a second. Even though it was his last chance, forever. Still, there's right and there's wrong, and he liked to think he knew the difference.

"So that's what the man in the moon really is," she said. "Don't get me wrong. I knew it wasn't really a man. But now I can see what makes it look that way. Those are actual land features on the moon, right? I never saw it up close like this. Not even in a picture. Not that I can remember. And I think I would remember."

"The dark places that look like eyes are seas. Not seas like we have here on Earth. No water in them, but they still call them a sea, or a mare. They have names, like Mare Serenitatis, the Sea of Serenity, and Mare Frigoris, the Sea of Cold. I couldn't tell you off the top of my head which of those seas look like the eyes. I'd have to look at my book again."

"And that crater-looking thing? With the lines coming out from it?"

"That's Tycho. It's just what it looks like it is. A crater."

She straightened up suddenly. As if she'd seen something that troubled her. But when she spoke, he knew immediately that her trouble was on the inside.

"I can never sleep when I'm scared," she said.

He took a step over, so that he was standing right beside her, nearly shoulder to shoulder but not touching. They stared at the moon together with only their unaided eyes.

"Why are you scared?"

"Because tomorrow everything changes. I have to go to a town I've never seen, to sleep on a couch of a friend I haven't seen in years, and then I have to get a job doing something I probably don't even know how to do yet. The only thing in my whole life that feels familiar is this apartment, and you. And now I have to walk away from that."

They stared at the moon together while Anton didn't answer.

It moved him in a way he could not have explained to have her confess that he was her whole familiar world. Even though he knew she meant it in a different way than he would have, if he had dared discuss the same subject. If he could have said anything at all, he would have told her he was afraid, too. Above and beyond the pain of losing her—or underneath it, it was hard to tell—was a pool of pure terror. Maybe because it was the first time since Greg's death that he had opened the door to emotion—the first time he had felt something other than a sense of his body being filled with quickly setting concrete. He had allowed himself to feel because he felt for her, because he hadn't been able to prevent it. But for all that time he had felt *only* what he felt for her, because it was overwhelming and left no room for anything else. Now she was leaving. So what would he feel? He was afraid the answer was "everything," but he had no way to know. There didn't seem to be a road map anywhere in the world for the path he was navigating. Or, if there was, he had no access to it.

He didn't tell her about his fear. Not because he didn't trust her with it, but because he was afraid words spoken out loud would solidify it, make it more real. Then he could never withdraw his thoughts about the fear, or claim he no longer believed them.

He suspected that maybe he couldn't anyway, but still he didn't dare.

All he said was "Stay awake and talk to me, then."

"I was hoping you'd ask," she said, and her voice sounded a little more secure.

—

They sat together, cross-legged, each with their lower backs propped against opposite arms of the couch. They had turned on no lights, but the moon was shining strongly through the living room windows. He was facing the moon; she had her back to it. So it lit up the front of him and the back of her, making him feel cheated. Then again, it might have been unbearable to see her so clearly as their time ticked down to nothing.

His right wrist was laid out in front of him, plainly exposed, in a way he wasn't used to displaying it. But he was talking about it, which made its display feel appropriate.

"People don't quite understand," he said. "They think it's about something different than it really is. They say, 'You can get a prosthetic.' Or they say, 'You'll learn to grasp things in a different way.' But that's not the hard part. The hard part is that every time I meet a new person, or even pass a stranger on the street, there's this moment. This shocked moment, where they expect to see something and it isn't there. If my hand had been mangled nearly beyond recognition but was still there, I swear people would have an easier time. People don't like to see parts of a person missing. It's something that happens in the caveman part of our brain, I guess. I know you had a little of that, too, when you first met me, and I'm not blaming you. I'm not saying there's anything wrong with it. I'm saying that as long as I live that's always going to be the first moment I have with anybody I meet. It just feels like looking down a really long road from where I am now. Sometimes I get tired just thinking about it."

He stopped talking, and she waited. Maybe to see if he was really done.

Then she asked, "You worry that's going to make it hard to meet a girl?"

That hadn't been a specific worry, probably because he couldn't currently imagine that he ever would. That he would ever be interested in anyone else.

"Among other things."

"There's a silver lining to that. Don't get me wrong. I hear what you're saying. I'm not trying to be all Pollyanna about it. I believe you, that it's hard. But sometimes the hard parts of our lives come with something valuable attached."

"That's what my grandmother says. So what's the silver lining in this?"

"You'll end up with a girl who's not shallow. It's hard to find someone to love you for who you are. Most people have this image of the person they wanted to love—that they always imagined themselves loving—and they just love you for fitting with that. Which is dangerous, because they'll try to avoid the parts of you that don't fit. But the girl you'll marry, she didn't imagine a husband with one hand. She'll have to look past that to who you really are. And that's how you'll know you got a good one."

He still didn't believe any of it would happen.

"What time is it?" he asked, because she could see the clock on the kitchen stove from where she sat.

"After two."

"What time is your train?"

"Six. But I'd like to be out of the neighborhood long before that."

They sat silent for several minutes. Either absorbing that their time was almost up, or trying not to absorb it. Anton knew only that he was in the latter category.

"What are you wearing around your neck?" she asked him after a time. "As long as I've known you, you never wore anything around your neck."

His hand instinctively came up to touch the leather cord. He grasped it and pulled up on it. He was wearing a T-shirt over his pajama bottoms, and he pulled until the ring she had given him popped out into view.

"I had this leather cord," he said. "It had a big jade pendant on it that my parents brought me from New Zealand. I took it off and put your ring on the cord so I couldn't lose it."

"*Your* ring," she said, her voice soft.

"I still feel bad taking it from you."

"And I feel bad taking money from you, but we're friends, and we're going to accept the gifts. Right?"

"I still don't see myself meeting a girl."

"I know. You have to trust me. Life brings all sorts of situations we never saw coming."

"We haven't really talked about ourselves much," he said, surprising himself with the conversational turn.

"I don't know what you mean. What have we talked about if not ourselves?"

"I mean . . . I still don't know much about your life before I met you."

"Don't you think that's purposeful, though? We're freezing time here. Just living out a piece of life that's separate from everything that came before it. Or anything that'll come after it. Because our time is almost up. What else do we need to know?"

"I hate that our time is almost up."

"Me too. I wish I didn't have to go."

"Then don't go."

"How?" she asked.

Her voice sounded like she was stretching to hear his answer. She wasn't being rhetorical or sarcastic as far as he could tell. She seemed genuinely to want him to know the answer. He sat silent a moment, hitting one brick wall after another in his mind.

"Oh," he said. "That's right. There is no how. I forgot."

———

He jumped awake, still cross-legged on the couch. His back was stiff and his legs almost completely asleep. He tried to launch himself off the couch to check the time, but ended up falling and hitting his ribs on the coffee table when his numb legs refused to support him.

The thump of it woke her.

"What?" she asked. "What just happened?"

"We fell asleep. What time is it?"

She craned her neck and peered into the kitchen. "Uh-oh. It's after four."

"Can we still get out while he's asleep?"

To his shame, Anton very much hoped the answer would be no.

"Barely," she said. "But we really have to fly."

—

They slipped out the back door of the apartment building and into the alley, then broke to the right. A cab could be hailed on either side street. Anton didn't know why he chose the direction he chose, or how she turned with him as if she knew his thoughts. They seemed to be operating together in some thrilling way, like the birds that swoop and dive and turn in perfect symmetry with their flock. They broke into a run.

She was wearing his mother's winter coat and floppy hat, with two knitted mufflers wrapped around the bottom part of her face. It was hard to see much of anything about her in the dark, other than the coat flapping out behind her as she ran, which was exactly how and why they had planned it that way.

As they sprinted toward the lighter street, into the glow of a streetlamp, she reached out and grabbed his hand with her right. And they ran together that way, joined.

His ribs ached where he had hit them on the coffee table, but it didn't feel important. His hat was not seated as firmly on his head as he might have liked, but he had to trust it to stay put. No way was he going to let go of her hand.

Anton wasn't sure what caused the intensity. Were they thrilled to be back outdoors and moving? He knew he was. It reminded him of his days running track, back when everything had been normal. Were they desperately afraid that her husband was somehow right around the corner, waiting for them, even though it made no sense to think he would be?

Maybe both, he thought.

They sprinted out into the street, his bare hand still in hers, and nearly ran right in front of a cab. The driver slammed on his brakes and blared his horn.

Anton opened the back door of the cab, and they piled in.

"Grand Central," Edith said. "As fast as you safely can."

Anton sat back and felt his elation drain away. Her hand was gone from inside his. More importantly, they had successfully made it out of the neighborhood in safety. The sun would come up in a couple of hours, and it would be far too dangerous to retrace their steps for any reason—which meant he could no longer hope that something went wrong and she had to stay. They had passed the point of no return. Their time together was all but over, and he knew it.

—

He sat on the train platform, bent over his own aching ribs. He more or less held his head in his hands—in his hand on the left and braced by his wrist on the right.

Edith had gone to buy her ticket. She had said she wanted to go by herself and had instructed him to wait on the platform. She hadn't said straight out that he couldn't come because, if he did, he might overhear her destination. Then again, she hadn't needed to.

Her train was already there, waiting—which was why he kept his head down, refusing to look. Passengers bustled by, most boarding. He could feel their slight hesitation as they walked by him. That pause as they took him in. Because he wasn't hiding his stump. At least, that was what his senses told him. And what they told him was consistent with the reality of his past seven or so months of life.

He looked up and saw a porter hurrying along the platform.

It struck him that he could ask the man where the train was headed.

He leapt to his feet, but then froze. He'd be doing the opposite of what she had asked him to do. Then again, if he asked, he could always decide to ignore what he learned. If he didn't ask, there would be no do-overs. He would have missed his chance for all of time.

He walked up to the short, beefy man, who was now arranging luggage into the compartment under the train. He opened his mouth to speak, but the truth he had foolishly overlooked flooded into his head and stopped his words. The train was not headed to any one destination. It was headed to dozens of them. And any number of those stops would offer an opportunity to transfer to a different train, headed to dozens more destinations.

It overwhelmed him to take it in. He had grasped at this idea as a last chance. Now he could feel the emptiness left inside him when that last chance melted away.

"Yes, son?"

"What time does the train leave, sir?"

The porter glanced at his wristwatch. "Four minutes."

Anton took a step back and was seized with a truly horrible thought. Edith might not be coming back. She might purposely have directed him to sit on the wrong platform, in front of the wrong train, while she slipped out of town without saying goodbye. Maybe she couldn't bear to say goodbye. Maybe it was his fault. Maybe it was that temper tantrum he'd unleashed on Christmas morning. What if it had convinced her that he could not be trusted to act like a gentleman at the last minute and let her go?

But she'd told him she would never leave without saying goodbye.

Maybe she was just late. Maybe she would miss her train. It would be unsafe to go home, but they could get a hotel room. He could go to the bank and get more money. No, it was Sunday. He couldn't. But they could spend the money he'd given her on a hotel, and he could get more in the morning. Maybe they would have to be together another day.

Or maybe he had already seen the last of her and simply, pitifully, didn't know it.

His wildly disturbed mind flew in circles, careening back and forth from one apparent truth to another. Then a hand touched his shoulder, and he jumped.

"Sorry," Edith said. "I didn't mean to startle you." She held two Danish pastries on napkins, one on top of the other. She tried to offer him one, but he waved it away. "Take it for later," she said.

He only shook his head. Words were not coming to him. He had lost his words somehow.

They sat on the bench together. She ate one pastry, and left the other sitting next to his hip. She said nothing because her mouth was full. He said nothing because he had forgotten how that speaking thing had used to go.

"Maybe you should go over to your grandmother's house after I leave. Or your uncle's. It would be good to be around someone right now. Don't you think?"

He didn't tell her what he thought. He didn't even know what he thought. And he didn't know how to speak anymore.

Someone called "All aboard," and they both jumped to their feet.

"I need to give you back your mother's coat and hat. And her mufflers."

"No, you can't," he said, dragging words up because he needed them. For her. "You'll freeze."

"I'll be on the train. It'll be warmer where I'm going."

"But you have to get off. At least to go into the station. When the train stops."

"What will you tell her?"

"I don't know. The truth, I guess. I'll buy her new ones from my allowance if she insists."

She tried to catch his eyes, but he only looked down at the filthy platform. While he was looking away, she embraced him. He softened in her arms, and held her in return. He couldn't think—his mind was too much of a muddle. He was too utterly overwhelmed. He knew he was feeling emotions but his brain couldn't process them. They seemed to be running amok in his world without him.

"I'll never forget you," she said, her mouth close to his left ear. He could feel the brush of her breath as she spoke. It tickled slightly. "You'll have to use that as consolation. You won't know where I am but you'll know that, wherever I am, I'll never forget you."

He unlocked his ability to speak again because he had to. Because it was too important an opportunity to miss. And he didn't have much time. "Promise?" His voice sounded rusty to his own ears. As if that had been the first word he'd forced out in decades.

"How can you even ask that, Anton? How could I forget you? After everything you've done for me, how could I possibly forget?"

Someone called "All aboard" again, but they remained in the embrace for a beat or two.

"I have to go," she said against his ear.

"I love you."

Because . . . well, there was every reason in the world to say it and no real reason not to. There would be no repercussions for the bold act, because she was about to jump on a train. And besides, she already knew. And how could he let her go without saying it? He'd regret the missed opportunity for the rest of his life.

"I love you, too," she said.

It was so quiet. Barely a whisper. So quiet that he wasn't even positive he'd heard it correctly, or heard it at all.

"Wait, what?" he said, a bit louder.

She pulled out of his arms and ran for the train. He ran after her, but she was up the steps and on board. She paused, holding on to the handrail, and looked back at him.

"Wait. You love me?"

She only smiled sadly. Then she disappeared for a moment, reappearing behind a window, settling into a seat.

"You love me?" he called out with as much volume as he could muster.

The train had begun to move now. It was pulling out of the station, and, almost without realizing it, Anton was running along with it. He picked up speed as the train did.

"Did you say you love me?"

He knew she couldn't hear him, so he tried to articulate the words clearly with his lips. Maybe she could read them. She raised one hand in a stationary wave. Anton kept running.

A moment later he saw her face change into a mask of alarm. She gestured wildly to him, as if trying to warn him about something. He looked in the direction she seemed to be indicating and saw that he was about to run smack into a post.

He tried to jump around it, because it was too late to stop. His momentum would have carried him into the collision anyway. He missed the post with the bulk of his body, but it caught his knee and foot and sent him sprawling.

He fell hard, feeling the breath forced out of him. Feeling the jarring of his bruised ribs.

When he had absorbed the impact, he looked up. His hat had come off and was rolling toward the edge of the platform. He reached out and caught it just in time. Before it could roll onto the tracks and be lost to him forever. He could still see the back of the train disappearing, but he could no longer see Edith. She was too far away.

He lay still, telling himself it was time to get up. That the obvious next move was to get up. That sooner or later he would have no choice but to get up.

He did not get up.

# Chapter Eleven

## *He Thinks He Broke*

Anton's consciousness rose up through a murky sea of . . . something. Something that felt like sleep but was not. Maybe it was a cross between sleep and forced unconsciousness. It felt like that.

He was still down on his side on the platform, and a uniformed police officer was crouched over him. He was a big man with broad shoulders and beefy hands. He was squatting on his considerable haunches over Anton. With one hand he reached out and physically opened one of Anton's eyes.

It struck Anton as odd that the man did that, because Anton had just opened his eyes on his own. And yet the sense of oddness was distant. Anton felt as though he were watching a movie about a young man down on a train platform. All the details were there, but they did not feel as important as things tended to feel when they were happening to him personally.

The policeman pried Anton's eyelids wide open and peered inside, his face alarmingly close. Or at least, it would have been alarming if it had been happening to Anton and not to the random boy in the movie.

Anton wondered what the policeman thought he could see. Did he think Anton was something like a car, and he could lift the hood and peer into the engine to see why Anton wasn't working properly? Or was there helpful information written in there somewhere, and, if so, why was it not helpful to Anton himself?

"What seems to be our situation here, son?" the policeman asked. "I been talking to you a long time and nothing. I don't smell alcohol. Your pupils aren't dilated. Trying to decide whether to arrest you or call an ambulance for you, and I could use a little help here. I'm not trying to bust your chops, kid. I'm trying to get you whatever help you need, but you're not making it easy to know what that is."

But Anton had no helpful information to give the man. He had no voice. Someone or something had reached inside him and removed his words. He had no idea how or why. He knew only that they were gone. He could feel the still, cool, empty space they had left behind.

The officer sighed and began calling the situation in from some kind of walkie-talkie on his belt. "Yeah. Miller. Got a kid here. Older kid. Down on a platform at Grand Central. Couple o' witnesses say he fell, but that doesn't explain everything. Not sure what we're dealing with here. Maybe a concussion. Because he's not fully with us. I think we need an ambulance here. Let me get up and get you some specifics on where we are. Might be overkill, but I think we need to play it safe."

Anton felt relief when the officer drew away. Partly because the man was gone. Partly because someone else was going to take care of the next move for him. Thinking about taking a next step himself—even something simple like standing up and making his way home—felt so overwhelming that it threatened to send him back down into that soup of unconsciousness. He clutched the hat tightly in his hand in the hope that it would go with him, wherever he went from here.

He didn't remember much more from that morning. Only a vague awareness of being lifted, but with a stiff board supporting him as he was carried away. And the only thought that crossed his mind was that he should stay right there on the platform because she might come back. Because she loved him. She had said so. And maybe she hadn't realized it until she heard herself say it, but maybe now that she realized it, she would get off the train and come back.

But he had no way to say that, and no control over the situation, so he found himself carried away all the same.

—

He opened his eyes again. Tentatively. As though it might be a dreadful mistake. He was in some kind of hospital room. There were other beds—beside and across from him—but they lay empty. In his peripheral vision he could see an IV drip running into the back of his hand.

"Ah," a familiar male voice said, from close by. "There you are."

He turned his head to see Uncle Gregor sitting by his bedside. It seemed like an effort, turning his head. As though his neck had partially seized up from lack of use.

Uncle Gregor held an unlit cigar clenched in his teeth. It struck Anton that his great-uncle was nervous, maybe even afraid, and was using the cigar as a kind of pacifier. Even though Anton guessed he couldn't light it in a hospital. And that *he* was the cause of all that worry. It felt mildly surprising. Yet, at the same time, it didn't feel like much. He simply wasn't able to feel much. Everything felt muted and far away, as though covered in a thick film of mud.

"How did you know I was here?" he asked.

Gregor pulled the unlit cigar from his teeth and heaved a great sigh of relief. "Oh, thank goodness!" he said on the rush of his exhale. "You're talking. They told me you weren't talking, and I didn't know what to make of that. They actually asked me if you were a deaf-mute. That scared me, let me tell you. They said you were awake and responsive, but you just stared at their lips as they spoke and never said a word. And then finally you wrote down my name and phone number for one of the hospital administrators. They said you had no physical injuries and no sign of a concussion. So then what happened, Anton? Can you tell me what happened?"

Anton lay quietly for a moment, wondering why he had no memory of people talking to him. Then he said, "I think I broke."

Uncle Gregor sat back and sighed. "I thought as much. I thought it might be emotional. Anxiety. I asked them to give you a sedative. Valium, I think they gave you. I thought it might help."

Anton only continued to lie still, trying to get his bearings. Wondering if the Valium had given him his voice back. It stood to reason that it had.

Then he was hit with a series of thoughts. The first, oddly, was that he had left the Danish pastry Edith had given him on a bench at the train platform. And now he wanted it back. Because it was from her, and he wanted anything that was from her. Then he realized that if she decided to come back, she would never find him here at the hospital.

Then, suddenly, a third thought: when the hospital staff took him out of his clothes, they might have taken the ring off from around his neck. He reached up with his hand, careful not to disturb the IV needle. It was still there.

"What's that you have around your neck?" Uncle Gregor asked. "I've never seen that."

"I have to go home," was all Anton said.

"I'm . . . not sure if I can make that happen. You've been ordered to stay for a three-day psychiatric evaluation. I might be able to override it, being a licensed psychiatrist, and get them to release you into my care. But I haven't succeeded in doing that yet."

"No, I need to go home *now*."

"I'm sorry. It might not be possible."

They sat in silence for what felt like several minutes. Anton was aware of panic. Distant panic, but panic nonetheless. It was under the Valium, which was weighting it down, but it was there. And it was attempting to struggle out and break free.

"Is this about Edith?" Uncle Gregor asked. "Or is this about Greg?"

Anton opened his mouth to answer, and, much to his alarm, burst into tears. Violent tears. A storm of them. Zero to a hundred percent breakdown in no time at all. It frightened him to hear his own noises. He sounded like a wounded animal bellowing in pain.

"I wanted to save him," he sobbed, his words sounding nearly unintelligible to his own ears. "I lost so much trying to save him but he didn't get saved. Why didn't he get saved? Why did I have to lose my hand and still not get to save him? Why did it have to happen like that? I can see losing *something* but why did I have to lose *everything*? It's not fair!"

His great-uncle slid his chair closer and placed a hand on Anton's arm.

"No," he said, his voice deep and soft. "No, you're right. It's not fair."

They sat that way for a time. Until Anton's nose became problematically runny. Gregor took a tissue from a box beside the bed and held it to Anton's nose and waited for him to blow. The way one does with a toddler. But it was likely not because his great-uncle meant to treat him like a child. It was probably because Anton's only hand was tethered by an IV drip.

"If you think you'll be okay here by yourself for a few minutes," Gregor said after a time, "I'll go look into whether they might be willing to release you."

Anton nodded, because he wanted to be alone. He wanted his uncle Gregor to go away.

The minute the older man did, Anton tugged at the IV until the tape pulled away and the needle popped out. Then he slipped out of bed, pressing a tissue against his bleeding hand.

His clothing and outerwear were lying neatly folded on a chair in the corner, with the hat perched on top. He picked them up and slipped into the bathroom, dressing as quickly as he could in his sedated state.

Then he rushed out of the hospital alone.

As he trotted down the street looking for a subway station, he wondered if he had already missed her. If it might be too late. Or, worse yet, if there had been nothing to miss. Could she possibly have told him she loved him and then not turned around and come back? It seemed hard to imagine. Then again, she had told him she loved him and then jumped on a train. But she would have had so much time to think while on her trip.

All he knew is that he needed to be there when she arrived.

If she ever did.

———

He was sitting in his living room, on the edge of the couch, when the knock came at the door. He was leaning forward, staring at the front door, as he had been for some time. As if waiting for it to do something. When it finally did, it startled him onto his feet.

He ran to the door to open it for her.

He knew it might not be her. He could feel the irritation of the spot in the back of his consciousness that said it might not be. But he refused to pay direct attention to it.

He tried to call through the door to ask if it was her, but he could not. His voice was gone again. Maybe the Valium had worn off, or maybe it was just gone anyway. So he only opened his mouth and pushed out nothing. A perfectly silent rush of air.

He had purposely left all the locks undone.

He threw the door wide and stood face to face with his great-uncle Gregor.

He tried to slam the door closed again, but Gregor physically stopped it. Braced both hands against the door, held it half open, and slipped in.

"Oh no you don't. I'm coming in and that's that. You can't avoid this, Anton, and you can't run from it. You need help. Why did you run away from the hospital? I was working on getting them to release you to me, but now you've gone and ruined it. Now you've made it clear that you're a danger to yourself, sneaking away against advice. Now we have no choice but to keep you under observation for three days at a minimum. I know you're upset, and I understand you're not thinking clearly right now. And I'm sympathetic to that—I am. But you're a bright, responsible young man, and I need you to help yourself here as much as possible. Why did you take off like that?"

Anton stood mute and frozen, unable to speak to explain why he couldn't speak.

"What do you have to say for yourself?"

He opened his mouth and genuinely tried. Tried to say he couldn't risk missing Edith. In case she came back. But no words came out.

"Oh," Gregor said. "Oh dear. It's like that, is it? Well, we'll get you some help. I know a good facility. Very clean and the staff is excellent, and you'll be treated well there. You don't have to be afraid."

Anton shook his head.

"And you don't have to be ashamed, either. Anyone who went through what you went through can expect this kind of break. It's not weakness. You just tried too hard to be strong."

Anton shook his head again.

Uncle Gregor sighed. Then he reached inside his unbuttoned coat, into the breast pocket of his suit jacket, and pulled out a thin, flat leather case full of note cards. Anton recognized it. It had been an anniversary gift from his wife, Mina, and he was quite proud of it. It had a small silver pen in a clip on one side. Gregor withdrew the pen, clicked out the writing tip, and handed both to Anton.

Anton carried them to the hall table, because he couldn't hold the card and write on it at the same time. He steadied the card with his right wrist, then wrote, *I have to be here in case Edith comes back.*

He handed it to Gregor, who frowned when he read it.

"Why do you think she's coming back? I thought she'd gotten away forever, and couldn't come back because it wasn't safe. What happened to make you think otherwise?"

Anton only shrugged, hoping it would be enough. He felt weak, as though suffering from a dreadful case of the flu. He felt panic just under the surface of his consciousness. It sounded like a relief to go to a "facility." Because they would take care of things. They would know what to do. But he couldn't go.

The shrug wasn't enough.

Gregor handed him back the card.

Anton sighed, and carried it to the hall table again. There he wrote, under his previous message, *I'd rather not say.*

He handed the card to his great-uncle, who frowned again. Gregor's brow furrowed into lines that Anton could never imagine unfurrowing. It made him worry that he might have broken his uncle, just as surely as he had broken himself.

"Here's what we'll do," Gregor said. "I'll write a note with the address of the facility. And I'll leave it on the door with her name on the outside. That way if she does come back, she'll know where you are."

Anton opened his mouth to object, out of force of habit. He had forgotten that his mouth was out of order.

"I won't say it's a mental facility," Gregor said. "Don't worry. I'll just give the address where you'll be and ask her to come there to see you." He looked up from the card and viewed Anton with a look that Anton could only describe as slightly suspicious. Then he added, "In case she really does come back."

Gregor seemed to know that the possibility of her arrival was suspect. He seemed to be temporarily viewing Anton as an unreliable narrator of his own life. At least, Anton hoped it was only temporary. It stung, but in another way Anton felt relief. He could go. He could go to this place where they knew how to fix him. He could give up now, and admit how much help he really needed to get his life back into some kind of equilibrium.

At least, he could admit it if and when he ever found his misplaced voice.

———

On his third day in the facility, the door to the appointment room opened, and a doctor came in. It was not the doctor Anton had been seeing. The man was tall and thin, with a receding hairline and a serious expression. It looked as though he hadn't combed his hair for days, which struck Anton as an odd trait in a professional man.

The doctor sat in a chair across from Anton and crossed his legs at the knee. He stared at Anton, who stared back.

"My name is Dr. Spiegel," he said. "Dr. Avery asked me to come and meet with you. I'm guessing you know why. Do you know why, Anton?"

Anton stared and said nothing.

He could have spoken had he chosen to. For three days he had been given a particularly helpful blend of sedatives, and they made it easier to function. But so far he had chosen not to let on that his words were back. It seemed safer not to go wherever they wanted to take him—the words and the doctors, both.

The doctor spoke again. "He feels he's making no progress with you. He's not sure where you are in there. The three days are almost up, but he doesn't feel as though we've helped you. We could order you to stay longer, but we don't really feel you're a danger to yourself or others. We just feel that you're traumatized and need help. Your parents could order you kept longer, but we have no way to get in touch with them. Or your great-uncle could, temporarily, in their absence, but he doesn't want to. He doesn't want to do anything against your will if he can help it. He wants you to *want* to connect with some kind of help. We all do. But we're not seeing any connection so far."

He allowed a pause. Anton did not fill it.

"So let me ask you a question, then, Anton. Your great-uncle tells us that when you first landed in the hospital, when nobody knew what was wrong, they gave you Valium, and you spoke normally to him. We're giving you quite the cocktail of sedative medications in the hope that you'll communicate with us. So I guess my question is . . . can you really not speak? Or are you choosing not to speak?"

He stared at Anton. Anton stared back and said nothing.

"Right. Well, I might have seen that coming. Let me try this another way. Is there anything on your mind that feels important enough to inspire you to say it out loud? It doesn't have to be about your trauma or your emotions. Could be a complaint about the facility, or something you feel you need to be comfortable. Anything at all weighing on your mind?"

It tapped into a need in Anton. Immediately. Without pause, without thought or fanfare, he opened his mouth and spoke. "I want my ring back."

Dr. Spiegel seemed surprised. He sat silently a moment, hands clasped around one knee. Then he said, "All of your belongings will of course be returned to you upon your release."

"No," Anton said. "I want my ring back now."

Anton felt he could almost see the thoughts and potential decisions swirling in the man's head.

"Let me see what I can do," the doctor said at last.

He got up and left the room.

Anton waited, doing nothing. Thinking nothing. Looking at nothing. It was a luxury—one he would miss when he was gone from here. The medication made it possible to hang in a state of stasis. He had never experienced anything like it before. It amounted to a much-needed vacation from his ever-present stress.

The doctor opened the door and stuck his head back inside.

"Seems the problem is the leather cord. Because it's on a leather cord, they're not keen on your having it back. A cord around your neck is something we traditionally associate with self-harm. I'm not saying you'll use it that way, but we have our policies. We have to think of your safety and well . . . our own liability if I'm being perfectly honest. So that's why they're not giving in on that."

"Fine," Anton said, noticing that he was blinking too often but not knowing why. "Take the ring off the cord. Keep the cord. Give me back the ring."

The doctor stood perfectly still for what felt like a full minute, though it might not have been that long. Then his head disappeared again.

Several minutes later he walked back into the room and held out his hand. Anton reached out with his left and felt the ring drop into his palm. He closed his hand tightly around it and savored the relief it brought. Simply holding it changed something inside him. Something that had desperately needed changing.

Dr. Spiegel sat across from him again, and Anton knew he would have to talk now. A tacit understanding had been reached. He had traded away his silence for this favor. And it had been worth it.

"So tell me about your brother," the doctor said.

"But you know all about that. Because my uncle Gregor told you."

"I'd rather hear it from you."

"I don't know what you want me to say about it."

"Did your parents get you any help afterward?"

"But you know that, too. Because that was something you asked my great-uncle. I know you would ask that first thing, because it's like a medical history. If I'd been seeing a counselor of some sort, you'd want to consult with him immediately."

The doctor sat back in his chair and sighed. "Let me phrase this a different way. Were your parents any help to you at all after your brother's death?"

Anton heard himself laugh out loud, but it sounded distant and foreign to his ears.

"I'll take that as a no," Dr. Spiegel said, and scribbled some notes on a pad.

"People always ask me that," Anton said. It was the first time he had said anything voluntary and unsolicited since he had lost Edith.

"Of course they do. Your parents are supposed to be guiding you. It's their job to offer you help with anything you're not yet ready to handle on your own."

"See, I don't understand that. Everybody is always like, 'Your parents are good parents, right? They're just what they're supposed to be, aren't they?' There's this *idea* of what a parent should be and everybody is so shocked that my parents are not it. But we all know the world is full of lousy parents, so I'm not sure what all the surprise is about."

The doctor scribbled more notes.

"Did you ever discuss with them the idea of . . . outside help?"

"No. Why would I?"

"Because . . . you needed some?"

"I'm not sure I knew I did. I mean . . . if I was being straight with myself, then yeah. Maybe I could have seen that. But I think . . . I thought I could just . . . stay away from it. Like I could put it over *there*, and then I could live over *here*. And then after some time it would get easier."

"Okay. Understood. I think that's what most people your age would try to do, given the lack of a better set of options. So no one is faulting you for the way you tried to handle it. But now I guess my question is . . . what changed?"

Anton sat still, strangely aware of his body, and did not answer.

"It might be a hard question," Dr. Spiegel said. "And there might be no real answer. Maybe nothing changed. Maybe you just held it in until you couldn't hold it in any longer. But I don't mean to talk over you or answer for you. Was there some kind of incident that precipitated this break?"

Anton held the ring more tightly in his palm. He could feel the edges of the diamond pressing into his flesh. It hurt some, but it felt perversely good at the same time. To feel that little bit of discomfort. To feel.

"I fell in love," he said.

The doctor set down his pad. "Oh. I see." Then, after a pause, he added, "Well. We're going to need a lot more time, then, aren't we?"

———

Anton had just found himself a seat in the lunchroom with his sandwich when he looked up to see Uncle Gregor sit across the table from him. It was early, a minute or two before they were supposed to start serving lunch, and all the other tables were empty.

"Hey," Anton said. A light, comfortable personal greeting. He purposely looked away from his great-uncle's face as it lit up at the sound of his voice. And he wasn't even sure why.

"You're talking."

"I guess." He wanted to take a bite of his sandwich, but he had the ring still clutched in his hand, and he didn't care to let it go.

"I heard good things about your last session. Nothing that breaks patient confidentiality, mind you. I just heard it was productive, and that Dr. Spiegel was pleased."

"Is the note still there?" Anton asked, ignoring all that had just been said.

Gregor had promised to check the note on Anton's apartment door daily. So that if Edith had come back and seen it, Anton would know.

"It hasn't been touched. I'm sorry."

Anton dropped his eyes to his sandwich, sitting uneaten on his plate. He had suddenly lost his appetite for it.

Uncle Gregor had gotten a bowl of soup for himself, and he sipped at it from what looked like a teaspoon. For a time, neither spoke.

Then Anton said, "I think I want to stay on longer here."

Gregor set down his spoon. He looked into Anton's eyes, or tried to. Anton avoided his gaze. "I'm happy to hear you say that. You feel ready to talk about what happened?"

"No. Not really. I really don't feel ready at all. But it's not going away, so . . . I figure I'd better talk about it anyway. You know. Ready or not. It's just time." He set the ring down on his thigh and took a bite of sandwich. It tasted like nothing. "Before the day my parents get back, take the note down, please. I don't want them to know about the whole Edith thing. And if she's not back by then, I guess she's not coming back at all."

# Chapter Twelve

## The Win

Anton was asleep when his mother burst into his hospital room. She had apparently hit the door with her solid hip, or maybe both of her hands, as a way of forcing it open. That was the only thing Anton could imagine—the only thing that could account for all that noise.

Fortunately he had been placed in a private room.

It was not yet six o'clock in the morning.

She crossed the room to his bed, her feet stamping on the linoleum, and threw a bundle of his clothes at him. Literally. He had to pull a pair of boxer shorts off his face to speak.

He was still as much asleep as awake. She beat him to that speaking thing.

"Get dressed. We're taking you home."

He blinked at her a few times. She had not bothered to turn the lights on when she came storming in. It was before dawn. She appeared only half there, due to the lack of proper lighting. It occurred to Anton that she might only be a dream.

"You're back," he said.

"No, I'm still in South America. Of course I'm back. You're looking at me, so I'm back. Now get your clothes on so we can get out of here."

Anton made no move to get his clothes on. He looked past her to see his father standing inside the door of his room. His father shrugged, an exaggerated gesture in the dim light. Anton took it to mean something along the lines of "What can we do? Your mother has spoken."

Anton looked to his mother again. Her face was fierce in the near-darkness. But he felt detached from her anger. He did not feel ruled by it because he did not feel connected to it.

"I'm going to stay a little longer," he said.

To his surprise, she did not explode with rage. Instead she collapsed into a sitting position on the edge of his bed, like a tire quickly deflating. "What happened, Anton?"

"Well. Greg shot himself. And the shot destroyed my right hand and now I've lost it forever and lost him forever and after all that I didn't even manage to save him."

"But we *knew* that. That's all a given. What happened while we were *gone*?"

"It caught up with me."

"But you were fine."

"I wasn't fine."

"You said you were fine."

"I said I was okay. You asked me how I was and I said I was okay. I meant under the circumstances. I trusted you to know I meant I was doing pretty okay all things considered."

"How can I know that if you don't tell me?"

"Because you knew what I'd been through."

"We shouldn't have left you alone," she said.

Anton nearly said, "Duh." He opened his mouth to say it. But he left it unsaid. Because she knew she'd been wrong and she'd said so out loud. For his mother, that felt like a lot.

—

They were in the cafeteria together, having breakfast, when Uncle Gregor arrived. He got a cup of coffee for himself and sat down with Anton and his parents. They had been eating in silence before Uncle Gregor arrived. They continued to eat in silence.

Anton raised his eyes to his great-uncle and asked him a silent question. Had he taken the note down? Anton figured he must have, since his parents had not confronted him about it—had not demanded to know who this Edith was. But he needed to know for sure.

Gregor answered with a barely perceptible nod.

"Why is it so important to you to take him out of here?" Gregor asked, shattering the silence.

There were other patients at other tables, and even a couple of doctors and visitors, but no one was making much noise. There just was not a lot of chatting going on.

"It's embarrassing," Anton's mother said.

"Embarrassing how?" Gregor asked. "Why is it embarrassing?"

For a time, she didn't answer. She had a strip of crisp bacon in one hand, and she seemed to be staring at it. As if it were important to consider her food carefully.

Then she said, "You know. Having a son institutionalized. It's just embarrassing."

Anton felt himself come apart. He leapt to his feet, banging the table with his thighs as he did so. Coffee and orange juice lapped onto its surface.

"Greg is dead!" he shouted. Shouted. It felt strange. He couldn't remember the last time he had raised his voice to his mother. "Dead! He's never coming back. And you never had to see it. I had to see it! I have that picture in my head now, and for the rest of my life I'm maimed because of what happened. And you find it embarrassing that *I mind*?"

He allowed silence to fall, but not because he felt done. Because the next thing he would have said was on the other side of a line he was not about to cross. It would have been too cruel. Too much. He almost said, "Is that why you never got help for Greg? Because it would have been embarrassing? Did he die to spare you that embarrassment?"

He said nothing more.

Every eye in the cafeteria was turned to him. But he did not feel embarrassed.

His mother stood, wiping her mouth on a napkin as she did. "Come, Abel. We'll go home and unpack. Give him time to settle down. Then we'll come back and get him this afternoon."

"I'm not going home this afternoon," Anton said. Calm now.

"We're your parents and we say you are."

"He's legally an adult," a new voice said. Anton whipped his head around to see Dr. Spiegel standing behind him. "If he thinks he needs more time here," Dr. Spiegel continued, "that's his choice."

"But we're the ones paying for it!" his mother shouted.

"His insurance is paying for it," Uncle Gregor said, clearly careful to sound relaxed.

"And we pay for his insurance!"

"But it's covered now," Gregor said. "And will continue to be covered even if you take him off your insurance at the end of the month. He probably only needs another week or two. And if you do somehow manage to get him off your insurance plan before then, *I'll* pay for it."

They all stood in silence for a moment. Everyone but Uncle Gregor, who had remained seated. Then his mother stormed out. Anton's father raised his eyes to Anton's face, offered his signature shrug, then followed his wife out of the room.

Anton flopped into his chair again.

"Was that bad, what I said to her?" He was speaking to both his great-uncle and Dr. Spiegel. But he was staring down at his uneaten food, so he wasn't sure if they knew.

"I thought it was excellent," Uncle Gregor said. "I was proud of you."

"Good progress to express that out loud," Dr. Spiegel added. "And a truth I feel she needed to hear."

———

Anton sat in the window seat, staring out, with one shoulder facing Dr. Spiegel and his face turned away. He was holding the ring tightly in his hand. It wasn't a defensive pose. He'd just learned that it was easier to talk that way, with his eyes elsewhere, looking at something unrelated. It was easier to *feel* that way. And the doctor didn't mind.

The facility was well outside the city, so Anton had a view of rolling hills and a duck pond. Or, at least, he had been told it was a duck pond. Now it was frozen solid, and the ducks had all flown south for the winter. Still, he imagined them behind his eyes. Eating, flapping their wings. Quacking, mating. Anything but fighting. He never wanted to imagine anything fighting.

He thought he might have been there ten days. Maybe even closer to two weeks. But he hadn't been counting, and the days were hard to keep separate. There was nothing very distinct about them as individuals.

"We've talked about your parents a lot in these last couple of weeks," Dr. Spiegel said. "Not to suggest that we're done, or that there's nothing more of importance there, but right now I want to take this in a different direction. Ask a different sort of question. So here goes. Do you ever get mad at Greg?"

"How can I get mad at Greg?"

"How can you not? Your life would be so different if he hadn't done what he did."

"But he had a mental illness. He didn't *want* to have a mental illness. He didn't ask for it. There was just something running around in his head that he couldn't get under control."

"You could get mad at mental illness."

"Yeah. I could do that all right."

But somehow he could find no anger, even though he felt around inside himself.

Snow began to fly outside the window. The hills and the pond had been white; now the whole world was white. Even the sky. It felt like an endless winter to him. As though his life were frozen here. He could barely remember what it felt like to stand in the sun.

"You don't seem angry," the doctor said.

"I think I got tired of being angry. Now everything just seems incredibly sad. And I like that better."

"Why is sadness better?"

"Because . . . you don't have to do anything about it. You can just hold still, and it's not so tiring all the time. Nothing needs fixing. It just is, and it's sad."

He stared out the window for a few moments in silence. The snow swirled faster.

"Do you ever feel fear?" Dr. Spiegel asked.

"All the time."

"What are you afraid of?"

"Going home. I think I might be staying here now because I'm afraid of going home. Going back to my life."

"Well, here's some news for you, Anton, and hold on to your hat for this one . . ."

It hit Anton like a bolt of lightning to hear that expression again. It made him miss Edith so much it felt like a cramp of pain in his midsection. It took him back in time to that little lunch café. The way the food smells wafted from the kitchen. The way she looked sitting across the table. The sunlight through the window falling on her hair. The light in her eyes when she took him in.

Meanwhile the doctor had been talking. And Anton had no idea what he'd said.

"I'm sorry. What did you say after the 'hold on to my hat' thing?"

"I said you're normal."

"I am?"

"I believe you are, yes."

"Then why do I feel this way? And what am I doing here?"

"You're here because when normal people have traumatic experiences it leaves them traumatized. And because, when you're traumatized, and a place like this offers you safe harbor, it feels scary to think of going it alone again. This is all normal stuff, Anton. It's pretty much what anybody would feel given your circumstances. It's hard to set down a crutch."

"So it *is* a crutch!" he said. "Being here."

"Of course it's a crutch. You have a broken leg. Figuratively speaking. There's no shame in using a crutch when you have a broken leg. It's what crutches are for. You just have to be willing to set them down again after you heal. Which is a little trickier with a broken psyche than a broken bone. But in time you'll learn to function around it."

"Do you think I'm ready to go home?"

"I think you're ready when you tell me you are."

Anton stared out the window for another minute or two. But he wasn't thinking about whether he was ready. He wasn't thinking about anything.

The doctor spoke again. "You don't have to go cold turkey. You could be an outpatient."

"What would that look like?"

"You'd live at home but still see a therapist regularly."

"But I'd still be with my parents. That sounds hard. Although . . . I was thinking maybe I could start college more or less now. Pick up this second semester. Do you think the '66 semester has already started? I don't know what the date is."

"I guess it depends on the university," Dr. Spiegel said. "Where were you accepted?"

"More than one place. More than two, actually. I have options. All out of state. I did that on purpose."

"The trauma over your brother is something you might be able to trust an admissions board to understand. They might let you start late."

"Or I could just audit some classes and then get up and running for real in the fall. Assuming my parents are willing to pay for it."

"You've been thinking about this. That's good."

"Is it?"

"Absolutely. You've been envisioning your life beyond right now. You can start over fresh in a new place. Make new friends. Maybe even date a little."

"No," he said. And squeezed the ring more tightly. "I won't date."

"Dating, Anton. Just dating. Not falling in love or even necessarily getting serious about anybody. Going out to coffee with a girl, or taking her dancing. Just to see what it feels like to be social, the way a young man your age normally would. I hate to break out the big guns . . ."

Anton waited. But the big guns did not seem to emerge.

"I give up. What are the big guns?"

"You know it's what Edith wants you to do."

Anton sighed and squeezed his eyes shut. "Yeah," he said in a breathy whisper. "Those are the big guns all right."

This is what you got when you told people about your life, Anton realized. Then somebody knows. They know you. Still, in that moment, it didn't feel altogether unpleasant to be known. It felt a little bit like being found after having been lost for too long.

He opened his eyes and stared out at the falling snow again. It had become a full-on squall. He could see nothing but white. Swirling white.

Finally he said, "I'd do just about anything for her, but I'm not sure I can do that."

———

His father pulled the car up into the circular driveway at the front of the hospital, and Anton climbed in. The car was still warmed up from his father's drive out from the city, and the heater was on high blast. He struggled out of his coat as they drove away.

"You know what I feel like doing?" Anton asked. "When we get back to the city?"

"I wouldn't even venture a guess."

"Taking a walk."

"In this weather?"

"I just feel like I've been cooped up too long."

"A word to the wise," his father said. "You'll start by coming upstairs. Your mother has plans."

"What sort of plans?"

"You are not to tell her you heard this from me. But she has a welcome-home party planned. Small. Just the immediate family. She wanted to invite your friends, but they've all gone back to their various universities. But she got a banner, and she's baking your favorite cake, so start by coming upstairs. And by all means, act surprised."

"Huh," Anton said. He was watching fence posts rush by the window, their tops mounded up with freshly fallen snow.

"Meaning what?"

"I guess I thought Mom was still upset with me."

"Your mother is more or less perpetually upset, but I wouldn't take it personally." He fidgeted with his hands on the steering wheel for a few seconds. Then he added, "Your mother is what she is. People are exactly what they are."

Anton answered with something that sounded like a soft snort. No words.

"You doubt me that people are exactly what they are?"

"It sounds like you're saying nobody ever changes."

"I *am* saying nobody ever changes. That's exactly what I'm saying."

"*I've* changed."

"Then you are the odd duck, my friend."

They drove in silence for a time. Many miles. Anton was thinking about the ducks in the duck pond at the hospital, and how he never got to see them. Underneath that, it struck him as sad that he and his father had not seen each other, then barely seen each other, for many weeks, and they had already run out of conversation.

Driving through the Holland Tunnel, his father spoke again. Just out of nowhere. "Your mother and I are having trouble with what happened, too. You know that, right?"

"Yes and no," Anton said.

"What kind of an answer is that?"

"An honest one, I guess. I figured you must be. Because he was your son. But just looking at you and Mom, it's . . . hard to tell."

"We all go through things in our own way. Your mother and I have our way of going through things. You think your mother is being thoughtless and cruel but she's trying to cut herself off from what happened. She's trying to cope."

"I guess I thought all of the above," Anton said.

"Can you let us be different from you in how we handle things?"

"I guess I don't really have a choice," Anton said. "Seeing as nobody ever changes." Then, with the lights of the tunnel flashing by, shining through the windshield at him, so ugly compared to fence posts and frozen ponds, he added, "Except me."

—

When he stepped into the living room, he almost expected everyone to jump up and yell something in unison. "Surprise," maybe. Though of course they weren't hiding. Gregor and Mina were sitting together on the couch, heads leaned close in conversation. Grandma Marion sat in the wing chair, appearing lost in her own thoughts. Over their heads was a draped, professionally printed banner that read, **WELCOME HOME!**

In a way it was nice, but Anton couldn't help noting that they hadn't bothered to have it personalized with his name. Didn't welcome-home banners usually specify who was being welcomed home?

His mother got up and ran to him, throwing her arms around him. Anton found it surprising. He couldn't recall the last time either of his parents had embraced him.

"I'm sorry about what I was like at the hospital," she said directly into his ear. But it was not a whisper, so it felt as though it knifed its way through his eardrum. "I said some things I'm not proud of. The main thing is, you're home and you're okay." She unwrapped herself from around him and held him by the shoulders, at arm's length, as though he were an article of clothing she might consider buying. "I made your favorite dinner. Pot roast with mashed potatoes. And German chocolate cake for dessert. But it all needs another hour or so."

"It sounds good," he said, wishing he had his shoulders back but not taking them back. She was being kind, and he didn't want to discourage that. "Maybe I'll take a walk while it's cooking. I've been feeling cooped up."

"Nonsense! You can't take a walk now. Everybody is here and wanting to see you."

She let go of his shoulders and grabbed his hand, towing him deeper into the living room. His uncle Gregor rose from the couch to greet him. Anton looked into his great-uncle's face and, in the moment before he moved in to embrace the older man, felt tears spill over.

"Oh, what is this?" Anton's mother bellowed. "You're home. You're fine. What was the point of all that time in the hospital if you're not halfway sorted out when you get home?"

But, though Anton had no words for it, his tears had nothing to do with things not yet sorted out. They were happy tears, brought on by his gratitude for the presence of Uncle Gregor and Grandma Marion in his life. He had looked at them and felt their support for him, and it had brought up positive emotions. But it would not have been easy to explain that to anyone. It might have been impossible to explain it to his mother.

Uncle Gregor said everything that needed saying. "Vera. Leave the boy alone."

Anton sighed with relief and embraced his great-uncle and then his grandmother.

Uncle Gregor grabbed him by the hand and pulled him out onto the balcony, closing the sliding glass door behind them.

"Don't you need your coat?" Anton asked him.

Anton still had his coat on from the walk up from the parking garage.

"I'll go in and get it in a minute. Right now I have something I need to ask you. Have you considered going to college more or less now? This semester, rather than in the fall?"

"I have, actually. I even talked to Dr. Spiegel about it a couple of days ago."

"Good. Run, boy. Run for your life. This is not a good place for you. You shouldn't have to walk by Greg's room every day and you shouldn't have to be around those people who shoot down everything you try to feel on the way to healing. Where will you go? Have you decided among your acceptances?"

"I was thinking Stanford. Only . . . if I go all the way to California, will you help me find a good therapist out there? I don't want to just stop therapy cold. I want to keep getting better."

He watched his great uncle's face and knew he had said the right thing.

"I can and I will, my boy. It will be my honor."

"Now I'm going in to get your coat for you. Before you freeze."

Before he could even reach the balcony door, it slid open and his mother stood face to face with him.

"Here's a mystery," she bellowed, seeming not to know how much volume was needed. "Any idea where my good winter coat and scarf have gone? I left them hanging in the hall closet. You know something about this?"

"I . . . ," Anton began. "Yeah. I do. I sort of . . . gave them away."

"You gave my things away."

"Yes. I'm sorry. I'll replace them out of my allowance if you want me to. But it's just that I . . . met somebody who needed to keep warm."

He watched her forehead knit into furrows. Watched her try to decide whether to be angry or not. "You mean like a homeless person?"

"Yeah. Someone who had lost their home and hadn't managed to find a new one yet."

Silence reigned as she chewed that over. When she finally opened her mouth to speak, Anton expected her to bowl him over with her outrage. Instead she said, "Well, that was kind. You're a kind boy. You don't have to replace them. Your father makes good money. The factory is booming. Why do you think I married him? Why do you think I stay?"

Then she turned and disappeared back into the apartment again. Anton looked over his shoulder at his uncle Gregor, wanting a second opinion on what he had just heard.

Uncle Gregor mouthed the words "Run for your life, son" without any volume at all.

—

"I'll bring the cake out," Anton's mother said.

"Don't bring the cake out," his father shouted. "You fed us too well already. We're too stuffed with pot roast to even think about cake."

"I didn't make that cake from scratch for nothing, Abel."

"All I'm saying, Vera, is we need time. Let us digest for a minute, will you?"

Uncle Gregor injected himself suddenly into the conversation. "Why didn't you tell Anton that he was to have Christmas with us?"

All conversation stopped. His father stared at his mother, who stared back.

"Abel told him. Didn't you, Abel?"

"You never told me to tell him! You said *you* were going to tell him."

"I said no such thing. I was doing all the packing. That's the one thing I asked you to do. Everything else you left to me."

Anton felt himself rise from the table. It was a move he hadn't planned out in advance. "I'm taking that walk now," he said.

But both his great-uncle and his grandmother had joined the argument now, and everybody was shouting to be heard over everybody else, and Anton couldn't tell if anyone had heard him or not. He sighed, and walked into the entryway of the apartment, where he got his coat out of the hall closet.

"Where are you going, honey?" he heard his mother's voice ask.

He turned to see that she had followed him to the door.

"Just out," he said. But she looked devastated, so he added, "I just need a walk. I'll be back in time for cake."

———

He walked along the avenue, breathing the freezing-cold air into his lungs. He hadn't bothered with gloves, so he plunged his hand and wrist deep into his coat pockets.

He reached the corner and stopped. Looked down the block at the newsstand, and the little coffee shop where he and Edith had gotten to know each other. He wanted to walk down there and look in the windows, but he wasn't sure if his heart could take it.

Then he decided to live his life by a lesson he'd learned in his sessions at the hospital: His heart could take more than he'd once thought. And turning his heart directly toward pain was better somehow. It had seemed counterintuitive at first, but he'd come to realize that looking directly at a painful truth hurts less than being stalked by it. At least, in the long run.

Maybe he would even go in and have a cup of coffee.

He began to walk down the block. Before he could reach the door of the restaurant, Anton heard an alarming thunder of running footsteps. Before he could even turn to see who was there, he felt himself grabbed by the coat and roughly thrown against the brick facade of the building. He hit the back of his head hard on the bricks, and thought he felt a trickle of blood begin to flow. He had no time to investigate. Someone had him by the throat.

Anton looked into the eyes of Edith's estranged husband—the man who had been such an enormous peripheral character in his world, but whose name he didn't even know.

The man's voice was a threatening hiss, delivered directly into Anton's face, complete with bits of flying spittle.

"You have ten seconds to tell me where she is."

In that moment, Anton was seized with a surprising wave of calmness. He scanned the inside of himself, expecting to find something volatile. But all he could find was the calm.

He had won. He had beaten this man by getting Edith safely away. He was about to pay a price for it, but he couldn't bring himself to care. He had saved the woman he loved. What could be more important? What price could this man mete out that would be too high? That would outweigh this victory?

"You're running out of time," the man growled. He seemed to sense that Anton was not cowed. Which apparently made him feel the need to posture even more threateningly.

"I don't know where she is."

"Liar!" the man barked, and pressed more tightly on Anton's throat. "I saw you with her. I saw you talking to her. You told her to leave me, didn't you? You stuck your nose where it didn't belong. And now you're going to tell me where I can find her."

The man's breath billowed out in steamy clouds that swirled around Anton's face. Anton noticed, in that disconnected way you notice things in lightning-fast moments, that the man had a slight widow's peak on his furrowed forehead. Anton pointed to his own throat with his cold, ungloved left hand, to indicate what he would need if he were expected to speak. The hand disappeared from his throat.

"Yes. I talked to her. Yes. I told her to leave you. Yes. I did. I stuck my nose right where you didn't want me to. I even got her safely out of the city." Anton knew as he spoke that anyone listening would think he was insane to say these things. They would view it as poking an angry bear. But Edith had befriended Anton, and trusted him. And he needed this horrible man to know that. Whatever it cost, he would pay that bill when it came in. But it needed to be said, because Edith's ex needed to know that Anton had bested him. "But I don't know where she is. She wouldn't tell me. Because she was smart enough and knew you well enough to know this moment would happen. She wanted me to be able to look you in the face and tell you honestly that I don't know. And it's playing out just the way she thought it would."

For a moment, the man said nothing. Did nothing. Just blocked Anton's exit. The man seemed to be losing his will to threaten Anton. Or, at least, Anton could feel that will waver. He could feel a truth that Edith's ex likely did not want him to know: that if Anton really didn't have the information he needed, this man was deeply lost.

"You really don't know?"

"I really don't know."

For a moment, nothing. The whole planet just seemed to hang still. Nothing moved in the universe.

Then a fist slammed into the bone at the outside of Anton's left eye. Hard. He swayed, his head whiplashing on his neck. He felt himself land on his knees.

"It was none of your business!" the man shouted from above him. And he swung his fist again, just as hard, hitting the same bone. "You needed to stay out of it!"

Edith's ex raised his fist again. Anton winced and braced for the third blow. But then the whole man seemed to fly away. Fly backwards, out of Anton's view. That's how it looked from his vantage point. Anton's world flooded with light again. He heard the screeching of tires, and the squeal of brakes.

He saw two middle-aged men, and realized they had come to his rescue. One of them had apparently grabbed Edith's husband and hurled him away—hurled Anton's tormentor into the street, where he had very nearly been hit by a cab. In fact, he had one arm over his head on the tarmac, and for a moment Anton thought the cab had run over it.

*Wouldn't that be a weird bit of justice?* a disconnected voice at the back of Anton's head mused. *If he lost a hand, or lost the use of one.*

But Edith's husband sat up in the street, and he appeared unhurt.

Anton didn't think it out in words, but it struck him that it was rare to have an accident so serious that it resulted in the loss of a hand. He wondered again why he had been chosen for that lightning strike of unwanted fate. But again, it wasn't a thought so much. He just felt it all at once.

Meanwhile his middle-aged savior was standing in the street, screaming at Edith's ex-husband. "You can't do that to him!" he bellowed. "You go and pick on someone your own size! Or . . . you know what I mean. Pick a fair fight at least! Someone who can defend himself! How's that boy supposed to defend himself with only one hand?"

Anton felt someone grasp his elbow. The other middle-aged savior was helping him to his feet.

"Come on," the man said. "Let's get out of here while he's still down."

They ran toward the corner together.

"I don't want that guy to know where I live," Anton said as they ran.

"I can well imagine you don't. I wouldn't, either. Don't worry. My friend will keep him busy while I get you home."

———

Anton stepped into the living room, wishing there had been some kind of mirror in the entryway. Wishing there was some way to know just how bad he looked.

His eye hurt. And the area around his temple hurt. Acutely. Throbbingly. Also surprisingly, because it hadn't hurt before. Not that he could recall. When the fist had struck him, he could not recall feeling any pain. Either time. It must have been the adrenaline. And the adrenaline must have been wearing off.

The family was sitting in the living room drinking coffee and eating cake. They had started dessert without him. His special dessert, for his special welcome-home party, and his mother had felt free to serve it without him.

That seemed to sum up Anton's life in a disappointing nutshell.

When they looked up at his face, Anton felt he'd seen the mirror he'd been needing—in their eyes. He looked bad. He should have known. His left eye was swelling rapidly. It was already swollen nearly shut.

"Honey!" his mother shouted. She ran to him and grabbed his chin, angling his face for a better look. "What happened to you? Did you get mugged?"

"Yes," Anton said, feeling it was an honest enough description. "I got mugged."

"We'll call the police!" she said, and ran toward the kitchen.

"No. Stop. Don't call them. What can they do? I can't even give them a description."

Surprisingly, she stopped. "You call the police when you get mugged," she said simply.

"I can't tell them anything. Why even bother?"

"What did they take?" his father asked.

It struck Anton as an odd detail to care about.

"I had nothing," Anton said. "So they got nothing."

"I still think I should call the police," his mother said. "Are you sure you're okay? Do you need a doctor? What can we do for you, honey? We'll call the police."

"Oh, the police do nothing!" his father shouted, and Anton realized they were now fighting with each other again. As if Anton and his welfare had been lifted out of the picture entirely. "What do they ever do?"

Uncle Gregor stepped out of the kitchen, took Anton by the arm, and steered him out onto the balcony again. Anton couldn't help noticing all the dragging and throwing and pulling. Just in the last few hours, he seemed to have lost the ability to put his own body where he wanted it. Everybody else had other plans for it.

When Uncle Gregor had closed the sliding balcony door behind them, he handed Anton a dish towel full of ice, then sat in one of the outdoor chairs and began the process of trimming and lighting a cigar. He still wore no coat.

"Thank you," Anton said, and sat in the chair beside his great-uncle.

"Did you get mugged, Anton?"

"I did," he said, touching the ice pack gingerly to his eye.

"Just random like that?"

"Well. No. I got mugged by Edith's ex-husband."

"I see," he said, puffing out cigar smoke. "I suspected it might have been something like that. When you didn't want to bring the police into it."

They sat in silence for a minute or so. Anton could hear his parents' voices, muffled by the balcony door and the traffic noise below. They were still fighting, but he couldn't make out their words. A blessing, really.

"See, I'm worried now," Uncle Gregor said. "Because you were doing so well. And now suddenly there's this violent episode, and I worry it's going to be a setback."

"Actually," Anton said, "it's just the opposite."

"The opposite of a setback? How? How does this move you forward?"

"Because I won."

If Gregor failed to understand the logic, he seemed to trust Anton to clarify.

"I won because I did what was best for her, even though it wasn't what I wanted. I put her first and I got her away from him, and that makes me a better person than him, and he knows it. We both know it. I beat him. And I told him so, even though I knew he'd get violent over it, but I did it anyway and I'm not sorry. I told him that I won, and it was worth it."

"You're a better person than most people I know, Anton. Congratulations on that big win. Painful though it must have been."

They sat quietly for a minute more.

Then his uncle Gregor said, "Another very good reason to move to California."

"Yeah, I think I'll do that pretty soon," Anton said.

# WINTER OF 1980

## MY NAME IS ANTON

# Chapter Thirteen

## I'm Sorry. Have We Met?

Anton stood shirtless in front of the mirror, shaving. He had placed the ring on its leather cord around his neck, as he always did when he got up and got dressed in the morning, but he had not put on his shirt yet because it worked better to strap his prosthetic hand in place at the elbow first. Amy liked it best when he did not walk around the house with the ring in full view. But she was in the kitchen, hopefully too far away to notice and be offended.

He rinsed and toweled off his face, then stepped into the bedroom, where three neckties waited for him to make his selection. He had a special rack for them that allowed him to tie their Windsor knots before slipping them around his neck.

He glanced at the bedside table, but the prosthetic hand was not there. He opened the top drawer of the dresser, but did not find it. There were a limited number of places it could be. It was important to his life, and he did not leave it just anywhere.

He stuck his head through the open bedroom doorway and aimed his words in the general direction of the kitchen. "Honey? Did you move my hand?"

"I would never touch your hand," Amy called back.

"I can't find it. And I don't want to leave for DC without it."

"Have you looked under your dog?"

It was such a strange thing to say that he did not answer for a time. He had no idea what to say in response to a question like that. He saw her step into the kitchen doorway. Her eyes slipped down to the ring, and she frowned. Then she looked up at his face again.

"You didn't know she takes it sometimes?"

"No. And I can't figure out how that can be true without my knowing it."

"I only saw it happen once. I took it back from her. But it was also on a day you were leaving. If you would leave your suitcase open, maybe it wouldn't happen. She'd rather park her butt right in the middle of your suitcase. But once you close it, well . . . she's a very emotional dog, in case you hadn't noticed."

"She couldn't have been chewing on it. I would have seen the teeth marks."

"No, she didn't chew it. Just curled up with it underneath her. You'd think it would be too uncomfortable, but who am I to say? I'm not a dog. I guess it smells like you. Either that or she's smart enough to know you don't want to go to DC without it."

Anton couldn't tell if she was kidding or not. He didn't pursue finding out. He stepped shirtless into the living room to look for his dog. The collie was curled up on the living room rug, but not asleep. She raised her eyes to him, looking noticeably guilty.

"Hannah," he said, keeping his voice gentle. "Did you take my hand?"

The dog dropped her eyes and stared at the carpet in shame. Anton walked to her and sat cross-legged on the rug by her side. He stroked her ears until she relaxed some. Then he slid his hand underneath her, plowing through all that long collie coat.

"I'll be damned," he said when his fingers bumped the prosthetic.

He pulled it free and held it up in front of the dog. She averted her eyes in shame again. She touched the carpet with the tip of her elongated muzzle and looked at him from the corner of one big, sad brown eye.

"I'll be back in two days," he said to Hannah. "Amy will take care of you. I won't even be gone that long."

"You do know it's almost seven o'clock," Amy said from over his shoulder. "You don't want to miss your train."

—

Anton found a seat in the business-class section of the train, which was surprisingly uncrowded. He took off his grandfather's fedora and set it on the seat across from him, along with his briefcase. There were enough empty seats. It was not too selfish to request that no one sit right across.

He glanced around to see if he felt safe leaving the hat and the case alone while he went to get a cup of coffee. Satisfied that no one was paying attention to him or his belongings, he moved to the front of the car. He left his leather driving gloves on, because he was mildly self-conscious about the artificial look of the prosthetic hand.

He poured himself a Styrofoam cup of black coffee and carried it back. Then he realized he had forgotten to pick up a newspaper, so he placed the coffee in the cup holder by his seat and walked toward the front of the car again. But he stopped, and changed his mind about leaving the hat alone a second time. The briefcase he could almost bear losing. But the hat was irreplaceable. He walked back to it and snugged it onto his head.

The newspapers sat stacked on an oval table in the middle of the coffee area. Anton reached out with his left hand to take a *New York Times*. Just as he did, a woman on the other side of the table reached for the same paper, and his gloved left hand bumped her bare one.

They both pulled back as if burned.

"Excuse me," the woman said.

"Not at all. My—"

But he never reached the word "fault." By then it had caught up with him. It took a second to register, because he hadn't looked at her yet. But he had heard her voice. And his reaction to it had come from behind and tackled him before he could finish speaking.

He looked up and took her in, to see if what he was sensing was the truth.

She was wearing a stylish-looking hat at an angle on her auburn hair, and reading glasses on her long, distinctive nose. She looked back at him but seemed to have no reaction to what she saw. At least, none that he could see.

His body broke into a sea of gooseflesh, leaving him feeling as though he were being mildly electrocuted. His head throbbed suddenly, and he felt a wave of dizziness seize him. He could feel the little hairs standing up at the nape of his neck, and all along his arms.

"Edith?" he asked, his voice breathless.

While he waited, it raced through his mind—lightning fast, like his life flashing before his eyes—how many times in the past fifteen years he had thought, if only for a split second, that he had seen her. Each time, ultimately, it had not been Edith. When the woman had turned her head, or smiled, or spoken, it had shattered the image. This time, though it was only a second or two before she answered, the image was strangely slow to shatter.

"I'm sorry," she said, and she was unmistakably Edith. "Have we met?"

Everything inside Anton fell downward, as if rushing into his shoes. Not just his heart—everything. His stomach, his guts, his hope for the world. It all fell.

He looked away, down at the newspapers, as a way of hiding his devastation.

He opened his mouth to say something. Some deep objection. Something like "How could you forget? You swore you would never forget. That was the second-to-last thing you said to me and I remember it word for word. You said, 'I'll never forget you. You won't know where I am but you'll know that, wherever I am, I'll never forget you.' And then, when I asked you to promise, you said, 'How can you even ask that, Anton? How could I forget you? After everything you've done for me, how could I possibly forget?' So then . . . how could you possibly forget?"

But before he spoke, he glanced up at her again. She was staring intently at his fedora. Fascinated, as if reading breaking news on its crown or brim. Her mouth was slightly open, as if in shock. He heard her draw a sharp breath. She directed her gaze slightly down, and met his eyes. Then she looked in the direction of his right hand. His prosthetic hand. Her face fell.

He reached out his right arm. Reached it out in her direction. To show her. His leather driving gloves had elastic at the inside of the wrist. He grasped it with his left hand and peeled back part of the glove. At least, as far as it would peel back—enough for her to see the milky plastic where someone else would have living flesh, and to show part of one of the straps that ran up to his elbow to hold the prosthetic in place.

They both stared at the glimpse of his man-made hand together for what felt like a strangely long time. She reached out and touched the gloved prosthetic, which was hard and unyielding. It did not feel like a human hand at all.

Then she said, her voice a reverent whisper, "It's *you*. It really is *you*."

Their eyes came up again, and met.

Then she leapt into his arms. Literally. She jumped up, both of her feet fully off the ground, held herself up with her arms around his shoulders—and kissed him squarely and fully on the mouth. Her head knocked his fedora off. It fell to the floor of the train behind him, and her reading glasses landed somewhere nearby. He heard the soft taps of them. But in the moment he could not bring himself to care.

When she pulled away and dropped back onto her feet, Anton had to steady himself. And not because of the weight of her, or the sudden absence of it. His knees were less than stable and his brain felt foggy, as if he might be about to pass out. He braced himself against the newspaper table because it was the only thing around to steady him.

She reached around him, bent down, and picked up his hat and her glasses. She snugged the fedora back into place on his head. Then she reached a hand up and wiped off his lips with the soft pads of her fingers, as if she could clean away the kiss she had just given him. And as if it was important that she did clean it away.

"I shouldn't have done that. I'm so sorry. I probably shouldn't have done that. Right? You must be married by now. I stepped over a line. Forgive me?"

Her eyes flickered down to his left hand, but he still wore the gloves. He pulled off the glove by placing it snugly under his arm and extracting his hand. He held the hand out to show her. No ring.

She didn't comment on the lack of ring directly. She only said, "I can't believe I'm seeing you again. After all this time."

Anton said nothing in reply, because he seemed to have lost his words.

———

"I didn't recognize you," she said, her words tumbling out fast. Tumbling all over one another. "When you said my name, I couldn't see it at first. I couldn't see you in there. You've changed so much. You looked like a boy when I last saw you. A big, mostly grown boy, but still a boy. And now you must be . . . what? I was thirty-three then and now I'm forty-eight so you must be . . . Oh! That's so strange! You're thirty-three. Aren't you? You're the age I was at the time. And it felt so old to me back then, to be thirty-three. It doesn't seem so old to me now. But you just looked so different at first. You've changed so much."

"You haven't changed at all," he said.

She had changed a little. Not changed "at all" had been a mild exaggeration. She had traces of crow's-feet around her eyes, and a few expressive lines at the corners of her mouth. But it was nothing that changed her in any meaningful way, so he felt the statement carried at least the beating heart of the truth.

He could still feel the kiss on his lips. He'd been too shocked to process the sensations at the time. Now he felt a ghost sense of tingling, with a strange warmth. So he hadn't spoken much since they had sat down together. It had taken him a few minutes to find his words again. Fortunately she had plenty of words in the meantime.

"First of all," she said, "I don't believe you. Of course I've changed. I'm forty-eight; how could I not have changed? But what I mean to say is that people change more between eighteen and thirty-three than between thirty-three and forty-eight. It's a more developmental time."

"You don't look forty-eight," he said, and it was utterly true. If she were a stranger he had just met, he might have guessed her age as forty, or possibly even a year or two younger.

"You're too sweet," she said. "*That* hasn't changed a bit. But I guess what I'm trying to say is . . . I saw that terrible, terrible look in your eyes when I asked if we'd met, and I'm so sorry. Of course I didn't forget you. I thought about you so often. I just didn't recognize you at first."

His eyes darted to her left hand, because he had been struck by a horrible thought. But there was no ring on it.

"No," she said, watching him check. "I'm not. I haven't had men in my life for a really long time. I tried to. A year or so after I left, I tried to start over, but then I was seeing these hints that maybe the guy had a temper. And then I started getting this feeling like I was stuck in a pattern that I was never going to get out of, and besides . . ."

She paused. Cut her eyes away. She looked out the window for a few beats in silence. They were sitting directly across from each other, facing, so they could look straight ahead at each other or turn their heads and watch the scenery. Mostly they had looked at each other so far. In his peripheral vision, Anton could see power poles racing by outside.

"I probably shouldn't say it," she said at last, her voice barely above a whisper.

"No, you *should* say it. You should say whatever you're thinking. What?"

But, while he waited, it struck him that he might not like it. The subject was, after all, other men.

"He wasn't *you*," she said, still in a near-whisper. "I kept thinking I could find somebody who was as good and unselfish as you. The way you put aside what you wanted to make sure I'd be okay. I kept thinking I could find that in somebody else, but I never did. In fifteen years, I never did. That thing you said—how you wanted what was best for me, even if it didn't include you. Most people aren't like that, Anton. I don't think you know how special you are."

"I have a confession to make about that," he said. Because he wanted to be the totally honest person she saw him to be. "That actually wasn't original. It was something my grandmother said to me."

She raised her eyes and looked straight into his, and his gooseflesh rose again. And the hairs stood up along his arms. "That makes no difference at all, Anton. None. I don't need to believe that you *invented* unselfishness. You *did* it. You *practiced* it. That's more than enough."

—

"You need to tell me everything," she said.

It was a few minutes later, after a lull in the conversation. But not an awkward lull. Their words had not frozen or stalled. They seemed to have rediscovered the simple fact that they could be together in silence and be comfortable. At least, that was how it felt from Anton's side of the equation.

"Everything?" he asked, turning away from the window to look at her face.

"Yes. Everything. The whole fifteen years. And we shouldn't waste too much more time because it's not that long a train ride."

Anton turned his face to the window again. He might have been feeling something uncomfortable, but if so, it was very far away, and he was happy enough to leave it there.

After a minute or so, she spoke again.

"I'm sorry. Did I say something wrong? Is it bad, the fifteen years, and you don't want to talk about it? What just happened there?"

He shifted in his seat, deeply uneasy for the first time since he had seen her again. "I just didn't like what you said about the train ride."

"What about it?"

"That it's short."

"Well, I'm not really in charge of the geography here," she said, clearly trying to joke away the tension.

"You made it sound like if I don't tell you everything before we get to DC we'll be out of time. Are you going to disappear out of my life again as soon as the train ride is over?"

She brought one hand to her mouth, then moved it away to speak around it.

"Oh, no. I'm sorry. I didn't mean it that way at all. I just meant . . . I was just trying to be light. How long are you in DC? We'll get together for dinner if you have time. I'll write my address and phone number down. We'll stay in touch this time. I promise."

He looked out the window for another minute or two in silence.

"That didn't seem to fix anything," she said.

He could hear a slight strain in her voice. She seemed upset not to be able to fix whatever rift she had created.

"It's just . . . if it's that easy. You know."

"No, I don't know, Anton. I'm not following you at all."

"If it's that easy to come back into my life, why didn't you? After some time had gone by, and you knew your ex-husband had moved on without you. You knew where my parents lived. Why didn't you try to get in touch? Why didn't you find me again?"

He had been looking out the window as he spoke, watching the state of Maryland slide by. Watching the scenery urbanize as they grew closer to Baltimore.

He heard her sigh.

"Two reasons. And it seems like they contradict each other, but I swear they're both the truth. I figured you were married and had a couple of kids by then. And who was I to come along and upset your applecart? I figured I'd caused enough pain and heartache in your world for one lifetime. But then another part of me said you didn't even care anymore. That it wouldn't mean much to you if I did. You were eighteen, Anton. It was first love. Puppy love. People get over those things. They leave them behind as they get older. They think they won't, but then life goes on and they do."

Anton loosened his tie. Unbuttoned the collar button of his white dress shirt. Then he took hold of the leather cord around his neck and pulled upward until the ring popped out.

"Okay," she said, after staring at it for a few beats. "I guess I don't know nearly as much as I thought I did. I guess those were two epically bad guesses. But I swear I was just trying to spare you any more pain."

———

"So, here's what I'm thinking," she said, a bit hesitantly, as the train pulled out of Baltimore. "I still don't know if you don't really want to tell me about the fifteen years. About what's been happening since I last saw you. But there's one thing that just keeps coming back up for me. The last time I laid eyes on you, you were down on your side on the train platform, and you'd just taken what looked like a nasty fall."

"Yeah," Anton said. "I'm no Baryshnikov."

"Oh, who cares about that? I just worried you'd gotten hurt. I kept watching, even though you were getting farther and farther away. I kept waiting for you to get up. So I'd know you were okay. To this very day, I still don't know if it was one of those situations where time plays a trick on your brain, but it seemed like you were staying down longer than . . . seemed right. I thought maybe you'd hurt yourself. I almost got off the train to check on you, or . . . well, I guess it's more accurate to say I had this *urge* to get off the train, but how do you really do that once it's moving? And besides, I just knew that in a minute you were going to jump up, and maybe you'd have a banged-up knee or maybe you would have scraped the heels of your hands or whatever, but basically you'd be okay. I mean, you were a young, fit guy. A big, healthy guy. I knew you must be okay." Then, finally, the question. The one he'd heard in her voice as she spoke. "Right?"

Anton cleared his throat. Without meaning them to, his eyes angled away from her and toward the window again. "I had a hard time after you left."

For the moment, he didn't try to say more. He knew those words didn't answer her question. He really hadn't meant them to. It was a question with no easy answer.

"I'm so sorry."

"It wasn't your fault."

"Are you sure?"

"It was partly about your being gone, but . . . I couldn't really sort it out at the time, but I think losing you the way I did was something like a fuse. Like I was this big walking powder keg, and you were a fuse running into it, and when you left, it was like putting a match to that fuse."

A silence fell. He glanced briefly, half peripherally, at her face. She was looking out the window, too.

"Your brother," she said. "And your hand. I knew you were handling that too well."

"I was handling it the only way I knew how."

"Understood."

"I spent some time in a hospital after that." He waited, in case she wanted to reply. She did not reply. "So it was a very weird time. Very hard time. But it was good, in a way, because it forced me to get some help. I was an inpatient for a while, and then I kept going to counseling. I mean, for years I went to counseling. And I'm not sure where I'd be without that."

They rode without speaking for a mile or two. The scenery was becoming rural again.

"Ever run into my ex after I left?" she asked, seemingly out of nowhere.

Anton was relieved by the change in topic.

"One time," he said.

"Did he hurt you?"

"Only on the outside. And not nearly as much as I hurt him on the inside."

A pause. Then she said, "I'm not a hundred percent sure what that means. But I guess if you want to tell me more about it, you will on your own. I don't want to pry."

"Did *you* ever run into him again?"

"I sent him divorce papers from a friend's address in another state. He signed them and sent them back. No argument, but a few choice words. I don't know if you'd call that running into him or not."

# Chapter Fourteen

## *I Think I Went by It*

He raised the wine bottle in a silent question. She nodded, and he refilled her glass to about two-thirds full. She had set down her fork, leaving her chicken Kiev a little more than half-eaten. The restaurant was packed, and noisy, and the smelly haze from the smoking section was not clever enough or kind enough to stay where it belonged. He tried to narrow his focus onto her, and only her. Everything was good and right if he could squeeze his world down to her. He kept his gaze on her long, straight nose, because it was so distinct, and because he had missed it. Because it kept reminding him that she was really Edith. And because that way his gaze just barely missed her eyes, which under the circumstances might have been too intense for his poor, battered heart to bear.

"You never told me what you do for a living," she said, raising her voice slightly to be heard over the din.

"I'm an attorney."

"That's a coincidence," she said.

"Are you an attorney now?"

"Ha! No. I wish."

"Then why is it a coincidence?"

She never answered the question. Her mind seemed to have taken off in a different direction. "That I did not expect," she said, with enough volume to be heard over the din. "I would not have guessed that. I know a lot of attorneys and you don't seem like any of them. What's your practice?"

"Divorce." When she said nothing, he added, "I'm a divorce attorney."

"Did not see that coming. I'm trying to get that to fit."

He heard a lot in that second sentence. There was a weight and a truth to it. It struck him that she was poking around in him to see if he was entirely familiar. If she really knew him after all these years. At least, that was how it seemed.

"I'm not sure why that would be a weird fit. I help women. Sometimes men, but mostly women. I help women who've been abused in their marriages. I make sure they can afford to get away, and I make sure they don't get abused all over again when they get to court."

"Ah. Got it. You're right, that's spot-on. That's almost what the actors call 'too much on the nose.'"

"I don't know what that means."

"It's a little hard to define in words, but it means something like . . . almost a little too predictable and perfect to feel believable. Something that has a contrived feel to it, like it came out of the mind of a fiction writer who likes things neat and perfect."

"Oh," he said, not sure what to make of that assessment. "Well. It's what I do."

"I believe you." She almost shouted the words, just to be heard.

"You?" he asked, also raising his voice.

"Me what? Oh. What I do. Well. When I first got to Tucson I was working at a makeup counter in a department store."

"I didn't know you were in Tucson," he said. Loudly.

"Oh. That's right. I never said. Yeah, I had an old college friend in Tucson. And I was sleeping on her couch for almost a year. The job didn't pay well, so it was hard to get on my feet and get my own place. It was a terrible job, but I stuck with it for seven . . . no, closer to eight years. But I hated making so little money, so I went back to college at night, and I managed to work my way up to paralegal."

"Interesting," he said, understanding a little better about the law coincidence. "What brings you to DC?"

"Job interview. I wanted to stay in New York, but the pickings are slim right now. I was working for a one-attorney office in New York and the guy just went and got himself disbarred."

"Ouch. What did he do? Do you know?"

"Nice guy," she said. "Means well, but he drinks too much. Can't seem to stop. After a while even having a trial that day didn't slow down his drinking much."

"I'm sorry you ended up paying for his problems. I'm having trouble hearing you. I'm even having trouble hearing myself. Do you want to go someplace where we can actually talk?"

"That would help!"

He silently indicated to the waiter that he would like the check.

—

They walked together on a bridge over the Potomac River, in the dark. His shoulder was close to hers, and they both seemed aware of that, but neither moved closer or farther away. They passed two couples leaning on the concrete railing, staring down into the river, and possibly talking. It was hard for Anton to tell. His head filled with a sudden image of bursting out the back door of his apartment building with her, fifteen years earlier. The way they'd held hands as they ran for the street, and the safety of a taxi.

He wanted to reach out and hold her hand now, but he didn't. He couldn't. Yet.

"So how did your job interview go?" he asked.

"No idea. The interviewer was perfectly inscrutable. She went through the motions of liking what she saw, but I couldn't tell how genuine it was. She said they'd call me, but then they always say that, don't they? Might mean they'll call. Might mean 'Have a nice life.' I have no idea how many people applied for that position. I have no idea of anything."

They walked in silence for a few beats.

Then she asked, "Why did *you* come to town?"

They were wandering slowly in the direction of his hotel, and they both seemed to know it. It seemed to Anton that the closer they got, the slower they wandered.

"I have a hearing in the morning, and I had a deposition earlier this afternoon. They changed venues on me. We thought it would be in our jurisdiction, but opposing counsel managed to get it changed."

"I'm sorry for everything I did wrong," she said, sending the conversation careening in an entirely new direction.

"What did you do wrong?"

"I don't know exactly, but I look back and it feels like everything. That whole time is such a blur. It felt like my life was just running out of control at a thousand miles per hour. I just know that I hurt you, and that was the last thing I wanted to do. I really had no right to be in your life at all. You know. Things being what they were."

"Do you have a right to be in my life now?"

They ambled a bit farther before she answered. Three joggers passed them, but Anton saw them as a blur and nothing more. He could focus only on waiting for her reply.

"I suppose so," she said. "You're a grown man. You're thirty-three years old. If you're crazy enough to want to hitch your wagon to a woman who has fifteen years on you, I don't know who's going to say you can't."

That hung in the air as they walked, feeling brittle. Important, but also impenetrable. It was the first time either one of them had suggested out loud that a romantic relationship was still on the table for them. Anton felt the words as icy little needles tingling in his gut. He looked up suddenly, and was shocked to see that they were only two doors down from his hotel.

"You didn't wear your fedora," she said.

"I don't like to wear it to restaurants. I have to check it, and I hate to. It always feels like I might lose it, and it's so irreplaceable. Not that I think anyone would consider it worth stealing, but it could get lost, or . . . I don't know . . . checked out to the wrong person by accident. Oh, that's stupid, I know. None of those things would happen to it. I'm just protective of it, and I worry."

"It's very you," she said, "so I don't blame you one bit."

He didn't know what she meant was very him—the hat or the tendency to worry over more or less nothing—and he didn't ask. They stopped walking because they were in front of his hotel and there was no more walking to be done.

"I should have asked you where you're staying," he said. "Why are you walking me to my hotel? I should be walking you to yours."

"I'm not staying. I had to choose between a night in a hotel or business-class train fare. I guess I made the right choice, didn't I? Imagine if we'd been on the same train but in different cars. What a waste. But anyway, it means I have to go back tonight."

"Okay. We'll call a cab and I'll take you to the station."

"No. Don't do that. Too many bad memories. Just call me a cab and we'll say goodbye here. And you can call me as soon as you get back to New York. Unless . . ."

Anton thought he might know what the "unless" meant, but he wasn't sure enough, and he had no intention of guessing and possibly missing the mark.

"Unless you want me to stay," she added, when he didn't answer.

Anton's face grew immediately hot. Everything inside him—his heart and every inch of his gut—seemed to be trying to move in her direction. He hated what he needed to say next. Despised it. It felt like a straitjacket, and he felt a deep sense of claustrophobic panic, as if he desperately needed to struggle his way out of it. He had waited fifteen years for this moment. And in all those fifteen years, he never once believed it would arrive. And now here it was, and he had to turn it away. It was inconceivable. It made him a little dizzy just to contemplate it.

He tried a dozen avenues to work around the need to say no. But they all took him back to exactly where he stood. There was simply no way out.

Meanwhile the pause seemed to have telegraphed his answer.

"Never mind," she said. "I shouldn't have said that. I'm sorry. I always mess these things up, don't I?"

"No, it's not you. *I'm* sorry. There's something I should have told you. At least I should've told you over dinner, if not on the train."

"You're seeing somebody."

"Yes and no."

A doorman stepped out and offered to hold the door for them. Anton shook his head, and the uniformed man retreated into the building.

"Can't really be both." Her voice was low now, and sounded tightly controlled.

"Today I'm seeing someone. Tomorrow I won't be. But still I can't invite you up today. Because it's today. I haven't told her yet. So it would be cheating."

He waited almost breathlessly for her answer. That is, while waiting, he had trouble drawing full breaths. He couldn't see her face well in the dim street lighting. He tried to sense her energy but he couldn't get a clear read.

"You're still the same Anton," she said after a time. "That's good to know."

"Tomorrow night I'll go home. And I'll talk to her. And the night after that I'd like to be the night of our first date. If that's all right with you."

"You sure you want to break it off with her?"

"I've never been surer of anything in my life."

"If you're so sure you don't want to be with her, why are you? Why didn't you break it off before this?"

He thought a moment before answering, because he took her question seriously. He wanted what he said next to be honest and correct. "Remember that movie we watched together?"

"It's been a long time. Help me out here."

"The Marx Brothers."

"Oh! Of course."

"Remember that scene I thought was so funny? When Chico was playing the piano? And Groucho asked him where the end was to that piece and he said he thought he went by it already? Or words to that effect."

"I've only seen that movie about a dozen times," she said, her tone a little lighter now. "So I think I know the one you mean."

"I think it was like that. I let the right ending go by, and then I could never seem to get it to come around again so I could get out."

"What was the right ending?"

"She insists on calling me Anthony. She doesn't like the name Anton. She thinks it sounds too German and she thinks German is a harsh, unfriendly sounding language. I made the mistake of telling her I used to go by Anthony when I was young. It never occurred to me that she would hear it as a menu she could choose from. It doesn't sound like a big deal, but . . ."

"But you should be able to tell somebody your name, and they should take your word for it."

"Exactly. But that's not the important part. She wouldn't let me come to bed with the ring around my neck. She didn't understand about that. And she seemed to take for granted that I would propose. She told everybody we knew that we were engaged, even though I hadn't asked her. But then she made it clear that she wanted her own ring. And that was the ending, that last thing. The part about the ring. And I blew through it. And I'm kicking myself for it now."

"If you told her where you got the ring, you told her too much," Edith said.

"Fatally honest," he replied.

"Can you entirely blame her?"

"No. I don't blame her at all. It just wasn't . . . it was like a roadblock I knew we could never get around. And so after that we sort of . . . we had no real future, but every day that went by didn't absolutely need to be the day I said so. So it just kept . . . I'm not looking for someone who's perfect. It's not that. I'm not trying to hold her to an impossible standard. I just thought . . . I was hoping to find somebody who was more like . . ."

But then he didn't know how to finish the sentence.

"You," she said.

"I don't think that's where I was going with it, no."

"You're an unselfish man." She touched his cheek with one winter-cold hand. "You have a right to want as good for yourself." She leaned around him and caught the eye of the doorman, huddled just inside. He leaned his head out. "My friend is a guest here," she called to him. "But I need to get to the train station. Can you please call me a cab?"

"Yes, ma'am," he said, and disappeared inside the hotel.

"What if you hadn't seen me again?" she asked him.

"I don't know what you mean."

"I'm still talking about your girlfriend. Would you stay with her if you hadn't bumped into me on the train?"

Anton sighed, and the breath of the sigh puffed out in a frozen cloud, something he couldn't hide. Something anyone could see. Something Edith saw. It felt as though his confusion, his inability to deal with people and life situations, had stepped out into the light in a completely visible form. He felt embarrassingly revealed.

"Tonight, yeah. Tomorrow night, probably. After that, maybe. I don't know. I never know what to make of relationships. Part of me feels like they're not right, but then another part of me doesn't know how right it's reasonable to expect them to be. I don't know what that says about me. I don't know what that makes me."

"Human," she said. "It pretty much makes you human. And a grown-up. Congratulations. You grew up. You thought you'd understand relationships when you got older, didn't you? I think we all assume that. Well . . . surprise!"

She did a sort of jazz-hands double wave at the end of the sentence.

He smiled at her tone and her physical antics, and it felt good. It made him realize that he hadn't smiled—at least not genuinely and spontaneously—for a long time. Too long.

"I'll tell you this, though," he said. "Maybe I wouldn't have broken it off with her if I'd never seen you again. But that wouldn't have been right. It would've been me second-guessing myself and not knowing what to make of things. I hope that makes sense."

He stopped. Waited. But she seemed to have nothing to add. "I wish I hadn't had to say no to tonight," he said, feeling painfully desperate inside. The way he had used to feel every day through the first decade or so of therapy.

"Don't even go there," she said, holding a finger to his lips. "I'll look forward to our first date. Day after tomorrow."

He took hold of her hand and gently moved it away from his lips. But then he didn't let it go. He held it. He shouldn't have. But he did.

"You said you loved me," he said. "But I never really knew how you meant that."

"Neither did I."

On that note, a cab pulled up. Anton couldn't believe how fast it had arrived, and he cursed inwardly about it.

"But I'll look forward to finding out," she said. She pulled her hand gently away from his.

She jumped into the cab and slammed the door behind her. She offered him one wistful wave through the window, and he returned it. Then she was gone.

—

Anton showered for a ridiculous length of time, purposely keeping the water almost painfully hot, as if burning away everything he so wished could be different.

Then he dried off and went to bed, but not to sleep.

He lay in bed all night with his hand behind his head, staring at the ceiling. He never closed his eyes. Not even for a minute.

In the morning his muscles buzzed with electricity. His stomach was too rocky even to consider breakfast.

But he had a date with Edith the following evening, and the adrenaline of that knowledge would be more than enough to carry him through the day. And he knew it.

# Chapter Fifteen

## Here's the Thing

Amy turned her eyes up to his. She reached for his hand over the restaurant table, but he pulled his own hand back and hid it in his lap. He looked quickly into her eyes, then away.

What he saw there told him he had made a dreadful mistake. She seemed hopefully expectant about his reasons for taking her out for dinner and a talk. She was anticipating something wonderful. She probably thought he was about to propose.

"So what did you want to talk to me about?" she asked.

It made his heart feel as though it were falling. He glanced at her face again.

She still didn't know.

*This is part of the problem with Amy,* he thought, though he hadn't consciously acknowledged it until that moment. If Edith had reached for his hand and he had pulled it back and hidden it on his lap, she would have known something was amiss. She would have said something like "Uh-oh. What's the bad news?" But Amy wasn't sensitive to his clues. She didn't read him. Now that he stopped to reflect on it, she didn't even seem to try.

Then he felt guilty for criticizing her in his mind at a time like this.

He rested his forehead on his palm in a way that shielded his eyes from her. "I've really messed this up. I haven't even said anything yet and I've already made a mess of things."

He expected her to catch the mood in that moment. She did not.

"Did you forget to bring something?" she asked, her voice light and teasing.

His gut grew heavier, and more than a little unsettled—as though something big and dense and indigestible had sunk down into it.

"You think I brought you here to propose to you." He hadn't really meant to say it out loud, but there it was. Sitting heavily on the table. Impossible to take back.

"Oh. Well, it crossed my mind. Yeah. But go ahead. What did you want to say?"

For a moment, he didn't answer. Couldn't answer. All he could think was that he had stayed with her so as not to hurt her feelings. And now he was hurting her so much more deeply. In that heavy pause, she finally began to catch the mood of the moment.

"Here's the thing," he said. "Amy . . . here's the thing."

From under his hand, his view restricted to the area nearest the table, he noticed she was holding her fork like a weapon. Not literally threatening him with it, but holding it tightly and faced away from her. The exact opposite of how one would hold a fork to eat her dinner.

He opened his mouth to speak, but she cut him off.

"If you say 'Here's the thing' one more time . . ."

He closed his mouth again. Because that had been exactly what he'd been about to say.

"Oh, come on, Anthony. It can't be that bad. Right? Whatever it is, you can just tell me. But hurry up, okay? Because now I'm getting a little freaked out. I mean, it's not like you brought me here to break up with me. Right?"

Anton moved his hand away from his eyes. He opened his mouth to speak, but it didn't work. It didn't happen. They both just sat there, watching him not speak.

Finally, when the silence became unbearable, he braved a glance at her face.

"Is there someone else?" she asked. Her tone was flat. Flatter than he had ever heard it. It was alarming, really.

He didn't answer the question because there was no easy answer.

"Oh my God, there is, isn't there? You've been cheating on me?"

"No!" he said, suddenly and loudly. Couples at other tables glanced around to see if there was trouble. Anton lowered his voice. "Of course not. I would never do that."

"Well, what, then? I thought we were doing great. I thought we were going to get married. Oh my God, you brought me here to tell me out in public so I wouldn't make a scene."

"No. I wasn't thinking that at all. I just . . . I wanted it to be nice."

"Well, isn't that lovely," she said, her voice sarcastic and hard. "Isn't that nice of you to want me to look back on the night you dumped me and think what a nice occasion it was."

Anton said nothing. What did one say in response to a statement like that?

"Tell me why," she said.

"Okay."

But for a long and painful moment, nothing more would come out of his mouth.

"Tick tock, Anthony."

"Okay. Here's the thing. Oops. Sorry. I'm not supposed to say that. Yesterday . . . when I got on the train . . . I ran into somebody. Somebody I haven't seen in a very long time."

He stopped. Waited. He was careful not to look at her face. Finally he glanced at her peripherally. She had the upper part of her face in her hands—hiding her eyes, the way *he* sometimes did.

"If it's not Edith please tell me right now. Because that's where my mind just went."

He did not tell her it was not Edith. He could not tell her that. He waited again. It might have been a minute or two, though it felt longer. In time she dropped her hands.

"How much time do I have to get my things out?" she asked.

It surprised Anton, to say the least.

"I don't know. As much time as you need, I guess."

They picked at their food a long time without talking.

———

"I expected you to fight with me," he said as they walked home.

Actually, "walked home" was not a fair description. Amy was hurrying ahead, trying to stay a good five paces ahead. He was trotting lightly along behind her, purposely not catching up. Because she didn't seem to want him to. And possibly because he didn't deserve to.

When she didn't answer, he added, "You're not fighting with me."

She stopped so suddenly that he almost ran into her back. "I can't fight Edith." Her voice was . . . well, he had no idea how to characterize it. It was something he had never heard before. "How can I fight Edith? She's a royal flush. And I'm like . . . two pair."

They stood under the streetlight a moment, breathing steam. Careful not to look at each other.

"I'm so sorry," he said. "I didn't mean to treat you like two pair."

"It's not a matter of how you *treat* me, Anthony. If you're holding a poker hand you don't *treat* it like a royal flush. It just is or it isn't. I'm going home. Could you please not follow? Sleep at the office or something. Just one night. I'll have everything out tomorrow."

"What about the dog? Promise you won't go away and leave her all alone all night?"

"No. Of course I don't promise that. I'm not responsible for your neurotic dog anymore."

"Then I'm coming home to get her. And then we'll get out of your hair for a while."

"Where are you going to go with that damned dog, Anthony? A hotel won't take her."

"Then I guess we'll have to stay with my parents. And my name is Anton." He almost added, "At least have the respect to call me by my name." But he had hurt her enough.

She walked away without further comment.

He watched her grow smaller in the distance, thinking that, around and underneath all the ickier, heavier feelings, it felt good to be Anton again. In every aspect of his life.

———

When his mother opened the apartment door, it was clear he had wakened her out of a sound sleep. Her hair was up in curlers and then wrapped in some kind of kerchief. She wore an old blue terry-cloth bathrobe over her flowered nightgown. She held the door handle with one hand and scratched the small of her back with the other. She looked at him and then down at his dog. Then she yawned broadly. Almost theatrically.

"We were sleeping!" she fairly bellowed.

Anton glanced at his wristwatch. "It's 8:37," he said.

"And your point would be?"

"Never mind. I'm sorry to wake you. May I stay here tonight?"

She craned her neck and looked behind him, and down the carpeted hallway, as if expecting an invading army. "All three of you?"

"No. Just me and Hannah."

"Where's Amy?"

"We broke up."

She opened her mouth to comment on that announcement. Probably to blast him. But before she could, his father's voice bellowed out from the master bedroom.

"Who is that, Vera?"

"It's Anton!" she shouted back. Loudly enough to hurt his eardrums and make him wince. "And his dog!"

"What's he doing here at this hour?"

"If you'll shut up for a minute, I'll try to find that out."

A brief moment of blessed silence fell. She turned her disapproving gaze on Anton again.

"It's *your* apartment," she said.

"I know."

"Apparently you don't. She walks all over you. She always has."

"She just wanted one night. You know. With a little privacy. And then tomorrow she'll get her things out and I can go home."

Anton's mother narrowed her eyes at him. She leaned in and peered at him more closely, as if having trouble with her vision. "Who broke up with who?"

"I broke up with her."

"Then she has a right to ask that much."

They stood in silence for a moment. His mother yawned again. Anton was aware that he and his dog were still out in the hallway. It seemed odd, but he didn't want to push.

"What is *wrong* with you?" his mother asked.

"I'm not sure how to answer that."

"I thought you were going to marry that girl."

"I never said I was going to marry her. *She* said I was going to marry her."

"Perfectly nice girl. What if you don't find anybody better?"

"I've already found somebody better."

"And you've known this new girl for how long?"

"Since I was eighteen."

For a strangely elongated moment, no one spoke.

Anton had never told either of his parents about Edith, and he had asked his extended relatives not to mention her. He guessed his mother must be thinking he was referring to someone from Stanford. He didn't mind leaving the assumption right where it was. He also chose not to correct her assessment that his new love interest was a "girl."

Still he was out in the hallway with his dog.

He opened his mouth to ask if he could come in. And if maybe they could talk about it in the morning. He never got there.

"Well, I just hope you know what you're doing," she said.

She turned and marched back to the master bedroom, leaving Anton alone in the open doorway. Leaving him to let himself in.

"You never liked Amy anyway," he called to her retreating back.

"Maybe I'll like this next one even less." She didn't turn around to say it. Just threw the words back over her shoulder.

Anton looked down at his dog, who looked back up at him.

"That's a pretty good possibility right there," he said in Hannah's general direction.

The dog wagged uneasily, because it disturbed her when he spoke to her in words she could not understand.

Anton let himself in and locked the door. He unclipped the leash from Hannah's collar, then walked down the hallway toward his room. The closer he got to Greg's old room, the more an alarming knot of dread twisted into his belly. Hannah walked with him, so close to his side that she continually brushed his knee. Before they could quite pull level with Greg's room, she stopped. He looked down at his dog and she looked up at him.

"What?" he said.

But she only cocked her head.

"Yeah, I agree with you. Let's start in the kitchen."

Hannah flopped onto the kitchen linoleum with a deep sigh while Anton searched the crocks on the counter for his grandmother's chamomile flowers. She was still alive at a hair over eighty-five, and still came over to his parents' apartment regularly to make tea and chat.

He found it easily, then drew water in the teakettle and set it to heat on the stove.

He took out his wallet and found the scrap of paper that Edith had given him on the train. In a careful hand, she had written her address and phone number.

He took the phone receiver from its cradle on the kitchen wall and called her.

"Hello?" her voice said on the line, and it completely negated the ball of anxiety in his gut. Just melted it, or turned it into steam that rose into the air and was gone.

"Hey," he said. "It's me."

"Hello, you," she said, in a voice that made his neck hot under his collar.

For a moment he was almost too overwhelmed to continue. But he forced out more words. "Is it too late to call?"

She laughed, and the sound brought an unexpected smile to his face.

"It's not even nine o'clock."

"Right. That's what I tried to tell my parents, but they weren't buying it."

"Are you okay? Is everything . . . okay?"

"Yeah. I'm okay. A little shaken up, but okay. I just wanted to confirm our date tomorrow night."

"Wow," she said. Then she did not elaborate.

"Wow what?"

"You really did it?"

"Of course I really did it. You didn't think I would?"

"Most people would get home and they wouldn't. Then again, you're not most people, Anton. You never were."

He leaned on the kitchen windowsill, not knowing what came next in the conversation. And, in many ways, not caring. Any direction with Edith would do. He looked out over the avenue. The kitchen window faced in the same direction as Anton's old bedroom. In other words, it offered a view of the apartment where Edith had once lived, and the third window from the left, the window she had run past only to be dragged back across it by her hair. His whole body tingled with hard needles of physical emotion, remembering.

"How did she take it?" Edith asked.

Her voice was . . . everything. It was saving him. It was bringing him down to the ground, into the world, and he didn't even mind being there. He could listen to that voice all night.

"Not terribly well. But . . . actually . . . better than I thought she would. But I hurt her. And now I feel really bad. I made a mess of things with her."

"Are you there with her right now? Is it super awkward?"

"No. I went to my parents' for the night, with my dog. Just for the one night. She swears she'll have everything out by the time I get home tomorrow. I would've gone to a hotel, but it's hard with the dog. I try to come to my parents' as seldom as possible, but I didn't want to leave her alone."

"Aw. You have a dog. That's nice. I always wanted a dog, but I hated to think of one alone all day while I worked a full-time job."

In the silence that followed, it struck Anton that he now had a dog and a full-time job, and no one to look after Hannah while he worked. He pushed the thought away again. He could only do just so much in that moment.

"So, I was walking down the hall," Anton said. "The hall in my parents' apartment. Which, like I said . . . I don't come here very often, and when I do, I try not to go down there. You know, my old room, and Greg's old room and all, where . . ." But he couldn't bring himself to finish that sentence. "And my dog, Hannah . . . she got to Greg's room and just stopped. And she wouldn't walk past it. I don't know if there's literally some kind of bad energy there after all this time or if she was picking it up from me. But now I'm hearing myself talk and I don't know why I'm telling you all this."

On the avenue below, he saw a man step out of Edith's old building, turning his collar up against the winter cold. But of course it was not him. It was not anyone Anton knew.

"Because we tell each other things," Edith said into his ear. "We always did."

He tried to answer but there was too much emotion in the base of his throat, blocking the way.

"How did *you* feel about going by Greg's old room?"

"Not good," he said, his voice a little croaky from the blockage.

"Probably that. Dogs are sensitive to their owners."

"After all those years of therapy . . ."

"After all those years of therapy, things are better. They'll never be perfect. It'll never be like it didn't happen."

"But I have to go past there. I can't sleep in the kitchen tonight. I guess I could sleep on the couch."

"Is there a phone in your old room?"

"They put in an extension for me when I was in the hospital. No idea if they bothered to have it taken out."

"Set the phone down. Without hanging up. And walk in there. To your old bedroom. And pick up the phone if it's there. I'm right on the other end waiting for you."

"Okay," he said. "Here goes."

He set the phone on the cutting-board island, and turned off the fire under the teakettle. Then he walked briskly toward the bedrooms. Hannah jumped to her feet and trotted along behind him.

He closed his eyes briefly passing the door of Greg's old room. But he didn't hesitate. And neither did Hannah. When he opened his eyes again, she was right there beside him.

He cracked open the door to his old room and was flooded with memories. Though he had lived eighteen years in that room, the memories were almost entirely from those days when Edith was staying here with him.

The extension phone was still there, and he quickly grabbed up the receiver.

"I made it," he said, and sat on the bed with a sigh.

"I never once doubted you," Edith said.

A long silence. He looked out the window at the building across the street. The same window where his telescope used to sit. It was almost more of the past than he could bear to carry.

"Are you sure you want to hitch your wagon," he said, borrowing her expression, "to such an emotional basket case?"

"You're not an emotional basket case. You're just emotional. And anyone who tells you that's a bad thing should be avoided at all costs."

She didn't say specifically that she was sure she wanted to hitch her wagon to him, but that was okay. He hadn't expected her to. It was too soon.

"He punched me hard in the eye," Anton said. "Twice."

"Wait. Who did?"

"You said if I wanted to tell you more about that, I would. You didn't want to pry."

"Oh. That. Right."

"It didn't even hurt at the time. I guess because of the adrenaline. But he wanted to know where you were, and I told him I didn't know. He hit me because I infuriated him by telling him the truth—which I knew would infuriate him—that you trusted me and relied on me and I helped you get away."

"So that's why you said you hurt him worse than he hurt you. But on the inside."

"Right."

"I'm so sorry he hurt you."

"Don't be. It was one of the best things that ever happened to me. Getting hurt on the outside is nothing. It heals. It takes care of itself, no matter what. Just all on its own and really dependably like that. It's those inside hurts you have to watch out for." Then, after a pause, he added, "Thanks for getting me down that hall."

"You're in your old bedroom now?"

"Yes."

"I love that I can close my eyes and picture it perfectly. Right where you are. I stayed there, after all."

For a long time they said nothing. Just breathed into the line.

"Where do you want to go tomorrow?" he asked after a time.

"You choose. Just somewhere we can talk. Or be together and not talk."

Anton held the phone in the crook of his neck and looked down at the scrap of paper in his hand. He hadn't bothered to turn on a lamp, but he could see it dimly in the glow of light from the window—from the streetlights and the lights of apartments in the building across the avenue. He had crumpled it with the pressure of his hand without meaning to. He regretted having crushed it. It was Edith's address and phone number, in her own handwriting. He was more inclined to frame it or bronze it than mistreat it in any way.

"Pick you up at eight?" he asked her. "Or is seven better?"

"Seven is definitely better. Because it comes sooner than eight."

They breathed into the line for a minute more.

Then Anton said, "I hate to say good night."

"But go ahead and say it," she said. "And trust that we'll have more chances."

"Good night, Edith," he said. With a confidence and ease that could only have proceeded from her last sentence.

"Good night, Anton."

He hung up the phone and sat on the edge of his old bed for a long time, his body and gut buzzing. His brain buzzing. He thought about getting up to hang up the kitchen phone. He could have. He could have walked past Greg's room now—even twice—because of everything he had gotten from talking to her. But it didn't feel important. He couldn't imagine what would be lost if he left it off the hook until morning.

He stripped down to his underwear and climbed under the covers. Hannah jumped up onto the bed and he held the covers up again and allowed her to slither under with him. Amy hadn't allowed it. But the dog seemed to know that Amy was not here to criticize them, or enforce any rules.

Anton thought he would never sleep. But sometime around three in the morning he drifted off, and dreamed that he and Edith were on the phone together, breathing into the line. Saying nothing. Because there was nothing they needed to say.

# *Chapter Sixteen*

*Jumping into Fear*

"So . . . ," Anton said. "Do you have any regrets?"

Edith laughed. It was a bitter sound, and it surprised him.

They were sitting in a restaurant in Anton's neighborhood. It was a quiet little place, which was why he'd chosen it. They served upscale Italian cuisine, with classic white linen tablecloths and single candles in silver holders. When he'd come here in the past, it had been quiet. There were always people eating there, but they were never loud or boisterous, and the acoustics of the room were good. So conversations tended to remain at their table of origin.

"Is that a joke?" Edith asked him.

She had fixed herself up for their date. She was wearing a formfitting red dress, and she had put her hair up in a swirling style. And she had put on full makeup for him. Anton realized he had never seen her fixed up before. He had only seen her natural self, which was eye-popping enough. He had not been prepared for what she would look like if she was trying.

"No. Not at all. Why would it be a joke?"

"Because I'm *all* regrets, all the time. I'm a big walking, talking bundle of regrets. I thought I'd made that ever so clear."

"I don't mean just in reference to our situation."

"Neither do I. I regret everything."

"Can't be everything."

"We can call it close enough. But I think I regret how I handled the situation with you more than anything."

"What would you do differently if you could?"

"Now that's a very good question. I'd have to think about that."

While she thought, he refilled her wineglass. He didn't say anything, because she might still have wanted it to be her turn to speak.

"I guess maybe nothing. All these years I thought if I had it to do over, I would have left the city somehow without ever bringing you into it. I don't know how. But I still thought I should have. Because I know I hurt you. But if we hadn't gotten to know each other *then*, well . . . we wouldn't be here *now*. So now I'm not sure. Now I'm wondering if it was for the best."

"What if everything was for the best?" Anton asked. "What if it turns out everything always is?"

It had been a question that had been playing on his mind a lot recently. Some sort of life theory just dying to claw its way through.

She never answered. The question seemed to have caught her off guard.

"If everything is right because it ends up right in the long run," Anton said, "would you still have regrets?"

"I wanted children," she said. There was no hesitation. No moment for thought. That regret had been right under the surface, waiting to burst through. "Two, to be exact. A boy and a girl. I know that sounds trite."

"Well," he said, "maybe you still could?"

She blushed, and turned her face away. "Anton. I'm forty-eight."

"You could adopt children."

"Oh, no, it's not that easy. Believe me, I tried. They don't like to place children with single parents. They want nice, safe, stable married couples with good incomes."

Their food arrived—Anton's spaghetti and her eggplant Parmesan. They ate in silence for a minute. Anton did not feel as though he was thinking. At the same time, a process was undeniably taking place inside him—it just wasn't happening in his thinking mind. He set down his fork suddenly. So suddenly, in fact, that she looked up, seeming startled. He loosened his tie and unbuttoned the collar of his dress shirt. His left hand grasped the leather cord around his neck, and he pulled it free. Pulled it over his head so that the ring dangled between them, a foot or so over his plate. He pushed his chair back, and her eyes flew wide.

"Oh, wait," she said. "You are *not . . .*"

He fell to one knee in front of her chair.

He wanted to take the ring off its leather cord, but with only one hand that would have been awkward. He would have had to enlist the help of his teeth, which seemed boorish and unromantic. So he just held it up in front of her with its leather cord still hanging down.

She held her face angled partly away from him, her cheeks flushed red. Two couples at nearby tables seemed to be watching with approval, but Anton only noticed peripherally.

"You're insane!" she said, a little too loudly.

But her voice was so full of affection and good humor that he could only hear it as a blessing. It stoked a small, dense, glowing fire in his chest, like an old woodstove heating up to warm the whole house.

"We really haven't known each other that long," she whispered.

"Fine. Then don't marry me *today*. Or tomorrow. Just take the ring and say you will. We can be engaged for a year. We can be engaged for three years. Five years. Whatever you want. However long it takes for you to believe we know each other well enough. But the sooner we set a date the sooner we can go adopt that boy and girl you've been wanting."

"You don't want kids of your own?"

"I want kids with you. I want to raise them with you. I don't care where they started out."

She leaned in closer. As if protecting her next sentence from the ears at neighboring tables. "This is crazy. This is our *first date*."

"It is and it isn't."

She met his eyes, and for a surprising length of time she did not look away. She had stopped pushing against his idea. Stopped trying to send it back from where it had come. He could see that. She was considering it.

He moved the ring closer to her. "Just take it and say you will. We have time to work out the details later."

For what felt like several minutes she said nothing, and did nothing. She seemed to have frozen there, like some magnificent ice sculpture. He saw and heard her swallow once. He wasn't even sure he had seen her blink.

Then she wrapped her hand around the ring, and around his hand. "You're insane. But I guess I must be insane, too. Because my answer is yes. I will."

He slid the ring onto her finger, its thin cord still dangling, and the other diners applauded.

—

They walked beside the East River together in the dark. Anton had one arm around her shoulder as if to protect her from the cold.

"They applauded us," she said.

"People always do that when someone gets engaged in public."

"I didn't think they would for us, though."

"Why wouldn't they?"

"You know."

"Do I?"

"I think you do if you stop to think about it."

"The age thing?"

"Of course the age thing. What else? I figured they'd look at us and think, 'Ick. Why is he proposing to his mother?'"

"Stop it. You're not old enough to be my mother."

"I marginally am."

"Well, you don't look your age. You look barely forty. And I probably look like I'm in my midthirties. It's 1980. People aren't going to make a big deal about it."

"I guess not." They walked in silence for a few moments. Then she added, "I'm relieved."

He stopped and turned to her, and she stopped, too. Faced him. To hear what he had on his mind, from the look of it.

"I'm going to ask you something," he said. "It's honest. Honest like . . . letting you see more of who I really am. Not always putting my best foot forward. It'll help us get to know each other better."

"Okay . . ." But her voice sounded tentative. As if she feared what he was about to reveal.

"I have a dog."

"So you told me."

"Oh, that's right. I did, didn't I?"

"And I told you I love dogs, and that I'd have one myself if I didn't have to work all day."

"Right. Good point. That's kind of the issue here. I have this dog, and she's very attached to me and very . . . emotional. Some might say neurotic, but I'm trying to give her the benefit of the doubt. The person who used to be with her while I was away is out of the picture now . . ."

"Oh, I see," she said, and Anton knew she got what he was driving at. All the tension had dropped away from her voice. "You feel guilty because she's home alone. You want to get back to her? We can end the date now if you need to."

"No!" he said. Nearly shouted, really. "No, that's not where I was going with that at all. I don't want to end this date now. I don't want to end it ever."

"You want to go back to your apartment and talk there? So she's not lonely?"

"Exactly. Is that silly? Does that make me absolutely pathetic?"

"It makes you Anton. Which is pretty much the polar opposite of silly or pathetic."

———

"I don't want you to take this personally," he said as he unlocked his front door. "She really mostly likes *me*. Not so much anybody else. She's kind of a one-person dog. She never really took to my ex-girlfriend, even though we all lived together for two years."

Anton threw the apartment door wide.

Hannah ran to the door to greet him, her tail swinging so wildly that the whole back half of the dog seemed to be wagging. She jumped up on his good suit, which she knew she was not supposed to do. But she seemed unable to keep her relief in check.

He held her front paws in his left hand and leaned down so she could kiss his face. Then Hannah jumped down and turned her attention to Edith. Edith dropped to her knees to greet the dog face to face.

"Aw. She's beautiful. She looks just like Lassie."

Hannah sniffed Edith's face carefully, as if tallying up information to form a conclusion. Then the dog jumped up and draped one paw over each of Edith's shoulders. She gave Edith one wet kiss on the cheek, then buried her long face in the crook of Edith's neck, hiding her eyes.

Edith looked up at Anton. "Now what were you saying?"

"I'll be damned."

It struck him that all those times he'd said his dog didn't like anyone else, he might simply have been overlooking or avoiding the fact that she didn't like Amy.

Or maybe Edith was just special, and his dog knew it.

———

"Is it okay for her to be up here with us?" Edith asked, her mouth close to his ear.

They were sitting on the couch together. He had one arm around her. She had her cheek against his shoulder. Hannah lay on the couch on the other side of Edith, her head on Edith's thigh. They had been sitting that way for a long time without speaking.

"Amy didn't like her to be up on the couch. I never cared. She seems to have caught on that the rules have changed. She knows Amy is gone."

Anton wondered if it had been a mistake to mention his recent ex by name.

"You can tell she just recently left," Edith said after a time.

Anton followed her eyes around the room. Books had been pulled out of bookcases in wild patterns. Nobody had bothered to move the bookends, so the remaining books—Anton's books—had fallen all over each other in erratic piles. A lamp had been taken, its shade inexplicably lying on a table alone.

"I'm scared," Edith said suddenly.

"Of what?"

"Tonight," she said, her voice scratchy with the stress of the thing.

"Well, tonight doesn't have to be anything we don't both want it to be. We can talk. We can watch movies. We can go out again. Whatever you want."

"I don't know. I don't know what I want."

Then they didn't talk again for a time.

"You didn't seem . . . ," he began. But he had trouble finishing the thought.

"What? I didn't seem what?"

"When we were in Washington . . . you didn't seem . . . you just threw out the idea of staying like it was nothing."

"I know!" she said, her voice full of something like awe. "How did I do that? I can't remember how I did that. I guess I hadn't really had much time to think about it. And now it's all I've been thinking about.

How you've been waiting fifteen years. Wanting that all this time. And how you sent your girlfriend packing like it was nothing. For me! Do you know how scary that is? You've probably imagined this a thousand times. What if I can't live up to that? Don't you see how huge that is?"

For a time he just waited. To see if she planned to say more.

"Actually," he said, "I didn't have those kinds of fantasies."

She picked up her head and stared at the side of his face. He closed his eyes to avoid being too deeply seen, too suddenly.

"Are you kidding me, Anton?"

"Strangely not. I'm not saying my mind didn't try to go there. But I put a lid on it. I didn't let thoughts like that play out very far."

"How does that even work? I have no idea."

"Hard to say. I just know putting a lid on things was my specialty back then."

"But why? Don't tell me you're such a gentleman that you wouldn't even *think* something without my consent?"

"You think you're kidding, but that's part of it. But mostly . . . I think it would have hurt me too much. To think how much I wanted someone I knew I'd never see again. Never have at all."

She waited in silence for a moment, then set her head back on his shoulder. She nuzzled her forehead more deeply into the crook of his neck.

After a time she said, "You do realize that only makes it scarier. Right?"

"Yeah. Sorry about that. Looking back, I do see it."

———

Anton woke suddenly from a dream. Not a good one. A dream in which Amy had been following him around the living room, furiously hurling books at his back.

He opened his eyes.

He was on his back on the couch, but he had no memory of ever falling asleep. There were no lights on, but he had no memory of turning off any lamps. The only light in the room was a glow from the clock on the kitchen stove, and a glint of a distant streetlight through the window. Edith was straddling him, hovering above him. She was not touching him with any part of her body, but she was leaning lightly on his torso, one hand on each side of his rib cage.

He looked up into her face, but it was too dark. His eyes had not had time to adjust to the lack of light. But there was something immensely Edith-like about her. He didn't need to see her to know. She radiated Edith.

It made his belly buzz with warmth and the beginnings of excitement.

"You awake?" she whispered.

"I am now."

"We're engaged to be married." Her voice was reverent and low.

"We are," he whispered back.

She leaned down and kissed him. The weight of her hands on his rib cage grew as she leaned in, but it was not an unpleasant sensation. In fact, it felt strangely welcome. It felt like being anchored to the earth after too much floating around for too many years.

The kiss was long and soft, more personal than any kiss she had offered him before—than anyone had offered him before. She pulled away and looked down at his face, her hair falling all around hers. His eyes had begun to adjust to the light. He could see she was smiling.

"Did you stop being scared?" he asked her.

She shook her head. "Nope."

"Decided to jump in anyway?"

"Yup."

Then they didn't talk again, after that.

# Chapter Seventeen

## The Canary Eater

When Anton woke in the morning, Hannah was under the covers with him. He could feel her long collie coat draped over one of his bare legs. He opened his eyes, but there was no one else in the bed with them. Edith was nowhere to be seen.

It hit Anton like a baseball bat to the gut. She had left quietly. Vacated his life again. As familiar as he was with losing her, he wondered why he hadn't seen that coming. Then he realized he had her address and phone number. So she couldn't be completely and utterly gone. He could find her again. Talk her into coming back. He would because he had to.

But he smelled coffee. A moment later he heard noises in the kitchen. Plates and glasses being taken down from the cupboard. He breathed deeply, grateful that he still had Edith. Then, as a wry afterthought, he felt grateful that he still had plates and glasses. He really had no idea yet what Amy had taken.

He rose and slipped into a pair of sweatpants.

Edith was in the kitchen, dressed only in the shirt he'd worn on their date the night before, staring into his refrigerator. He stepped up behind her and put his arms around her, and she leaned back into his chest and sighed.

"You scared me," he said. "I thought you were gone."

"That's in the past."

"Good."

She handed him an empty mug. "There's coffee."

"So I smell." He let go of her, took the cup, set it on the counter, and began to pour. "Sorry about Hannah. You know. Getting under the covers with us. Not everyone is into that with a dog, I realize."

"I thought it was sweet."

She was preparing some kind of egg dish, from the look of it. Scrambled eggs, or omelets. She had a glass bowl and a whisk out, and was counting out how many eggs to break.

"It didn't bother you?"

"Not at all. She likes to cuddle. Who could be bothered by that?"

Anton barked a short, sarcastic laugh without meaning to.

"Oh. Don't tell me, let me guess. Your recent girlfriend didn't want dogs in the bed."

"Or even *on* the bed."

"Don't take this the wrong way . . . and I could be mistaken, because you've only told me a little bit about her . . . but . . . she doesn't sound like the nicest person, this ex of yours. What was her name again?"

"Amy."

"Right. Amy."

Anton sighed. He sat at the kitchen table with his coffee and took a sip. It was perfect. It was that perfect cup of coffee that he hadn't had in as long as he could remember. But he had always known it was out there. Waiting for him.

"She wasn't the worst person. But not the nicest, I guess. She was high maintenance, I'll say that. She had a lot of rules. But there are good things I could say about her."

"But *you're* the nicest person," Edith said. "So why not ask for more?"

He looked down at the end of his right wrist. He hadn't bothered to strap on the prosthetic. The amputation scar was so completely healed that it looked as though no hand had ever existed there, and Anton could almost believe that. He remembered the hand, but the memories felt hazy and almost artificial, as if he had only dreamed such a thing.

"Not as easy as you make it sound," he said. He watched her break eggs into the bowl in silence. Then he added, "I remember you telling me that some girls I'd meet would be shallow. And they would mind about the hand. And then I'd know when I found the right one, because she wouldn't be shallow. But . . . you know what? More people are shallow than I realized at the time. It's hard. Back when we first talked about it, I didn't realize how hard it was going to be. Going out on first dates, and watching a girl catch on that the right hand is fake. And then waiting to see if there'll ever be a second date. It throws people. I'm not even saying it's only with terrible, shallow people. People just don't know how to react. They don't want to focus on it too much, but they're not sure how to focus *off* it. It gets awkward. And on a first date, when you really don't know the person at all . . . just how uncomfortable are most people willing to be?"

She looked up at him, the whisk in her right hand. "Okay. We'll give Amy a couple of points for not being shallow."

"Right. But on the other hand . . . I always got this nagging sense that she wanted credit for the fact that she was overlooking it. But I feel bad saying these things about her. I feel bad about the whole Amy thing. The way I ended it. So I'm going to stop talking now."

He watched her brow knit down, but she said nothing.

His dog came wagging into the kitchen. He got up to get Hannah her breakfast.

"Poor girl," he said to the dog. "I feel bad for you. You'll have to be alone all day today."

"That's not how you do it," Edith said.

"What's not how I do what?"

"That's not how you keep a dog calm. They'll think something is terrible if *you* think it is. If you telegraph to them that it's terrible. So if you're going to leave them, you never want to say, 'Oh, this will be terrible.' You want to say something more like 'You'll be just fine and I'll be home before you know it.'"

"But she'll still be unhappy when I'm gone. Because I'm gone."

"But you don't want to make it worse."

He opened a can of dog food in silence and spooned it into Hannah's clean bowl. Set it on the kitchen linoleum for her.

"How do you know so much about dogs?" he asked Edith.

"My parents used to raise Irish wolfhounds."

He sat at the table and sipped his coffee again. Watched her pour beaten eggs into a hot skillet. Watched Hannah eagerly scarfing her food. He felt happy for the first time in as long as he could remember.

"I don't want to lose you again," he said.

He hadn't meant to say it out loud. But it was too big to keep inside, unsaid.

"I'm not going anywhere," she said. "I'll stay with Hannah today if you want."

"Don't you have someplace you need to be?"

"I'm out of a job, Anton. And I have no more interviews lined up, I'm sorry to say. I have to be somewhere today. Why not here?"

"That would be . . . amazing."

"I'd actually like it, too. I'll go to the market and get a few nice things for dinner. And when you get home, I'll have cooked. I'll light candles on the table. It'll all be very . . . domestic. How does that sound?"

He rose and walked to where she stood at the stove, and took her into his arms. She held him in return, still holding a spatula in one hand.

"I think it sounds like my cue to suddenly catch on that I died without knowing it. Like in the movies. Like I wake up thinking it's just a regular day, but then something tips me off that this is the other side of the Rainbow Bridge and I'm in Heaven."

She held still in his arms and said nothing in reply.

"I'm burning the eggs," she said after a time.

It was probably the only thing she could have said that would have inspired him to let her go.

———

"What the hell is wrong with *you*?" his secretary, Marlene, said.

It was a bit bold, even for her. She tended to be brassy and a little sarcastic, and Anton had never really minded. But something had turned up the volume on her rhetoric.

"I have no idea what you mean."

He took off his fedora and hung it on the coatrack outside his office door. He could see her watching him, her eyebrows arched upward.

"You got high before work," she said.

"I did not get high before work."

"What, then?"

He didn't answer. He tried to duck into his office but she stopped him.

"Wait."

"What, Marlene?"

"Come here."

Against his better judgment, he walked closer to her desk.

"Go like this," she said.

She made a broad gesture of showing her teeth, as if asking him to be sure she didn't have spinach stuck in them before a big date.

"And why would I do that?"

"I want to see if you have any canary feathers stuck in your teeth, you old sly cat, you."

Anton sighed, but he was not entirely displeased by the exchange. "Can't a guy be happy?"

"Can't his secretary be nosy and pry?"

"I'll be in my office," he said.

———

He stepped into the boardroom at 9:30 sharp for the regular partners meeting. Took a seat at the long table. Then he looked up to see everyone staring at him.

"What?" he asked.

At first no one said a word.

Then one of the senior partners, John Edwards, said, "I think we're just not used to seeing that look on your face."

"What look is that?"

For a moment, no one answered.

Then Laura Tapper said, "Did Amy bring home one of those women's magazines with tips on how to please your man?"

Anton felt his face flush humiliatingly red. "Now you're embarrassing me."

John didn't seem pleased with her remark. He pasted a scowling look on his face. "Back to a little decorum," he said.

"I just wanted to share in the happy news," Laura said.

"Maybe he and Amy won the lottery," Jack Watson added.

"I didn't win the lottery. And Amy and I broke up."

For an odd length of time, nobody said a word. Anton was aware of dust motes floating in striated shafts of light through the half-closed window blinds. He could feel all eyes on him.

"Well, I must say you're taking it well," John said.

More silence.

"Okay," Laura said suddenly. Decisively. "When he's ready to tell us, he'll tell us. Let's get this meeting started so we can get it finished."

—

On his way back into his office, his secretary addressed him again.

He found himself inwardly leaning away, wishing she wouldn't.

"Hey. Mr. Addison-Rice."

He stopped, but did not go closer. Whatever it was, he wanted her to say it from that distance. She had other ideas. She beckoned him closer with one crooked finger. Anton sighed. He decided the fastest way out of the situation was probably to keep moving through it.

He walked to her desk and leaned forward slightly, looking right into her face. "What? Go ahead and get it out of your system."

"I know I teased you before. I'm good at teasing. It's kind of where I live. But it's actually nice to see you happy." She didn't literally say "For a change." Then again, she didn't need to. They both knew it was a change. "You're a nice guy. You deserve to be happy."

He leaned back, nursing a stunned feeling. It had been the last thing he expected to hear. It was a side of her he had not seen in all the years they had worked together.

"Thank you, Marlene."

She offered a little salute, but no words.

As he disappeared into his office, he expected her to fling some parting rejoinder at his back. Just to get the last word in. But she let him go in silence. She let her kind words be the sum total of what he took away from that encounter.

—

Edith greeted him at the door in a different dress from the one she'd worn on their date the previous evening. She had tied an apron on over it. She kissed him briefly on the lips.

Hannah wagged up to him. But something was different. She seemed gratified to see him, but not beside herself. Not desperate in her joy. She did not jump up on him.

"I hope you don't mind. I took Hannah on a walk to my apartment to get a few things."

"Of course I don't mind. Why would I mind?"

He patted his dog on the head and scratched behind her ears.

"Well, I didn't specifically ask you if I should be taking her places."

"It's fine."

"Are you hungry? You can sit right down at the table. It's ready anytime. I made Hungarian goulash."

"I *am* hungry," he said, and followed her into the kitchen.

She had the table covered with a powder-blue cloth, set with his good china and silver. Two taper candles sat in the middle, along with a small arrangement of flowers that she must have purchased while out that day.

She lit the two candles with a paper match and swept off the apron.

She dished up Anton's dinner from two separate pots on the stove.

"Are you Hungarian?" he asked, because it struck him that there could still be a great deal they didn't know about each other.

"I'm not. I just like their goulash."

She dished up her own dinner and set the pots back on the stove. Then she turned off the kitchen light, leaving only the candles to illuminate the table. She sat across from him and they both shook out their napkins and set them in their laps.

They met each other's eyes and stuck there, smiling in a way that felt vulnerable and a little bit silly.

"How was work?" she asked, when they finally broke eye contact.

"Kind of weird."

"In what way?"

"I guess I must've had a different sort of look on my face all day, because people wouldn't stop staring at me and making comments."

"Different as in . . . happy?"

"Must have been. Because I sure was happy. *Am. Am* happy. But I was talking about today at work—that's the only reason for the past tense." He took a bite of the goulash. It was surprisingly good. "This is wonderful."

"Glad you like it. They're not used to seeing you happy?"

"I guess not."

"Were you ever happy in all the time we didn't see each other?"

He chewed and thought for a moment, to be sure he was giving her a well-considered, honest answer. "I don't think so."

"When were you last happy? I mean, before these past few days."

"When you were spending the holidays with me at my parents' apartment. But even then . . . I always knew you were leaving, so they were just flashes of moments when I managed to put that out of my head."

He took another bite. He had been too excited and wired to eat much that day, and the food was helping to settle him. It was turning his elation into a quiet satisfaction that felt hugely welcome. Like the difference between Hannah greeting him at the door that day, and the way she always had in the past.

"I was happy today, too," she said. "I walked the dog and bought flowers and food and cooked for you and waited for you to come home. Like I said, all very domestic. And I didn't think about my own problems. I didn't think about what I would do for a job, or the rent coming due. I just gave myself a day off from all those worries. Like a vacation. I was just at your house, and there was nothing to worry about at your house. So I didn't worry. Now I'm kind of dreading the vacation being over."

He wiped his mouth with his napkin and set it beside his plate. "Don't go," he said.

"Sooner or later I have to find a job."

"Why?"

"So I can pay the rent."

"Why?"

"Because landlords really, really hate it when you don't."

"I guess I'm not expressing myself very well. Why don't you go back to your apartment and get your things and bring them here and put them in all the empty spaces left from Amy's stuff? And not pay rent. And not get a job unless you decide you want to."

He was looking down at the tablecloth as he spoke, but he braved a quick look into her face. Her eyes were averted as well.

"You're asking me to live with you? Starting right now?"

"Why not?"

"Maybe because . . . three mornings ago we didn't even see any of this coming?"

"So it's a surprise. So what? It's a *great* surprise. And it's not like three mornings ago I didn't know I wanted to live with you. I just didn't know I was about to get the chance."

She picked up her fork again and took a few bites in silence. Then she cleared her throat. "It *would* take a lot of pressure off me. It's wild to think of every day . . . you know . . . being as happy as I was today. Still—"

"Don't go to 'still.' Don't even go there. You're just going back up into your head to see what caution signs it has there for you. Ask your gut. Just go into your gut and see what it wants to do. And if it says yes, then say yes to me."

A beat or two of silence.

"Yes," she said. Then they both fell silent again. "You're insane," she added after a time. "But I'm so glad you are, Anton. It's one of the best things about you, and there are a lot. What the hell? How many chances like this do you get in one life? We'll give it a go."

# Chapter Eighteen

*Flush*

A knock on his apartment door brought Anton out of sleep. He opened his eyes and looked through the open bedroom doorway and down the hall. As if that would help. As if his apartment door were wide open and he could see who was knocking. Then he realized he was looking over Edith's bare shoulder, and for a moment everything else dropped away.

He wasn't accustomed to it yet, and he thought maybe he never would be. Never could be. He hoped he would never take it for granted. Every time he woke, he thought for a moment he was in his normal, dull world—that reuniting with Edith had been a thrilling dream. Then he'd realize it had happened. Was continuing to happen. It was his life. And it was astonishing.

He completely forgot someone was at the door until the second knock jarred him out of his elation.

He sighed. He slid out of bed, careful not to wake her, and pulled on a pair of sweatpants. He quietly closed the bedroom door behind him and walked shirtless down the hall, scratching his head and grumbling to himself.

"Who is it?" he called through the door.

"It's your mother."

Anton sighed again, and leaned his forehead on the door. Then he undid the locks and opened it. She looked surprisingly put together considering it was . . . well, he didn't know what time it was. He hadn't bothered to check. He glanced sideways into the kitchen to see the clock on the stove. It was barely six thirty.

"It's six thirty in the morning," he said.

"And your point would be?"

"People are asleep at six thirty in the morning."

"I'm not."

"That's because you're asleep at eight thirty at night."

"You're actually going to make your own mother stand out in the hall just because it's early? You're not even going to invite me in and offer me a cup of coffee?"

"There's no coffee made. How can there be coffee made when I was sleeping?"

"There can be coffee made starting now, Einstein."

The Einstein comment was over the line. It caused him to raise his voice to her. It was one thing to wake him at this hour, quite another to insult him for being less than fully sharp.

"Seriously, Mom, what are you doing here?"

"You don't have to raise your voice at me," she said, shifting her considerable weight from one foot to the other. For a moment Anton thought she was preparing to retreat. Then he realized he was unlikely to get that lucky. "You must've known I'd have more questions sooner or later. You haven't called in days."

"I go weeks without calling."

"Let's review," she said. She banged into him and used her shoulder to push him out of the way. "You come to our apartment. You have no place to sleep. You say you broke up with Amy and there's already somebody new. But you don't say who. I was waiting for some more news or an introduction or something. Anything. But I've been waiting for days and nothing."

She walked into his kitchen, looking up and around as though inspecting the cleanliness of his ceiling. Anton sighed and followed her in. He began making a pot of coffee.

He looked up to see her staring at an area around the upper part of his chest.

"Wait a minute," she said.

"What?"

"Where's that . . . ?"

"Where's what?" he asked. But he knew.

"This," she said. She indicated the spot on her own collarbone where the ring would normally have rested on his.

"You're not making yourself clear," he said as he dropped a filter full of ground coffee into the basket.

"That ring. That ring that you had around your neck since you were a teenager. The one I asked you about a hundred times and never got a straight answer."

"I would think by now you would have gotten the hint."

A toilet flushed at the back of the apartment.

They both looked in the direction of the bathroom, then at each other.

"I see," his mother said.

"I'll be right back."

He turned on the coffee machine and walked down the hall, letting himself into the bedroom without opening the door any more than necessary. Edith was just coming out of the bathroom, wearing his blue terry-cloth robe.

"I'm sorry," she said in a whisper. "I'm so sorry, Anton. I had to go, but I was going to flush later. I was just going to put the lid down quietly and not flush. I don't know what happened. Force of habit."

"It's actually a desirable habit in a mate. That flushing thing."

He watched her face soften. Watched her return to the Edith he knew. "Oh good, you're not mad."

"Of course I'm not mad. You're not a secret."

"But that's your mother, right?"

"Unfortunately, yes."

"And you probably aren't ready for me to meet your mother."

"I think what we have on our hands is a ready-or-not moment. So go ahead and get dressed and then come on out and have coffee. You live here. I won't have you hiding like there's something wrong with that."

"But she might not approve."

"I guarantee you she won't approve. She never approves. Of anything. And I never let that stop me. And I'm not about to start now."

—

Edith came out to the kitchen a few minutes later, walking slowly, as if on the way to her own execution. She was fully dressed in a khaki skirt and white blouse, a far nicer outfit than he expected her to wear around the house. Anton saw her before his mother did. He caught her eye and smiled in a way he hoped looked reassuring. She smiled back, but it only looked tight and afraid. For a moment he felt guilty for having asked her to come out. Seconds later it was replaced by a flash of anger at his mother for forcing them into this situation so soon.

Something derailed in Anton regarding his mother. He was thirty-three years old, and would guide his own life. In the past he had simply moved farther away from her when she tried to lay her hands on his world, but now he was prepared to push back hard. In fact, he would push her entirely out of his life if needed, to keep Edith safe.

He would do anything to keep Edith safe.

His mother looked up and noticed Edith in the room. For a bizarre—and frankly rude—length of time, she only stared at Edith, who seemed to grow increasingly uneasy under her microscope. "Well, hello," his mother said at last.

Her voice carried a note of derision, almost sarcasm, that Anton knew well. He could only hope that Edith would be less familiar, and less able to interpret it.

"Hi," Edith said quietly.

"Mom, this is Edith. Edith, this is my mother. Vera." He waited, but no one said a word. "There's coffee."

Something caught his mother's eye. She turned her gaze from Edith's face. Downward. It took Anton a moment to realize she was staring at the engagement ring on Edith's left hand. Anton watched as she looked up at the spot on his collarbone where the ring had used to live, then back down to Edith's hand.

Anton had no idea if Edith was noticing. Her gaze was purposely averted.

Anton's mother tried to catch his eye, but he did not allow it. He watched Edith pour herself a mug of coffee. They both did. The silence in the kitchen felt positively toxic.

"So," Vera said. "Tell me how you met my son all those years ago."

"No," Anton said.

It was loud and it was firm. It took his voice down into a low register, the way you speak to your dog or child when you want him to know you mean business.

His mother turned to stare at him. "Excuse me? I wasn't even talking to you. I believe I was talking to your friend."

"And that's what I'm saying no to. First of all, she's not my friend. Well, she is a friend, but more importantly she's my fiancée, and the love of my life, and you don't get to grill her. If you have questions about the relationship, you ask *me*."

As he spoke, he watched Edith's face. He was worried that the conversational turn would upset her. Instead her face seemed to be relaxing.

"Well!" Vera said, with her signature huffiness. "I believe I know when I'm not wanted."

She headed for the door, leaving her half-drunk mug of coffee on the table, marked by an orangey lipstick smudge. Anton followed her down the hall. When they reached the door she turned back to him, then leaned in as if about to share a secret.

"How old is that person?" she asked in a scratchy whisper.

Anton leaned in return and imitated her whisper. "She is exactly none-of-your-concern years old," he said.

He had thrown off the last of his restraints. There was officially nothing he would not say to his mother now—no depths of honesty he would not plumb. It felt wonderful. Freeing. He wondered why he hadn't done it years ago.

"I see," Vera said, no longer whispering. "So you tell me quite rudely in front of your friend . . . your fiancée, I guess I mean . . . that I should ask *you* if I want to know something, but now I ask you and you don't want to say."

"You want to know how we met?" Anton asked, feeling the delicious comfort of not caring what she thought anymore. It felt like the clean air after a storm. "Fine. I'll tell you. When I was eighteen and you and Dad went off and ditched me for the holidays, she was one of our neighbors. She was just getting out of a bad marriage, and I helped her, and we became friends. There was nothing between us at the time except friendship, but I loved her. I've always loved her and I always will love her, and nothing is going to get in the way of that, and nobody is going to speak ill of it. Anybody who has issues with any part of my life just won't have a space in my life anymore, because nothing is more important to me than Edith, and nothing ever was, not since the day I met her. So you'll just need to decide which is more important—having a relationship with your only living son, or expressing your disapproval."

He fell silent, half watching her face. She was staring down at the Persian carpet runner in his hallway, betraying nothing.

"I see," she said after a time. "The walls are really down now. Suddenly everything you've ever wanted to say to your mother feels appropriate to you. Anything more you'd like to get off your chest at my expense?"

"She was staying in our apartment while you were in South America."

"You'd better not say you put her in your father's and my bed. Because you know that's one thing I won't stand for."

*One thing?* Anton thought. *There are quite a number of things you won't stand for.* He didn't share the thought out loud. The idea was to be truthful, not to bait or insult her.

"I put her in my bed and I slept on the couch."

"Right. Got it. Anything else you've been dying to say to me? Go on, Anton. Get it all off your chest."

"One thing," he said, and leaned in a little closer. "Why didn't you get him some help?"

"Who? Why didn't I get who some help?"

"Your only other son. Why didn't you help him?"

He watched her face absorb the blow. When her voice came out, it sounded like a dry, dead hiss. Like the skeleton of a voice, with all the flesh and muscle removed. "He didn't need help! He was fine!"

"If he was fine he'd still be here."

She teetered in the doorway for a second or two. Then she said, "I just came close to slapping you for the first time in my life. But I'm not going to do that. I'm just going to go. When you decide to return to civility, let me know."

She walked out, crossing the hallway and ringing for the elevator.

Anton turned back to see Edith standing at the end of the hall, watching. He had no idea how much she had heard, but it filled him with a deep fear. What if he had gone too far? What if she thought he'd been horrible to his mother? What if she was right? He had suddenly lost perspective on the situation by trying to see it through Edith's eyes.

He walked to her, frozen in that fear. He stopped, and stood in front of her, waiting.

She threw her arms around him.

"What are you feeling about all this?" he asked, holding her in return.

"Relief. I knew your mother was a tough customer. Most men won't stand up to their mothers. I don't think I ever met a man who didn't turn to jelly in front of his mother. But that was not jelly. I didn't hear everything, but you stepped right in and rescued me from her. It was amazing."

He sighed out a long breath and they just stood there in the hallway, holding each other for the longest time.

"I might've gone a step too far," he said into her ear, after a time.

"The part about your brother?"

"Oh. You did hear that. I think that hurt her."

"Probably. I'm sure she still carries a lot of pain from that. Then again, so do you. It's a valid question, Anton. I think you just had it locked up in there waiting for too long."

—

He was in his office when Marlene buzzed him. It was five or ten minutes earlier than he needed to leave for court, but he was already packing files and legal pads and pens and pencils into his briefcase. Being early and overly organized was something of a curse for Anton.

He leaned over and hit the intercom button on his phone.

"Yes, Marlene?"

"Your wonderful grandmother is here to see you."

"Oh," he said, feeling confused. It was unlike Grandma Marion to pop in on him at work.

He always found it odd that Marlene called her his wonderful grandmother, as though she had known the other one. His maternal grandmother had died when Anton was eleven. But, oddly, Marlene had guessed correctly. His other grandmother had been terrible.

"Send her in."

He looked up and watched Grandma Marion let herself into his office. She was more stooped than she had been a few years earlier, but she still overflowed with energy and intensity. She was still a force to reckon with—maybe more so than ever.

"Are you busy?" she asked, leaning her palms on his desk.

"I have to leave for court in about five."

"I'll make this quick."

But for a moment, she didn't make it anything. Whatever she had come to say, she didn't begin it at all. Or maybe it just seemed like a significant pause to Anton, who was now intimidated by the visit.

"Your mother is worried about you," she said.

Anton sighed deeply and said nothing.

"And normally I wouldn't mix in." She unbuttoned and loosened her winter coat as she spoke. "But some of the things she told me did seem rather alarming. Are you having trouble coping again, Anton?"

"No. Not at all. I've never been happier."

She stared at his face for a moment, as if measuring the truth of his claim. "You look happy. But it doesn't all add up. She says you broke up with Amy about four days ago, and now you're already engaged to somebody else. Somebody she thinks is too old for you, but that's nobody's business but your own. But the speed of the thing . . . it seems unlike you, Anton. You're usually so deliberative. It made me wonder if she's worried about you for good reason."

"She didn't tell you who it was?"

"Who it was?"

"She didn't tell you the woman's name, or how we met?"

"No. Why? Who is it?"

"Grandma Marion . . . it's *Edith*."

"Edith," she repeated, not seeming to make a connection.

"Edith. You met her. You had Christmas dinner with her that first year after Greg died. You brought Christmas dinner over while my parents were in South America."

He stopped talking, and she did not start. She only stood there, as if waiting for the facts to catch up. When they did, Anton could see it on her face. He could see it flare up in her eyes, like a fire in a gust of wind.

*"Edith?"* she asked, her voice full of awe.

"Yes. Now do you get why I'm so happy?"

"She found you again?"

"We ran into each other."

Another pause, during which no one moved or spoke. Then she rushed to him, her open coat flapping, and threw her arms around his waist. "Oh, Anton. I'm so happy for you!"

"You are?"

"Of course I am. She was the love of your life. You think I'm too blind to see that?"

"I just thought . . . I mean, before . . ."

"Before, you were a boy. Now you're a man and you can make your own choices."

"You don't even have any words of caution for me?"

He wasn't sure if he was dreading hearing her answer or not. The exchange had turned so positive. It was hard to feel afraid. She let him go and backed up a step.

"Well, possibly one word of caution. You know your grandpa Anton was quite a bit older than me. Everybody said I would be a fairly young woman when I lost him and then I'd end up alone in my old age. I wish I could say they were wrong, but that's more or less what happened. But, changing the subject for a moment, take my advice about one thing, Anton. When the time comes to marry, elope. I'll do well enough just seeing the photos. Your mother and father will only ruin everything. Gregor and Mina are not here to see. Don't have a formal wedding just for me. Make it clear that you're free agents. You'll do exactly as you wish."

"One question, though." He glanced at his watch, knowing he had to wrap up quickly. "About the age thing. With Grandpa Anton. Do you regret it?"

"Marrying your grandfather?"

"And ending up alone in your old age."

"I wouldn't trade the time I had with Anton for anything. For any reason."

"It's not much of a word of caution, then. Is it?"

"No," she said, and patted his cheek. "I suppose it's not."

# SPRING OF 1981

## HEART CONNECTION

# Chapter Nineteen

*Rash*

They stepped out of a cab together in lower Manhattan. Edith walked on his left, as she tended to do, so she could hold his hand.

Anton could see which building was the correct one, because it had a small concrete play yard on the side, with a high chain-link fence. He could see children toddling around, some playing, some fighting, others huddling in the corner as if hoping to disappear.

He glanced over at Edith, who was also watching the children.

When they reached the doorway of the building, she stopped walking. He kept going, thinking it was only a pause. Thinking she would restart herself momentarily. After all, she must have been as anxious as he was to take this meeting. He reached the end of the tether created by their linked hands. He watched Edith's face, wondering if she would volunteer what kind of trouble she was having. She was staring in the direction of the play yard, despite the fact that they were standing too deeply inside the entryway of the building to see the children.

"Tell me what's making it hard to go in," he said.

She looked at him then, and in her eyes he saw a fear he had never seen there. No, he had, he realized. Just not for many years. Not since the day her husband had shown up at the diner and caught them having lunch together.

For a moment she didn't answer.

"What are you afraid of?" he asked, keeping his voice soft.

She opened her mouth to answer. But a few ticks of time passed, and she did not speak.

"Are you afraid they won't approve us to have a child?"

Edith nodded, looking as though she might be about to cry.

"Well, look at it like this," he said. "I don't know what's going to happen when we go in. They might let us adopt a child and they might not. But we have a chance if we go. If we don't go in, we don't have much hope. I only like our chances at all if we take this meeting."

She smiled at him, but it was a sad-looking thing, and seemed to require effort. When the smile fell away from her face, it left her looking tired.

He tugged gently at her hand and she followed him inside.

———

He stood in the far corner of the playground, his shoulder against the brick of the building, watching Edith speak to a child. A girl. Mrs. Hazelton, the woman who had agreed to interview them and show them around, was standing near his left shoulder, watching with him.

"She's going to be a good mother," Mrs. Hazelton said. "Isn't she?"

It wasn't a bland compliment, or any sort of tossed-off comment, as far as Anton could tell. It sounded like a genuine observation. As though the woman had noticed something about Edith and it had impressed her so deeply that the words simply had to come up and out into the air and the light.

"She will be," he said. "I know she will. But I know her. I'm curious as to how you know."

In the silence that followed, they watched the scene together for a moment longer.

The girl looked to be about five years old, with dark hair and huge, dark eyes. She was wearing a yellow dress with white trim, and an expression that seemed to be made from equal parts sadness and intensity. Edith was sitting on the bench of a picnic table. The little girl had climbed up onto the bench seat with her and sat down cross-legged, as close to Edith as possible, pulling at one knee of her red leggings. Then she leaned in closer, as if to tell Edith a secret. Edith never took her eyes off the girl's face. She was speaking to the child, but in a voice that did not carry to where Anton and the administrator stood.

"I watch a lot of prospective parents meet children," she said. "It almost never looks like this."

"What does it look like?"

"Usually stiff and formal. Most adults are self-conscious around a child who's clearly a stranger to them. But your wife seems to have made a real heart connection already."

He opened his mouth to correct her. To tell her that Edith would be his wife at some point in the future, but was currently his fiancée. Then he closed his mouth. Edith had already made a deep connection with a child. How could he forgive himself if he said the wrong thing?

"I'm supposed to conduct a first interview today," Mrs. Hazelton said. "But I hate to break this up. Maybe I could just ask you a few informal questions."

"Okay."

It did not feel okay. He was now lost in his fear of saying the wrong thing and spoiling their chances. Then again, nothing would be worse than a lie. So he had to truthfully tell her what she wanted to know. He stuck his hand in his pocket so she wouldn't see it shaking.

"How long have you two been married?"

Anton squeezed his eyes shut. Then he forced himself to open them quickly, so she wouldn't see his hesitation. "We're actually engaged."

"Oh. Not yet married?"

"No, but soon. Soon enough that we wanted to get the process started."

He watched her make notes on her clipboard. He felt his sense of dread increase.

"When's the big date?"

"Just a few days away."

It was the closest he had come to a lie, but he would turn it into the truth. He would rearrange their lives to make it that way, because now he had to.

"Good," she said, still scribbling. "Because that definitely increases your chances. How long ago did you meet?"

It seemed, to Anton, a question made in heaven. He had expected her to ask how long they had known each other. Could he really have said they'd known each other for fifteen years? They had not known each other for the vast majority of that time. But she had asked how long ago they'd met. Anton almost could not believe his luck.

"Fifteen years ago."

"Good. That shows stability. Unless it was a long engagement for a reason."

"We were friends first," he said simply.

"Excellent. I like that. Is there a specific reason you chose adoption over having children of your own?"

"Edith is forty-eight." He watched her write that down. "Is that a problem?"

"Not much of one, no. Sometimes age is a factor, because some people are old enough that they might have trouble taking care of a child within an eighteen-year time frame. But if you're willing to adopt a child who's four or five, well . . . forty-eight is not an issue." She looked up from her clipboard and drilled her gaze into his face. "And you? You seem younger."

"I'm thirty-three," he said, feeling his face burn. "Is *that* a problem?"

"Quite the opposite, actually. One younger parent helps allay fears that there won't be enough health and energy to raise a child."

"Huh," Anton said. "So that actually helps us here. It sure hurts us everywhere else."

Then he wished he had said less.

Mrs. Hazelton smiled at his remark, but she seemed to be only half listening.

"The girl she's talking to, Jenny, can only be fostered at present. Her mother hasn't signed away her parental rights yet. She's been trying for a year to get sober, the mother, with no good result. She swears if it doesn't work this time, she'll sign the papers. My suggestion? Come back after the wedding. Don't fill out an application today. Do it as a legally married couple. Your chances of being approved will be better. There's a whole series of hoops you have to jump through. Background checks, and a number of home visits. If you're both sure Jenny is the child you want to adopt, hopefully by that time she'll be adoptable."

Anton looked across the playground again. Jenny had climbed into Edith's lap and was resting the side of her face against Edith's collarbone, staring up into her face.

"I have a strong feeling Jenny is the child we want."

"*You've* hardly spoken to her."

"I support my wife in whatever decision she makes," Anton said.

———

They stepped out onto the street together, and Edith took hold of his hand and held it firmly. He felt something like a buzz of energy through her hand. As though she was so excited that even her hand knew it. Anton stepped off the curb to hail a cab, but she pulled him back.

"Let's take the subway." Her words energized into a tone of voice he had never heard. "Too much traffic. A cab will take forever."

They set off toward the subway station together, still hand in hand.

"I need to tell you something," she said. "I wouldn't tell it to most people, because they'd say I'm getting ahead of myself, or I can't really know. But I think I can tell you."

"You can tell me anything."

"That little girl . . ."

"Jenny."

"Yes. Jenny. She's the one. I can feel it. She was meant to be my daughter."

"Our daughter," he said.

"Yes. Of course. I didn't mean we both wouldn't be her parents. Of course we will be. I just mean . . . I don't have a right to say what's meant to be in *your* life. Only my own."

Anton stopped. He tugged on her hand to stop her and turn her around to face him.

"What?" she asked.

She gazed up into his eyes in a manner that was utterly unguarded. She trusted him now. Or maybe she always had. In any case, it made him inordinately happy.

"Right at the moment Jenny can only be fostered. Her mother hasn't signed away her parental rights yet." He waited to see how the news settled in. To see her elation sink. But nothing sank. At least, nothing Anton could see. He verbally raced on. "But Mrs. Hazelton thinks it could be soon. She thinks if we come back and fill out an application and then go through the whole process with the home visits and all . . . maybe by then she'll be adoptable."

"She will be," Edith said. There was not the slightest note of doubt in her voice.

She turned to walk again, but Anton pulled her back around.

"Let's get married."

She stood on the sidewalk staring up at him and smiling wryly. As if he'd told an only slightly amusing joke. "Déjà vu," she said.

"What does that mean?"

"You don't know what déjà vu means?"

"No, I do. Just . . . why is this déjà vu?"

"Because you already asked me to marry you and I already said yes."

"No, I mean . . . I asked you to marry me . . . you know. Someday. Now I mean . . ."

"Oh. You mean let's get married *now*."

They stood in silence for a moment, if one can refer to the traffic noise of a busy Manhattan street as silence.

"Are you not sure yet?" he asked her.

"I'm sure."

"Then what are we waiting for?"

"If I'm being honest . . . I guess I'm waiting so other people won't say we're being rash."

"Let's be rash, then."

"Is this because we have a better shot at adoption as a married couple?"

"Yes and no. Marrying you is because I've wanted that my whole adult life. Marrying you right now is so we have a better chance at adopting Jenny."

She cupped a warm hand against his cheek. "I'm not sure what I did to deserve you. But I'm glad I did it. Okay. Let's get married now. But don't we have to plan something and invite your parents and all that?"

"No! We're definitely not inviting my parents. They ruin everything."

"What about your grandmother?"

"It was her idea not to invite them. I promised her we'd elope."

"Okay. Fine." He noted that her face had now caught up to the tone of the conversation. The vague look of doubt had disappeared, and her face now glowed with something like joyful amusement. "I still think you're crazy, but it's what I love about you. We'll go get a marriage license and then . . . let's elope."

—

Four mornings later, they showed up at Grandma Marion's door, in front of her little row house in Astoria, Queens. Edith had an overnight bag looped by its straps over her shoulder, because she had brought an outfit for the wedding that Anton was not yet supposed to see. Anton wore his best gray suit, and carried only a camera bag.

As he raised his hand to knock, he briefly hoped it had not been a mistake to surprise her. What if she was still in her nightgown, hair undone, or not feeling her best?

He took a deep breath and knocked anyway, then gave his hand back to Edith to hold.

Grandma Marion opened the door, and her face lit up to see them. Anton's fears about catching her at a bad time had been misplaced. She was fully dressed, with her hair nicely done. She even had stockings and shoes on.

"Oh my!" she said. "This is quite unexpected."

"I hope it was okay to surprise you," Anton said, feeling like a little boy again for reasons he did not entirely understand.

"Well, I think so. Tell me what the occasion is." As she spoke, she glanced at Anton's familiar fedora. As though admiring it all over again.

"Edith and I are eloping. Just like you suggested. But we can't imagine doing it without you. You're really the only family member I have who supports me. Now that Uncle Gregor is gone. So we're hoping you'll come to city hall with us and be our witness. We need to provide our own witness. And maybe you can even be our wedding photographer. What do you say?"

"When and where is the honeymoon?"

"We're leaving this afternoon for Hawaii," he said.

"Okay, fine," Grandma Marion said, her face alive with amusement. "I will be honored to be part of the wedding. But when the time comes for the honeymoon, you two are on your own. And I must not appear in any of the photographs, because if your parents can ever prove that I was there and they weren't, they'll kill me."

"Your secret is safe with us," Edith said.

———

It was Grandma Marion who eased open the door to the clerk's office and peered in at the spot where Anton stood waiting. "Are you ready?"

"Anytime."

Edith stepped into the office and Anton literally needed to catch his breath. For a moment she almost stopped the natural processes of his survival. Breath and heartbeat.

She was wearing a beige off-the-shoulder dress that snugged in at her waist. Her hair had been done up in an up-and-back style, crowned with a fine ringlet of flowers—probably baby's breath. She smiled at him, and his knees felt as though they were melting.

The clerk seemed to be in a bit of a hurry. But Anton didn't care, and Edith didn't seem to mind, either. As long as they ended up married, the process didn't trouble him much.

"Do you, Edith Renee Faber, take this man, Anton Edward Addison-Rice, to be your lawfully wedded husband, to have and to hold, from this day forward, for better, for worse, for richer, for poorer, in sickness and health, to love and to cherish, till death do you part?"

Edith looked directly into his eyes and smiled that smile again. This time it was his belly that turned to liquid heat.

"I do."

Then Anton lost track of the proceedings, looking into her eyes. Feeling that smile. It was warm and hot at the same time. It answered a question he had been afraid to ask. It told him, beyond a shadow of a doubt, that she felt the same. Or nearly the same. Nearly the same would do, because he accepted that nobody loved anybody quite the way he loved Edith.

Silence fell, and it struck Anton that everyone was staring at him. Edith had been all along. But now the clerk and his grandmother-witness were staring at him, too.

"You're supposed to say 'I do,'" Edith whispered.

"Oh. I'm sorry. Is it time for that? You distracted me by being so beautiful." He looked up at the clerk, who seemed impatient. "I do," he said. Loudly and firmly.

"I now pronounce you husband and wife. You may kiss the bride."

Anton leaned in to kiss her and she met him halfway. It was just a light, nearly chaste kiss, because they were so aware of his grandmother watching. Anton could hear her applauding in the background. He broke away and pressed his cheek against Edith's, and held her for a moment, despite knowing that the clerk wanted to wrap this up.

"I love you," he whispered into her ear.

"I love you, too," she whispered in return.

It took him back suddenly to the scene at the train station fifteen years earlier. It was a nearly perfect repeat of that moment. Except this time she remained in his arms.

———

Grandma Marion took pictures of them out in the hall, using Anton's camera.

"Scooch closer together," she called.

They did.

"Now kiss her again," Grandma Marion called.

It embarrassed Anton slightly, because there were people in the hallways. Lots of strangers. But he did as she instructed.

"Now like you mean it this time!" she shouted.

Anton felt his face turning red. But, to the best of their ability, they kissed as though no one was watching.

"Okay, I think I got some good ones," Grandma Marion said.

She walked the few steps to where they stood, the newly married couple, and handed Anton back his camera.

"Thank you," Anton said.

"It's just too bad," she said.

It surprised Anton. He almost didn't want to know what she meant. But he had to ask. "What?"

"Oh, I don't know. I was just . . . I shouldn't say it."

"Now I think you have to," he said, his arm firmly around Edith's shoulder.

"I was thinking about when I first met Edith. You were so in love and everybody was saying it was just a youthful thing and she needed to go away so you could forget her. And now I'm wondering if we gave you the best advice. Oh well. Water under the bridge, I suppose."

"We'll take you home," Anton said, eager to change the subject.

"I can see myself home. Go get ready for your nice trip."

"We'll at least put you in a cab," Edith said.

"Okay, fine. Whatever. Why should I argue?"

They walked together down the big stairwell. Out onto the street.

Now and then Anton glanced over at the side of Edith's face. He wasn't able to see into her eyes. Still, he thought he saw a sadness there. Something that was setting up camp and wanting to stay. He wasn't even sure how he knew. It just didn't look like a passing thing.

—

When they arrived in their honeymoon suite, Anton felt awkwardly aware of the fact that this was their honeymoon night. It shouldn't have mattered, since they had been living together for a few months. But it seemed to matter anyway.

He couldn't tell if it felt awkward for her, too.

There was a lot he couldn't gauge about her mood. She had seemed absent on the plane, and through dinner. As though her thoughts had been elsewhere. Now and then he had felt her try to drag her attention back to the moment, but it had never seemed to last.

They stood together at the end of their hotel bed, and he wrapped his arms around her.

"We should get you out of this dress," he said.

"Okay." Her face was buried in the crook of his shoulder.

There was something wrong with the word. It shook a little. For a moment he held her in silence, afraid to confront what was happening.

"Are you crying?" he asked after a time.

She sighed deeply. She still did not show her face. "I'm sorry. It's stupid. It's our honeymoon. And now you're probably wondering why you married such an emotional basket case."

"No." A tension was building in his chest. It was hard to talk around it. "No, I'm not. Just . . . I need you to tell me what's wrong."

She pulled away from him and walked to their big glass patio door. The one that opened out onto the lanai. She pulled the curtain back, and looked out at the beach. He came up behind her. With each moment that passed he felt more and more like a ticking bomb. Like he would explode if she didn't hurry up and tell him. He could see the reflection of her face in the glass. It was streaked with tears. He could see them drip off her jaw and onto her dress.

"What if I should've taken you with me?" she asked.

"When?"

"You know when."

"You mean all the way back?"

"Yeah. All the way back. You wanted me to take you. Why didn't I? Even your grandmother doesn't know anymore. I sort of know. I remember. You were only eighteen. We all thought being in love was a passing thing for you. But we were all wrong. And now I look back and I made a decision and it wasted fifteen years we could've had."

"You were doing what you thought was best."

He dared to wrap his arms around her again. She leaned back onto his chest.

"I was trying to. But I was wrong. You weren't a minor. You were a legal adult. All those years putting makeup on impatient rich ladies and working my way through school and thinking I had to be alone even though I'd already met the most wonderful, unselfish boy in the world and he adored me. We could be raising our own children right now, Anton. We'd have teenagers. How do you make up for a mistake that huge?"

Anton breathed quietly for a moment, looking for the right words. "But if we'd had our own kids, then you never would've met Jenny. And you said she's the one. You said she was meant to be your daughter."

"Our daughter," Edith said. Anton thought that was a good sign, but he didn't answer because he wasn't sure. "Maybe. Maybe this was right. I don't know. I feel like I don't know anything anymore. Oh, hell. Who am I kidding? I'm not sure I ever did."

"All I know," he said, "is that we have a past. And we have right now. And then we have what comes after this. Two of those things we can actually do something about." He felt the breath sigh out of her, and knew, in a rush of relief, that he had said the right thing. "And another thing. Tell me what I did to make you love me."

"Lots of things."

"The main one, then."

She didn't seem to need time to think. "You let me go. Because it was safer for me. And it was the most unselfish thing anybody had ever done for me. Oh. I think I see where you're going with this."

After that they stopped discussing the past and let the "right now" of their situation be something better. They allowed it to be their honeymoon in all the best senses of the word.

—

It was after three when she rolled over, woke up enough to look at his face, and realized he was awake. He had been up all night, watching her sleep and thinking. Or maybe not thinking. Maybe just allowing thoughts and feelings to wander through.

"You're not sleeping," she said.

"No."

"Thinking?"

"I guess."

"What are you thinking about?"

He opened his mouth to say, "So many things." But what came out was a reference to one thing only. "I'm wondering if this means you really love me."

The words ricocheted around in the dark for a few seconds. Then she reached over him and turned on the lamp, blinking into its sudden glare.

"You didn't think I really loved you?"

Anton sighed. Pulled his words together for a moment. "I believe you love me more than you've loved most people you've met. I didn't realize you loved me enough to cry over the fact that we lost all those years."

She blinked too much for a moment, and when she held her eyes open into the light, they looked sad. "Then I've really let you down. And I'm sorry. From now on I'll do a better job of making sure you know. Telling and showing. Both."

"It's probably mostly me. I didn't figure you could love me the way I love you because . . . who does? Who loves anybody the way I love you? It's not even fair to ask anybody to try."

She smiled, but it still looked sad. "No. It's me. It's my fault. It's my job to let you know. And I've been falling down on the job. And I promise you it won't happen again."

# Chapter Twenty

## The Last Ally

They arrived home a mere three days later—there was only just so much time Anton could take off from work on short notice—to find seven messages on the answering machine.

He began to play them one by one. They were all from his mother.

"Anton. Where are you? Are you ignoring me? Or are you out of town or something? And why did you go out of town without telling me? You need to call us right now. *Right now!*"

That was the third. After that, they grew more desperate.

Edith abandoned her unpacking and stuck her head into the room. "What's she all upset about?"

"I have no idea," Anton said. "You just never know with her. I'll call them."

He picked up the phone and hit number two on the speed dial.

"Anton?" she barked into the phone. In place of *hello*.

"Yeah, it's me."

In his peripheral vision, he watched Edith watching him.

"Where the hell have you been, young man?"

"I was on a little vacation. Can you please tell me what's going on?"

"Oh, nothing important," she said, her voice dripping with sarcasm. "Just your grandmother died and now we're holding up planning the funeral until we hear from you. Nothing big at all."

He let the phone sink down past his waist.

"What?" Edith asked. "What is it?"

"Grandma Marion."

He watched her face fall. She came to him and held him. He kept the phone receiver in his left hand, the line still open, and held Edith in return. He could hear the scratch of his mother's distant voice, shouting at him. Trying to get him back.

"At least she got to come to our wedding," Edith whispered into his ear. "If you hadn't gotten it into your head to get married suddenly like we did, she'd have missed it."

"We should have gotten her in one of the pictures," Anton said. "Because there's nothing they can do to her now."

"Anton!" his mother bellowed.

He put the phone back to his ear. "I'll be over in a few minutes. As fast as I can get there." Then he hung up.

"You want me to come with you?" Edith asked.

"I'd love to have you there. Come later if you want. But the best thing you could do for me is go get Hannah back from the kennel. That would be the biggest help right now."

———

He'd been sitting with his parents in their living room for nearly an hour when his mother noticed his wedding ring. They had been discussing flowers and churches, and predictably arguing over the smallest details. At first he'd been prepared for her reaction to the ring, but he had let his guard down as the conversation dragged on.

"Her church is all the way in Astoria!" his mother shouted. "Who wants to go all the way to Astoria for a funeral?"

He glanced at his father, who had been uncharacteristically silent. Just mostly staring off into space as if barely present. Then again, his mother had just died.

"Think about what you're saying," Anton told her.

"What am I saying? I'm saying who wants to go to Queens?"

"And who's going to be going to her funeral?"

"Family and friends."

"The only family she had left are the three of us. And her friends live in Queens."

"I'm just saying. She hardly ever went to church anyway. Maybe we don't have it at a church. Maybe we have it at a nice funeral home."

Anton dropped his head into his hands, real and prosthetic. One could drop one's head into that plastic hand. He'd done so many times. Usually in the presence of his parents.

"You're making this harder than it needs to be," he said.

He heard nothing in reply. He looked out through the hands to see her staring at his ring. For a moment no one moved or spoke.

"You got married, Anton?"

"Yes. I got married."

"Without telling us?"

"Yes. We eloped."

"After a handful of months with this person? Abel, wake up. Are you in a trance, or what? Are you hearing this? Your son got married without us."

His father only grunted.

"I told you," Anton said. "I've known her since I was eighteen."

"Forget that. How could you do this to us? Forget us. How could you do this to your grandmother? You don't think she would have wanted to see you get married?"

Anton pulled a deep breath and let the truth fly. "She *did* see us get married."

For a long moment, only silence. Then it was broken by a knock on the apartment door.

"I'll get that," Anton said. "It's probably Edith."

At least, he hoped it was Edith. He needed rescuing. As he walked to the door, his mother broke her trance and began yelling after him.

"I don't believe you! I don't believe she would do that to us, because she would know how that would make us feel. I think you're making it up to be cruel."

Anton undid the locks and opened the door. Edith stood on the mat, looking up into his face. She had Hannah on a leash by her side. It rocketed him back in time to the night she first knocked on his apartment door, because she had left her husband. His whole life had changed in that moment. Hannah wagged wildly at him, and he stroked her head and face. A voice in his gut was trying to tell him it was time for his whole life to change again.

"She would not have approved of this marriage!" his mother shouted, her voice closer.

Anton turned to see her standing at the end of the entry hall, and knew she wasn't done.

"Because that person is too old for you, and everybody with eyes in their head can see it!" she added.

In a strange and twisted way, Anton was almost glad she'd said it. Because it clarified that voice in his gut. He understood, in that moment, what it was telling him to do.

"But she *did*," he said. "She'd known Edith for fifteen years, too. And she *did* approve. And she was the one who made me promise we'd elope, and not invite you and Dad. Because she said you ruin everything. And she was absolutely right. She only wanted to see photos, but we picked her up and took her along because she was my grandmother and she always had my back and I couldn't imagine getting married without her. And now I'm glad I did. So I'm taking Grandma Marion's advice. Edith and I are going to have an adopted family, and I won't let anybody ruin that. So plan the funeral yourself, or turn it over to me to plan on my own. You decide. I'll see you at the funeral, but not after that. After that we're done."

For a long, silent moment, his mother only stood at the end of the hall with her mouth open. Then he could see her gather herself to speak. "What do you mean 'done'?"

"I think you know what I mean."

"You think you'll be done being our son? You can't be done with that. You'll always be our son. We'll always be your parents."

"You'll be my estranged parents."

She didn't answer. Just stood frozen like a statue. He took Edith gently by the elbow and they walked away, leaving the apartment door wide open. Anton rang for the elevator, and the doors sprang open immediately. They stepped on. As the doors closed, he saw that his parents' apartment was still standing open.

"I'm sorry about that," he said to Edith as the elevator descended.

"Not your fault."

"Thank you for picking up the dog. Was she a wreck?"

"She was awfully happy to see me. I'll just leave it at that."

"It was nice of you to bring her. She would have hated being left alone at home so soon after the kennel. Not sure how you did it, though. Did you get a cab to take her?"

"We walked. She needed it. It was good for her. She started to settle down on the walk."

"That's forty-two blocks."

"I know. I just walked it."

The elevator stopped in the lobby and they stepped out. Walked onto the street together. The weather was brisk and cool, and it felt new to Anton. The way weather should feel when you've just changed your life.

"Should we try to see if a cab will take her?" Anton asked his wife.

"No, let's walk. Something tells me *you* need it. Maybe *you'll* settle down on the walk."

They walked in silence for several blocks, Edith holding his left hand and the dog's leash. She seemed to be purposely giving him space to work things out inside himself. They crossed streets at corners, dodged turning cabs. Wove in and out of pedestrian traffic.

"Can I *do* that?" he asked after a time.

"I think you just did."

"But I want to know from you. If it's okay."

"You don't need my permission."

"I know. I didn't mean permission. I'm not making myself clear. I was just thinking . . . you lost your parents when you were young. You'd probably do anything to see them again. Is what I did a slap in the face to somebody who would do anything to see her parents again?"

"The reason I'd do anything to see them again is because they were helpful and kind."

"My parents are neither helpful nor kind," Anton said.

"I would tend to agree."

"Grandma Marion was right. They ruin everything. And I won't let them ruin us. It's too important. And the children we're about to adopt. Why would I even subject them to people who aren't helpful or kind?"

"Based on my experiences looking into Jenny's eyes, I'd say she's already had experience with people who are neither helpful nor kind."

"Then why put her through it again?"

"You don't have to convince *me*," she said.

And they walked in silence for another block.

"So you think I can do it," he said.

"I think you already did."

———

The first person Anton saw when he walked into the Methodist church was his mother, but she cut her eyes away. Edith had her arm through his, and he held it more tightly, and she gave him a squeeze in return. Then an older woman he thought he didn't know filled the church aisle in front of him and addressed him in a booming voice.

"You're Anton!"

"I am," he said, still not knowing who she was. "And this is my wife, Edith."

"So pleased to meet you, Edith," the woman nearly shouted. Granted there were quite a few guests, most talking, and some extra volume was required. But this seemed like too much even under the circumstances. "So glad Anton finally popped the question. We thought it might never happen."

Anton winced inwardly. He purposely did not look over at Edith to see how she felt about being confused with his ex-girlfriend. He opened his mouth to ask the woman, in a polite way, to help him place her. She didn't give him the chance.

"I know. You don't remember me. And I don't expect you to. I'm Esther, from her bridge club. We met a few times, but you were very young. I know you better than you know me, because your grand-mother talked about you all the time. She was so proud of you. She just adored you. But I can't believe how big and handsome you got. She tried to tell me you were a grown man, all big and handsome. But I still wasn't prepared. Ladies!" she called, looking all around herself. "Look who it is! It's Anton!"

The ladies began to move in his and Edith's direction.

"If you haven't seen me since I was a boy," Anton said, "how did you know it was me?"

Her eyes flickered immediately downward to his prosthetic hand.

"Oh. Never mind. That was a silly question."

"Such a tragedy. I don't know how one single member of your family made it through all that pain. Especially you, because the pain was not all emotional for you. But Marion had a terrible time with it, too, because she loved your brother, but she also loved you, and hated to see you suffer. She never felt like there was enough she could do to help you."

"She helped me a lot," Anton said.

Now there were four more ladies gathered around him in the small aisle, all standing too close. Anton felt as though he might cry. But he held it back, because he didn't like to cry around people he didn't know. Or people he did know. Or just people. Or even himself.

"She loved you so much," one of the ladies said.

"The feeling was mutual," he said, still managing to hold it in.

"And she told us how much you looked like Anton the elder in that hat," another lady said, reaching up to touch it. "I thought she was exaggerating. She was *not* exaggerating!"

He felt himself being pulled backward by the fabric of his suit jacket. He half turned his head to see that his mother had gotten hold of him, and was roughly pulling him back out of the crowd of his grandmother's friends.

"We're sitting!" she hissed near Anton's ear.

"Fine. Edith and I will go sit."

"No. Edith will go sit. You'll go get up on the altar and speak about your grandmother."

Anton just stood a moment with his mouth open. Edith's arm was still firmly hooked through his. He glanced at her, and she returned a barely perceptible shrug. "Now?"

"Yes, now. We're starting."

"Doesn't the minister say something first?"

"There's no minister. She never went to church, so the minister hardly knows her. We're only hearing from people who really knew her. Starting with you."

"You couldn't have told me this?"

His mother punched him on the shoulder surprisingly hard.

"Ow," he said.

"*Someone* made it very clear that we were to plan the service without him."

"Oh," Anton said. "Right."

He walked with Edith to a front pew, and she sat and used her purse to hold a place for him. Meanwhile Anton could hear his mother rudely clapping her hands to get everyone's attention, and demanding they sit.

He stepped up onto the altar in a mild state of shock. He had no idea what to say about his grandmother. He'd had no idea he would be encouraged, or even allowed, to speak. He took a deep breath and realized he had so many good things to say about her that it couldn't be a problem. It would be more of a problem to edit them down, so the gathering would not be here listening to him all day. He stepped behind the podium, squeezed his eyes closed, and decided that he would say only what he thought would please his grandmother if she were alive. In other words, he would be honest.

He opened his eyes to see everyone in attendance seated, staring at him. Waiting for him to begin. His mother was miming that he should take off the fedora. He did not take it off.

"I didn't realize I was going to be asked to speak." He paused and listened to the expectant silence. Realized everyone in the room was hanging on his words. It was unnerving. "But it's not a problem, because I could fill hours with all the good things I remember about my grandmother."

He paused again, trying not to look at his mother. She was still gesticulating wildly to try to get him to take off the hat.

"My mother wants me to take off the fedora," he said, and her hands fell still. "But I'm not going to. Even though I know it would be a common courtesy to have my hat in my hands as I do a eulogy. But this is not just any hat. This is my grandpa Anton's hat. The one that makes me look so much like him as a young man that I take people's breath away. And Grandma Marion gave it to me. I think she'd want me to have it on."

He pulled a long breath, realizing that he hadn't been breathing enough. He plowed on.

"I remember the day she gave it to me. She said she wouldn't have parted with it for anyone else. But she said I was his namesake, and growing up in his image, and that made me its rightful owner. What she didn't say—but I think she didn't need to—is that he was a role model for me. My goal was to grow up to be just like him, not because I was expected to, but because 'like Grandpa Anton' was a good way to be. Grandma Marion was my role model, too. She taught me to be honest. The older she got, the more honest she was. She was kind in every way she could be. But if she had a choice between kindness and honesty, she'd be honest in as kind a way as she could manage. She wouldn't hold back."

He took a deep breath. Leaned on the podium. He could see his parents in his periphery, but he was careful not to look at them directly. His father was crying. He had never seen his father cry. His mother sat with her arms crossed over her chest, as if ready to defend herself.

"I'm sure I don't have to tell anyone that the year my brother died and I lost my hand was a very bad time for me. Someone told me just before I got up here that it was hard for Grandma Marion, too. Well, of course it was. That goes without saying. But for a reason I hadn't known. Because she thought she couldn't help me enough. I wish she were here so I could tell her how much she helped me. I guess she wanted to put an end to my pain or fix it for me, but of course she couldn't do that. Nobody could do that. But she was my ally. At a time like that, some people are your allies and some are not. And it's not always who you might expect."

He glanced sidelong at his mother. She looked angry. He kept talking anyway.

"Grandpa Anton was my ally, but he was gone by the time we lost Greg. But I had Grandma Marion and I had my late uncle Gregor, and they got me through it. They didn't make it easy, because nothing and nobody could, but they had my back. Uncle Gregor is gone six years. So I guess you could say Grandma Marion was my last ally."

He stopped talking. Looked up at Edith in the front pew. She smiled back at him. Even though what he'd just said was wrong.

"That's not entirely right, though. She was my last ally from my original family. But I'm married now, and about to start a family of my own. And I was fortunate enough to've had Grandma Marion there at the start of that union, at least. To give it her blessing."

His mother leapt up from her pew and flounced out of the church.

"I've upset my mother. But I decided I would be completely honest, because that's how my grandmother was, and that's what I think she would've wanted." He watched her go for a moment. Then he said, "My kids are not only going to have allies, they're going to be surrounded by people who really, sincerely have their backs. Not that I can reorder the whole world for them, but I can be brave enough to protect them in ways I didn't protect myself."

A long pause. Long enough that the congregants began to shift in their seats, wondering if he had more to say. Anton removed the fedora and held it over his heart.

"My very first memory of my grandmother and grandfather, they were dancing. It was some kind of outdoor event. At night. Under the stars. I might have been four or five. And they were waltzing. And I was watching. Because even though I was very little and didn't understand much, I understood love. I could see how they had not one bit of attention left over for anything else but each other. I could feel their devotion. So I just want to thank them for modeling love for me, the real thing. Grandma Marion was the one who taught me that selfish love isn't love at all. She said—and I'll never forget this—if I wanted to be selfish with love, then what I felt would be what ninety-nine percent of the world was satisfied to call love. But for her it wasn't good enough. And I want to thank her for that, because that's the kind of love I want in my life. And I have a chance at that now. She taught me what that looks like, and that's no small favor to do for a confused boy."

He stopped. Looked up. Directed his remarks to the ornate ceiling of the church.

"I'm sorry your great-grandchildren won't know you, Grandma Marion, but they'll know your version of love. I'm glad you and Grandpa Anton get to have another dance now, after all this time."

It made him cry to say that last sentence. This time he didn't try to stop it. He couldn't have if he'd tried, and anyway, it didn't matter.

He opened his mouth to say more, but there were no more words. Just more tears.

So he took his seat beside Edith, and she held his hand tightly.

"I'll be your ally," she whispered in his ear.

"I know you will," he whispered back.

# SUMMER OF 1981

## WHY IS THIS?

# Chapter Twenty-One

## Why Is This?

Anton stepped into the living room to see Edith frantically pushing and pulling the vacuum cleaner. He watched in silence for a moment, wondering if he dared say anything.

"What?" she asked after a time.

"Are you breathing?"

She stopped all motion, and he saw the beginnings of a smile crack onto her face. "Well, I'm not dead, if that's what you mean."

"I guess I meant are you breathing *enough*?"

"Oh." She leaned on the handle of the vacuum for a moment. "Probably not, no."

"Is there anything I can do to help you relax?"

"Got a fast-forward button for life?"

"Sadly, no." He crossed the living room and took her into his arms. "How can anybody not think this is a great home for a kid? Why would they think that?"

For a moment, she seemed to relax in his arms. Then he could feel her go rigid again. "I'm worried about the dog," she said, pulling away.

"What about her? You can have a dog and kids, both. It's done all the time."

"What if she snaps at Jenny?"

"Why would she do that?"

"She might be jealous."

"Hannah's never snapped at anybody or anything in her life. Not even once. And she's not jealous of *you*. She knows how much I love you but she doesn't see you as a threat. She treats you as another person to love."

"I'm turning myself inside out over nothing, aren't I?"

"Pretty much. Yeah. No offense."

"It's just so hard to—"

Her thought was interrupted by a knock on the door. *The* knock.

Edith scrambled to put the vacuum away. Hannah woofed in a deep voice.

"I have to do something about my hair," Edith said. "Let her in, okay?"

Her hair looked perfect to Anton, but he didn't argue. He just answered the door.

Mrs. Hazelton stood on the mat, poised to knock again. She had Jenny with her. She hadn't promised to bring Jenny for the first home inspection, but of course they had both hoped she would.

Hannah came barreling down the hallway, barking, scrambling for purchase on the slippery hardwood. Jenny grabbed tightly to Mrs. Hazelton's legs.

"She's friendly," Anton said. "She just didn't know who's here."

He reached out to grab the dog's collar. To stop her. But she had already stopped. She stood near Anton's legs and wagged her tail tentatively, sniffing in the direction of the little girl.

"Promise?" Jenny asked.

"I promise."

The little girl let go and took a tentative step forward. Hannah matched it with a tentative step of her own. The dog sniffed around the girl's neck and belly with her absurdly long muzzle. She sniffed at the side of her head, blowing locks of curly hair around on the out breaths and making Jenny giggle. Finally Hannah offered the girl a single lick on the ear.

Jenny's face lit up. "She kissed me!"

"That means she likes you."

"I *know*!"

"You should both come in," Anton said.

———

Jenny was sitting on the couch between Edith and Mrs. Hazelton, but closer to Edith. But her attention seemed fixed on Anton.

"We might be able to work out a foster arrangement in as little as five or six days," Mrs. Hazelton said.

Anton watched his wife's face. Watched the battle taking place inside her. She wanted to be elated but she didn't dare. Not yet. It was too important. Scary important.

"No signing of papers yet?" Edith asked, clearly coding her discussion for the girl's sake.

"Not yet. We were told it might be Friday. But we were told that once before. Jenny? Would you like to come stay here and have these two nice people be your foster parents?"

"Now?" Jenny asked. She sounded hopeful.

"No, not now," Mrs. Hazelton said. "They need a license to foster you, and it hasn't come through yet."

"I don't know what that is," Jenny said, and frowned.

"It's just paperwork. We just have to do some more paperwork. But we might be able to have you here in less than a week."

"Okay."

To everyone's surprise, she slid down from the couch. She patted Hannah firmly on the head twice. The dog both winced and grinned. Jenny walked right up to Anton. She pointed at Anton's prosthetic hand. Without a glove—which he would have felt self-conscious wearing around the house—it was easily identifiable as a prosthetic.

"Why is this?" she asked.

It was an oddly phrased question. But she was five. And besides, Anton understood.

"Jenny!" Mrs. Hazelton said, her voice scolding. "That's not polite."

"No, it's okay," Anton said. "You can't blame her for noticing. Grown-ups notice too, but they don't ask. And that's not really much better from my end of the thing. Kids appreciate honesty, right?"

At least, Anton knew he would have appreciated some when he was a kid. Edith nodded. Mrs. Hazelton only shrugged. Anton turned his attention back to Jenny.

"The reason this hand looks different is because it's not a real hand. It's what's called a prosthetic hand, which is just a big word that means fake."

"Why is it fake?" she asked, turning her huge, unguarded eyes up to him.

"Because I don't have a real one."

As if this were a game or a test, she pointed enthusiastically to his left hand.

"Right. Yes, I do have a real hand on the left. I meant I don't have a real one on this side." He unbuttoned the right cuff of his shirt and rolled it back to show her the straps. She reached out and touched them. "Will it scare you if I take it off and show you what it's like without the prosthetic? Because I don't always wear it around the house."

"I don't know. What's under it?"

"There's nothing *under* it, exactly. Just, without it, there's nothing there on the end of my wrist. Does that sound scary?"

Jenny shook her head, her eyes still wide. Anton glanced up at Edith and then at the social worker, but saw no messages of caution. So he undid the straps and set the prosthetic on the coffee table. Jenny reached out and touched the end of his wrist.

"Did it used to be a hand?" She was clearly not afraid. Fascinated, but not in a bad way.

"Years ago, yes. I had a hand there."

"Where did it go?"

"Some doctors had to take it off, because it was so badly injured."

"You hurt it?"

"Yeah. I hurt it too badly for them to save it."

"Does it hurt?"

"Not now. It's all healed now."

For a moment the little girl just stared at the empty space where Anton's right hand had once been. Then she said, simply, "Oh," and walked back to the couch, where she jumped up between Edith and Mrs. Hazelton again.

Anton looked first at his wife, then to the little girl's social worker. On both faces he saw a satisfied confirmation that he had done well.

"We'll hurry up the fostering paperwork as much as we can," Mrs. Hazelton said. "Because Jenny's not thriving at the agency. I think she'll be happier here."

———

Anton was not asleep, but he could tell by Edith's breathing that she was. She was behind him, pressed up close to his back. One of her arms was under his neck. The other was thrown over his shoulder.

Then, with no change to her breathing, she began to stroke the end of his right wrist. The stump. Which was an accurate word, but also one he tried to avoid. There was something negative and harsh about it. Mostly he just called it his wrist, and so did she. She had done it before, but always seemingly in her sleep, or at least when she was half-asleep. He had never said or asked anything about it.

In time she stretched, yawned. Moved her hand away from his wrist. She hugged him more tightly. "You're not asleep," she mumbled. It didn't sound like a question.

"No."

"Are you worried? You shouldn't be worried. It went great."

"I'm not worried. Just thinking, I guess."

"What were you thinking?"

"I was wondering why you touch the end of my wrist while you're sleeping."

"I do?"

"Yeah."

"Often?"

"Not too often. It's happened a few times." She didn't answer right away, so he added, "I don't think of it as being the most appealing part of me, so I guess that's why I was curious."

They lay quietly in the dark together for a time. Anton could hear traffic noise ten stories down, and the beeping of a garbage truck that told him it was nearly morning.

"If I'm asleep at the time," she said, "it's hard to know."

He didn't answer. Just gave her time.

"But if I had to guess . . . I figure it's probably because that's how I know it's you."

"Oh," he said. "Okay."

"Does it bother you?"

"Not now that you've said *that*."

They lay quietly for another moment.

Then she said, "We're really getting our daughter, aren't we?"

"Looks that way."

"I love you so much, Anton. You know that, right? How many men would put aside having their own children for me? But I don't mean that the way it sounds."

"How do you think it sounds?"

"I mean . . . I don't mean I love you because you do what I want. Or do things for me. I love you because that's who you are. I love you so much it scares me sometimes. I'll think how much I love you and for a minute it's hard to breathe."

Anton smiled in the dark, but he knew she couldn't see. For a moment he was simply happy in his own life, and nursing a warm, full feeling in his chest. Feeling as though he had arrived someplace he had been running toward for as long as he could remember.

"Welcome to my side of the fence," he said.

——

Anton met them for lunch at a restaurant on Central Park East, five days later. It was Jenny's first day with them, but Anton had needed to be at work when she arrived.

They were standing outside the Italian restaurant waiting for him, and Anton was surprised to see that they had brought the dog. Edith was beaming as though she had some internal light source shining out through her eyes.

He hugged Edith, and almost hugged Jenny. But it might have been too much too soon, and he didn't want to scare her. Instead he reached out his left hand, and she shook it with her left. She did not seem to need a moment to break the right-hand habit as most grown-ups did.

"The dog was an interesting choice," he said.

"Jenny insisted we bring her. I brought a tablecloth and some silverware in my purse. I thought you could go in and order lunch to go and then we'll go to the park and have a picnic. It was Jenny's idea. She said it had been too long since she'd had a picnic, and that dogs can be invited to the park."

"Is it okay?" Jenny asked, turning her big eyes up to Anton.

"I think it's a great idea," he said.

—

"We need to buy her a lot of things," Edith said.

Anton was sitting on one hip on the grass, half-worried about grass stains on his good suit pants. He took off his jacket, set it on the ground with the lining side down, then sat on that. He gazed out over the lake.

"Well, that's no problem," he said.

"You should have seen what Mrs. Hazelton brought. It was . . ." He thought she was going to say some harsh word like "ridiculous" or "pathetic." Instead she glanced down at the girl, who was clearly listening, and changed her tone. ". . . not enough. Just enough clothes to fit into two paper grocery sacks, with a comb and toothbrush. Grocery sacks! They don't even give her a suitcase."

"We can get her a suitcase," Anton said, and took a bite of his sandwich.

"She doesn't need one now. Because she isn't going anywhere. I have some good news to tell you about that. About her not going anywhere." But she seemed hesitant to discuss it in front of the child. "Papers have been signed."

"You mean . . ."

"I mean what you think I mean. A certain party was told the details of her having a family who wants her. And this party did the right thing. So we can begin the adoption process."

"That's great!"

"It is. It's wonderful. We talked it over with Jenny, and she's okay with being adopted."

"I don't like that place," Jenny said.

"The place you've been staying? With Mrs. Hazelton?"

"Right," Jenny said. "That. I don't like that."

"Don't worry," Edith said. "You're with us now. But we need to get you more clothes."

"You can take the credit card," Anton said. "Get anything you need. Only, you'll have to leave the dog at home."

"No," Jenny said, sounding quite firm. "We'll go when you get home from work. She doesn't like to be alone. It makes her sad."

———

"You have to see this," Edith said. She had stuck her head into the living room to speak to him.

"Okay."

He rose and followed her down the hall, Hannah trotting along beside him, her nails clicking on the hardwood. They stepped into Jenny's room together. They hadn't had time to do much with the room, but Anton had spent the weekend re-wallpapering. The walls were now covered with images of balloons in bright primary colors. Jenny was fast asleep in the single bed, covered by a store-bought quilt printed with frolicking puppies.

He felt Edith take his left hand and give it a squeeze.

"Look at that face," she said. "Have you ever seen anything more beautiful in your life?"

"There *is* something special about a sleeping child, isn't there?"

The night-light in the corner illuminated her tiny, upturned nose. Light wisps of dark hair fell across her face, lifting and falling with her breathing.

"I just feel so . . ." But then she didn't finish the thought.

"I hope you were going for 'happy.'"

"Yeah. Happy. Sure. But also scared."

"Why scared?"

"Don't you get scared when you're happy?"

"I don't think so. Why would I?"

"Because when everything is so good like this . . . when you just feel like life is perfect and you have everything you want . . . don't you ever feel . . . like you're waiting for a shoe to drop?"

He thought a moment. But the feeling didn't sound familiar.

"I don't think so. I think I'm just happy."

"I'm surprised. Because of that terrible experience you had when you were seventeen. I thought you'd know better than anybody how it feels to be scared that what you're happy about could be taken away."

"Oh, I was never happy before Greg died."

"Never?"

"I don't think so."

"So when were you happy?"

"After I ran into you on the train."

"That was just a few months ago."

"Right."

She squeezed his hand again. "Well, I'm not going anywhere."

"I didn't think you were. And neither is Jenny."

"You're right. I'm just being silly. I'm not going to worry anymore. I'm just going to be happy."

# WINTER OF 1981

## THE SECOND SHOE

# Chapter Twenty-Two

## Hero

Anton was in his office waiting for a client when his secretary buzzed him. He assumed it meant the client had arrived a few minutes early. He pressed the intercom button.

"Yes, Marlene?"

"You have three beautiful girls here to see you."

He tried to ask more, but she had clicked off the connection. He glanced at his watch and then hurried to his office door and threw it open. Edith and Jenny were waiting in his outer office, and Edith had Hannah on a leash. Anton met his wife's eyes, and enjoyed that warm spark he always felt when she looked straight into him.

"Sorry," she said, indicating the dog with a movement of her head.

She didn't need to say more. They both knew Jenny strenuously objected to the dog being left alone for anything but the shortest of errands.

Anton glanced at his watch again. "I have three minutes. Unless my next client is late."

"We'll talk fast," Edith said.

He stepped back from the doorway to allow them into his office, and closed the door.

"Nice surprise," he said, and kissed her briefly on the lips. Then he bent down and kissed Jenny on the top of her head for a longer time. Her hair smelled fresh, like baby shampoo. "Nice surprise . . ." He paused as though he couldn't recall her name. It was a little game they played. ". . . I want to say . . . Germy."

She giggled as he straightened up. "No," she said, drawing the word out long.

"You sure it's not Germy?"

"Germy is a *boy's name*."

"No, not Jeremy . . . It's . . . never mind."

"It's *Jenny*!" she nearly shouted, followed by another squeaky laugh.

"Oh, that's right." Then he looked to Edith. "Nothing's wrong, is it?"

"No. It's good. It's very good. It's kind of exciting."

He glanced at his watch again.

"Short version," she said. "More later. I have to share this with you now because it's so exciting."

"Must be if you walked all the way down here."

"You know Mrs. Kressler from our building?"

"I do."

"And you know her daughter Yvette."

"Not as well, but yes."

"And you know she's eight months pregnant."

"That would be hard to miss, yes."

"She's not keeping the baby."

"Oh," Anton said. It dawned on him for the first time where this might be going.

"She's only seventeen. And the father took off for California and doesn't want any part of parenthood. She's scared to death. She's been trying to find a family she trusts. She doesn't want to give the baby to an agency. She wants to choose for herself. She wants to feel like she picked a family she knows is the right one, so she can sleep at night. I talked to her for three hours this morning."

"Wow," Anton said.

That word just hung in the air for a moment. The conversation stalled, and they allowed it to, even though they both knew Anton was running out of time.

"We won't know if it's a boy or a girl," he said after a time.

"No. We won't."

"Does it matter? You wanted a boy."

"No. It doesn't matter. You just have this image of what your family will be."

It rocketed Anton back to one of their earliest conversations. She had told him that shallow girls would have too inflexible a mental image of what their husband should be.

"Like wanting to marry a boy with two hands but being willing to adjust?"

He watched her connect it up in her brain. Watched her turn it into a knowing smile.

Marlene buzzed him again, and he knew it meant his client had arrived.

"So what's our next step?" he asked.

"I think we get a babysitter and take her out to dinner. And talk."

"Shouldn't Jenny be there for the talk, too?"

"Yes. Of course."

"Oh. You meant a babysitter for the dog. Because Jenny thinks she's sad without one."

"She *is* sad without one," Jenny said, her voice a bit whiny.

"Okay, we'll get out of your hair," Edith said, and kissed him quickly.

He walked them to the office door. His client, a woman in her fifties, watched them leave, a sad smile on her face. Then she looked up to Anton, who waved her into the office.

It would be a challenge, he knew, to be fully present in this meeting. To listen, keeping his mind off Edith's sudden news. But he would have to try.

"Your family?" she asked as she sat in front of his desk.

"Yes."

"It's a lovely family."

"Thank you."

"You should feel very fortunate."

"I do," Anton said. "Not a day goes by when I don't."

——

The girl, Yvette, was sitting at the bar when they arrived. Crying.

She looked up suddenly when she saw them. As if they had startled her.

"It's just a soda," she said, nodding down toward her glass. She wiped her eyes with her hands and sniffled. "I'm sorry. I don't want you to think of me like this. You must think I'm some kind of emotional basket case."

Anton exchanged a glance with his wife, and they both smiled.

"What?" Yvette asked. She was obviously watching their reactions.

"Nothing about you," Edith said. "It's just that I'm always saying that to Anton."

"Oh," the girl said, and sniffled again. "That makes me feel better. More . . . normal."

"Why were you crying?" Jenny asked. She had her small hand in Anton's, and had only been staring until that point.

Yvette didn't answer.

"She's going to have a baby," Edith said. "And when a woman is going to have a baby, it makes her emotional. But I'm sorry." She directed the last sentence to Yvette. "Maybe I shouldn't have answered for you."

Silence reigned for a time. Then Yvette began to cry openly.

"I thought he loved me," she said. "I'm such an idiot. But you don't want to hear about that. Let's get a table, and we'll talk about happier things."

———

"So Jenny is your adopted daughter?" Yvette asked.

She was buttering a roll, and she had her head bent so far forward that her long, straight hair swept across her arms. Anton kept expecting to see the ends of it land in the butter.

Edith passed the rolls to Anton while she answered. "Technically we're fostering her. But the adoption is in process."

"How long have you had her?"

"About six months," Edith said. Then she added, "It's slow."

"I know," Yvette said. "I've heard that. That's why I don't want to put anybody through that. All that red tape. Especially the baby. That's why I want to pick a family, and then when the baby's born, I don't even want to see it. I'm not calling it an it. I just don't know whether to say he or she. I don't want to see it until it's already part of a new family because it'll only break my heart. I want to have a family picked out and the nurses can put the baby in *their* arms right from the start and it'll just be so much simpler that way."

Anton was breaking open and buttering a roll. It involved steadying it with the outside of his prosthetic, so the process drew a certain amount of attention. Yvette was watching him in apparent fascination.

"It's not quite that easy," he said. "But easi*er*, absolutely. There should still be an attorney involved."

"I can sign the papers before I have the baby. Wait. I thought *you* were an attorney."

"I am. But I don't know anything about adoption law. But it's fine. I can find somebody who does. And we'll take care of all those expenses. I mean . . . if you choose us, we will. I didn't mean to get ahead of myself."

He took a bite of the roll, holding it in his left hand, and dropped the prosthetic back into his lap again. It was a relief, because she had been staring at it.

"I didn't know about *that*," she said, pointing to her own right hand. "When I saw you in the hall you must've been wearing gloves. Or had your hands in your pockets. Or . . . hand. You know what I mean. Is it hard to do things? Because with a baby you have to do a lot of things."

Anton swallowed hard. For a moment, he felt their objective slipping away. He felt Edith tighten at his side. She wasn't touching him in any way, but he knew her well enough to sense the shift in her energy. As he opened his mouth to answer, he found himself thinking, *Seriously? We're going to lose the baby over my hand? Like I haven't been through enough just being without it?*

"Not at all," he said. "I can do everything I need to do. I lost it when I was pretty young. Only seventeen. So I've had a lot of time to adjust. You learn how to do everything you need."

"Anton is only thirty-four," Edith said, her voice a little fast and desperate. "He's very strong and has lots of energy. We both do. We're both up for this."

But Yvette did not appear to be paying attention to her. "How did you lose it?"

"I was trying to save my brother's life."

Yvette covered her wide-open mouth with one hand, pantomiming her shock. Then she moved the hand and said, "But you didn't?"

"Didn't save him? No. Sadly, I was not able to save him."

"But you lost your hand trying?"

"Yes."

For a maddening length of time, no one spoke. Anton watched Jenny spear little tubes of pasta with her fork and chew with her mouth half-open. He tried to read Edith's tension without looking over at her.

Finally, finally, Yvette spoke. "If that's true, what you just told me, then you're a hero."

"It's true," Edith said.

"Then you're a hero. To do that for somebody you love? That's a hero. So that does it, then. That decides it. I want to give my baby to you."

———

They walked down the street together in the dark. Strangely slowly, hand in hand. Jenny was riding on Anton's shoulders. He was using his right arm to secure her legs to his chest, for safety. She was stroking his prosthetic hand, as though it soothed her. She never had before, so now Anton wondered if it was connected in her mind with heroism.

"Penny for your thoughts," Edith said, breaking the stillness.

"I was just wondering why my parents never treated me like a hero. I always got this vague sense that they considered me part of the mess and tragedy of the whole thing."

"I'm sorry. You got more than your share of bad breaks." They walked in silence for a time, then she added, "You might want to see them sooner or later. I mean, it's up to you. But just so you always have that sense that you did your best with them."

"I've thought about it."

"You don't have to bring the kids."

"I would definitely not be bringing the kids. So . . . you seem . . . happy. But not really surprised. Was this another one of those things you knew was meant to be?"

"Pretty much," she said, and gave his hand a squeeze.

"When did you know?"

"Early."

"Like when you first talked to her about it?"

"Like when she started showing."

"How do you do that?"

"No idea."

They reached their apartment building and unlocked the outer door. Anton ducked down getting into the elevator, so Jenny wouldn't hit her head. "Waiting for a shoe to drop?"

"Not really," she said. "I just feel happy."

———

They had been standing in the kitchen talking quietly, leaning on the counter, for several minutes when they realized Jenny had been in her room for too long.

"I'll go check on her," Edith said.

She walked to the door of their daughter's bedroom and just stood, staring. As though she couldn't believe what she saw. Anton ran down the hall to her side. He looked in at Jenny. She was sitting on the edge of the bed, hands neatly in her lap. Staring at the rug. On either side of her was a paper grocery sack filled with the little girl's belongings. Not all of them, of course, because they couldn't possibly all fit anymore. But Anton recognized a yellow dress that she had owned when she arrived.

For a moment Anton wondered why they hadn't noticed her coming into the kitchen for the paper bags. Then he decided these were the original ones. Somehow she had stored them in her room all this time without anyone noticing.

"Honey," Edith said. "What are you doing?"

"Getting ready to go." She did not raise her eyes.

"Where are you going?"

"I don't know. Back to the place, I guess."

"But you don't like it there," Anton said.

"No," Jenny said.

"So why go there?"

"Because you're adopting that baby now. Everybody wants babies. I know that from the place. People always want babies."

Edith went to her, and sat with her on the bed. "Honey, did you think we were adopting a baby *instead* of you?"

No answer.

"Honey, we're adopting a baby to be your little brother. Or sister. Not instead of you. In addition to you." She raised her eyes to Anton, and they looked desperate. "Holy cow," she said. "Did we mess this up or what?"

"We forgot to explain it to her. We forgot to look at her and see it. Honey. Jenny. Are you okay with having a little brother or sister?"

Jenny nodded almost imperceptibly.

"But we still want you!" Edith said, almost too stridently.

"But you didn't adopt me yet."

"But we're trying! We're doing everything we can to hurry it along. It takes a long time to adopt a child. There's lots of paperwork and legal mumbo jumbo. I thought you knew that."

Silence.

Then Jenny said, "I figured you weren't sure."

Edith lost it then, and began to cry. Anton sat on the bed, on the other side of their daughter, so they could talk it out. Fix what they had broken.

———

"She's asleep," Edith said, joining him in the kitchen. "Finally." She reached for the glass of wine he had poured for her. "Heartbreaking. Utterly heartbreaking. If you thought it couldn't get any worse, I helped her unpack those two bags. She'd saved the bags she'd brought her belongings in when she first showed up. Like it had occurred to her that she might be needing them again. And the only things she'd packed were the things she brought. Nothing we bought for her. Like she thought she didn't get to keep any of the new things."

"That makes my chest hurt," he said, rubbing a spot over his heart.

"Tell me about it. I'm just sick over the whole thing."

"You think she believed us? And felt better?"

"I think so. But, wow. That really shook me up. I started thinking maybe we shouldn't even be allowed to raise children. That was such a colossal mistake. I lost track of her. I mean, we brought her with us. To discuss it. I knew where she physically was. But I lost track of what she was hearing. Whether she understood. Or whether she needed help understanding. Who *does* that, Anton?"

He set down his wineglass and took her into his arms. It took her a few moments to soften and dissolve, and to hold him in return.

"We're rookies," he said, close to her ear. "We've only been parenting for six months. Most people with five-year-olds have five years' worth of experience."

"But she deserves better."

"Then we'll learn to do better. We're doing better than her first mom. We're doing better than *my* mom."

She snorted a bitter bark of a laugh against his shoulder, and he knew she would be okay. Given time. "Maybe I'm being too hard on myself," she said.

"Parents make mistakes. We just need a lot more experience."

# Chapter Twenty-Three

*Include Us*

Marlene slammed the door of the conference room open. All the meeting attendees jumped.

"Mr. Addison-Rice," she barked. "Code red."

Anton looked to the faces around him, but silently. Almost apologetically.

Laura was the first to speak. "Well, don't just sit there looking at us, Anton. Go!"

Anton went.

———

He flew down the street, his jacket blowing out behind him. His chest began to ache, but he didn't stop running. He kept one eye on the traffic, in case a cab started looking like a better option. But the cars and cabs were stalled in a dense pattern of gridlock, and running felt like the only answer.

By the time he saw Jenny's school at the end of the block, he felt nearly desperate to stop, lean on his knees, and gasp for air. He didn't stop. He could breathe while the office staff pulled her out of her kindergarten class. For the moment he had to keep running.

Fortunately the office was on the first floor.

The woman behind the desk looked up at him and seemed quite alarmed, as though Anton might need her to call an ambulance for him immediately.

"Anton Addison-Rice," he said, but it came out impossibly muted and obscured.

"I'm sorry?"

She had a legal pad on the desk in front of her, a pen in her hand. He turned the pad around and reached his left hand out for the pen, which she quickly handed over.

"Anton Addison-Rice," he scribbled. "Need Jenny from kindergarten."

He turned the pad back to face her. Her face remained in a frown as she struggled to read his scrawled handwriting. Then it suddenly lit up. "Oh, the baby's coming!"

Anton could only nod. But he was grateful to be understood at last. And he could feel his own face light up as well.

The baby was coming.

———

They rode the subway together, Jenny sitting in perfect silence at his right side. He had one arm draped over her shoulder, because the world seemed unpredictable to him, and he wanted to protect her from it. She had taken to absentmindedly stroking the plastic of his prosthetic, as she tended to do. As if it were a magic lamp, or otherwise contained superpowers.

When she finally spoke, it startled him out of his thoughts. "So is it a brother or a sister?"

"We don't know."

"You said it was here."

"I said the baby was coming."

"Why don't we know boy or girl if it's coming?"

"Because we have to see it first. When a baby comes out of its mommy, then you can just look down and see—boy or girl. But until you see the baby, you don't know."

"Oh." She sounded disappointed. As if the whole birth experience was not measuring up to her expectations.

They rode in silence for a few minutes more. Anton was beginning to feel lulled by the motion of the train car, and the clacking of its wheels on the tracks. Now and then the lights of the car would flash off and then on again. Jenny seemed to find it concerning.

"Why are you scared?" she asked after a time.

It was a surprising question. At least, from a five-year-old it seemed surprising. He found himself sitting with it, weighing and balancing his feelings. "Am I scared?" It was a perfectly ingenuous question.

"You seem scared."

"Well . . . a baby is a lot of responsibility. But maybe that's too big a word."

"I know what responsibility is."

"You do?"

"I think so. It means what you're supposed to do, and doing it right. Was *I* a lot of responsibility? Was *I* scary?"

"A little bit. Not as much, though. The younger the child, the more they need taking care of. You knew how to hold your own head up. And walk without falling down. And drink from a cup without choking."

"So that's good about me."

"Very."

That seemed to satisfy her, and lighten her mood.

"Oh," he said suddenly. "This is our stop."

—

Anton couldn't run anymore. Especially not with Jenny riding on his shoulders, her hands on either side of his temples like blinders on a carriage horse. So he just walked as briskly as possible down the street and into the hospital lobby.

The woman behind the desk grunted at him without even looking up.

"Yvette Kressler," he said.

She blinked a few times, still looking at a list on the desk in front of her. She did not seem to have registered his words.

"Maternity ward. My wife is up there with her now. We need to go up and see her."

The woman looked up. Her eyes skirted past his face and up to Jenny, still perched on his shoulders. She frowned at the little girl. "No children under fourteen above the first floor."

Anton stood mute and stunned for a moment. "Why not?"

"They carry infectious diseases."

"So do grown-ups."

"They carry *more* infectious diseases."

"But—"

"Hospital policy."

Anton sighed. "Can you at least get a message to my wife that we're here?"

"I'm only allowed to page doctors. But if somebody comes through the lobby on their way up there, I'll ask them to take the message."

Anton sighed again. All the excitement of the day was draining out of him fast, leaving him discouraged and more than a little sad. He had thought they could be there for this moment. Be part of it. It was a moment that would never come again.

He lifted Jenny down from his shoulders and took her hand, and they walked to a seating area with vinyl couches.

"I guess we just sit for the time being," he said.

A woman of about forty on the couch across from them smiled sadly at Anton. "I couldn't help overhearing," she said. "I could watch your daughter while you go up."

Anton's mind ran in several directions at once. He wanted to jump at the idea. It would be such a relief to be able to join Edith upstairs on the maternity ward. But leave Jenny with a stranger? What if he came back down and they were gone? Or if they were there but Jenny seemed terrified to have been left?

"That's nice of you to offer," he said. "But what would really help is if you could go up to the maternity ward and tell my wife I'm here. Her name is Edith. If you find Yvette Kressler, that's where she'll be."

"I could do that. But if my husband comes to pick me up, you have to tell him where I've gone and ask him to wait."

"Will do. Thanks."

He watched her walk toward the elevators. Then he looked down at Jenny, who looked back at him. She smiled, but it was a scared, sad smile. Anton smiled in return, but it probably looked the same.

A child *was* a lot of responsibility. Even if she was already five.

—

He looked up to see Edith standing over him. He jumped to his feet. For a moment he couldn't read what he saw on her face. It was intense emotion, but he could not get a feel for whether it seemed intensely good or intensely bad.

She placed a hand on each of his cheeks, and her hands felt dry and warm. "It's a boy," she said in an awed whisper.

"Healthy?"

"Absolutely. Eight pounds two ounces and perfect in every way."

"So we have a boy and a girl. Just like you wanted."

She nodded, seeming unable to speak.

"And Yvette didn't change her mind."

Edith shook her head, clearly holding back exhausted tears.

"She had the nurses put him in your arms and didn't even look at him, just like she said."

Edith nodded, still mute and tearful.

"When can we take him home?"

She only shrugged.

"Okay," he said. "I'll see what I can find out."

Edith seemed to gather herself, almost shake herself, to find words. "And I'll see if I can bring him down here for just a minute. Or even bring him somewhere where you could see him through glass. Or . . . I don't know. I'll try."

"Jenny!" Anton said suddenly, remembering Jenny. "You have a little brother!"

"Oh," Jenny said. "Okay." She didn't seem elated. Neither did she seem to mind.

———

They stepped into the apartment with the baby the following morning, while Jenny was away at kindergarten. Anton was holding him with almost ridiculous care, staring down into his sleeping face. His eyes appeared hooded, the skin bluish at the lids. He had tiny soft hairs between his eyebrows and his hairline, and a perfectly shaped nose with a round bulb at the end. And plump, full cheeks. Anton could not stop staring.

He carried the baby over the threshold with a certain energy. It reminded him of carrying a bride over the threshold, which he had not thought to do with Edith. It meant something. It meant the child was home, and was theirs.

They walked into the master bedroom with him, and Anton set him gently in the crib they had placed near their own bed. They watched him sleep in perfect silence for several minutes, the dog wagging continuously at Anton's side.

"We should move to a bigger place," he said, keeping his voice soft.

"Three bedrooms would be nice," she whispered. "But can we afford it?"

"I could pick up some extra clients. I think we could manage it. What would you think about getting out of the city? Maybe someplace in New Jersey or Connecticut? With a backyard full of grass for Hannah and the kids."

"You'd have to commute on the train."

"People do it all the time. I'd manage. I could have a telescope again. There's still dark sky out there somewhere."

"It *would* be nice."

"What are we going to name him? We haven't talked about it."

"No," she said. "I didn't want to talk about it until I knew he was real. I have an idea for a name. But I think maybe you won't like it."

"Try me. Just not Anton, because that's too hard on a kid."

"I was thinking Leo. It was my father's name. But if you don't like it . . ."

"Leo is fine," he said. "I like Leo. It's strong, like a lion. And it's a constellation. How can I not like that?"

———

They were sitting at the kitchen table drinking coffee and holding hands when the knock came at the door. Well, Edith was doing both. Anton had given her his left and did not wish to take it back, so his coffee was only sitting on the table getting cold.

They looked at each other, perfectly silent and still, waiting to see if the knock had wakened the baby. But Leo made no sound.

"I'll get it," she said.

He followed her to the door as if lost in a dream, Hannah wagging at his heels. Because life had taken on a dreamlike quality. Because he now lived in a fairy tale.

When she opened the door, he saw Mrs. Hazelton standing on their welcome mat. And, because he assumed she had come to tell them that Jenny's adoption was final, or ready to finalize, he fell even more deeply into his fairy tale. Even though, in retrospect, he would realize he'd had to ignore the look in her eyes to do so.

"May I come in?"

They walked with her into the living room, where she sat with her hands neatly folded on her skirt. Anton perched on the arm of a reclining chair. Edith stood. It was dawning on him, and he guessed on her as well, that this might not be a happy visit.

"I wanted to talk to you in person," she said. "So I'm glad you're both here."

"Is the adoption ready to be finalized?" Edith asked. But her voice sounded tight.

"We were right at that point, yes. But now something has come up."

Anton felt himself falling and spinning, as if he were a feather floating to the bottom of a deep well. Mrs. Hazelton was still speaking, but her voice sounded far away.

"Jenny's birth mother knows the adoption was about to go through. She's been calling. She's been sober for two months. She feels like she has control of her problems now."

"She wants to see her?" Edith asked, clearly trying to minimize the gravity of the news.

"She wants Jenny back."

In the silence that followed those four horrible words, Anton hit the bottom of the well. He no longer felt like a feather. A feather would have touched down softly.

He reached out for Edith's hand, but she darted away and began pacing.

"Well, she can't *have* her back," Edith barked. And paced. "She signed away her rights."

"Yes she did," Mrs. Hazelton said.

"So that's that."

"I wish that was that. But she'll take it to court. She doesn't have much money, so you'll have better attorneys."

"But the judge will see that she signed away her rights."

"But she'll say she did that for the good of the child. Because she couldn't take care of her. And now she feels she can."

"But the judge will see how much we love her."

"Yes. And he'll also see how desperate her birth mother is to have her back. And the courts tend to skew toward keeping birth mothers together with their children. It's not an absolute. Just a bias. I'm not saying she'll win. But I have to be honest and say you need to start preparing yourself for the fact that she might."

Edith stopped pacing. Anton watched her, helplessly, and felt as though he were watching all of something drain out of her. Quickly, like water from the bathtub when you've pulled the plug. It might have been her life force. It might only have been all her hope.

She plunked down hard in the chair next to Anton's perch. He put his arm around her, but she didn't seem to notice.

"But . . . that's not fair." Her voice sounded five years old. As if she were channeling her beloved Jenny.

"I realize this comes as quite a blow," Mrs. Hazelton said. "We hate it when things like this happen, but sometimes they do. Child protection can be messy. If you decide you want to fight this, we'll help in any way we can. But it'll be a long and contentious battle and it will be expensive. And it'll take a lot out of everyone involved. Battles like this tend to be particularly hard on the child. It's almost as though each set of guardians have hold of one of their hands and won't stop pulling. And ultimately the child feels pulled apart. But I'm not trying to influence your thinking. I'm just telling you what I've learned in my experience. I'm sorry to be the bearer of such dismal news." She pulled to her feet and smoothed out her skirt. "I'm going to go and give you two time to think and discuss."

Anton walked her to the door.

"Thank you for coming over in person," he said as he let her out. But his voice sounded unfamiliar to his own ears. As if he'd become someone different since she'd arrived.

She looked down at the welcome mat and frowned. Then she walked away.

Anton locked the door and joined Edith in the living room. She was still seated on the edge of the recliner, staring out the window. Except the curtains were closed. Her face looked utterly blank to Anton.

"We'll fight it," he said.

She looked in his direction without quite connecting. She opened her mouth to speak and began to cry. "We can't," she said, as the tears spilled.

"Of course we can. Why can't we?"

"Because we have to do what's best for Jenny. Even if it doesn't include us."

Anton stood a moment, feeling dizzy. Then he sat on the arm of the chair again. "We don't have to do that. Just because I did it that once."

"You do it all the time."

"We don't have to. It's hard and you don't owe it to anybody."

"But I *do*," she said, the words bent by quiet sobs. "That's exactly it. I *owe* it. When the world does well by you, you have to do well in return. I can't just take unselfish love and give back crap. Well. I could. But what would that make me?"

"Maybe it's best for her to stay with us."

"Maybe. We'll go pick her up from school and talk to her."

It was a devastating thought. To imagine seeing her. Telling her. Asking her to make a decision so earth shattering for all involved. But it could not be avoided. They had signed on for this responsibility, and now had to do whatever was required to see it through.

They were halfway to the door when Edith said it. "We're forgetting something."

"What are we forgetting?" But before she could answer, it clicked in. "Oh. Right. You want to go pick up Jenny? Or you want to stay here with the baby?"

He almost said, "Leo." ". . . stay here with Leo." But in the moment, he couldn't bring himself to fully own the child sleeping in the next room. Maybe he would find the courage later. But in the moment it only felt like setting himself up for another loss.

"You go, please," Edith said. "I'll stay here with Leo. But don't talk to her. Just bring her home. We'll talk to her together."

"Of course."

As he walked out the door he admired Edith, even more so than usual. For having the courage to claim Leo as her own at a time like this.

# Chapter Twenty-Four

## Hard Sometimes

They walked down the street together, Jenny holding his left hand. The traffic noise was bothering him in a way it normally didn't. He wondered if the simple act of setting his sights on a move to the country had eroded his ability to tolerate city life—as though he already lived in Connecticut in his head, and wasn't used to the din.

It struck him that they might not need an extra room anymore. He felt it in his gut as though someone had punched him.

"Why are we sad?" Jenny asked, her voice small.

"Are we sad?"

"Seems like we are." He didn't answer for a time, so she asked it again, a different way. "Is something bad?"

He had promised not to talk to her without Edith, but neither did he want to lie.

"I'm not sure about bad. I have stuff on my mind. We'll talk when we get home."

"Okay."

She didn't say more. Or ask more. Anton had to assume that children hated, as much as adults did, the experience of being told there's something to talk about but having to wait.

If she hated it, she did not complain.

———

"So, I realize it's a hard thing to have to decide," Edith said.

Jenny sat in a stuffed chair and stared intently at the carpet. She had her hands cupped over her tiny kneecaps, which were covered in patterned white tights. She seemed determined not to meet anyone's eyes.

"And there may be more to the decision than just what sounds best to you," Edith continued. "We have to think about where you'll be safe. Where you'll be happy. But we need to start by hearing you say what you want."

The girl seemed aware of both sets of eyes watching her. Hannah slunk over and set her narrow chin on Jenny's knee, and Jenny leaned over and kissed the end of the dog's snout. But she did not look at them. And she did not speak.

"So what do you want?" Edith asked, her voice heavy with pain.

Jenny only shrugged.

"You can talk to us," Anton said. "You can tell us what you really think."

Jenny shrugged again.

"Do you understand the question?" Edith asked.

No reaction. They waited in silence for a moment or two. Then the baby began to fuss in his crib in the next room.

"Oh," Edith said. "I have to go tend to Leo. It's too much for a five-year-old. We shouldn't be asking her to do this, Anton. It's too hard for her. I don't know what we do now."

"You go look after Leo. I'm going to take Jenny out for ice cream."

Jenny's head jerked up expectantly at the suggestion. Then she looked down again.

Edith stood still, staring at him. But the fussing was quickly becoming full-blown crying.

"Okay," she said. "Fine. If you think it'll help."

———

He watched Jenny stare at her strawberry ice cream. She was not *only* staring at it. She was spooning it into her mouth. But she never took her eyes off the shrinking scoop in the bowl in front of her.

"Life is hard sometimes," Anton said. "Isn't it?"

Jenny offered a barely perceptible nod.

"You know what you want to do. Don't you?"

Another faint nod.

"Why didn't you say so?"

She surprised Anton by speaking. "She doesn't want me to say that."

"I think she wants you to say what's true."

"No." She shook her head. Spooned up another bite of ice cream. Spoke with her mouth full. "She wants me to say I want to stay with her and you."

"But you want to go live with your mother."

Another barely perceptible nod.

Anton felt the root beer float in his belly. Suddenly it felt dense and weighty. Undigested. Almost as though it might choose not to stay down. He would have to go home and tell Edith. It would be the hardest thing he'd ever had to say to her. But who could blame the child? It was a woman who had shared a body with her. A woman she'd known for years, not months. Of course she wanted her mother. But he couldn't think of a way to say it that would not be a slap in the face to Edith. She knew the advantages of birth mothers, and she would never be one. And he didn't want to be cruel.

"When you finish your ice cream, we'll go home and talk to her again."

"She doesn't want to hear that."

"Then I'll be the one to tell her."

That seemed to settle the girl, and put her more at ease. Anton thought he heard her breathing in a way that was looser and deeper than he'd seen before. Maybe ever.

———

"There's more involved than just what she wants," Edith said. Her voice was almost too composed, but she couldn't stop the tears. She was pacing with the baby in front of the living room windows, swinging him back and forth to soothe his fussing. Anton could see tears falling onto the blanket in which Leo was wrapped. "Kids want things that are bad for them. We have to make sure she'll be safe."

"That goes without saying," Anton said.

"But I need to *say* these things!" she fairly bellowed.

With that she stopped pacing and swinging. Both mother and baby stood still by the window, openly crying. Anton walked to her. Wrapped his arms around her as best he could without squishing Leo. But the baby seemed comforted by the close, dark space between them. His crying faded to a series of comfortable noises.

"Shh," Anton whispered into her ear. "Please let's not let Jenny hear us fighting."

He had set Jenny up in her bedroom with a coloring book and crayons.

"I'm not fighting with *you*," she said through sobs. "You know that, right? I just hate the world right now."

He said nothing. Just held them both.

"How will we know if she's safe?" Edith whispered into his ear. "What if her birth mother goes right back to her old ways?"

"I don't think they just give a child back to a mother . . . you know . . . after they've been taken away . . . and then walk away and hope for the best. I think they keep looking in to see how things are going. If she slips and isn't taking care of Jenny, maybe we could get her back."

"Will you find out?" Her voice was small, like a child's.

"Of course."

He reluctantly let them go. He looked down to see that Leo had fallen asleep.

———

"I'm afraid I said too little when I was there," Mrs. Hazelton told him over the phone. "I was aware of the impact of my . . . news, and I wanted to leave you two alone to talk. Frankly, I didn't think you'd make the choice to allow her to go home. So I haven't filled you in on another big choice you'll have to make. Even if there's no court battle, we're in no way prepared to place Jenny back in the home yet. There will be a period during which the birth mother will have to demonstrate that she's capable of caring for a child."

"How long does that usually take?"

He could see Edith watching him, but indirectly. He could tell by her expression that she was straining to listen. She was standing by the window, making a show of looking down onto the street. But Anton imagined there could be a parade of dancing elephants going by out there without capturing her attention.

"At least a year."

"A year!" Anton repeated. He hadn't meant to. It just popped out. He wasn't sure how to take the news. Was he glad to hear this or not? His gut and brain felt muddled, and it was impossible to tell.

He saw Edith turn to look directly at his face.

"Or longer. There are a lot of factors. We don't place a child back in a home unless we're as sure as it's possible to be. It might be too heart-breaking to keep her for another year and then have to lose her. If you choose to have us place her in a different foster home in the meantime, I'll certainly understand."

"Can you please hold on a minute?" He covered the mouthpiece with the fingers of his left hand. "It could be a year or more until they're sure enough to place her back with her birth mother. And we have to decide if we want to keep her that long and then lose her, or if we want her placed in a different foster home in the meantime. What do I tell her?"

"You tell her there will be no other foster homes for that little girl. She'll be right here."

"Are you sure? You sure that won't break your heart?"

"Of course it'll break my heart. But that's the way it's going to be."

"You don't want more time to think about it?"

"There's nothing to think about. We take care of her as long as we can."

Anton took his fingers off the mouthpiece. "She'll be here with us," he said.

———

They went to bed that night without having discussed it again.

They lay awake, Anton watching the side of her face in the soft light through the bedroom window. It was obvious that they were not sleeping, and not likely to sleep, and the weight of holding it all in was too much for him.

"You know," he said, "we could keep her for a year and her birth mother might not get her back. She might not do well enough."

"I've thought about that." Her voice was calm, almost emotionless. But Anton knew she was not without emotions. More likely she was worn down by them. "But I can't really bring myself to lie here and hope for somebody to fail."

Anton smiled slightly. Almost more on the inside. Because he was so happy to be married to her. A memory had come rushing back.

Something she'd said to him shortly after they'd met up again. "You're an unselfish man." She had touched his cheek. He remembered the words so clearly. He could almost feel the wintry coldness of her hand. "You have a right to want as good for yourself."

"Hard to know what to hope for," he said. "Life is just hard sometimes."

She never replied.

"If we do end up having to send her home . . . would you want to adopt another girl?"

Edith shook her head with surprising vehemence, considering how tired and dispirited she seemed. "Absolutely not. Jenny is our daughter. Wherever she is. Whether she gets to live with us or not, she's still our daughter. She can't possibly be replaced."

—

They walked to school together, Jenny and Anton. Hand in hand. She had taken to walking on his right side, because she seemed to prefer holding hands with his prosthetic.

For the first few blocks they didn't speak.

Then Jenny said, "When do I get to see her?"

"Your birth mom?"

She only nodded.

"Well, I'm not sure. It could be a long time. Mrs. Hazelton needs to make sure she's really better before she can let you go back. And that she stays better. That takes time."

"But when can I *see* her?" Jenny asked, sounding a bit whiny.

"Oh. You mean for a visit?"

"Right."

"I'm not sure."

"Can you ask?"

They stopped at a corner before crossing the street. Waited for the light to turn green, though no cars were coming.

"Yeah. I could ask Mrs. Hazelton."

"You have to ask Mama, too."

Jenny had taken to calling Edith "Mama." Possibly a way of differentiating Edith, in her mind and speech, from her other mother.

"That's true," Anton said.

He dreaded having to bring it up. But it seemed important to Jenny, and not an unreasonable favor to ask. So he would.

"She might not want that," Jenny said.

"I guess we'll see."

The light turned. They walked again. Anton could smell the sewer each time they walked across the grates. It made moving to the country seem like a more and more desirable option.

"So you'll ask her?" Jenny asked, her voice anxious.

"Yes. I'll talk to her."

"Good. You're good at that."

———

By the time they went to bed that night, he had broached the subject with Edith, but not gotten a firm answer. But he trusted her to tell him, in her time.

They lay together in silence, not talking. Not sleeping. Not touching. It struck Anton that they had been spending quite a bit of time lately doing just that—nothing.

Edith spoke, softly but suddenly. "What if we send Jenny there for a visit and that woman never returns her?"

He dared to move closer to her and wrap one arm around her, pressing up close to her back. She didn't move away.

"I don't think we just send her there. That's not how I was picturing it. I figured it was more like . . . we arrange with Mrs. Hazelton for Jenny to have some supervised visits. You know. At . . . 'the place,' as Jenny calls it. Take her there and let her birth mom come visit, and then pick her up later."

He wanted to ask, "Would that be okay?" Or something else that would force an answer. But he didn't want to force an answer. He wanted to get one from her, but not by force. The conversation fell away again. Anton felt almost as though he could hear her thinking.

"On one condition. Are you willing to be the one to take her there? Because I don't want to meet that woman. I don't even want to see her. Ever."

"I'll take her."

Edith never replied. They went back to doing nothing. Not talking, not sleeping. Their bodies were still touching, though, which seemed like an improvement.

He took a few minutes to gather up his courage to ask a question that had been on his mind since the adoption blew apart. "Are we going to be okay?"

She sighed. "Oh, I don't know, Anton. I suppose. It's hard on both of us, but people get through things. What choice do they have?"

"That's not what I meant. I didn't mean are you going to be okay and am I going to be. I mean are *we* going to be okay? *Us.*"

She rolled over to face him, and took him in her arms, and he returned the favor. He wished he could see her eyes, her face, in that moment, but it was too dark. Once she turned away from the window, her expressions were lost to him.

She kissed him on the mouth, a soft, almost thoughtful kiss.

"Anton. If I made a list of all the things in life in the order I was willing to give them up, you'd be the last entry. Right after oxygen."

He felt himself exhale a breath he hadn't known he'd been holding. "Glad to hear that."

"I'm falling down on the job again, because I should have made sure you knew."

"Don't worry about it. Just get through this any way you can."

"No," she said. "Not good enough. *You're* how I'm able to get through this. I need to make sure you know it. To this very day I have no idea what I did to deserve you, Anton."

It made him feel a little shy, so he made a conversational turn. "Did this turn out to be the worst time in the world to adopt a baby?"

"No. Just the opposite. The best. He needs attention every minute, whether I feel like it or not. He gets me out of myself. I have to go on for him. It's perfect. Between him and you, I sometimes almost feel like I might get through this."

———

Anton took Jenny down to "the place" on foot, because he felt like a long walk might do both of them good. She held tightly to his prosthetic hand with both of her own.

"I just want to make sure you know you're not staying with her today," he said as they waited for a traffic light to turn.

"I'm staying with her some."

"Yes, some. An hour, or maybe an hour and a half. But then you're coming home to live with me and Mama some more."

"I *know* that," Jenny said, chastising him in her impatience.

"Just making sure."

"You only told me like *a hundred times.*"

They crossed the street. Walked a block in silence. Turned the corner, bringing the familiar building into view. The sight of it sank into Anton's belly like an undigested meal, sickening him. The day he and Edith had first seen the place had held so much promise. *But not every promise is kept,* he thought.

It struck him that this might be a mistake. Maybe he should never have agreed to this. Never brought her here. Maybe they should simply have kept her until they couldn't keep her a minute more.

"Why are we stopping?" Jenny asked, tugging at the prosthetic hand.

"Oh," Anton said. "Sorry. I didn't notice we had."

———

"So just leave her here with you?" he asked Mrs. Hazelton.

"Yes, I purposely asked her mother to come a little later. I thought you might be uneasy running into her. If I'm wrong, and you want to sit down and talk to her, let me know."

"No," Anton said. "That's okay."

"Come back and get Jenny about ten."

Anton turned his attention down to the girl, who looked equal parts excited and nervous. "You okay here without me?"

She nodded.

"Okay, then. I'm going to go now."

He turned and walked away without betraying his unease by looking back. He trotted down the stairs, out the front door, and onto the street, squinting into the light. He felt someone take hold of his prosthetic hand. He could feel the weight of someone tugging at it. He looked around to see that a small woman had grabbed him by it. Someone wanting money, he thought. Until she spoke.

"You're him, aren't you?"

"Who?"

"The husband. Of the . . . you know. The couple. Who've been looking after Jenny."

He took her in for a moment with new eyes. She was not at all what he had expected. She was neatly dressed, with her hair up in a careful style. She looked put together. Not like someone who would panhandle on the street. Also not like a woman who would have her child taken away, though Anton realized, to his shame, that he was wrong to think such situations followed a type. Still, she seemed mousy and shy, like someone who would be prudent about everything. Like a store clerk who was always polite, said little, and balanced her cash drawer to the penny at night. Or an accountant who was a bit too drab but did the job well.

As these thoughts ran through his head, he was able to see a dawning on her face regarding the hand she was holding.

"That one's not real," he said.

She immediately let it go. He did not care to touch her or be touched by her, but she seemed desperate for some kind of approval, so he reached out his left hand, which she took. He didn't let her keep it, though. Just squeezed and shook her hand, then made a point of taking his own back.

"I know I'm not supposed to come up to you or say anything," she said. "But I just wanted to say thank you. I couldn't believe it when Mrs. Hazelton said you weren't going to fight me on getting Jenny back. I just had to see for myself what kind of people could be so unselfish. I don't know why you decided it, but thank you."

"We just want what's best for Jenny."

"Unselfish, like I said. Look, I'll let you go now. I don't want it to be like I'm accosting you. If you don't want me talking to you, I'll go in now. I just wanted to say thank you, and that I won't let you down. And I won't let Jenny down. Again, I mean. And I hope you'll tell your wife I said thank you to her, too."

He did not mean to telegraph a reaction to her mention of Edith, but apparently he did.

"Unless she doesn't want to hear anything at all from me," she added, her eyes trained down to the pavement.

"I'll have to play that by ear," Anton said.

"I'll leave you alone now. Stop bothering you."

She trotted up the stairs of the building and disappeared inside.

—

He sat at the breakfast table with Edith, drinking coffee and eating the omelet she had made. At first they didn't talk, and Anton thought she was silently asking him not to. But in time he decided it was too important to leave unsaid. It was rare for him to go against what she seemed to want, but it felt warranted in this case.

"I'm actually thinking . . . you might want to meet her."

He watched the muscles around her mouth and eyes tighten.

"Why would I want that?"

"She's just . . . different than what you're picturing."

"How do you know what I'm picturing?"

"Good point. She's different from how *I* pictured her. She's just . . . very . . . real."

"I pictured her as real," Edith said, seemingly to joke away his message.

"I think she might be even more real than you're picturing."

They ate in silence for an awkward length of time. Three or four minutes, maybe.

Then Edith said, "Okay, I'll think about it."

Leo began fussing in the bedroom. She had to go to him, leaving her food to get cold.

——

More than a year went by, and if she thought more about it, she never said as much to Anton.

# SPRING OF 1983

## THE LOCKET

# Chapter Twenty-Five

*Secret*

They were rushing to get ready, and to get the babysitter up to speed. Anton was running through the huge country house, up and down the stairs, carrying carefully packed boxes of Jenny's belongings and leaving them in a pile by the big oak door.

She had so many belongings after living with them for a year and a half. They had bought her so much. Now there were deliverymen coming to get it all, so Jenny could take it with her. And they had a train into the city to catch.

Anton dropped the last box by the door, nearly tripping over the dog, then looked around the house for Edith. He found her in the huge, skylighted country kitchen. She was making notes for Leo's babysitter. It would be the first time they'd left him with anyone, and Anton knew it was a situation—one of many—that was causing her stress.

He tapped his fingers on the kitchen doorframe to get her attention. "How're you holding up in here?"

"Don't make me hold still and think about it, or I might find out."

"We've got ten minutes to get out the door if we want to catch that train."

"If we're late then we just are."

"Wouldn't it be better to get this over with?"

She sighed, and set down her pen. "I suppose. Where's Jenny?"

"Up in her room."

"But it's empty. There's nothing up there."

"I know. But she wanted to say goodbye to her room."

The phone rang. It made them both jump.

"I'll get it," Anton said, and grabbed up the receiver.

"Anton," a gruff male voice said.

"Right. Who is this?"

"It's your father."

Anton mouthed the words to Edith. *"My father."* She watched in horrified fascination. She seemed to be expecting bad news. Her face registered what he was only just beginning to feel: something big must be happening, because his parents did not call. They had, up until that moment, respected his wishes and stayed out of his life.

Meanwhile his father was berating him on the other end of the line. "You don't even know your own father when he calls on the phone? Who doesn't know his own father?"

"We don't talk much," Anton said.

"And whose fault is that?"

"Did you just call to give me grief? Because it's a bad morning over here. We have a lot going on and we don't need any more grief, thank you."

"Your mother is dying."

Anton stood a moment, processing the words. Waiting for feelings to come up and fill in the spaces around them. But he only felt numb. "Of what?"

"Is that really the most important question? Look. Anton. I just called because I thought you might want to see her. We've all had our differences, but maybe we can put them behind us at a time like this. But if you want to see her, come soon."

"Is she in the hospital?"

"No. She's at home."

"Why isn't she in the hospital?"

"There's nothing they can do for her at the hospital. She wanted to be home."

"Okay. Well, it can't be this morning. Too much important stuff going on this morning." He glanced at Edith, who was clearly listening. Could he really bring himself to leave her alone on the day they lost Jenny? "It might not even be today."

"Then you might not see her. You're rolling the dice, my friend."

"Why didn't you tell me sooner?"

"Because *somebody* said to stay out of his life and not get in touch."

"But—" Anton began. He wanted to say, "But you did get in touch. You knew you'd call once, when time was running out. So why not sooner?" But none of it felt useful. "Never mind. Please tell her I'll come. If it was any other day I'd come now. But I'll come as soon as I can."

His father hung up without saying goodbye. Anton let the receiver droop.

"You should go see her," Edith said.

"I'm not going to miss our last time with Jenny. I'm not going to make her think anything is more important than seeing her off."

"You might miss your chance with your mom. What if you always regret it?"

"I'm putting my own family first. Whatever happens, I'll live with that."

———

They rode the train, looking out the window—all three of them—until it dove underground and left them with nothing to see.

Jenny was the one who spoke. "Will you come see me?"

It was a question Anton had been dreading, and he knew Edith had been dreading it as well. He answered, to take Edith off the hook. "We might not be able to."

"Why not?"

"It might be against the rules."

"What rules?"

Edith roused herself from a seeming dream state and spoke. "It's up to your mother. We can only visit if she says we can."

Anton caught her eye. Her words were outside the boundaries they'd agreed to. She answered his look as though he had spoken.

"Well, I don't care. I won't let her think we don't care enough to come see her. If we don't get to, I want her to know why."

"I'll ask my mom," Jenny said.

Silence fell.

Then Jenny added, "Please don't be sad."

It brought Anton's sadness into such sharp focus that it was all he could do not to cry. But he didn't cry. He held it inside.

———

They turned the corner, and "the place" came into view—the drab-looking brick of the building, the play yard full of uncertain-looking children. It took effort for Anton to keep walking. He wanted to stop the world. Press a pause button on everything. The Earth would no longer turn. They would never have to go inside. The next part of life would never happen.

He glanced over at Edith, but she was betraying nothing of what she felt. She must have buried it deeply.

She stopped at the door and crouched to Jenny's level. "I'm not going to go in," she said. "I'm going to say goodbye to you here."

"Why?" Jenny asked, a little whiny.

"It's just better that way." Anton understood that Edith didn't want to run into Jenny's birth mom. Jenny likely did not. "But Daddy will go in with you. And we'll say our goodbye right here. I have a present for you."

She reached into her purse and took out a jewelry store box. Anton had not seen it before, or heard about it. This was all Edith. She opened the box and showed Jenny a gold locket on a chain.

Jenny reached out and touched it with one finger. As if it might not prove real.

"It's pretty."

"It's a locket. Do you know what a locket is?"

Jenny shook her head.

"It's like a holder for things. For secrets. You can put something inside it, and close it up, and wear it around your neck, and you have the secret with you all the time."

"Is there a secret in there now?" Jenny asked, her eyes wide.

"There is." Edith opened the locket, revealing a picture of their little family.

"It's us," Jenny said. "And baby Leo."

"So you can take us with you everywhere you go. And if you ever need to see us, we'll be right there. Right around your neck. But there's another secret. Don't tell anyone, and don't look unless you need to. Don't take the picture out. Leave it right where it is. But if you're ever in trouble, or you need us for any reason . . ." Anton heard her voice crack. But she pulled herself together. She was doing an amazing job of holding it in. ". . . I wrote our address and phone number on the back of the picture. Nobody needs to know except you. Just in case you need us."

"I won't tell," Jenny said.

"Good girl." Edith kissed her on the forehead, her lips locking and pausing, as though maybe the goodbye kiss never needed to end. Then she rose to her feet. Anton could see she was crying, but she turned her face away. "I'll be right here," she said.

Anton breathed deeply and walked the little girl—his daughter—inside. It struck him, though not for the first time, that she was his daughter. Fully and completely. She was Edith's, and his. They were a family. They had made her their own. And people are not supposed to have to give their daughters back. This was not the way the world was supposed to work.

He needed to say something to her. Some final words. But he had no idea what they should be. He had nothing prepared.

Anton was overwhelmed by the need to tell her everything she would need to know to grow up safely. How to navigate dating, and do well in school. How to make sense of life when it seemed random and cruel. How to be kind, and how to survive emotionally when others were not. But he didn't have much time.

Mrs. Hazelton met them at her office door. "Are you and your wife okay?" she asked.

"No." Anton got down on his knees to address his daughter. "I just want to say . . ." But what did he want to say? ". . . be patient with your mom."

"Why?"

"Because she's trying to do something really hard."

"What?"

"She's trying to quit drinking for good, which is hard. And raise you on her own. And . . . just . . . have a life."

"Is that hard? To have a life?"

"Oh yeah."

"Is it hard for you to have a life?"

"Very."

"I'm sorry," she said, and hugged him.

"You don't have to be sorry. Just be a good girl for your mom."

"I will."

"Bye, Jenny girl. We'll never forget you."

Anton rose and walked away. It was hard not to look back. But, as with all difficult things, he did it anyway.

—

He met Edith out front, and she was not crying. Her face was a mask, as though all emotion inside her was dead, or at least shackled. Imprisoned. He held her, but it brought no cracks in her armor.

"Go see your mom," she said into his ear.

"I need to get you home."

"I can take the train by myself."

"Don't you need me to be with you right now?"

"In the medium run, yes. But all I'm going to do now is go home and have the cry of the century. Put the baby down for his nap and drink a glass of wine, or three, and cry for hours. That's a pretty good solitary activity. You're right here in the city. Less than thirty blocks from their apartment. Go visit her and I'll see you later at home."

"If you're sure."

She kissed him firmly. He thought he felt everything through that kiss—all the heartbreak she was keeping inside. But when she pulled away, her face appeared composed.

He watched her walk away, a lead weight sinking deeper and deeper into his gut. Then he hailed a cab.

—

His mother was in bed, in the master bedroom. But if the familiar location had been subtracted, he might not have known her. She had lost what looked like half her body weight. Her hair was dry, straw-like. Her cheekbones protruded under skin that looked papery in its thinness. She had clearly been sick for a long time.

"Sit, Anton," she said, her voice a deep, familiar croak.

He pulled up a chair. For a moment they leaned closer together without talking. For the second time in less than an hour, Anton needed to say goodbye to an important person, and he had no idea what his last words should be. He had not prepared.

Then, after nearly a minute of silence, they both opened their mouths at the same time.

"What?" he asked.

"No, you go."

"Okay. I'm sorry for what I said to you."

"Which time?"

"The one you almost slapped me for."

"Right," she said. "I remember."

They fell into silence again. Anton thought he could see her gathering something in her head. But he had no idea what it was or when it might emerge.

"This may be hard for you to believe," she said, "but I adored your brother. Not more than you. But not less. I know you think I made a terrible mess of that situation. I'm not even saying you're wrong. But I did the best I could at the time. I'd like you to forgive me."

A wave of vertigo passed over him. He squeezed his eyes shut to keep the room from swaying. He felt a sickening sense that she'd asked him to come not because she loved him and wanted to see him, but because she wanted something from him. His absolution. It felt uncomfortable, but not surprising. It fit with who she had been his entire life.

"Okay," he said, his eyes still closed.

"Meaning what?"

"I forgive you."

"Really?"

Anton wanted to say, "Don't push your luck." He didn't. "I believe you gave the situation everything you had to give it. At the time. None of us really knew what to do to help him." *Though I would have let Uncle Gregor get him some professional help,* he thought. But he kept it to himself, because it was his last chance not to hurt her. "So I forgive you."

Truthfully, he didn't. He wasn't sure he ever could. But if he ever could, anytime in his life, it seemed a shame to miss his deadline for letting her know. So he borrowed from a future event that might or might not arrive, and gave her what she wanted. It felt less selfish than what he was genuinely feeling in the moment. It felt like a lie that served the greater good better than the truth could have done.

He wanted to say more, or for her to. But when he looked up at her face, he saw she had already slipped into a noisy, drugged sleep.

—

Edith was upstairs in the master bedroom when he got home, sitting in the big window seat, gazing at a view that consisted of first his carefully covered telescope on the rear balcony, then down to the barn below. She wasn't crying, but it was clear by her face that she had cried—a lot—since he'd last seen her. Hannah thumped her tail.

"Want some company?"

"On one condition. That you don't try to tell me I'll get over it."

"I wasn't going to say that."

He walked to her. She straightened up to allow him to sit behind her, then leaned back on his chest and sighed. He put his arms around her. To his mild surprise, she undid the straps of his prosthetic hand and tossed it lightly onto the bed. He never asked why.

"Because you don't think it's true?" she asked. "Or because you don't want to tell me something I don't want to hear?"

"I'm not a fan of the concept. 'Getting over it.' Makes loss sound like a brick wall, and like somehow you'll scramble over the top and drop down on the other side and keep going, and then it's all behind you. It never worked that way for me. Like Greg. Every day, my brother is still dead and my hand is still gone. How do you leave that in the past? It's not the past. It's my present-day reality, and it doesn't end."

"So if we don't get over it, what do we do?"

"Learn to live around it, I guess."

They stared out the window in silence. The scene was quiet and still, save for a light wind in the trees, and a gray squirrel jumping from branch to branch.

"We have a barn," she said. "We should own something that lives in barns."

"Maybe when Leo is old enough we can get him a pony."

"You think we'll ever get her back?"

"I don't know. Possibly."

"When you did your unselfish thing and let me go, you got me back."

"But it was a long fifteen years."

"I want you to promise me it'll happen if I wait. But I know you can't."

"If we wait twelve years, she'll be a legal adult. Maybe we can see her then."

"She'll have forgotten us," Edith said, and her voice shook with the words. Then her shoulders. Seconds later she seemed to pull herself back together.

"It's okay to cry," he whispered.

"I'm so exhausted from it, though. How was your visit with your mother?"

"Strange. She wanted me to forgive her."

"For something in particular?"

"Yeah. The big something."

"Did you?"

"I said I did."

"But you don't?"

"Not really. I'd like to, but I'm not quite there yet. But I figured maybe I will be eventually. And she doesn't have that kind of time."

"You never cease to amaze me," she said.

"In a good way?"

"Of course in a good way. I don't know what I'd do without you, Anton."

For a split second, Anton felt lucky. Because it was something they wouldn't need to find out. They had losses, but in that moment he was able to be deeply grateful for what was not lost.

Later he would feel the loss, and the gratitude would remain beyond his reach. But in the meantime, he had that moment.

# SUMMER OF 1995

## WE ALL GOT OLDER

# Chapter Twenty-Six

### Older

Anton was taking a meeting with a client when Marlene buzzed him. "Mr. Grable on the phone for you," she said through the intercom.

Anton grabbed up the receiver. He addressed the woman across the desk. "I apologize for this. Normally I wouldn't take a call during your time. But this is urgent. I'll keep it brief." Then, into the phone, "Martin." His heart hammered as he spoke.

"I think I got something," Martin said.

"I was hoping." He could barely breathe well enough to speak.

"Got a pen?"

"I do. Go." But he was still scrambling for a pen. He simply couldn't bear to wait to hear the news.

"She's going to college in Maryland. Towson. Housing on campus. I have no idea what her plans are for the summer. The semester ends after next week, so I wouldn't waste time if I were you."

Martin read him the address and room number of the dorm, and he scribbled it down.

"Thanks, Martin. Bill me."

"Lemme know how it works out. So I know whether to keep looking."

"Will do."

He hung up the phone and addressed his client. "Again, sorry. Please go on with what you were saying."

The problem was, she did. And Anton had to listen.

It wasn't easy.

—

Leo was lying on his belly on the living room rug when he got home, eating microwave popcorn. Doing his homework in front of the TV. Anton's ears were assaulted by a raucous laugh track. Leo had taken to wearing his hair down over his eyes, a waterfall of dark bangs to signal his membership in the difficult teenage years.

"Where's your mom?" Anton asked. But he couldn't be heard over the TV. He grabbed the remote and muted the volume.

"Hey!" Leo shouted. "I was watching that!"

"And what does she say about homework in front of the TV? Which is how I know she must not be home."

"She went into town to get groceries."

"Okay, give her a message for me."

"Sure. Whatever."

"No. Not 'whatever.' It's important. I have to drive down to Maryland. For business. I probably won't be back until tomorrow. I'm taking the car."

"She has the car."

"No, not *her* car. I'm taking *my* car."

"Whatever."

"It's important. You can't forget."

"I won't forget. Now could you put the show back on?"

Anton unmuted the volume on the TV. He looked down at his son and knew there was a fifty-fifty chance he would forget.

He wrote Edith a note, and left it on the kitchen table.

337 _ My Name is Anton

He called her from his car phone, somewhere along the I-95 south, through Pennsylvania. Just to be sure she'd seen the note.

"Hey," she said when she picked up the phone.

"Hey," he said, overwhelmed by the sound of her voice. He had never lost that feeling, even after so many years together.

"On a Friday night? That doesn't seem fair."

"Just something I have to do. Sorry."

"Are you coming back tonight?"

"I doubt it. It's a four-hour drive. Each way. But I'll be home tomorrow."

"Okay." It didn't sound okay. Her voice sounded tight.

He was lying to her, though only in the most peripheral way, and for the purest reasons. Could she tell? He had never lied to her. Maybe she could hear the difference.

"Bye," she said.

"Love you."

But she had already hung up the phone.

—

Anton knocked on the dorm-room door, his heart hammering. It hit him that the chances of her answering were slim. She might be out. She could be anywhere. She could have left town for the weekend. He might have driven all that way for nothing.

The door flew open, and there she stood.

"What?" she said.

Her hair was curly and long, partly covering her face. It was curlier than when Anton had known her, so maybe a perm, he thought. She was slight. Not as tall as he'd expected. But there was no mistaking that it was her.

"You're Jenny."

Her eyes narrowed in suspicion. "Who are *you?*"

"I used to be your foster father. You lived with my wife and me for a year and a half. You were only five or six, so maybe you don't remember."

Her hand came up to the collar of her T-shirt. Anton watched as she took hold of a gold chain and lifted it. The locket Edith had given her popped out into the light. Jenny opened it. She looked inside, her eyes narrow, then at him. Then at the photo. Then at him.

"You look different," she said. "You got older."

"We all got older."

"Your hair is gray. You look really different."

"It's been twelve years."

"Why did you wait so long?"

"We figured your mother didn't want you to see us. So I waited until you were an adult and could decide for yourself."

"I'm still not . . . how can I be sure it's you?"

Her eyes fell to his right hand. He wore no gloves. He had a new, better prosthetic. If someone only glanced peripherally, it might not catch their attention. Considered directly, it still did not look like a real hand.

"It *is* you," she said. "What can I . . . I mean . . . why did you . . ."

"Have you had dinner yet? Can I take you out someplace and we can talk?"

—

"I remember this." She indicated her own right hand. She was holding her menu but ignoring it. "It's the main thing I remember about you."

"Did it scare you?"

"No. It was what I liked about you. It was the first time I knew I liked you. And, you know . . . trusted you. Because I asked about it and you didn't get mad. You showed me and explained about it and let me ask questions. Most grown-ups don't do that. They get really ticky about things like that, and they want you to pretend you don't see. But you weren't like that. And I remember that pregnant lady. The one who gave you Leo. She said you were a hero, because you lost it trying to save your brother. So after that I thought you were a hero, too. What do you want from me? Oh, I'm sorry. That came out wrong. I didn't mean that the way it sounded. I just meant . . . you drove all the way down from New York, right?"

"More or less. We live in the country now. Connecticut."

"So you drove for hours. Wanting . . . something. What?"

Anton sighed. He tried to gather his words, but the waiter arrived.

"I haven't really looked at the menu," Jenny said. "I was talking. You want to get pizza? I feel like pizza. We could split one."

"That's fine."

"Pepperoni, large," Jenny said, and handed the waiter both menus.

Then, when he was gone, she sat staring at Anton. Waiting.

"It's been hard for me," he said. "But it's been harder for my wife. Mama, you used to call her. It's just who she is. She's a natural mother type. She never stopped worrying about you. I mean, in some ways you get on with it and live your life, because . . . what choice do you have? But in another way she never quite let it go. It's like this hole in her life. So part of my being here was just to see you and know you're okay. But I think what we both really need to know . . . did we do the right thing?"

Jenny blinked for a moment. She did not seem to connect to the question. "With what?"

"Giving you back."

"But you didn't have a choice. Did you?"

"We sort of did. Actually. Your mother signed away her parental rights. We could've fought it in court. We wanted to keep you. We thought we were going to be adopting you. We wanted you to stay with us so badly, but we thought a drawn-out legal battle would tear you apart. And you said you wanted to go back to her. We just wanted what was best for you."

"Oh," she said. She had one hand over her mouth, as if in shock. She had to move it to speak. "I didn't know all that."

"You were too young to understand all that context. So?"

"So . . . what?"

"Did we do the right thing?"

"Yeah. Absolutely. I would have hated never seeing my mom again. Especially after she got sober. I would've resented that. Yeah. You did."

"Your life with her was okay?"

"It was fine. It was just . . . normal. I mean, I think it was normal. I went to a million AA meetings with her and sat in the back doing my homework or reading or whatever. Half the time I wanted to strangle her, because she made everything harder than it needed to be, but . . ."

"But she didn't drink again?"

"No. She stayed sober."

"Sounds pretty normal to me."

"All my friends wanted to strangle their parents. So I figured."

"I'm sure if you'd stayed with us, you'd have wanted to strangle us. Leo wants to strangle us. He's a teenager now. I can see it in his eyes."

"It was nice of you," she said.

"What? Giving you back?"

"Yeah. Most people wouldn't. Most people just want what they want. And you said it was really hard for you. And her."

"I was hoping . . ." Then he almost couldn't bring himself to ask. There was so much riding on the answer. "I want her to be able to see you again. I want to give her that. I think it would mean everything to her to see with her own eyes that you're okay, and to hear you say what you just said to me. Is that something you could make time for?"

"Like . . . when?"

"I don't know. You tell me. Anytime you're willing."

"It's the weekend."

"It is," he said, barely daring to hope.

"When are you driving back?"

"Maybe tonight. Or I could get a room somewhere and go back in the morning."

"If I come back with you, will you get me back here by Monday classes? You don't have to drive me. You could put me on a train."

"Anything. Anything you want."

"Okay. Let's go now. Well. Not now. There's that pizza. I'm not going to walk out on a pepperoni pizza."

———

"What is that?" she asked, and pointed to the knob on his steering wheel.

They were on the I-95 north, in the dark. A river of red taillights ahead of them. A river of white headlights on their left. Anton was sipping a cup of gas station coffee, steadying the wheel with his new and improved prosthetic, which gripped.

"It helps me make a turn. I can turn the wheel a full couple of turns with only one hand."

"Oh. That's smart."

He sipped and drove for a few minutes. Then he looked over to see that she had fallen asleep. Her head was leaned against the window, her mouth open. It rocketed Anton back to the times when she was a little girl and Edith would tow him into her room to see how beautiful she was when sleeping. To see her perfect face by the night-light. The lights of the highway showed just about as much detail, and made him ache for the nights he'd missed. Then he decided it was wrong to ache over something that was right in front of his eyes.

Thinking so didn't change the feeling.

Somewhere north of Philadelphia he heard her shift around. He looked over to see her gazing out the window, half-awake.

"How did you find me?" she asked.

He'd been hoping she wouldn't wonder.

"I had to hire a PI."

"A what?"

"A private investigator. I hope that doesn't seem . . . I don't want it to feel like an invasion of privacy. It wasn't meant that way. I just . . . I love my wife. More than anything. I wanted it for myself, yeah. Of course. I wanted to see you. But for her . . . I'd do anything for her."

He waited. To see if he was forgiven.

"If it's for Mama," she said, "then it's okay."

They didn't make it home that night. Jenny fell asleep again. No amount of coffee could make Anton feel safe on the road. He stopped at a motel, where he got two rooms. He didn't call Edith, because it was late. He wanted to hear her voice, but he didn't want to wake her.

—

They arrived at Anton's house the following morning. Anton unlocked the door with his key. But when he pushed it open, Leo was running to the door as if they had knocked. Leo was wearing jeans and no shoes, his white socks sliding on the shiny hallway floor.

When he saw Jenny, he stopped cold, save for a few final inches of sliding. He stared at Jenny and she stared back.

"You're baby Leo," Jenny said.

Leo turned his gaze downward, hair spilling over his face, and frowned. "I'm not a baby."

"She means she knew you when you were a baby," Anton said.

"Well, now I'm not."

"Duh," Jenny said. "I can see that with my eyes. Where's the dog? Oh. Wait. Never mind. That was too long ago, wasn't it?"

They stepped into the house and Anton closed the door behind them. "Where's your mom?" he asked Leo.

"Upstairs. She's in a bad mood."

"About what?"

"I dunno. But she was crying."

"Oh. Okay. I don't know, either. I'll go get her."

But when Anton looked up, she was there. Halfway down the stairs. Frozen, staring. Anton couldn't tell if she had made the connection or not.

"Mama," Jenny said.

Edith broke loose then, and moved. She rushed down the stairs, taking the girl into her arms. Burying her face in Jenny's hair. When she showed her face again, Anton could see she was crying. Without letting Jenny go, she reached out one hand and cupped Anton's cheek.

"*This* is where you were?"

"I didn't want to tell you yet. It might've been the wrong girl. Or she might not have wanted to come back, or . . . I'm sorry. I didn't want to get your hopes up until I heard what she had to say."

"Come in the kitchen," Edith said. "I'll make us all some breakfast and we can talk."

———

Jenny stared out the window at the barn as she ate. "Do you have horses?"

"No," Edith said.

"You have a barn. You should have horses."

"We had a pony for Leo." Anton glanced at his son, who was pretending not to stare at Jenny from behind his waterfall of hair. "But it turned out to be . . . not his thing."

"And I'm sixty-three," Edith said. "Might be a little late to learn to ride."

Jenny chewed at a strip of bacon, staring out the window. "You could get a *quiet* horse," she said after a time. "An older one, maybe.

When the semester is over, and I'm off for the summer, I'll be back in New York with my mom. Maybe I could come out again."

Anton wasn't sure if Jenny was saying *she* wanted a horse. But he would get her one without hesitation if it meant she would visit.

Before he could answer, Jenny said, "Here's the thing. I sort of feel like I don't know you guys. I mean, not entirely. Part of me feels like I know you. But another part of me feels like I don't. Does that sound mean? I don't want it to sound mean."

"It doesn't sound mean," Edith said. "It's honest. We'd love it if you came to visit. We're not saying you're supposed to feel like family after all these years. But if you came and visited, you'd *get* to know us."

Jenny chewed thoughtfully for a moment. "I want to know you. Because I haven't met too many people who would do what you did."

"Jenny didn't know," Anton told Edith, "that we had a choice about giving her back."

"No," Edith said. "Of course she didn't. She wasn't meant to. I wouldn't put that on a child. I didn't want her to have to feel guilty over what she wanted."

"See?" Jenny said. "That. That's what I'm talking about. Most people aren't like that."

"Do you *want* a horse?" Anton asked. "Because we would get one, if you'd ride when you come out and visit."

"Yes! Absolutely. I'd be here a lot if I had a horse here. But I don't mean to get ahead of myself. That's getting ahead of myself, isn't it? I guess I should just start by visiting again and we'll see how things go."

Anton—who was generally a fan of not getting ahead of himself either—made a mental note to at least research how to shop for a quiet older horse. For later. Maybe. Hopefully for later.

—

He sat on the edge of the bed in the master bedroom, watching Edith undress and step into her nightgown in front of the big closet-door mirror.

"Why were you crying?" he asked.

"How could I not cry? Seeing her after all these years?"

"No, before that. Before I got home. Leo said you were crying."

She cut her eyes away from his in the mirror. "No need to go into that."

"But that worries me. Especially if you don't want to talk about it."

Edith sighed and settled next to him on the bed. "I feel silly about it now."

"But go ahead and tell me. Please."

"I thought you were having an affair."

*"What?"* Anton surprised himself with his own burst of volume. "How could you . . ."

"All of a sudden you're going to be gone for the night and I can hear you not telling me the truth about why. Of course I feel like a fool now. You were going off to do this wonderful thing for me. For us. But I . . ."

"How could you possibly think I could do that? Or even *want* to do that?"

"I'm sixty-three, Anton. You're not even fifty."

"Oh. You're fifteen years older. What a shock." He threw an arm around her shoulder and pulled her close. Pointed to the mirror. "Look at us. How much do we look like we go together? I'm completely gray. You're completely not. Have you ever seen a better looking sixty-three-year-old woman in your life? People never register our ages now. We just fit." They stared at themselves for a moment. "It really hurts me that you could think that."

"I'm sorry, Anton. My insecurities got the best of me."

"Promise me you'll never make a mistake like that again. Ever."

She smiled at him in the mirror. A little sadly, but seeming fairly sure. "Okay. I promise."

—

In the morning, Leo pulled him aside. Literally pulled him by his sleeve, before he could join Jenny and Edith in the kitchen. "Is she my sister?"

"Pretty much."

"Does she *have* to be?"

"Yeah. Really no getting out of that. Can you deal with it?"

Leo sighed with the grandeur only a teenager could master. "Well . . . if it's only weekends . . . I guess."

# WINTER OF 2020

## EVERYTHING

# *Chapter Twenty-Seven*

## *The Whole Universe*

Anton hovered over his telescope, on the balcony outside their bedroom, trying to decide whether to take more images. He was tired, and he wanted to check on Edith. He also wanted to shoot the Sombrero Galaxy. Still, he knew from experience that the camera might bump up against the leg of the tripod while trying to achieve that extreme angle. Then he would have to align his equipment all over again.

It felt like too much trouble.

He loosened the screws that held the camera's T-ring adapter in place. He returned the tracking mount to the zero position, but did not turn it off. If he uploaded his images and nothing turned out, he might come back and try again.

He stepped in through the sliding glass door.

Edith was in bed. There was nowhere else she would, or could, have been.

"Get anything good?"

"Remains to be seen." He picked up his laptop computer from the dresser. "Before I settle, do you need anything? More pain meds?"

"I do need some, actually, but it's awfully soon."

"What difference does it make? The idea is to keep you comfortable. That's what the hospice experience is about."

"You're right. Yes, then. Pain meds."

She had a fentanyl patch on her hip, but also hydrocodone tablets in the bathroom medicine cabinet. He fetched her one with a glass of water.

"Tell me honestly," he said. "Is it time to call the kids? Ask them to get out here?"

"No. Soon but not now. Now I want to see the universe."

He settled next to her on the bed, moving the computer onto his lap. He popped the memory card out of his camera and into the card slot. Watched the RAW files load.

"I hope my tracking isn't off again tonight. That's so frustrating."

"But you have that guide scope now."

"But I'm still waiting for the guide *camera*. It's back-ordered. The guide scope has to have a way to communicate with the mount."

"Too complicated for me," she said.

"On most nights it's too complicated for me, too."

He opened his first image in the photo app. Edith leaned over to look.

"Oh, I see something. Right in the middle."

"That's a good sign. I was aligned, at least." He played with the brightness, the curves tool. The color balance. "This is good, actually."

She slid her arm through his. "It's great. Look at the stars. How round they are. The tracking is almost perfect. You got the focus, too. I love how the stars have points of light around them. What am I seeing?"

"That's M51. The Whirlpool Galaxy. But it's really two galaxies interacting."

"I can see that."

They stared at it together for a moment—the bright-centered swirl of the larger galaxy, seeming to pull matter from the smaller one. It was a good image. It was worth the aggravation Anton had endured.

"I love that you show me the universe." They stared a few minutes more without speaking. Then she said, "Remember when we had dinner that first night in DC? After we ran into each other on the train? You asked me if I had any regrets. Do you remember what I said?"

"You said you regretted everything."

"Ask me again."

"Okay. What do you regret now?"

"Nothing. Not one damn thing."

"Marrying that awful man?"

"It's how I met you."

"You don't regret giving Jenny back anymore?"

"She adores us for it, so that would be hard. What about you? Now that you're about to be . . . alone . . . do you regret anything?"

"Nothing about forty years with you. Who could regret that?"

"Anything, though?"

He didn't answer.

"I know. You still wish you'd been a second faster the night your brother died. At least you didn't add any more regrets later in life. Are you going to be okay now, Anton?"

He sighed. Closed the lid of his laptop. "I'll be . . . different. It'll be different. But, yeah. I'll be okay."

"You could get married again."

Anton snorted laughter, then realized she might not be joking. "Oh, that was serious? At seventy-three?"

"People get married at seventy-three."

"This person doesn't. You know what? The fact that you're even talking about this makes me think it's time to call the kids."

"Not yet. We have time. Show me another galaxy."

"I might have a nebula in here to show you."

"I like that you show me the universe," she said again.

"Then I'll go out and get more shots."

"No. Stay here. Show me everything you've ever taken."

"Even though you've seen it before?"

"Even though."

They sat together most of the night, touring the universe. Because he was almost out of time. But not out of time. Not quite. In that moment, she was there with him. Later, when he, too, wrapped up his life, maybe she would be again. There was nothing he could do to prepare for the time in between. So he stayed in the moment with her, looking at images of celestial objects millions of light-years away.

He was showing her the whole universe. It was everything. All of creation. That's how he knew it would be enough.

# BOOK CLUB QUESTIONS

1. At the start of the book, Anton prefers to be called Anthony. Eventually, he finds his way back to his original name. What do you think each name represented for him, and why did he choose Anton by the end?

2. Anton suffered tremendous trauma with the death of his brother. Even though they are part of the same family, and suffered the same loss, Anton's parents handle their grief in very different ways. What do you think his parents' choices say about their ability to cope and take Anton's needs into consideration?

3. Throughout Anton's life, his great-uncle and grandmother act as allies, each in their own way. What do you think their challenges were in trying to be there for Anton without interfering in his family life and with his parents' wishes?

4. Anton witnesses Edith's domestic violence. At first, he can't understand why she would continue to allow that abuse. Shortly before Edith finally leaves her husband, she tells Anton, "Now there's somebody watching it happen. And that's just . . . unbearable." Why do you think having a witness to her situation made such a monumental difference?

5. Anton hides Edith and eventually helps her escape. Later in the book, when they reconnect, they both question whether they made the right decision back then to part instead of staying together. Do you think it was the right or wrong choice for both of them at the time?

6. After Edith disappears to escape her husband's abuse, Anton is heartbroken. Then he remembers something from his sessions in the hospital: "That looking directly at a painful truth hurts less than being stalked by it." Do you agree with this philosophy? Do you think it helped him in the long run?

7. In trying to teach Anton about true love, his grandmother tells him the story of when his grandfather was dying and she really wanted him to stay with her. She says, "I let him make a decision to go forward to a future that did not include me. Because I loved him that much." How did Anton's understanding of his grandmother's words affect the decisions he made in the future?

8. Many years later Anton is in a romantic relationship with a woman named Amy. When he unexpectedly runs into Edith again, everything changes. Up until that time, he didn't know which hurt worse, staying with Amy or leaving her. Do you think he made the right decision in the end?

9. The celestial beauty of the stars and the universe are a thread that runs through the entire book. In the final pages, Anton must face that Edith, the true love of his life, is dying. In what ways did this final scene together bring the book to a poignant closure?

# ABOUT THE AUTHOR

Catherine Ryan Hyde is the author of forty published and forthcoming books. An avid traveler, equestrian, and amateur photographer, she shares her astrophotography with readers on her website.

Her novel *Pay It Forward* was adapted into a major motion picture, chosen by the American Library Association (ALA) for its Best Books for Young Adults list, and translated into more than twenty-three languages for distribution in over thirty countries. Both *Becoming Chloe* and *Jumpstart the World* were included on the ALA's Rainbow list, and *Jumpstart the World* was a finalist for two Lambda Literary Awards. *Where We Belong* won two Rainbow Awards in 2013, and *The Language of Hoofbeats* won a Rainbow Award in 2015.

More than fifty of her short stories have been published in the *Antioch Review*, *Michigan Quarterly Review*, *Virginia Quarterly Review*, *Ploughshares*, *Glimmer Train*, and many other journals; in the anthologies *Santa Barbara Stories* and *California Shorts*; and in the bestselling anthology *Dog Is My Copilot*. Her stories have been honored by the Raymond Carver Short Story Contest and the Tobias Wolff Award and have been nominated for Best American Short Stories, the O. Henry

Award, and the Pushcart Prize. Three have been cited in the annual *Best American Short Stories* anthology.

She is founder and former president (2000–2009) of the Pay It Forward Foundation and still serves on its board of directors. As a professional public speaker, she has addressed the National Conference on Education, twice spoken at Cornell University, met with AmeriCorps members at the White House, and shared a dais with Bill Clinton.

For more information, please visit the author at www.catherineryanhyde.com.